SHATTERED NEXUS

KEN LOZITO

ACOUSTICAL BOOKS LLC

Published by Acoustical Books, LLC

KenLozito.com

IF YOU WOULD LIKE TO BE NOTIFIED WHEN MY NEXT BOOK IS RELEASED VISIT

WWW.KENLOZITO.COM

Paperback ISBN: 978-1-945223-83-9

Book Cover © 2025 Ivan Zanchetta & Bookcoversart.com

CHAPTER 1

SEAN STEPPED through the heavy doors into General Hayes's office and immediately sensed that something was wrong. The transparisteel windows stretched from floor to ceiling along two walls, offering him a view that still took his breath away even after all these years. Sierra's military district spread out below like a carefully orchestrated dance of purpose, while the orbital defense platforms hanging in the distance were reminiscent of stalwart sentinels.

It was times like these when he was planet-side that he sometimes found himself trying to recall the earliest days of the colony. He'd been seventeen and among the first group of early risers. The New Earth landscape had been untamed and free, despite the battle scars of a civilization that had collapsed long before any humans had set foot there.

Sean had been in this office before but never failed to notice how it reflected Hayes himself—controlled, deliberate, and impressive without being ostentatious. The holographic battle displays cast their blue glow across polished walls, and Sean recognized several of the tactical maps from campaigns he'd personally fought in. The Krake War scenarios still made his jaw tighten slightly, but it was the Vemus invasion that threatened to drag him back to those desperate times and the battles he'd fought on the ground, leading soldiers and citizens alike as they fought for their own survival. Those days had become a distant memory.

Hayes's desk commanded the center of the room. It was made from New Earth oak, harvested from the early days of Sierra's rebuilding efforts. The desk's surface was characteristically clean, except for the subspace comms array and a few personal items that Sean had glimpsed during previous visits—a lunar rock, a model of an early CDF destroyer, and a physical photograph that Hayes had never explained.

The silence struck him most of all. The sound-dampening was so complete that Sean could hear his own heartbeat, making every word that would be spoken here feel weighted with significance. He'd stood at attention in many offices over his thirty years of service, but this one always reminded him that decisions made in rooms like this shaped the fate of entire worlds.

Sean straightened his shoulders and waited for the General to acknowledge him, knowing that whatever had brought him here today would likely change everything.

General Hayes was staring at a vid comlink display. "Understood, Governor Blackstone."

He disconnected the comlink and turned toward Sean. "Thanks for coming down, Sean." He walked around the desk and extended his hand.

"Congratulations on your appointment, General," Sean replied, shaking his hand.

Nathan's mouth twitched. The law allowed the colonial government to appoint the head of the CDF from a pool of very limited candidates. Nathan had been in his current role for a very long time, since the Krake Wars.

"I was the easy choice. After all these years, they know what they're getting."

Sean smiled. "That's not a bad thing."

"It could just as easily have been you, General Quinn."

Sean shook his head with a grin. "Not anytime soon."

"Don't want to be stuck planet-side?"

Sean shrugged. "I'll serve where I'm needed. Why would they need me here when they have you?"

Nathan rolled his eyes and glanced at the time display. He walked over to a glass bottle of bourbon and poured them both a finger's worth, handing one to Sean.

"Thanks for that," Nathan said.

Sean raised his glass and drank. The brown liquid warmed his mouth and throat—smooth with a pleasant aftertaste that reminded him why Nathan preferred the authentic varieties over synthesized alternatives.

"Are you looking for a change?" Sean asked.

Nathan shook his head. "Not really. Connor and I have things divided up pretty well, but the CDF is growing. With the Confederation, they're looking for representation from Old Earth."

Officers recruited from Old Earth had been admitted to the Confederation, but their influence was small.

"Nothing stays the same. One day, both of us will be replaced," Sean said.

"But not yet," Nathan said and set his glass down. "Our timetable to return to the Aczar homeworld has to be moved up."

The Aczar were a species from a world called Ichlos and had come to New Earth with Connor nearly two years prior.

"We'd promised to bring them back home once we better understood the new Infinity Drive protocols and had tested them out on our ships."

Nathan nodded. "And they've helped us understand the Phantom ship that Connor and Noah brought back with them from the outpost."

Connor, who at one time had been both their superiors and

recruited them both to the CDF, had found himself thousands of light years from home when an I-Drive utilized experimental protocols to increase its range. Phantom interference was also involved, but that remained a topic for quiet conversations. No one liked to think about a powerful race of beings that existed outside normal space. They'd taken an interest in humans and Connor in particular.

"What happened to move up the timetable?" Sean asked.

Nathan chuckled. "Something we should have anticipated, but I'm afraid it's caught us all by surprise, including Phendran."

Phendran was an Aczar Loremaster and the leader of the four Aczars who had helped Connor escape Ichlos. Nathan gave him an expectant look and he frowned. Two of the Aczar were younger than the others. They were students of Phendran.

"The young ones... I can't remember their names," Sean said.

Nathan nodded with a smile. "Kholva and Vorix. Vorix is pregnant, and with the Aczar's accelerated physiology, we don't have a lot of time."

"What do you mean? Couldn't we just duplicate an environment similar to Ichlos?"

Nathan stared at him for a second and shook his head. "It's not an entirely scientific question to be answered—create an artificial environment and their baby should be fine."

Sean didn't have a family. He and his wife had decided to wait. Given that the average human lifespan was well over two hundred years, approaching two hundred and fifty, they had plenty of time.

"Their baby must be delivered on Ichlos. In fact, Vorix and Kholva must return to complete their marriage rites, but it's more than that. The longer she's here, the more risk to the development of the baby while in her mother's womb. This is no longer just a diplomatic promise; it's now a life-or-death medical necessity."

Despite the fact that Sean didn't have a family of his own, he knew that children were the lifeblood of the colony. The human population was increasing, but it would be generations before it reached the population at the height of Old Earth—at least before the Vemus had spawned on their planet, decimating the human population, and then traveled to New Earth to do the same.

"Accommodations specific to Ichlos's atmosphere is required for proper Aczar fetal development. Matching the gravitational needs is easy, but it's the specific minerals, radiation levels, and electromagnetic fields on Ichlos that need to be carefully configured. Their SRAs allowed them to artificially adapt to our atmosphere, but Vorix's baby doesn't have an SRA."

Saruvian Robotic Assistants (SRA) was technology given to the Aczar from Salpheth, who was some kind of pre-ascended Phantom. Salpheth had been a prisoner of the Aczar for hundreds of years. Phendran had explained that SRAs were sentient beings who partnered with the Aczar shortly after they were born. Their SRAs helped them with communication, as well as working with and understanding technology, and could defend them from attack.

Sean had seen Connor's SRA, and there was a preliminary rollout of the new technology among the colonists.

Nathan watched him for a few moments. "It's important for their baby to be born on Ichlos so they will be accepted into Aczar society."

"I understand."

"I thought you might. We've created an artificial environment for Kholva and Vorix on the lunar station. That HAB unit will need to be brought to the *Odyssey*, and now we've come full circle to why I've brought you here. You're to lead the mission to return Phendran and the other Aczar to their homeworld, Ichlos. A small diplomatic envoy will go with you to help establish diplomatic relations between our two species."

Sean pressed his lips together in thought. "When Connor left their star system, a civil war was starting."

Nathan nodded. "And we have no way to communicate with them until we return to their star system. The mission is not without its risks. We have no way of knowing what the situation is on Ichlos. Phendran has given us possible scenarios, which he'll review with you while you're en route there."

Sean eyed his superior officer for a long moment. "There is more to the mission than this, not to diminish the importance of what needs to be done."

"You're right. In addition to returning to Ichlos and establishing a comms buoy network between our two worlds, you're to investigate the Phantom outposts that were detected on the *Pathfinder*," Nathan replied.

"Five thousand light years from home."

Nathan dipped his chin once. "Like you've done throughout your career, you'll be a trailblazer, Sean. You led our fleets through the space gates during the Krake War. You've traveled to Old Earth." He arched an eyebrow. "You were even on the first ship to ever use the Infinity drive."

Sean chuckled. Technically, he hadn't been authorized to go on the *Infinity* but had navigated the gray areas of command to finagle his presence for the mission to investigate the second colony. It was the circumstances that had necessitated his authority.

"You're the best person I've got for this mission," Nathan said. "If it were as simple as escorting the Aczar back to their homeworld, I could assign it to someone else, but there's more to it than that. The implications of what you might find will shape our security posture for years to come."

"How much of a skeleton force will I be working with?"

"How many do you think you'll need?"

"This has the hallmarks of a deep-space exploratory mission, so a Voyager class heavy cruiser with six support cruiser class ships. That would give me some flexibility to cover the star system and send a scout team to investigate the other Phantom outposts."

Nathan regarded him, and Sean didn't like what he saw in his friend's eyes.

"How bad is it?" Sean asked.

Nathan rubbed his beard, giving him a knowing look. "I can give you three ships for this mission. Due to the time constraints we're being called to work within, it's the best I can do."

Half the number wasn't as bad as it sounded, but when he considered the vast distances they'd be traveling, it was enough to give any space veteran pause. For all intents and purposes, he would be on his own.

Nathan gestured toward the nearby holotank and three ships appeared. The data beneath showed their current armament and crew information. Sean studied the information for a minute. He was familiar with the commanding officers of those ships.

He looked at Nathan. "I want Ethan Gates to command the *Ascendant*."

"That might be difficult—more so than you think it is."

Sean shook his head. "Is this going to be my mission? Do I have final say on who is on the team?"

"No, you don't."

Sean bit his lower lip for a second, eyes narrowing thoughtfully. "Do you?"

"Due to the diplomatic nature of the mission, there are other cooks in the kitchen."

"Those are CDF vessels." An uneasy silence expanded between them. "Ethan has essential command potential and is an asset. His records support this."

"His record is exemplary. It's the fact that he's still a hybrid that makes people nervous. Me, included."

"I trust him."

"It's not that simple. For the record, I trust him, too. He's a rising star, just like you used to be in the beginning."

"I have spoken to Ethan about this a lot. Does the review board or Governor Blackstone understand what he's sacrificing by remaining a hybrid? This isn't some kind of selfish indulgence on his part. It's personal. He believes it gives him unique insight into the Vemus—insight we'll need to glean whatever edge we can against them."

Nathan looked away and sighed. "That's exactly the problem. The Phantoms advised us to limit our exposure and build ourselves up, and there's a growing sentiment that we should comply with this advice. They believe it's in our best interest."

"You've got to be kidding me. That's akin to burying our heads in the sand and hoping no one comes by to kick our exposed posterior."

Nathan chuckled, and a grin bubbled out from Sean's chest.

"Nathan, I need Ethan for this mission."

"You just found out about the mission."

Sean waved away the comment. "This mission has been in my purview since Connor returned. I knew two things: one, that I was going to lead the mission back to Ichlos and certainly to investigate those outposts, and second, that I was going to need Ethan with me for it."

"In the off chance that you encounter the Vemus at one of these outposts?"

"Salpheth was aware of the Vemus, which means that their presence in the galaxy is far older than any of us realized. Has it occurred to you that we've only found remnant civilizations? Any civilization that has encountered the Vemus was wiped out—mostly wiped out. There was that race of beings whose fleet gave their all to stop the Vemus Alpha. Ethan led that mission. Even if we're just going to scout the area, I want the best scouting force with me, those with the most experience. Right now, he's been sidelined, except for short duration missions."

Nathan tipped his head to the side. "Would you make him your XO?"

Nathan was testing him, seeing how much he would fight to have Ethan on the mission.

Sean shook his head. "No, he's not ready for that yet, and he doesn't have the rank. He's best suited to being the tip of the spear. You could say I can relate to that."

Nathan exhaled through his nostrils. "Well, you're not wrong about that."

"And I'm not wrong about needing Ethan for this mission." Nathan gestured for him to continue. "Three ships. That's all I'm allotted for this mission. I'll need at least two ships to approach the planet, which leaves me only one available for scouting. Connor's report had the Aczars without any space presence, despite having abundant technology available that was capable of getting them there. Depending on how their civil war was resolved, I would anticipate at least some changes on that front. Phendran's account is that there was a movement gaining traction to reduce Salpheth's influence and for the Aczar to abandon their isolationist ways. I'd rather bring more of a battle group with me, but given our timetable, I take it this isn't an option."

"Correct, the return mission is a humanitarian priority, not just political."

"How much time do I have?"

"Three days. The *Odyssey*, the *Horizon*, and the *Ascendant* are being prepped as we speak."

He needed to review the preparations, and three days wasn't enough time. It wasn't impossible, but he would've preferred more time.

Nathan watched him for a few moments. "Want a piece of advice?"

"Of course."

"That bond you have with Ethan, I have it, too. I remember when he was born. I need to warn you about those strong bonds, especially when there might be a need to sacrifice a ship or soldiers to achieve an objective, even if it's so the rest can survive. I know you're no stranger to making those calls, but things are different now. The CDF that we came up in isn't the same."

Sean nodded. "If this was war time, we wouldn't allow families to come on the ships for the exploration initiatives. We know what we might have to sacrifice going out there. Ethan knows it, too. He might've beaten the odds a few times, but he's aware that eventually the cost will catch up with him. He's more mature than he used to be. Seasoned."

The edges of Nathan's lips lifted, but it wasn't a smile. "He'll need that."

"So, who do I need to speak to in order to justify adding Ethan to my team?"

"Not necessary. I'll take care of it."

Sean raised his eyebrows in surprise.

"You weren't expecting that," Nathan said.

"No, I wasn't."

"Maybe I was testing you."

"Did I pass?"

"With flying colors."

It didn't feel like he had.

Nathan shrugged. "You've commanded large fleets and smaller battle groups. The fact is that this is a small mission with limited resources, but the implications could be far-reaching. Members of the security council will probably think you're overqualified, and they'd be right about that. However, the reason I'm sending you on this mission is that one day you'll be the general in charge, and you need to know first-hand what you'll be facing."

Sean inhaled a deep breath and sighed. "Going somewhere?"

"Not that I know of, and neither is Connor, but we need to groom our senior officers for the challenges they'll face in the near future. I still remember when traveling 0.7 C was the fastest we'd ever been. Now we travel thousands of times the speed of light, and not only that but it didn't require untold amounts of energy to achieve. In that respect, both myself and Connor are dinosaurs. The best we can do is prepare the torch to be passed. You're next." He paused with pursed lips. "Well, you, and some others. Ethan's generation will follow after that. But, you have the advantage of being there at the forefront of it all. You were there when Connor put the CDF together, and then we made it into what it is today. One day, the responsibility will rest on your shoulders and those of similar rank but different experience. You'll have to be the voice of reason in a room full of people who don't have more than a cursory knowledge of what we do."

"I don't think we're there yet."

"Stranger things have happened."

Sean narrowed his gaze. "Are you sick? Do you have some kind of disease I don't know about."

Nathan chuckled. "No, but I've been thinking about the future a lot lately."

Sean knew he wasn't the only one thinking along those lines. His recent conversations with Connor had been similar. Sean wasn't naive enough to think that both Nathan and Connor, the two most senior and experienced officers in the CDF, would always be there, and that there wouldn't come a time when someone else would have to carry the torch they'd lit. Deep down, he knew he would be the one to whom the torch was passed—maybe not this year or next, but sometime soon.

"I understand. I'll be ready for it when it comes, but I know it's not today," Sean said and paused for a few moments. "Thanks."

"For what? Sending you on a long-range mission that'll have significant historical significance with limited resources that would make anyone in command feel ashamed?"

"I've done more with less."

"Yeah, but we're supposed to be better at preparation now."

Sean chuckled. "Have you seen the *Odyssey*? Or the other ships? Their capabilities are unmatched in both the CDF and Old Earth

Alliance militaries. They're built on everything we've learned thus far. Trust me, Nathan, you're not sending me out there with nothing. You're sending me and the others out there to stand on the shoulders of all who came before. It's a legacy we can be proud of, as well as a firm foundation from which we embark on this next great mission."

Nathan blew out a long breath and slowly shook his head. "Are you sure you're not related to Connor? Sounds exactly like something he'd say."

"Well, if I'm going to emulate someone, I choose the best."

"True. Now get out of here. I can see you're already inching toward the door."

Sean straightened and snapped a salute. "I'll get it done, General."

Nathan returned the salute, and Sean left the office.

CHAPTER 2

GENERAL CONNOR GATES stepped out of the transport shuttle and into the bustling heart of Sanctuary's Colonial Research Institute, feeling like a relic from another era. The campus sprawled before him in all directions, a carefully orchestrated complex of gleaming research towers, sprawling fabrication complexes, and tree-lined walkways where some of the Confederation's brightest minds moved with purposeful energy.

Connor remembered when this had all been frontier territory, little more than hastily erected prefab structures and muddy paths carved through New Earth's untamed wilderness. The Ovarrow archives had been discovered by his wife, who had led a team of researchers to learn all their secrets, which had been instrumental in alerting them to the Krake. The Ovarrow were the original inhabitants of New Earth, which they now shared with humanity, and most had become part of the colony. The Krake were an interdimensional alien race who traveled through different universes conquering the Ovarrow. The Krake had never anticipated a human colony, and despite being a technologically superior race, the colony had triumphed against them through ingenuity, building a resistance across multiple universes, and clandestine operations to study their enemy. After the Krake Wars, those alliances had disbanded, and travel through the multiverse was prohibited.

As Connor surveyed the large campus, he noted how it had grown over the years to rival the other more established colonial cities as a center of learning and innovation. Sanctuary's skyline was dominated by the distinctive spiral architecture that had become the city's signature, buildings that seemed to grow from the earth rather than being imposed upon it. It was an architectural nod to the Ovarrow civilization that had once flourished on this planet, who, much like humans, were rebuilding their population one generation at a time.

Connor paused on the shuttle platform, searching for the escort that should've been waiting for his arrival. He looked at his companion.

Major Tyler Kincaid held his finger to his ear and nodded. "Understood. I'll inform him," he said and looked at Connor. "They're almost here."

"Let's go, we'll meet her along the way," Connor said, walking down the steps to the pathway near the pad. He was on a tight schedule and wouldn't allow it to slip for any reason.

Kincaid snorted. "Not sure why they insisted on an escort this time. It's like the coordinator doesn't realize you live in the area and have been here many times."

Connor shrugged. "It's probably just an oversight. The conference has a lot of distinguished guests on their roster."

A familiar chuckle sounded from around the corner. "Then I guess we're in the wrong place."

Noah Barker smiled a greeting and looked at Kincaid. "Congratulations on your promotion to major."

"Thank you, Noah," Kincaid replied.

Noah gave Connor an appraising look. "No Jacob? I was hoping to see the little guy."

Connor smiled. "Seventeen pounds of pure determination. I left him with Lauren for the afternoon, but I'll need to pick him up later."

His one-year-old son spent a lot of time with his older sister Lauren, who had a family of her own. Connor often joked with them that they all needed was a compound of their own to live in.

"I saw Lenora yesterday. She looks like she's ready to pop," Noah said.

"She's ready, that's for sure."

"She told me you guys were waiting to find out what the sex of the baby is."

Connor nodded. "Decided to do it old-school this time. Juan's suggestion. Whether we have another boy or girl, it'll be a welcome surprise. How's Kara feeling?"

"Morning sickness has passed, and she's much happier now," Noah replied.

Kincaid was unusually quiet, surveying their surroundings.

Noah lifted his chin toward the CDF Major. "Having more kids isn't contagious."

Kincaid grinned. "Yes it is, and no, not yet. And no, don't put any ideas in Cass's head about starting a family now."

Noah's eyes widened and he gave Connor a conspiratorial look.

Connor shook his head. "Trust me, Cass doesn't need us to put any ideas in her head. Those ideas are already there."

Kincaid nodded. "Where is our escort? She should've been here by now."

"Oh, that. I told them it wasn't necessary. I'm your escort," Noah said.

Kincaid frowned with disapproval. "They're supposed to tell me."

Kincaid was part of Connor's protective detail and was coordinating with the conference organizers.

Noah raised his eyebrows. "Aren't I on the approved list?"

"Of course you are. I just don't like the break in protocol."

Noah nodded and glanced around for a second. "Where's your backup?"

Kincaid smirked. "Oh, they're around. Not too far and not too close for anyone to notice."

Noah gave Connor a questioning look.

"They're testing some new equipment from R&D and from a friend in the Intelligence Bureau."

"Isaac?" Noah asked.

Connor's son-in-law was a good guess, but his contacts in Intelligence went all the way to the top. He gave Noah a slight shake of his head, and his friend shrugged, letting the matter go unanswered.

They walked toward the main research complex, Kincaid maintaining a discreet perimeter while keeping an eye on the mixed crowd of colonial and Earth scientists moving around them. The diversity still amazed Connor sometimes. When he'd helped establish the first settlements, everyone had been human. Now the campus hosted Ovarrow researchers and Old Earth exchange scientists and students, as well as colonial citizens.

The Old Earth scientists and students spent anywhere from six months to a year on New Earth before returning home. Breakthroughs in subspace communications allowed them to interact with people on Old Earth with relative ease and in real-time.

"How are the Earth scientists adjusting to working with our people?" Connor asked, noting a group clustered around what appeared to be a holographic star chart.

Noah's expression darkened slightly. "They're eager to catch up to us, and sometimes," he paused for a moment, pressing his lips together, "they're just frustrated. They feel that they're so far behind us technologically that they must do everything they can to regain what they think they lost."

The survivors of the Vemus Wars on Old Earth had spent over two hundred and fifty years carving out an existence while either trapped on the planet or trapped in old space stations throughout the star system. Mixed among the settlements were Vemus-occupied areas—remnants from the war.

The colonists had learned there were actual survivors on Old Earth, and with the development of FTL technology, returning was within their grasp. An expedition was launched and they were able to liberate people from the terrible living conditions they'd been in.

"I've seen the recent vids from Old Earth," Connor said. "They've made remarkable progress with rebuilding."

"They want equal footing in the Confederation."

Connor gave Noah a knowing look, and his friend rolled his eyes.

"Probably more than equal footing," Noah said.

Connor nodded. "Well, that's not going to happen anytime soon. At least they have a seat at the table, just like the Ovarrow and, hopefully, the Aczar will one day have."

"Mutual cooperation, but we're not giving the keys away. All parties must contribute, and we do share, but with Old Earth it's different." Noah shrugged and shook his head. "Anyway, I'd expect you to receive a few questions when it's your turn to present."

"Good, they should be asking questions. That's what these conferences are all about," Connor said.

They entered the main research building through doors that recognized their biometric signatures, and their authentication was transferred through their neural implants. The lobby buzzed with controlled chaos. Holographic displays showed projects from across the Institute, researchers moved between collaboration spaces, and the constant hum of discovery seemed to permeate the air itself.

The bustle of energy and enthusiasm was infectious, and Connor allowed himself to take it in, making his chest swell with a little bit of pride. It was important to remember the reasons he'd chosen to protect the colony. Mostly, those reasons had to do with his own family and inner circle of friends but were also his moral compass—the part of him that made brave men and women go toward danger when others froze or ran away. It wasn't that he was fearless, far from it. It was that he knew the price to be paid if he failed, and there were some things that were worth the sacrifice of one's life. Witnessing people going about their lives with freedom, eyes turned toward the future—those were the fruits of their labor, and he wouldn't lose sight of that.

They took a lift that moved both vertically and horizontally through the building's complex internal structure, depositing them in a conference room with floor-to-ceiling windows that looked out over the campus. Below them, Connor could see research teams testing equipment in outdoor facilities, their work protected by energy barriers that shimmered in New Earth's afternoon sunlight.

The conference room was already occupied by dozens of researchers representing the cream of the Confederation's scientific community. Connor recognized several faces from previous briefings, but the man standing near the head of the table was new—tall, sharp-featured, with prematurely silver hair and the kind of intense focus that marked brilliant minds pushed to their limits.

"Dr. Sebastian Devakul," he said, extending his hand as Connor approached. "Terra Research Consortium. I've been looking forward to this meeting, General Gates."

"Doctor," Connor replied, shaking his hand while noting the calculating way he watched him.

"I saw that you'll be addressing the conference this afternoon," Dr. Devakul said.

"That's right, and I'm looking forward to listening to the presentations and noting the direction of current research trends throughout the Confederation."

Dr. Devakul's smiled. "Excellent. I'd like to get your opinion—"

"Actually," Noah said, gesturing to some seats farther away from them, "it looks like we're about to begin, and time is short."

Dr. Devakul frowned in disappointment, and his gaze slid

toward Connor's hands for a second. "Understood. Please don't let me keep you."

Connor frowned as he went to his chair.

Dr. Devakul has a small scanning device within his ocular implants.

Joshua's words appeared on Connor's internal HUD. Over the past two years, he'd gotten used to interacting with his SRA, or they'd gotten used to each other. Sometimes Joshua communicated via thoughts or impressions, but it wasn't intrusive.

They're interested in SRAs, Connor replied subvocally.

The scans were insufficient to detect anything. If he was interested in learning more about SRAs, why wouldn't he have asked you?

He might've been afraid he wouldn't get the chance, or they're going to try to duplicate the technology on their own.

Perplexing. Why duplicate what will be freely given?

The edges of Connor's lips lifted slightly. As capable as Joshua was, he still had a lot to learn about people.

We're not moving fast enough for him or whoever he's working with.

You're not surprised by this?

No.

Understood.

Joshua was content to observe and form his own decisions on the intricate behaviors of humans. Connor had discovered that not only his own SRA but others in the SRA pilot program didn't rush to judgment, and if their conclusions were problematic, short-sighted, or just incorrect, they were open to instruction. His experience with Joshua had helped further develop his own communication skills, which, according to his wife, was never a bad thing.

The conference was called to order and presentations of the various R&D initiatives were given. Connor didn't enjoy long meetings in general, but these presentations that showcased current findings across a vast array of fields were extremely interesting and were one of the reasons for his being here. Some of the research was on advancements in fabrications systems where materials could restructure themselves at a molecular level and energy systems that tapped into dimensional substrates they were only beginning to understand. And there had been more than a few researchers eager to be part of the expanding SRA pilot program.

Before long, it was time for Connor to speak at the presenter's podium. He wore his dress uniform, and a quiet murmur quickly swept across the conference room, disappearing into a hush as he came to the podium. They were eager to hear what he had to say.

Noah was already at the podium and was about to introduce him. "Ladies and gentlemen," he said, gesturing to Connor, "all of you know who the man to my right is—father of the Colonial Defense Force, a faithful and stalwart defender of not just the colony, but all of humanity." Silence blossomed in the room as all eyes went to Connor. Noah was enjoying this, and Connor hated the attention. "He has been both my mentor and dear friend since I was seventeen years old, newly come to the colony. As anyone who has ever worked with him can attest, he has a talent for seeing right to the heart of things and won't hesitate to share it with you. Sometimes, the things he says can be difficult to hear, but you'll never find a more honest and faithful companion anywhere. You know him as General Connor Gates, the man who happened to find himself in a place he never expected to be—a living legend. And trust me, he hates this. Just look at him. I'm going to pay dearly for this after we're finished here today. So, if I suddenly disappear, don't bother looking for me because you'll never find me."

Connor grinned, and Noah bobbed his head.

"It is my honor to introduce, and honestly, it's your honor to get to listen to, General Connor Gates."

Noah gestured toward the podium and extended his hand. Connor gripped it and leaned in. "Watch your six."

Noah laughed and returned to his seat.

Connor exhaled slowly and smiled at the audience. "What do

you say after an introduction like that? Noah was a bright young man with massive potential, which I fought to keep all to myself. Sometimes I won, and other times I lost as he was needed. The fact that we're all in this room together, traveling across vast distances, is due in large part to his work. If there is a legend among us, it's him."

He paused for a few moments while applause broke out and Noah's face reddened.

Connor smiled at him. "I'm not done with you, Noah." Several people chuckled at this. "Let me first say how impressed I've been with all the presentations so far from everyone in this room and those watching across campus and in the other cities. All of you have contributed to what we have here today. We can never forget the sacrifice of the people of Old Earth so that we were warned. We had just enough information to prepare. I'm not going to bring up all the history; you know it, but it's important to remember that we're all here standing on the shoulders of the generations that came before."

Connor paused and looked pointedly at the Old Earth scientists around the conference table. They sat straighter, looking more at ease and happy to be acknowledged.

"You might be wondering why I'm here. Specifically, why is anyone from the military here," Connor said, and waited a few moments. "We've partnered with institutions of higher learning and have good relationships with many here on New Earth. The CDF is opening certain research initiatives with the things we've learned about Phantom Technology. The purpose is to assist in continuing our efforts to reverse engineer the new technology we've been able to capture from the alien outpost." A buzz of conversation swept across those in attendance, and Connor imagined there were similar scenes occurring wherever this conference was being broadcast.

He cleared his throat and the conversations subsided. "Not all the tech we've discovered has a military application, but we need help with understanding the potential of our recent discoveries—technology like shapeshifting SRAs but with a more drone-like application, and adaptive repair drones that can merge to work on larger repairs, as well as reduce in size to deal with smaller issues. I've personally witnessed Phantom technology that pushes the boundaries of everything we thought we knew. A few years ago, we *thought* we'd maximized the speed of the Infinity Drive, only to learn that we'd underestimated just how limited our understanding of it actually was. At this moment, we've launched a mission to return the Aczar refugees back to their homeworld located over five thousand light-years from New Earth. Consider this: some of the people in this room, others on various campuses, and those who will later watch this broadcast could travel to the other side of the galaxy and maybe beyond. None of this will be possible if we don't pool our resources. Not just ours," Connor said, and looked at several Ovarrow who were sitting around the conference table, "but anyone who joins the Confederation. I've witnessed teleportation capabilities, which I believe are tied to the development of the SRA." He lifted his arm to show the silvery band that covered his forearm. "No, I can't teleport from here, and Joshua doesn't know how to do it either. I've asked him." Several people chuckled. "But maybe one of you will figure this out. However, with any R&D endeavor there are ethical considerations that we need to weigh, and access to certain technologies are restricted."

A woman raised her hand. Connor had been planning on taking questions and was nearing the end of his presentation. He gestured for her to speak.

Her eyebrows peaked in surprise. "Thank you, General Gates. I'm Dr. Caroline Lockwood, and I specialize in cooperative and cohesive interactions across species."

"I'm familiar with your work. I've read your research on the data we collected about the various Ovarrow civilizations we encountered during the Krake Wars, as well as your more recent work submitted to the Confederation," Connor replied.

She smiled. "I had no idea you were so familiar with my work. I understand that the CDF wishes to share some of the things it has discovered with various academic and private research firms. I also understand the need for discretion, but how can we petition the CDF for increased access?"

"We review requests through the standard submission process."

"Yes, this is exactly my point. I think that sometimes there is a lack of understanding by the review board before it makes its way to you. If you'll allow it, I'm willing to give you a short example."

Connor considered it for about half a second and then nodded. "Okay, go ahead."

"My specialization stems from psychology. On the surface, myself or a team of researchers wouldn't require access to the Phantom ship that is currently docked in a secure location. However, we're trying to improve life aboard our fleet, and as we expand with even more ships traveling farther away and perhaps even establish space stations or outposts of our own, the things we can learn just by being granted access to the Phantom ship would put our efforts ahead by years. By all accounts, the Phantoms have been around for thousands of years. I expect that their ship design represents the pinnacle of all that development. I conclude with the hope that access to these new discoveries will become open to scientists such as myself that are outside the expected disciplines."

Connor regarded her. "You know, I won't make any promises in a venue like this, but I do acknowledge your feedback. I'm aware of the value of your work, and I think there is indeed something to your request that is worth considering. I'll have someone under my command liaise with you and what I expect are similar types of requests." He paused and turned his attention to the room. "I imagine that everyone here and on campus can raise similar issues. That's why I've made available to you some guidance that contains examples of what is appropriate access to sometimes dangerous technology, but a more accurate description is less-understood technology. For some of the things we have, there are no replacements."

"General Gates," Dr. Sebastian Devakul said, hand raised. "I'd like to ask a follow-up question, but this is in regard to technology we're quite familiar with."

Connor noted that several people leaned forward as if they knew what Dr. Devakul was going to ask.

"Alright, ask."

"The consortium has been aware of Space Gate technology for some time, but access to it has always been denied."

Connor stared at him and waited. He'd anticipated what was going to be asked but wasn't about to fill the gap and do Dr. Devakul's work for him.

"We'd like access to Space Gate technology to use on Earth."

"As you're already aware, this is not possible."

"How can we make it possible?"

"This isn't the correct forum for this kind of request."

"On the contrary, General Gates, this *is* the perfect forum for it. We're all peers here. There's a general knowledge of the Space Gates, but by all accounts they haven't been used for decades, not since the end of the Krake Wars. I'd like to make a case for why this should be reconsidered."

Connor was shocked by the question. The subject of Space Gates hadn't been raised in a very long time. "The only thing I will say on this is that your request should go through diplomatic channels, which will be reviewed by the Colonial Security Council."

"Yes, where it then gets bogged down and eventually denied."

"Then that's the decision."

"Why isn't this technology freely shared like the others?"

"Because it's a technology that has destroyed entire civilizations, and the fact that we've used it doesn't mean we completely understand the ramifications of its use." Dr. Devakul was about to speak but Connor held up his hand, his expression hardening. "This is as far as this conversation goes. If you'd like to set up a meeting with me, contact the CDF and we'll discuss it."

Dr. Devakul leaned back in his chair. "Very well, General Gates. I will do that."

Connor turned his attention to the others. His allotted time was just about over. "Some technologies are too dangerous to share widely, no matter how beneficial they might seem. I thank you all for your attention and I look forward to continuing the work we've done and will continue to do in the future."

Connor watched Dr. Devakul gather his materials with deliberate precision, noting how the man's colleagues clustered around him in hushed conversation. The tension in the room was palpable. Some researchers looked uncomfortable with the confrontation, while others seemed energized by it. Connor had made his position clear, but he suspected this was far from over.

As the meeting broke up and researchers began filing out, Noah approached Connor with a concerned expression.

"You know he's not going to give up," Noah said quietly. "The Terra Research Consortium has significant political influence back on Old Earth. They could make things difficult for the Confederation."

"Let them try. Some principles are worth defending, even if it makes our lives more complicated."

Connor had faced many challenges over the decades, but sometimes the most challenging things came from within their own civilization. The Security Council could decide that Old Earth was entitled to the use of Space Gates, and it was his job to remind them that this should not be allowed. Some people hated being denied access to the things they thought they wanted, but Connor's experience during the Krake Wars and all the atrocities that alien race had visited upon countless Ovarrow civilizations made him determined it would not be permitted again, not even by humans.

CHAPTER 3

MAJOR ETHAN GATES stood in the center of the training facility's combat simulation chamber, sweat beading on his forehead despite the climate-controlled environment. The metallic band around his wrist—his Saruvian Robotic Assistant, Atlas—pulsed with a faint blue glow as nanoscale tendrils extended across his forearm like liquid mercury taking form.

"Ready when you are," he said, rolling his shoulders to work out the tension that had been building there for the past hour.

From the observation deck above, Cynergy leaned forward against the reinforced transparisteel barrier, her honey-brown eyes tracking his every movement. Beside her, Phendran sat with characteristic Aczar stillness, his large triangular ears occasionally twitching as he monitored the biometric displays. The Loremaster's own SRA had formed a subtle chrome accent along his uniform's sleeve, barely visible unless one knew what to look for.

"Begin simulation," the facility's AI announced. "Combat scenario seven-alpha, multiple hostiles detected."

The chamber's holographic projectors came to life, transforming the sterile white walls into the twisted corridors of a derelict space station. Emergency lighting cast everything in harsh red shadows, and the sound of hull breaches echoed through hidden speakers. Ethan's enhanced senses immediately catalogued the simulated threats—three Vemus fighters materializing from the alcoves thirty meters ahead, their exoskeletal forms moving with predatory grace.

Embracing his hybrid nature, Ethan felt the familiar surge as his physiology shifted. His perception sharpened, and time seemed to slow as enhanced reflexes and strength flooded through his system. His skin darkened to its characteristic hybrid pattern as his eyes took on their jade coloration.

That's when Atlas pulled back.

The SRA's tendrils retracted so quickly that Ethan stumbled, losing the tactical overlay that had been feeding directly into his upgraded neural implant. The shared consciousness network that should have expanded awareness collapsed like a punctured lung.

"Atlas?" Ethan's voice carried an edge of frustration as the first simulated Vemus fighter reached him. Without his SRA's enhancement, he had to rely purely on hybrid reflexes to dodge the creature's clawed strike.

The Vemus fighter lunged, and Ethan quickly moved to the side around a support strut. The fighter shifted at the last second, using the strut to pull itself around and continue its pursuit of Ethan. The combat simulations were connected to his neural implants, so despite being a simulation, it felt real, including the pain.

The Vemus fighter dove, claws extending, and Ethan leaped into the air, using his feet to push off the fighter's head.

A second fighter blindsided him with a tackle, and they both hit a steel support beam, hard. His armor absorbed some of the blow, but pain registered along his back as the Vemus fighter opened its wide mouth filled with savage teeth and snapped, trying to bite Ethan's neck.

Gritting his teeth, Ethan used the creature's momentum, slamming its face into the steel pillar. He shoved the creature with enhanced strength, sending it flailing into the other fighter.

The metallic band around his wrist pulsed erratically. *I'm... I'm sorry, Ethan. Something's wrong. When you change, I can't... I lose track of where I end and you begin.*

Ethan dove behind a support strut, breathing hard. This was the third time this week Atlas had disengaged during hybrid transformation.

"End simulation," he called out.

The derelict station vanished, replaced by the chamber's white walls. Ethan slumped against the nearest surface, running a hand through his dark hair. His skin was already returning to its normal pale coloration, the hybrid state receding like a tide. He'd thought the stress of a combat simulation would have forced Atlas to overcome whatever was hindering him, hoping the SRA's protective instincts would keep their connection intact.

The chamber door hissed open, and Cynergy descended the steps two at a time. Her long, dark-blonde hair was pulled back in a practical ponytail, and she wore the standard gray training fatigues that had become her uniform since... since she'd stopped being a hybrid. The reminder still twisted something in Ethan's chest sometimes.

"Same thing?" she asked, though her expression said she already knew the answer.

Ethan nodded, studying his SRA. Atlas had reformed into a simple band, but Ethan could sense the artificial being's distress through their neural link. "It's getting worse. Atlas can't maintain coherence when I'm fully transformed."

Phendran approached with measured steps, his brown fur-covered hands clasped behind his back. The Aczar Loremaster was shorter than both humans, standing barely five and a half feet tall, but his presence commanded respect. His large tan ears swiveled forward as he spoke.

"This is not uncommon in the early stages of SRA bonding," Phendran said, his translated words carrying their characteristic rapid cadence. "Your neural implant is functioning perfectly—I can see the data streams. But the integration between hybrid physiology and SRA consciousness presents unique challenges."

"How unique?" Ethan asked. After his father, Ethan had been among the first non-Aczar to receive an SRA, part of the technology exchange following his father's return from the Phantom outpost. Neural implant upgrades had been necessary to interface properly with Saruvian technology.

"Consider this," Phendran continued, "when you embrace your hybrid nature, your brain chemistry alters significantly. Neural pathways that were accessible to Atlas suddenly become... turbulent. It's like trying to maintain a conversation during an earthquake."

Cynergy crossed her arms, pursing her lips in thought. "But Ethan's neural implants are supposed to compensate for that, right? The Distributed Consciousness Warfare protocols should create stable pathways regardless of physiological state."

Ethan's enhanced neural implants were indeed revolutionary. Unlike the previous generation that simply interfaced with ship systems, these created a mesh network capable of sharing sensory input, tactical analysis, and even decision-making processes across multiple users in real-time. In theory, a squad or even a platoon equipped with such technology could function as a collective intelligence, adapting faster than any traditional command structure. The technology was also being tested with bridge crews on CDF warships, quickening analysis and decision-making capabilities, and leveraging the might of their formidable computing cores beyond anything that had come before.

The implications for tactical command were staggering. A ship's commander could share perceptions with ground forces in real-time, while soldiers could tap into orbital reconnaissance as if it were their own eyes. Ethan had experienced glimpses of this potential during testing—moments when his awareness expanded beyond his physical form to encompass data streams, sensor networks, and even Atlas's artificial consciousness.

But those moments when he embraced his hybrid nature were becoming rarer. Sometimes, when he was completely human, the efficiency of his connection with Atlas was diminished, as if it had to be reconstituted. Atlas claimed that the old connections weren't the same, and Ethan believed him. Transitioning into a hybrid had an impact on his physiology, like a slider that he had to move back to a region that allowed him to become human again. At least that's what he thought, and Cynergy confirmed. According to Atlas, there were differences, tiny variations that must add up and cause their link to wobble until it was lost.

"The implants themselves function flawlessly," Phendran said, gesturing toward the readouts still displaying on his personal holo-screen. "The issue lies in the interaction between three consciousness types—human, hybrid, and artificial. Each operates on different wavelengths, if you will."

Atlas pulsed against Ethan's wrist. *I want to help. When we're connected properly, it's like... like I can see the universe through your eyes. It's an additional context that I cannot accomplish on my own. But when you change, it's as if you're becoming someone else entirely.*

Someone else? Ethan frowned. *I'm still me.*

Are you? When you're fully hybrid, your thought patterns shift. Your priorities realign. I've studied the data. When you're in that state, you think like a predator, not like the Ethan I bonded with.

The observation stung because it held truth. In his fully transformed state, Ethan's tactical thinking did become more aggressive, more direct. The careful analysis he prized in his human form gave way to instinct-driven decision-making. It was one of the reasons hybrid soldiers had been so effective against the Vemus. They could match their enemy's predatory mindset, and their hybridness acted as camouflage among the Vemus of Old Earth.

"Perhaps," Phendran suggested, "Atlas is attempting to protect himself from that transformation. SRAs bond with the core personality, not its variations."

"Core personalities change over time," Cynergy pointed out.

"Indeed, but the changes are smaller, incremental," Phendran replied.

"Is that fixable?" Cynergy asked.

"Time and practice," Phendran replied. "Among my people, full SRA integration takes years. You've been bonded for mere months. The relationship must evolve to encompass all aspects of your nature. Each personality variation, essentially, resets the relationship."

Ethan frowned in thought. "I keep thinking this is different."

"Please, go on," Phendran replied.

"What if it's some kind of security limitation built into the… base code that's part of an SRA's core. I know I'm oversimplifying how SRAs are…created. This is why Cynergy couldn't just use my SRA, and I couldn't use hers."

The Aczars believed their SRAs were entirely sentient, with full rights in their society, despite their artificial origins. It was a topic that was debated among Confederation scientists. Participants who were part of the pilot program to use the SRAs had to be open to the possibility that the Aczars were entirely correct in their assertions that SRAs were sentient. There were now over five thousand human participants who had an SRA, and after a certain amount of time, all had arrived at the same conclusion as the Aczar.

"I agree with you," Phendran said. "Salpheth helped us develop this technology, so it is of Phantom origin. Perhaps they had specific reasons for this kind of constraint. While Salpheth's motives are questionable, I am more open to the idea that Phantoms had more benevolent reasons for designing the SRAs the way they did."

"I wouldn't call Phantoms benevolent," Cynergy said.

Ethan nodded. "I agree. We can't be sure of their motivations for doing anything. They've helped, but they've also studied us, manipulated us."

Phendran gave them both a patient look. "I didn't say they were perfect. I don't understand their methods, but at least some of them had taken an interest in your species, or at least they did. Things have been quiet on that for a while."

"It would be easier to trust them if they didn't hide what they were doing," Ethan said.

"They're a superior alien race," Phendran said, and held up one of his hands. "Technologically superior."

"We're closing the gap, especially with your help," Cynergy said.

"The benefit was for us all," Phendran replied.

Ethan's wrist computer chimed with an incoming priority message. He glanced at the display and felt his pulse quicken. Recall notice—immediate reporting required.

"Duty calls," he muttered, then looked at Cynergy. "Want to grab dinner later? We can continue this conversation."

She nodded, though something in her expression suggested she had her own concerns about their evolving dynamic. Being the non-hybrid in their relationship created its own complications.

As they left the training chamber, Ethan's neural implant pinged with a secondary message, this one encrypted with command-level protocols—a priority vidcom request from General Sean Quinn.

Ethan's steps faltered. Sean Quinn requesting a direct call usually meant one of two things: either Ethan was in serious trouble, or something significant was about to happen. Given recent events, he wasn't sure which possibility concerned him more.

Whatever it is, Atlas whispered through their link, *we'll face it together.*

Despite his apprehension, Ethan smiled. At least some aspects of their bond remained constant, regardless of his hybrid transformations. He stepped off to the side, engaged his secure communications protocols, and activated the comlink.

Sean's weathered face appeared on the holographic display, his steel-gray eyes immediately focusing on Ethan with characteristic intensity. The general's office was visible in the background, the same office where Ethan had received both commendations and reprimands in equal measure over the years.

"Major Gates," Sean began without preamble, "how quickly can you assemble a crew and prepare the *Ascendant* for extended deployment?"

"Extended deployment, General?" Ethan's enhanced neural implants automatically began calculating logistics, crew rotation schedules, and supply requirements. "Depends on the mission parameters, but standard prep time would be—"

"You have seventy-two hours."

Ethan blinked. "Sir?"

"We're returning the Aczar to their homeworld," Sean continued, his expression serious. "Ichlos is about five thousand light-years from here, and we're operating under medical emergency protocols. One of the younger Aczar is pregnant and requires specific environmental conditions that can only be met on their homeworld."

Ethan glanced at Phendran, who was speaking with Cynergy, and then frowned for a moment. The implications hit him immediately. A mission to Ichlos meant traveling through largely uncharted space, far from any support networks. It meant potentially encountering whatever political situation had developed since his father's escape from the Aczar civil war. And it also meant...

"Sir, will this mission involve investigating the Phantom outposts?"

Sean's slight smile suggested he'd expected that question. "Among other objectives, yes. Which is why I specifically requested you for this mission, Major Gates. Your experience with both Vemus encounters and alien technology makes you invaluable for what we might face out there."

Ethan felt a surge of excitement despite the compressed timeline. Command of the *Ascendant* for an extended deep-space mission was the kind of assignment he'd been hoping for. He'd been sidelined while the CDF figured out what they wanted to do with him. He hadn't been stripped of command, but he hadn't been able to rejoin the expeditionary initiative either. Sean must've fought hard to have him added to the mission.

"I understand, sir. The *Ascendant* will be ready."

"Good. We'll have more detailed briefings once we're underway, but Ethan…" Sean's expression grew more serious. "This isn't just a diplomatic escort mission. Intelligence suggests the Phantom outposts may contain technology or information that could change our strategic position regarding the Vemus threat. I need my best people on this."

"Understood, sir. Thank you."

Sean regarded him and then leaned toward the camera. "I trust you, Ethan. I trust your instincts. That's why you're on this mission."

"I won't let you down, sir."

The transmission ended, leaving Ethan staring at the blank holographic display. He had seventy-two hours to prepare for a mission that could determine humanity's future relationship with both the Aczar and the mysterious Phantoms.

This should be interesting, Atlas observed through their link.

"That's one way to put it," Ethan murmured, already mentally organizing the thousand tasks that needed completion before departure.

Cynergy and Phendran waited for him, and he realized their dinner conversation had just become significantly more complicated.

"I've been recalled to the *Ascendant*," Ethan said, focusing on Phendran. "We're taking you home."

Cynergy smiled at Phendran. "This is wonderful news."

"Very," Phendran agreed. "I knew they were reviewing the request, but I'm still quite concerned."

Cynergy glanced at Ethan. "Why? What's wrong?"

"We only have three days until departure. Vorix is pregnant."

Her eyes widened and she looked at Phendran. A pair of CDF soldiers arrived. They were there to escort Phendran to his shuttle transportation.

Phendran looked at Ethan.

"Thank you for helping us," Ethan said.

"You are very welcome, and it's the least I can do for the son of a person I highly respect," Phendran said.

The Aczar gave Cynergy a nod and quickly joined the CDF soldiers.

Cynergy watched him go with a thoughtful frown.

"What is it?" he asked.

"Phendran didn't seem surprised."

"He said he put in the request, so he was aware of the situation."

The Aczars had been guests of the Confederation for the past two years. His father had promised to get them home once they'd worked out the new I-Drive protocols that allowed them to travel the vast distances that had been unthinkable just a few years ago.

"That's not what I mean. I think they've been wanting to return home for a long time, but the powers that be were dragging their feet."

Ethan arched an eyebrow. His wife had completed her training in intelligence analysis, so she could join him on the *Ascendant* or wherever he happened to be serving in the CDF. She wasn't in the military but was a civilian contractor.

"It takes time to upgrade ships, even with fully tested protocols."

"I don't mean to paint this in a malicious light, but I do think a certain amount of manipulation is going on here. Vorix suddenly becomes pregnant?"

"So cynical," he said with a disapproving shake of his head. "Vorix and Kholva are young and far from home. Aczar life spans aren't that long to begin with. I'm surprised it hasn't happened sooner."

Cynergy arched an eyebrow. "Exactly. It happened after the new I-Drive protocols were proven reliable and their effect on the drive core and power core requirements were accurately measured."

"Do you think Phendran encouraged this?"

She shook her head. "I don't think so, but they are his students. He must've known that this would happen sooner or later and didn't do anything to prevent it."

"What was he supposed to do?"

"It doesn't matter now. What's done is done."

Ethan's neural implants automatically began establishing connection protocols with the *Ascendant*'s central computer core. Even across the distance to the lunar shipyards where the *Ascendant* was docked, he could feel the ship's systems coming online, responding to his command authority like a living thing awakening.

The Distributed Consciousness Warfare capabilities might still be unreliable when he was in hybrid form, but his connection to his ship remained constant. In seventy-two hours, that connection would carry him and his crew farther from home than most humans had ever traveled. He just hoped Atlas would be able to keep up when things inevitably became complicated.

"Come on. We've got to get home and pack," Ethan said.

"Don't forget to send a message to your mother."

"My father will know about the mission..."

She gave him a disapproving look. "Ethan, it's better if she hears it from you. She's your mother. The fact that you would contact her, even though your father will also tell her the news, will still mean something to her." Her gaze narrowed. "Either you do it, or I will."

He smiled. "Great. I was hoping you'd say that." Her eyes widened, and he held up his hands in surrender. Cynergy's parents had both died when she was a little girl. Ethan's mother had welcomed her to the family with open arms, and the bond between them was strong.

"I'll call my mother. I promise."

CHAPTER 4

GENERAL SEAN QUINN emerged from his ready room feeling the burden of history pressing against his shoulders like a tangible weight. His conversation with Phendran had crystallized what he'd been trying to avoid acknowledging. They weren't just carrying passengers home; they were forging a shared future for two civilizations five thousand light-years from the nearest help. Walking beside him, Phendran's distinctive gait consisted of quick, energetic steps that made his chrome-accented uniform shimmer, which created an almost musical counterpoint to Sean's measured stride. The Aczar Loremaster's large, triangular ears swiveled constantly, processing conversations and data streams that Sean's merely human senses couldn't detect.

"Your fabrication systems have exceeded my expectations," Phendran said, his translated voice carrying undertones of wonder that the universal translator couldn't quite capture. "The atmospheric processors don't just replicate Ichlos, they harmonize with it. Vorix says the baby moves differently now, as if it recognizes home."

Despite being so early in Vorix's pregnancy, her SRA was able to help monitor the baby's development.

Behind them, Oriana lingered in the doorway of the ready room. Sean knew his wife was still processing the implications of what they'd discussed. Her dark eyes—the same eyes that had seen him through the worst moments of the Krake Wars—reflected both professional fascination and deep personal concern.

"The mineral particulate readings are perfect," she said, moving to join them. "Vorix's biometrics show the baby's neural development is accelerating to match normal Aczar patterns. But Sean…" She paused, and he heard the unspoken concern in her voice. "If something goes wrong, if we can't reach Ichlos in time, we'll be delivering a child that may never survive outside that artificial environment."

The Aczar species was short-lived in comparison with a human lifespan, even without life-extending treatments. Their race experienced rapid development almost from the time of conception, and Sean wasn't sure whether this was part of their natural biology or augmentations. Phendran had been particularly interested in how human prolonging treatments worked and hoped to reproduce similar results when he returned home.

But before any of that could happen, there was a tiny little life that was depending on them. The weight of that responsibility settled into Sean's chest like a stone. In thirty years of CDF service, he'd carried many burdens—the lives of his crews, the success of crucial missions, the fate of the entire colony while it fought to survive the Vemus invasion. But this felt different, more personal somehow. It was probably because he was old enough to appreciate what one person's… one being's… life was worth.

Sean looked at his wife, conveying reassurance as much as he could. "Then we don't let anything go wrong," he said simply.

They approached the bridge, and Sean felt the familiar pre-mission energy building, that electric anticipation that came before stepping off the edge of the known universe. The corridor's viewport showed New Earth rotating slowly beneath them, its blue oceans, dark continents, and silver rings a reminder of everything they were leaving behind.

"Ready to make history?" Oriana asked, falling into step beside him. Her hand briefly brushed his, a gesture that spoke of twenty years of partnership, both personal and professional.

"History's easy," Sean replied, feeling a familiar half-smile tug at his lips. "It's making sure we're around to tell about it that's the challenge."

Truth be told, they'd already made history. Both of their careers, military and professional, had placed them at the edge of most developments in the colony. It was the era they'd been born into, and Sean was happy they'd been able to meet the challenges they'd faced. Those accomplishments were shared across the CDF and the colony itself. It was a good legacy, and Sean would do everything he could to ensure that it didn't end with them.

Colonel Brad Sutton rose from the executive officer's station, his imposing frame and closely shaved head giving him the appearance of a man who'd been forged rather than born. At six feet, four inches, with deep-set eyes that missed nothing, he projected an authority that had kept the *Odyssey*'s crew sharp through countless deployments.

"General Quinn," Sutton said, his resonant voice carrying easily across the bridge, "all stations report ready for departure. The task force is standing by for your orders, sir."

Sean moved to his command chair, feeling the bridge's attention focus on him like a lens gathering starlight. The command interface responded instantly to his biometric signature, updating displays with his tactical preferences and mission parameters. Three ships showed on the main tactical plot—the *Odyssey*, flanked by the exploration cruisers *Ascendant* and *Horizon*—three ships to carry them across five thousand light-years of largely unexplored space. He should have felt woefully inadequate; instead, Sean felt the quiet confidence that came from commanding the finest crews in the Confederation.

"Captain Norquist," Sean said, addressing his tactical officer, "status of our escort vessels?"

Captain Jane Norquist looked up from the tactical station, her striking blue eyes catching the amber glow of the weapons displays. Despite her petite frame, she commanded the *Odyssey*'s devastating firepower with a precision that had impressed Sean since her assignment. Her shoulder-length blonde hair was pulled back in regulation style, but no regulation could contain the sharp intelligence in her gaze.

"Both escorts report green across all systems, General," she replied crisply. "Major Gates aboard the *Ascendant* has completed final crew briefings and reports readiness for extended deep-space operations. Colonel Torren on the *Horizon* confirms all departments ready for departure."

"Operations?" Sean turned to Captain Jake Lennox, whose angular features were highlighted by the blue glow of the Infinity Drive status displays.

"I-Drive operating within optimal parameters," Lennox reported, his slightly tousled hair and easy manner concealing one of the sharpest tactical minds in the fleet. "Fabrication systems have completed construction of the first deployment wave—twelve relay buoys and three subspace transceivers. Engineering estimates we can maintain the planned communications network deployment without impacting the mission timeline."

Sean nodded, satisfied. The communications network they would establish represented humanity's first permanent link to the far reaches of space. Subspace relay buoys deployed every hundred light-years would create a chain of connectivity stretching back to the Confederation. The larger transceivers, positioned every five hundred light-years, would boost and amplify signals across previously impossible distances.

It was audacious. It was also absolutely critical.

Major Wallace," Sean called to his engineer, "how are our Aczar passengers adapting to the environmental modifications?"

Only Phendran had kept his adaptations so he could live in a human-centric environment. The other Aczar had all gone to the artificial HAB unit.

Major Jamal Wallace turned from the engineering station, his warm smile visible even across the bridge. His lean frame and expressive eyes radiated the calm competence that had made him indispensable during the *Odyssey's* previous voyages. "Vorix and Kholva have settled into their modified quarters. Noxrey is as happy as I've ever seen him. I think they're ready to go home, sir," Wallace reported. "The atmospheric processors are maintaining Ichlos-standard conditions—twenty-three percent oxygen, specific mineral particulates, and 0.87 standard gravity. Medical reports indicate that our expectant mother is progressing normally and within Aczar parameters."

Phendran moved to stand near the main viewer, his SRA-enhanced uniform subtly shifting as the artificial being adapted to the electromagnetic environment. "Your people have shown remarkable dedication to accommodating our physiological needs. It gives me great hope for what our civilizations might accomplish together."

Sean felt the familiar pre-mission energy building in his chest—part anticipation, part fear, part absolute determination. It was time.

"Specialist Ramirez," he called to the communications station.

"Yes, General?" came the immediate response from the young specialist, whose rapid-fire competence had earned him a spot on the *Odyssey's* crew despite his junior rank.

"Open a channel to all ships in the task force. Full broadcast to all hands."

"Channel open, sir. All vessels receiving."

Sean rose from his command chair, aware of the bridge's attention focusing on him with intense concentration. Behind him, the main viewer showed New Earth in all its blue-and-silver glory, rings catching starlight like scattered promises. Soon, it would be nothing but memory and navigation data.

"Crews of the *Odyssey*, *Ascendant*, and *Horizon*," Sean began, his voice carrying the authority of three decades in uniform, "today we embark on humanity's longest journey into deep space, five thousand light-years from home. With the exception of the CDF ship *Pathfinder*, this is farther than our species has ever intentionally traveled."

He let the magnitude of that distance settle into their minds— five thousand light-years. Even with the new Infinity Drives, they were venturing into a realm where help was measured not in hours or days but in the fundamental assumptions of human civilization.

"Our primary mission is humanitarian," Sean continued, "returning our Aczar allies to their homeworld, where new life awaits birth under alien stars. But we carry responsibilities that extend far beyond a single journey, no matter how historic."

Sean gestured toward the main viewer, where New Earth slowly rotated beneath them. "We go as more than explorers. We go as ambassadors of everything humanity has achieved, our science, our values, our determination to reach beyond the comfortable boundaries of the known."

He paused, meeting the eyes of his bridge crew before continuing. "Every technological breakthrough since the founding of our colony has led to this moment—the Infinity Drive that will carry us across the impossible distance, developed from wreckage and wonder; the fabrication systems that let us create what we need from raw elements, refined through necessity and ingenuity; and the enhanced armor and weapons that protect us from unknown threats, forged in the fires of wars we barely survived."

Sean's voice grew stronger, more certain. "But our greatest

strength isn't technological. It's the bonds of trust and cooperation that let us stand here, human and Aczar together, preparing to face whatever lies ahead."

He looked directly at Phendran, then back to the camera pickup that would carry his words to every soul under his command. "We don't know what we'll find at Ichlos. When General Gates escaped that system two years ago, civil war was beginning, ancient isolationist policies were crumbling, and an entire civilization was questioning the foundational principles of their society."

Sean's expression grew more serious, his command voice taking on the weight of absolute authority. "We will proceed with caution. We will evaluate before we act. We will remember that our decisions may echo across generations of both our peoples."

The bridge had fallen into the kind of absolute silence that preceded momentous events. Sean could feel the attention of every crew member, not just on his ship but across the small fleet.

"We also carry a secondary mission that may prove equally significant," he continued, "which is the investigation of Phantom outposts detected during previous exploration. The mysterious beings who nudged us to re-examine our FTL technology that makes this journey possible remain largely unknown to us. What we learn about them—about their capabilities, their intentions, their enemies—could determine whether our species survives what's coming."

Sean straightened, feeling the familiar surge of confidence that came before any major operation. It was the feeling that had carried him through the desperate battles of the Krake Wars, through the exploration of hostile star systems, and through every moment when the impossible had to become merely difficult.

"Some of you have families back home—children who will grow older while we're gone, parents who will worry, spouses who will count the days." His voice softened slightly. "That sacrifice means something. It means we don't take unnecessary risks. It means we do everything we can to return home."

He let that promise hang in the air for a moment before his voice strengthened again.

"But it also means we don't shrink from necessary risks. This is what the CDF was created for; not just to defend what we have, but to extend our reach, to learn, to grow, and to face whatever challenges await us in the darkness between stars."

Sean nodded to Specialist Ramirez, who closed the general channel. The bridge crew turned expectantly toward him, and he felt the familiar weight of command settle onto his shoulders like an old, comfortable uniform.

"Helmsman Roberts," Sean said, settling back into his command chair, "take us out of orbit. Standard departure procedures."

"Yes, sir," Floyd Roberts replied from the helm, his hands already dancing across the navigation controls. "Maneuvering thrusters engaging. We are clear of orbital traffic patterns and moving to departure coordinates."

Sean watched New Earth shrink on the main viewer, its familiar continents and cloud patterns growing smaller until the entire world—everything humanity had built, everyone they'd ever known—became just another point of light against the infinite darkness.

"Colonel Sutton," Sean said, "signal the task force to form up for hyperspace transition. Navigation, lay in our first waypoint."

"First waypoint confirmed at one hundred light-years along our projected course to Ichlos," came the response from the navigation station. "Infinity Drive standing by for engagement."

"Major Nagata," Sean said, addressing his intelligence analyst, whose lean frame and precise movements concealed one of the most formidable analytical minds in the CDF, "continuous monitoring once we transition. I want to know about every anomaly, every signal, every piece of data we encounter. We're writing the book on long-range exploration. I want that book to keep future crews alive."

"Understood, sir," Hiroki Nagata replied, bringing additional sensor arrays online. "All analytical suites are active and recording."

Sean felt Oriana's presence as she moved to stand beside his chair. Her hand briefly touched his shoulder—a gesture that spoke of shared dangers, shared discoveries, shared faith in what they could accomplish together.

"All stations report ready for hyperspace transition," Colonel Sutton announced, his deep voice carrying the calm authority that had made him indispensable during the *Odyssey*'s most dangerous missions.

Sean looked around the bridge one final time, seeing the faces of the men and women who had volunteered for this mission knowing they might not return for months or even years. Each one had left behind everything familiar and comfortable. Each one had chosen to step into the unknown because someone had to.

Because it was necessary.

Because it was what humans did.

"Take us into hyperspace," he ordered.

The familiar sensation of the Infinity Drive engaging washed over the bridge—a subtle shift in perception as space-time bent around them like reality taking a deep breath. The main viewer displayed the characteristic swirling patterns of hyperspace, beautiful and alien and utterly inhuman. But this time felt different. This time, the patterns seemed to stretch farther, deeper, reaching toward distances that made previous jumps seem like stepping across puddles.

They were committed now. Behind them, New Earth had already vanished into the immeasurable gulf of space and time. Ahead lay Ichlos, ancient Phantom mysteries, and whatever other discoveries awaited them in the depths of a universe that was proving far stranger and more dangerous than anyone had imagined.

Sean Quinn had led many missions into the unknown but never one that felt quite like this. As the *Odyssey* and her escorts raced through hyperspace toward their distant destination—carrying diplomats and soldiers, scientists and engineers, the hopes of two civilizations and the dreams of a child not yet born—he found himself wondering not just what they would find, but what they would become in the process of finding it.

The greatest journey in human history had begun. And Sean was determined to ensure it wouldn't be the last.

CHAPTER 5

GENERAL SEAN QUINN stood before the main holoscreen on the *Odyssey's* bridge, transfixed by a sight that redefined everything they thought they knew about the Aczar. The Ichlos star system blazed before them in all its complex glory—thirteen worlds orbiting a G-class star that burned with fierce luminosity, casting shadows across a civilization that had utterly transformed itself.

"My God," whispered Dr. Samuel Chen from the auxiliary workstation, the xenopsychologist's composure cracking as the full scope of the transformation became clear, "they're well on their way to establishing an entire interplanetary infrastructure in just two years."

The tactical display revealed something that should have been impossible. Massive orbital platforms ringed Ichlos like metallic moons, their surfaces bristling with defensive arrays that pulsed with energy. Asteroid mining operations were detected in the inner-most belt, their automated harvesters carving wealth from stone and metal with mechanical precision. Most impressive of all, a kilometer-long shipyard hung in perfect orbit around Ichlos's largest moon, its construction bays revealing the skeletal frameworks of vessels that were impressive by Confederation standards.

"Sensor analysis complete, sir," Captain Jake Lennox reported from operations, his voice tight with barely contained amazement. "Confirmed artificial structures on forty-seven separate bodies throughout the system. Energy signatures indicate active civilizations on at least twelve major installations."

Sean's jaw tightened as the implication hit him. In his thirty years of CDF service, he'd seen civilizations rise and fall, and he'd witnessed the birth of technologies that reshaped entire species. But this was different. The Aczar hadn't just embraced space; they were conquering it with a speed that suggested capabilities far beyond what anyone had imagined.

"Captain Norquist," Sean called to his tactical officer, "threat assessment?"

Jane Norquist's striking blue eyes reflected the amber glow of weapons displays as she scanned the data streams flowing across her station. "Significant defensive installations near the planet. Exploration probes have been detected near seven of the thirteen planets in the system," she reported crisply. "Orbital platforms around Ichlos mount energy weapons with estimated yields in the teraton range. The mining installations appear to double as forward defensive positions, and I'm detecting what can only be described as mobile defense platforms—unknown range."

She paused, her fingers dancing across the tactical interface as new data arrived. "Sir, if these readings are accurate, the Aczar could field a defensive force that would make things difficult for us."

Sean scanned the data. Energy signatures indicated significant yield, which matched the intelligence they'd gathered about the Aczar. Their power systems were more efficient and smaller.

"How difficult?" Sean asked.

"Our weapons are superior, but their systems are more robust than we expected. Analysis indicates that an encounter wouldn't destroy our ships, but we would sustain significant damage."

Phendran moved closer to the main viewer, his distinctive gait bringing him within arm's reach of Sean. The Loremaster's large triangular ears twitched as he absorbed the tactical display, and Sean could see complex emotions playing across his alien features—pride, apprehension, and something that might have been fear.

"Salpheth's final gift," Phendran said, his translated voice carrying undertones of bitter irony. "He set us on this path knowing we would embrace it completely once we overcame our fears. My people do nothing by half-measures."

Ambassador Elena Vasquez stepped forward from the diplomatic workstation, her experienced eyes taking in both the tactical data and the body language of everyone around her. At fifty-seven, she had successfully navigated negotiations with species whose thought processes were utterly alien to human understanding—the Ovarrow colony disputes, the Terra Consortium trade initiatives, and the new Terran Alliance global power that had the majority representation of Old Earth in the Confederation. Her graying hair was pulled back in a practical style that suggested someone who had learned to prioritize substance over appearance, and her dark eyes held the sharp intelligence of a mind that processed information on multiple levels simultaneously.

"The technological advancement is remarkable," she said, her diplomat training evident in her controlled tone, "but it fundamentally alters our negotiating position. We're no longer approaching an isolated civilization seeking contact with the wider galaxy. We're dealing with a rapidly expanding space-faring power that may view us as either potential allies or potential threats."

Sean regarded them for a long moment. "We shouldn't get caught up in what we're seeing. The Aczar are inexperienced at exploration, and they lack FTL-capable ships. They're guarding against interstellar threats, which is to be expected, but I doubt that all this is because they thought we'd visit their star system. My guess is that this is meant to deter Salpheth from returning."

His statement seemed to put them at ease and bring into context the things they were seeing. But Sean also knew that every decision made in the next few hours could determine whether humanity gained powerful allies or created dangerous enemies.

"Colonel Sutton," Sean called to his executive officer, "deploy the final series of communications relays. When all the seed buoys and subspace transceivers become active, we'll at least have a link back to the Confederation."

"Yes, General," Brad Sutton replied calmly. "Deploying seed-buoys at our current position. Full subspace transceiver network should be online within thirty days, providing real-time communications capability across five thousand light-years."

Sean watched as the *Odyssey* released the final wave of automated communications nodes—sleek devices no larger than shuttlecraft that would unfold into full transceivers once they reached their designated positions. They were tiny construction platforms that would become part of the vast interstellar communications network. The technology still amazed him—human ingenuity merged with Phantom innovations to create capabilities that would have been pure fantasy just five years ago. Each relay buoy contained fabrication systems capable of constructing larger transceivers from local materials, creating a self-expanding network that could grow to span entire galactic regions.

"Comms," Sean said, addressing Specialist Danny Ramirez, "prepare to transmit using the protocols Phendran provided. Full diplomatic package—identification of the Confederation, detailed reference to General Gates's previous contact and the circumstances of their departure, and our current mission parameters. Let's tell the Aczar that they're not alone, and we'd like to be friends."

"Ready to transmit, sir," Ramirez replied, his fingers flying across the holographic interface. "Message formatted according to

Aczar diplomatic protocols, with cultural context markers as specified by Loremaster Phendran."

Sean looked at Phendran one final time before committing them all to a course that couldn't be undone. The Aczar Loremaster stood straighter, his SRA-enhanced uniform adapting to his emotional state with subtle shifts in color and texture. Despite his small stature, his presence commanded respect through sheer force of intellect and moral authority.

"Phendran," Sean said quietly, "any last-minute advice? We're about to announce the Confederation's presence to a civilization that appears to have undergone massive political and technological changes since you left."

The Loremaster's large ears flattened slightly—a sign Sean had learned indicated serious concern. "My people have always been... thorough in their transformations. When we abandoned space travel, we destroyed every ship and orbital facility with methodical precision. Now that we have embraced the stars once more, we appear to have done so with equal commitment."

He gestured toward the tactical display, showing the system's extensive defensive installations. "But remember, General Quinn, that transformation born from centuries of fear often swings too far in the opposite direction. They may see threats where none exist, or conversely, may underestimate dangers they have never faced."

Sean nodded grimly. "Understood. Transmit the message, Specialist Ramirez."

The communication raced across space at faster-than-light speeds, carrying with it the hopes, fears, and carefully crafted diplomatic language of two civilizations. Sean had worked on the message for days, balancing the need to establish Confederation authority with respect for Aczar sovereignty, while making it absolutely clear that they honored their commitments to allies and expected the same in return.

The response came with startling speed, far faster than even optimistic projections had suggested.

"Sir," Specialist Ramirez called out, his voice tight with surprise, "we're receiving a reply. Full audio and visual transmission from what they're identifying as Ichlos Defense Command. Signal strength suggests they're using communications systems with capabilities comparable to our own."

Another technological advancement that changed the strategic picture. The Aczar weren't just building defensive installations, they were developing communications networks that could coordinate military responses across interplanetary distances in real-time.

"On screen," Sean ordered.

The main viewer flickered, then resolved into an image that made several bridge officers draw sharp breaths. An Aczar wearing elaborate military insignia sat behind what was clearly a command station, his brown fur meticulously groomed and his large ears held in a position that Phendran had taught them indicated formal authority mixed with barely contained hostility. Behind him, Sean could see other uniformed figures moving with the purposeful efficiency of a fully operational military command center.

"I am Defense Coordinator Vaethis, serving under First Protector Korveth of the Ichlos Defensive Alliance," the figure said, his rapid speech automatically translated by systems that had been fine-tuned through months of interaction with Phendran and the other Aczar refugees. "We acknowledge the presence of the Confederation vessels *Odyssey*, *Ascendant*, and *Horizon*, and express our appreciation for your efforts in safeguarding our citizens during their unauthorized and illegal absence from Ichlos sovereign territory."

The formal, almost hostile tone sent a chill through Sean that had nothing to do with the bridge's climate control. This wasn't the grateful reception they'd hoped for; it was the opening statement of what might become a very dangerous confrontation.

Vaethis continued, his voice carrying the weight of absolute authority, "the individuals known as Loremaster Phendran, Engineer Noxrey, and Apprentice Loremasters Kholva and Vorix are currently classified as criminals under Ichlos Planetary Security Law for their flagrant violations of sovereign territory protection protocols and their unauthorized collaboration with potentially hostile alien entities."

The bridge fell into shocked silence. Sean saw Ambassador Vasquez's diplomatic composure crack for just a moment, revealing the outrage beneath her professional facade. Dr. Chen looked as if someone had struck him.

Beside the main holoscreen, Phendran's ears drooped in what was unmistakably despair mixed with resignation. The proud Loremaster who had helped save Connor Gates and his crew, who had shared precious knowledge with the Confederation, who had chosen exile over complicity with Salpheth's manipulations, had been branded a criminal by his own people.

"We require their immediate surrender to Ichlos authority for processing according to established justice protocols," Vaethis concluded, his tone suggesting that compliance wasn't really a request. "Once this preliminary matter is properly resolved, we may discuss potential diplomatic relations between our respective civilizations."

The transmission ended, leaving the bridge in a silence that seemed to pulse with barely contained emotion. Sean looked around at his crew, seeing his own mixture of outrage and disbelief reflected in every face. These people had volunteered for this mission knowing they might face hostile aliens, unexplored phenomena, or technical disasters. None of them had expected to confront the ugly politics of a civilization consuming its own heroes.

"Recommendations?" Sean asked quietly, his command voice carefully controlled despite the anger building in his chest.

Ambassador Vasquez cleared her throat. "Proceed with extreme caution, General. We're clearly dealing with a political situation that's far more complex and dangerous than our intelligence suggested. We don't know if the faction now in power views any association with outsiders as inherently treasonous, or if they're still working through their own political shift from isolationists to being more open."

She gestured toward the tactical display that still showed the system's extensive military installations. "More concerning is the speed of their technological development. Either they possessed capabilities we never suspected, or they've received assistance that enabled this transformation. Regardless of the impact on our negotiating position, both our species stand to gain if we can enter into a mutually beneficial agreement."

"Sir," Colonel Sutton added, his imposing presence somehow reassuring in the face of an increasingly volatile situation, "we have full authorization to offer asylum to any Aczar who requests it. Under Confederation law, we're not obligated to turn over individuals to face what may be politically motivated prosecution."

Sean had already been considering this but had kept it to himself. He looked at Phendran while the others continued to discuss the issue.

"No." Phendran's voice cut through the discussion like a blade, carrying a dignity that made his small stature irrelevant. "You must understand—I am a Loremaster. My knowledge, my experience, my very existence belongs to my people. I will not abandon them, especially now when they most need guidance."

Sean studied the alien, seeing something that reminded him of the best officers he'd served with—that absolute commitment to duty that transcended personal safety or comfort. It was the kind of dedication that came of serving something larger than themselves. Sean admired it, but he wasn't immune to the injustice of it all. "Phendran, they're calling you a criminal. You helped Connor escape wrongful imprisonment. You saved lives and protected innocent people from Salpheth's manipulations. Are you sure about this?"

"And I will answer for those actions according to the traditions and laws of my people," Phendran replied with a quiet dignity that made Sean's chest tighten with unwilling respect. "But first, there are things you must know about what was set in motion before Connor ever came here. Changes that go far deeper than the construction of orbital platforms and mining stations."

The Loremaster moved to stand directly before the main holoscreen, his gaze fixed on the distant blue dot of his homeworld. "Salpheth's influence didn't end when Connor Gates thwarted his escape attempt from Ichlos. If anything, his absence hopefully liberated my people to embrace changes they had been unconsciously preparing for centuries. But liberation without wisdom can be as dangerous as oppression."

Sean couldn't find any fault with Phendran's logic. He glanced at Elena, and the ambassador gave him a single nod.

Sean reopened the transmission, feeling the weight of diplomatic protocol even as every instinct screamed at him to take his ships and leave this increasingly dangerous situation behind. Defense Coordinator Vaethis waited with the rigid posture of someone prepared for confrontation.

"Defense Coordinator," Sean began, carefully modulating his tone to convey respect without subservience, "I appreciate your position and your concern for proper legal protocols. However, I must inform you that one of your citizens, Vorix, is pregnant and will require immediate medical evaluation before I will authorize any transfer to your custody. Additionally, I must respectfully but firmly disagree with your characterization of these individuals as criminals."

He paused, letting his words carry the weight of absolute conviction. "They assisted in preventing wrongful imprisonment of my people by your government and were cooperative when they learned that returning to Ichlos wouldn't be an immediate option. During their time with the Confederation, they've shared with us information about the Aczar culture and how Salpheth manipulated you for generations. Their actions demonstrated courage, wisdom, and loyalty to the highest values of civilized behavior. We've prepared a report for your review, the contents of which also contain the testimonies of Phendran and the others."

Vaethis's ears twitched slightly—a sign that might have indicated amusement, irritation, or calculation. In the background, Sean could see other uniformed figures leaning forward with interest, suggesting this conversation was being monitored by higher authority.

"We appreciate your concern for our citizen's welfare, General Quinn," Vaethis replied, his tone carrying the kind of reasonableness that made disagreement seem petty. "Appropriate medical facilities will, of course, be made available upon their return to proper Ichlos authority. However, their actions, however well-intentioned by your standards, violated fundamental laws regarding unauthorized contact with alien species and the disclosure of sensitive information to potentially hostile entities. Much has changed, but all actions and intentions must be weighed through the measure of justice."

The Defense Coordinator leaned forward slightly, his large eyes focusing directly on Sean with the intensity of someone who had fought battles. "Surely your Confederation has similar protocols regarding unauthorized disclosure of classified information. Citizens who violate such laws, regardless of their motivations, must face appropriate consequences."

Sean found himself nodding slightly despite his frustration. Vaethis had turned the situation around expertly, making Sean's defense of the Aczar refugees seem like interference in legitimate legal proceedings. The Defense Coordinator's comparison to

Confederation protocols for classified information was particularly skillful, forcing Sean to either acknowledge the parallel or appear hypocritical.

Behind the diplomatic language, Sean could see the political machinery at work amidst a new government consolidating power, needing to demonstrate strength and authority. Phendran and his companions were convenient targets, their absence making them perfect symbols of the old regime's failures.

"I understand your legal position," Sean said carefully, feeling the eyes of his entire bridge crew watching him. "But I hope you'll consider that these individuals may have prevented a larger catastrophe. The entity they helped escape, Salpheth, had been manipulating your species for centuries. Their actions may have saved your civilization from continued subjugation."

"That matter is also under comprehensive review by proper authorities," Vaethis replied, his tone suggesting that outside opinions were neither wanted nor welcome. "We have transmitted precise coordinates for the transfer of our citizens to Ichlos jurisdiction. We look forward to productive discussions regarding future relations once this preliminary matter is properly and completely resolved."

The transmission ended, leaving the bridge in a silence that seemed to throb with tension. Sean turned to face his crew and the diplomatic team, seeing a mixture of frustration and concern that mirrored his own.

"Options?" Sean asked, though he suspected he already knew what each of them would say.

"We could refuse to turn them over," Colonel Sutton suggested, his military background evident in the directness of his response. "Claim diplomatic immunity or invoke Confederation protection protocols. We have the legal authority and the military capability to enforce it."

Ambassador Vasquez shook her head, her diplomatic experience overriding any emotional satisfaction such a response might provide. "That would end any hope of productive relations with this government, possibly for generations, aside from the fact that Phendran and the others would like to return to their homeworld. They're prepared to face the consequences of their actions."

Sean nodded and looked at Phendran. "I wish there was more I could do for you, but once you're in their custody my hands will be tied."

"I appreciate all of your concern," Phendran said. "We all do, but as I have said before, my knowledge, my experience, including my experiences among you, will be shared with my people. That is worth more than a reprieve from whatever injustice we might suffer."

Phendran turned toward the tactical display, his gaze taking in the orbital installations and defensive platforms that represented his species' transformation. "My people are children playing with weapons they don't understand. Loremasters have the mandate to provide wisdom where there is fear. They need guidance now more than ever."

Sean felt a profound respect for the small alien's courage, even as he worried about the political machinery that would soon crush anyone associated with the previous regime's "failures." "This could be a show trial designed to discredit anyone who supported change, anyone who questioned the old ways."

Phendran's large ears flattened slightly, but his voice remained steady. "I don't think so." He gestured toward the holoscreen. "Change has already occurred. It does not come without cost, and wisdom is not gained without sacrifice. My people must learn to think beyond their fears, to see past the manipulations that have controlled them for so long. If my trial helps them understand the truth about Salpheth and about the larger universe we now inhabit, then it serves a purpose greater than my personal safety."

The Aczar turned back to face Sean, his alien features conveying both sadness and unwavering determination. "General Quinn, I ask only that you remember us as we were during our time together, as allies who chose to do what was right when doing right required courage."

Sean felt the familiar ache that came with watching good people make necessary sacrifices. He'd seen it with his own father, Connor, and others. In thirty years of command, he'd seen too many heroes walk into situations they wouldn't survive, driven by duty and honor to places where survival was less important than principle.

"We'll comply with their request," Sean said finally, the words tasting like ashes in his mouth. "But Ambassador Vasquez, I want you to make it absolutely clear that the Confederation will be monitoring this situation closely. These individuals are under our protection until they're safely delivered, and we expect regular updates on their welfare."

"Understood, General," Vasquez replied, already working on her diplomatic holopad. "I'll also request observer status for any legal proceedings. It's a reasonable diplomatic protocol, and their refusal would be significant in its own right."

Sean nodded, then looked at Phendran one final time, knowing he was about to hand over allies to face what might be nothing more than political theater designed to consolidate power.

"The offer of asylum remains open until you're in their custody."

Phendran's expression mixed gratitude with a kind of unwavering resolve. "Thank you, General Quinn. My people need to learn that the universe is larger and more complex than their fears, more dangerous and more wonderful than their isolation allowed them to discover. If my trial helps them understand that truth, if it forces them to confront the consequences of their choices, then everything we've done, everything we've sacrificed, will have been worthwhile."

"Very well," Sean said. "Helm, set a course for Ichlos. Ops, prepare a transport shuttle and escort for our diplomatic envoy to be ready when we reach the planet."

As the *Odyssey* and her escorts began their journey toward the inner system, their engines carrying them inexorably toward whatever waited on Ichlos, Sean couldn't shake the feeling that they were walking into something far more complex and dangerous than anyone had anticipated.

The Aczar had indeed embraced the stars, transforming themselves into a spacefaring civilization with stunning speed and efficiency. But in doing so, they had also embraced all the political complexities, military dangers, and moral ambiguities that came with a species in the midst of revolutionary change.

And Sean Quinn was about to learn firsthand just how treacherous those waters could be—for his mission, for the Confederation, and for the brave individuals who had chosen duty over safety in service of principles larger than themselves.

Sean stared at the blue dot of Ichlos growing larger on the main viewer, acutely aware that the next few hours would determine not just the fate of his Aczar allies but potentially the entire future relationship between their civilizations. Failure here might mean losing not just potential allies but any hope of standing united against the Vemus and other fallen Phantoms like Salpheth. The weight of that responsibility settled on his shoulders like a familiar burden—one he'd carried before, but never across such vast distances or with such far-reaching consequences.

CHAPTER 6

Ambassador Vasquez gave Sean a quick appraising look and then turned toward Phendran. "We only have a few hours left before you will return to your people. Would you please join me in the lounge to help me update our diplomatic approach given these new developments?"

Sean watched as Phendran considered it for a moment. "We understand where your loyalties are, and we're not asking you to compromise any of that. Your guidance has been and will always be welcome."

Phendran gave a small nod. "Thank you, General Quinn."

The diplomatic envoy left the bridge, and Phendran went with them.

Colonel Sutton came to stand next to Sean. "This changes things."

Sean nodded. "Indeed, it does."

"How do you want to proceed?"

"Combat shuttle escorts will go with the transport shuttles when we get there. I won't be at the mercy of the Aczar when we're on the planet. We'll need to be prepared to show our strength if the situation calls for it."

Sutton considered this for a few moments. "We'll gather much intel on our approach."

"I prefer a light-touch demonstration, but only if it's needed. However, we'll also need to be able to punch and run if the situation on Ichlos rapidly devolves."

"Should we hold off on the scout mission?" Sutton asked.

Sean's gaze slid to the icon representing the *Ascendant* on the tactical display. His brain was going through multiple combat scenarios given what they'd observed.

"I don't think so. Let's have tactical come up with firing solutions to incapacitate their defense enough to give us a window for withdrawal. We can easily escape them, so any retaliatory measures should be appropriate. I don't want to start a war, but if we need to show our teeth, I want it done in no uncertain terms."

"Understood. I'll put tactical on it and see what intel can come up with."

Sean went to the command chair. "Comms, open a comlink to the *Ascendant*."

A few moments later Ethan Gates appeared on Sean's personal holoscreen.

"Major Gates, you are authorized to begin your scouting mission."

"Yes, General Quinn."

There was no hesitation in Ethan's response, but Sean knew he had a few questions. Since there was no immediate danger, he could give him a few minutes. "What's on your mind, Major?"

"I just thought you'd want us to stick around. I could alter our deployment window so if you needed our help we wouldn't be as far away."

Sean quirked an eyebrow, and Ethan chuckled.

"But you probably already thought of that. Understood, General."

"Your mission is no less important than the diplomatic one taking us to Ichlos. We need to assess whether Salpheth has been active at any of the other stations or outposts or whatever leftover Phantom facility is out here. What the *Pathfinder's* out-of-date systems were able to detect is a miracle in and of itself."

Ethan nodded. "If there's anything hiding out there, we'll find them, sir."

"Happy hunting," Sean replied.

The comlink severed and Sean checked some of his messages that had been flagged as high-priority.

"General," Captain Lennox said from the operations station, "the *Ascendant* has transitioned out of n-space on the mission-specified trajectory."

"Understood," Sean said.

He looked at the main holoscreen, which showed a high-resolution image of the star system and their approach to Ichlos. It was still nothing more than a bright blue ball, barely discernible. He turned his attention to his own workstation holoscreen and looked at a star map of the area. It had been taken from the *Pathfinder's* data core, and the *Odyssey's* much more advanced sensor array was filling in the colossal gaps that had been there before.

The Aczar had traveled to this planet at least a thousand years ago and then abandoned the technology that brought them there. Sean didn't understand that kind of mentality. He understood the need to hide and conceal their presence, but to abandon any and all space travel? The idea was as foreign to him as giving up breathing. Just because he went on the occasional camping trip on New Earth didn't mean he had any illusions that anyone would be better off by abandoning all the technology that had allowed humanity to survive as long as it had.

They traveled to Ichlos much slower than they could have, gathering as much intelligence from their sensors as possible so they had as complete a picture as they could.

As they neared Ichlos, he noted the time. He would have just enough time to have a meal with his wife before joining the envoy going down to the planet.

Major Hiroki Nagata came out of CIC, along with Colonel Sutton. Nagata had a wiry frame and moved with quiet precision. His angular face, framed by high cheekbones and medium-toned skin, was typical of a descendant of Old Earth's East Asian region. Nagata came to stand a short distance from the command chair and waited for Sean to acknowledge him.

"Report, Major," Sean said.

"General, our analysis of the Aczar defensive capabilities is complete. We've assessed their defensive capabilities against the risk to our ships and the away teams. While their weapons can draw from a significant power source and must therefore have a tactical yield comparable to the *Odyssey*'s energy weapons, the materials used in construction are inferior to ours. There are limits to how long their weapons can sustain an ongoing attack. The design allows for this, so in essence they're relying on multiple energy weapons to create a defensive screen that will effectively cover the approach of an attacking fleet. They're also limited in range; hence, more of these weapons deploy on their lunar infrastructure. Their approach is interesting in that they're hidden within their various installations."

"Hiding weapons in plain sight is a good tactic as long as they're not hiding them within civilian installations. They're counting on us focusing our attention on the most obvious sources, which are those rings around the planet," Sean said.

Nagata nodded. "But it's obvious they're still new to what we know of as a change in their species philosophy. We can disable the power cores for these weapons systems, which would compromise their defensive capabilities. We're not exactly sure how long it would take their systems to recover and reroute power. We do know that the Aczar are highly capable of generating power from small power cores, so if they have redundancies in place for emergency power, their weapons could still be operational but in a diminished capacity."

Sean glanced at the main holoscreen. Then he looked at Nagata. "Do you think the targets are too obvious then?"

"It has occurred to me, sir. Different simulations do indicate that this is a possibility. We can account for it in our own defensive posture, but we'll also need to rely on new data as it comes in. Also, any tactic that we employ will also be evaluated by their military and they'll adapt as well."

Sean nodded. "Given the fact that they use their SRAs to communicate without even speaking, they can adapt faster than we can unless we allow for more control of our weapons systems to the computing core."

Colonel Sutton cleared his throat, and Sean anticipated what his XO was about to propose. "Sir, we've trained using the new protocols that allows for quicker communication among the crew. It's been effective at the platoon level and among bridge crews. I'd like permission to keep this as an option if the situation escalates."

Sean's lips tightened as he considered it. The term that R&D had been throwing around referred to this new technology as Distributed Consciousness Warfare. It was impressive both in the reports and in the field tests in certain tactical scenarios. Near instantaneous information sharing, adaptive learning acceleration, and collective problem-solving were among the gains afforded by their augmented neural implants. Those, coupled with the SRA pilot program where a subset of his crew was now paired with an SRA, yielded many benefits, but it wasn't without risks. Emotional-resilience sharing could strengthen the resolve of soldiers experiencing panic or other heightened emotional stressors during a conflict, but Sean knew the reverse must also be true. Panic could spread quicker than it could be stopped. For all the gains of quicker data analysis and response in any type of combat scenario, there was also the increased risk of a single point of failure that could greatly impede their ability to respond and would risk the lives of the crew and the ship itself.

"I'm well aware of the advantages and the vulnerabilities it introduces," Sean said.

Colonel Sutton nodded once. "Network vulnerabilities. We're entirely too comfortable that certain conditions will persist even in the event of a hostile conflict. All that can quickly change. The fact of the matter is that switching from distributed-consciousness protocols to something I'm much more comfortable with escalates the risk of further breakdown."

"Sir," Nagata said, "we could run a mixed crew, utilizing the secondary bridge with a crew that could take over in the event that this crew becomes incapacitated."

Sean exhaled sharply. He was somewhat skeptical of the ideas being presented to him, but he did remember pushing the envelope himself with some of the things he'd done to defend the colony and the riskier tactics he'd suggested to his own commanding officers.

"Colonel Sutton," Sean said, "you'll be in command of the ship while I'm on the planet. Authorization for use of the Distributed Consciousness Warfare tactics is granted, but I want redundancies in place to address the risks they introduce."

The edges of Sutton's lips lifted. "I won't leave you in the lurch, sir."

Sean chuckled and shook his head. "Just don't get lost in the virtual world."

"It'll never be a problem, sir. And I'll only use the DCW if I see a tactical advantage; otherwise, we'll rely on proven tactics."

"Carry on," Sean said, standing up.

Sutton took Sean's place in the command chair, and Major Nagata returned to CIC.

"Good luck, General. I hope the Aczar are more reasonable than they appear to be," Sutton said.

"We'll see," Sean replied and left the bridge for his quarters.

Oriana had arrived at nearly the same time as he did. They had a quick meal and discussed the mission. They'd been married a long time, and she was no stranger to potentially dangerous missions.

"As many times as we've been through this, I would rather someone else was going down there," Oriana said.

"They might get it wrong."

She rolled her eyes. "Then they shouldn't be on the team."

He smiled and she grinned. "What kind of message does it send if I stay up here safe and sound on my ship? I'm not indispensable. I'm going down there because I have every confidence that if the Aczar are unfriendly, they'll learn a very harsh lesson in becoming an enemy of the Confederation."

"It would be nice if an alien species were to accept an offer of friendship without us having to prove that we also have a big stick to beat them with if they attempt to take advantage of the situation."

Sean grinned. "I think we'll be successful. This is different than our other encounters. They're aware of the Vemus and know what's at stake. I don't like the thought of how they might treat Phendran, but there is very little I can do about it."

"We can't influence the conversation if we're not in it. I think we're right to rely on Phendran's judgement in this matter."

Sean shrugged. "It beats the alternative of abducting him against his will."

Oriana laughed and playfully slapped his hand. "Sometimes, Sean, you just distill these things to their simplest terms."

Sean reached over and gently rubbed the top of her hand. Her skin was soft and smooth. "I'll have *you* up here watching my back."

"I'll be on the bridge," she said, and glanced at his hand

lingering on hers. Her gaze narrowed. "We don't have time for that."

He chuckled. "It's not like they're going to leave without me."

She shook her head and stood up, taking her hand away. "Go to work, Sean. They need you."

Sean caught up to her at the door to their quarters, where he swept her up in his arms and kissed her. She clung to him for a long moment and then pulled away.

"Now that you've got that out of your system, you can get down to the shuttles."

"I needed something to think about while I'm away from you."

Her gaze narrowed playfully. "Wrap this up quickly and I'll make it worth your while."

She opened the door to their quarters and they stepped into the corridor.

Sean watched his wife disappear down the hallway and turned to his protective detail. "Time to go."

CHAPTER 7

THE *ODYSSEY*'s main hangar was bustling with coordinated activity as the transport and combat shuttles were prepped for departure. Sean walked up the loading ramp and approached the diplomatic envoy. They all wore EVA suits. These suits had changed quite a bit over time, going from simply protecting the wearers in space or other harsh environments to the latest augmentations that bridged the gap between flex-weave and nano-robotic mesh, which was the base for the multipurpose suits that had become commonplace for the people of New Earth. The EVA suits had the appearance of minimal protection, but they could protect the wearers even in some of the harshest environments. There were even safeguards that could deflect hostile SRAs if they needed to.

Clearance to depart was given from the bridge and the Confederation diplomatic envoy left the ship. Transport shuttles with the carrying capacity to safely move the Aczar HAB unit followed the main shuttle group.

Ambassador Vasquez looked at Sean. "I'm told that they were able to update the HAB unit's artificial environment to further mimic Ichlos's atmosphere at the landing zone."

Sean nodded. "We've made every effort to ensure that they can walk out of the HAB units without issue. How is Phendran?"

"I watched him enter the HAB unit and begin his transition to adjust to the atmosphere. It must have been painful for him, but he didn't show much discomfort."

Sean had once seen Ethan alter his physiology through his hybrid nature. The change was quick, but it didn't look comfortable. He'd imagined that Phendran using his SRA to re-acclimate to his native atmosphere would be easier on him than it was to adjust to New Earth, but perhaps he'd been wrong.

"He said he would be completely recovered by the time the shuttle reaches the planet," she continued.

"I hope his people treat him well," Sean said.

"Me, too."

The shuttle descended through Ichlos's luminous cloud cover, breaking into clear skies that revealed a world transformed beyond the video recordings from the *Pathfinder*. Where Connor had once seen hidden underground facilities carved into mountainsides, now gleaming spires of crystalline metal thrust skyward like monuments to ambition unleashed. The Aczar capital had erupted from its subterranean cocoon into a sprawling metropolis that married organic curves with geometric precision—towers that spiraled upward in helical patterns, their surfaces alive with the shifting blue-green glow of integrated Saruvian technology.

Sean leaned toward the video feed, watching as they passed over what had once been concealed mining operations. Now, massive extraction platforms filled entire valleys, their articulated arms reaching deep into the planet's crust while gravity lifts carried streams of raw materials toward orbital processing stations. The old philosophy of hiding from the universe had been replaced by something far more audacious—reshaping their world to support an interplanetary civilization.

"Incredible," Ambassador Vasquez murmured, her own gaze

fixed on the sprawling industrial complexes below. The metallic band around her wrist pulsed with a soft silvery glow as it interfaced with her neural implants. "In two years, they've accomplished what took us decades."

"I wonder how long their plans were in the works for this," Sean replied. "Connor's account was that they had extensive underground architecture. They might've just moved them to the surface. They had the technology to hollow out an entire mountain."

She nodded. "Leaves one to wonder how much of what we're seeing is new construction. Good point."

The shuttle's destination became clear as they approached a massive complex that crowned a flattened mountain peak. The structure defied easy categorization—part government center, part fortress, part technological marvel. Concentric rings of buildings spiraled outward from a central spire that stretched nearly a kilometer into the sky, its surface covered in what appeared to be living metal that shifted and flowed like mercury frozen in motion. Defensive platforms studded the complex's perimeter, their weapons arrays tracking the group of shuttles with mechanical precision.

Their shuttles touched down on a wide platform that accommodated the entire shuttle-group. The platform seemed to grow from the mountain itself. Its surface was composed of the same adaptive metal that characterized so much of Aczar architecture and resembled the recordings of the Phantom Outpost. How much Phantom technology had Salpheth shared with the Aczar?

The shuttle's hatch opened and a ramp extended to the platform. As Sean stepped out, he felt the material responding beneath his feet, becoming firmer and more stable with each step. He smiled. Aczar technology anticipated need and adapted accordingly. The Confederation had similar technology and had expanded its use by reverse engineering the Phantom ship that Connor had brought back to New Earth.

A delegation of Aczar officials waited for them, their chrome-accented uniforms catching the filtered sunlight that penetrated the perpetual cloud cover. At their head stood Defense Coordinator Vaethis, his military bearing unmistakable, even allowing for the differences in species. His brown fur was meticulously groomed, and the metallic components of his uniform seemed to pulse with contained energy.

"General Quinn," Vaethis said, his voice carrying clearly through the translation systems, "on behalf of First Protector Korveth, welcome to Ichlos. I trust your journey was without incident." Beside Vaethis stood two other officials. "Please allow me to introduce my companions. They've been assigned to assist you during your stay here. This is Senior Counselor Thyven, who will function as your liaison."

Thyven was smaller and more delicate in build, with fur that carried silver highlights and eyes that held the sharp intelligence of someone accustomed to managing complex details.

"And this is Zelara. She is a communications expert and was on the team that interacted with other members of your species during their last visit."

Zelara wore elaborate headgear that looked like a small crown of metallic filaments. Sean recognized this as the advanced interface with their communications networks. Phendran and the others had shared a lot of information with the Confederation over the past two years.

As the formal greetings began, Sean noticed Zelara's attention fixate on Ambassador Vasquez with unmistakable intensity. The Aczar's large ears twitched, and the metallic components of her headgear began to glow more brightly.

"Fascinating," Zelara said through the translator. "The human carries Saruvian technology. How is this possible?"

Vaethis's gaze sharpened, focusing on Zelara with disapproval before moving to the SRA band around Elena's wrist. "You possess our technology?" There was no hostility in his voice, but Sean detected a note of concern.

Sean knew the Aczar could communicate without speaking, and Vaethis's initial reaction to Zelara was one of disapproval. How many unspoken conversations were going on right now? Sean and the others could do this, but on a much slower basis using their own neural implants. The exceptions were those who were part of the envoy and soldiers in the CDF who had an SRA.

Elena smiled pleasantly at Vaethis. "A gift from Loremaster Phendran and also partially based on one of our own discoveries. The SRA has helped us understand your people and your culture during the time Phendran and the others spent with us."

The three Aczar exchanged rapid, untranslated communications. It looked as if they were speaking with their thoughts but sometimes vocalized them. Sean felt a moment of unease, realizing that despite their translation capabilities, there were levels of Aczar communication that remained beyond human understanding.

The CDF soldiers nearby watched the exchange, and Sean knew they were waiting for him.

"Defense Coordinator Vaethis," Sean said, and the three Aczar looked up at him at the same time. The Aczar soldiers nearby also watched with the intensity of a primed weapon ready to unleash. "Phendran has worked tirelessly to teach us about your culture. It was his intent to lay the groundwork for an alliance between us."

Vaethis regarded him for a long moment. "This information could've been coerced from him, given the fact that he had no other choice."

Elena turned sharply toward Sean, and he held up his hand. Then he looked at Vaethis. "You're correct. We could've coerced them, imprisoned and interrogated them, but we didn't. You'll find this out firsthand from Phendran and the others as you debrief them."

Elena cleared her throat. "We have an agreement with Phendran that in exchange for teaching us, we should, in turn, share some of our knowledge with you. This includes our recent discoveries with Phantom technology."

Vaethis's gaze narrowed.

"Salpheth," Sean said.

All of the Aczar in the area stiffened before letting out a shrill hiss.

Vaethis regarded Sean thoughtfully.

"There is a lot we should discuss, but I don't think this is the proper place for this conversation," Sean said.

Vaethis gave a slight nod. The Aczar in the area became quiet, and once again Sean was surprised at the speed with which they communicated.

Vaethis gestured toward several transport platforms that had some kind of antigravity emitters beneath them. The artificial HAB units were opened and Phendran, Noxrey, Kholva, and Vorix walked down the loading ramp. A mixture of awe and relief showed in their expressions as they stood on their homeworld.

Sean looked at Vaethis. "Would you allow me the courtesy of speaking with them before you take them all into custody?"

Vaethis looked as if he were going to refuse.

"We invite you to join us," Elena said. "We do not intend any kind of deception."

Vaethis glanced at Zelara for a brief moment, then gestured toward the Aczar protectors waiting near the shuttle. They guided Phendran and the others over to them.

Vorix had a swollen stomach, visibly showing signs of her pregnancy as she spoke. "General Quinn, please accept my sincerest gratitude for returning us to Ichlos."

Kholva nodded. "On behalf of my chosen, and my family, we will be in your debt for this great service you and the Confederation have done to ensure that our child has the best chance of survival."

Noxrey stayed by Phendran's side. "Thank you. I have learned much from our time together," he said and turned to Vaethis. "I look forward to sharing it all with you."

Phendran gave Sean an appraising look. "A promise kept. Please be sure to convey my appreciation of this to General Gates."

"I'll tell Connor, but hopefully when things settle down, you'll be able to tell him yourself once the communications buoys are brought online. I hope this isn't goodbye," Sean said.

"I share this hope with you. Remember, General Quinn, shared knowledge benefits everyone. What we have learned together serves a purpose greater than any individual fate," Phendran said.

Vaethis watched the exchange closely but kept his emotions hidden.

Phendran straightened. "Defense Coordinator Vaethis. Loremaster Phendran has returned and is eager to reacclimate with our brethren on Ichlos. We submit ourselves to your authority, willingly and without duress. We will share our actions and experiences while away from Ichlos to the fullest."

Vaethis stared at Phendran and something unspoken seemed to pass between them. "Thank you, Loremaster. I know the protectorate looks forward to hearing all you have to share, and now you will be taken for health checks and debriefing protocols for you and your SRAs, along with provisions and temporary housing."

Vaethis gestured toward one of the protectors, and they guided Phendran and the others away.

Sean and the rest of the diplomatic envoy, as well as a subset of their protective detail, climbed aboard the transport platforms. The artificial gravity field compensated for acceleration as the platforms rapidly moved away. There must've been multiple artificial gravity fields being used to achieve this.

The open-air transport platforms went down a main thoroughfare, taking them to the Aczar Government Complex. The complex dominated the flattened mountain peak like a technological crown, its architecture defying conventional understanding of how buildings should interact with the landscape. From the exterior, the structure appeared to grow organically from the mountain itself, as if the rock had been convinced to transform into something far more ambitious.

They passed through a main gateway area and saw that the complex's interior was as impressive as its exterior. The corridors were more than wide enough to accommodate the transport platform. They were lined with flowing metal that guided them through spaces that seemed to reshape themselves based on traffic patterns and need. Gravity fields allowed for multi-level transportation, with Aczar moving along walls and ceilings as easily as floors. The technology Connor had witnessed hidden underground had not merely been moved to the surface; it had been expanded, refined, and integrated into something approaching a technological singularity.

They passed through chambers where holographic displays showed the real-time status of the entire star system—mining operations, defensive installations, and communications networks—all coordinated through systems that processed information at speeds that even Sean could appreciate.

Thyven, their liaison, quietly watched their reactions as they traveled.

"Your technology has advanced remarkably in such a short time," Sean observed as the transport platform came to halt.

"Necessity drives innovation," Thyven replied. "When we abandoned our isolation, we embraced change with the same thoroughness we once applied to hiding from it."

"What about Salpheth and his escape?"

"We're better off now that he's gone. The direction of our society is our own and not under the purview of a dangerous prisoner who manipulated us," he replied. "Please, General Quinn, First Protector Korveth will speak to you about Salpheth and much more. We should continue to the inner chamber."

They were guided inside, far away from the landing platforms where the shuttles were.

First Protector Korveth waited for them in a chamber at the heart of the complex. The room itself was a marvel, with walls that displayed real-time feeds from across the star system, creating the impression of floating in space while surrounded by evidence of Aczar expansion. Korveth himself had the most elaborate stately outfit Sean had seen so far. He was larger than most Aczar Sean had encountered, his uniform bearing the intricate insignia of supreme military command.

"General Quinn, Ambassador Vasquez," Korveth said, rising from what appeared to be a command throne that seamlessly integrated with the room's technology, "your arrival marks both a significant moment in Aczar history and closes a loop that was opened two years ago when others of your kind were here. For the first time, we engage with alien visitors as equals rather than as a species in hiding."

Sean stepped forward, conscious that every word would be analyzed and weighed. "First Protector, we come seeking friendship and mutual understanding. The Confederation believes our species have much to offer each other despite the rockiness of our first meeting."

Korveth's expression was unreadable, but Sean sensed calculation behind those large, dark eyes. It had been a risk to remind their hosts that they'd intended to keep Connor and other prisoners here forever, but Sean thought it was best to lay their cards on the table. The fact that they'd come all this way to bring Phendran and the others back to Ichlos should speak to the sincerity of the Confederation's desire for an alliance.

"Perhaps. But first, there are matters of law and justice that must be addressed."

"About that," Sean said, choosing directness over diplomatic circumlocution. "I must speak for Loremaster Phendran and his companions. These individuals acted with courage and wisdom in preventing what could have been a catastrophe for both our species. Our understanding of the situation is that it was a time of upheaval for your species. Our own history has had similar events. Regarding your citizens that we've returned to you, they deserve recognition, not punishment."

Vaethis stepped forward. "Your sense of duty to our citizens is commendable, but the facts remain that they violated fundamental laws—"

"They prevented Salpheth from escaping to threaten your people again," Sean interrupted. "The situation was complex, and they made difficult choices under extraordinary circumstances. Surely your justice system accounts for such factors."

A long silence followed, broken finally by Korveth. "The laws exist for good reason, General Quinn. But we are not without mercy when circumstances warrant it." His gaze fixed on Sean intently. "You speak of these individuals as friends. This is significant?"

"Many in the Confederation count them as friends," Sean confirmed. "They've shared their knowledge, their culture, their perspective with us. They've helped us understand not just your species but the larger universe we all inhabit."

"There is also a medical consideration," Elena added. "Vorix is pregnant and requires careful monitoring during any transition to your custody."

Sean nodded. "That's right. In our culture we value the lives of the unborn as equals."

Korveth glanced at Vaethis, and then he looked at Sean. "I thank you for your care of our citizens, including Vorix's unborn child. We, too, value life as you do, and both she and the child will receive the very best care that we can provide. This is my promise to you."

"Thank you," Elena said.

Korveth nodded once. "We will conduct our own investigation into the actions of Phendran and the others. The investigation will be thorough, and actions will be weighed accordingly. We strive to be as fair in our rulings as possible. Should Phendran or the others feel that they've been treated unfairly, they will have the option to appeal the ruling. I'm afraid I will not make any promises beyond that. I have faith that both the results of the investigation and the subsequent rulings will be fair and just. Loremaster Phendran and his companions will be taken into custody, but they will not be isolated. If communication becomes necessary for our discussions, that will be available." He paused, his expression softening slightly. "Their treatment will be... appropriate to their service to both our peoples."

Sean couldn't think of a counter argument that would help Phendran, and Korveth's reply was an olive branch.

"I understand, First Protector," Sean said. "Would you be open to sharing the results of your investigation with us?"

Korveth's ears twitched in consideration and his gaze flicked toward Thyven.

Thyven stepped forward, consulting a holographic display that materialized at his gesture. "General Quinn, our long-range sensors have attempted to locate your homeworld based on our records from our previous encounter with your species. The distances involved appear... significant."

Sean nodded. "New Earth is approximately five thousand light-years from Ichlos. During our journey here, we've laid the foundation to establish a communications network, but real-time contact remains challenging—one which I hope we can overcome."

The revelation sent a ripple of reaction through the Aczar delegation. Five thousand light-years represented a journey that would take their current technology generations to complete.

"Such distances," Zelara murmured. "Your species has truly mastered interstellar travel."

"Indeed. This is quite impressive," Korveth said. "Could you show us your homeworld?"

Sean activated his holoscreen and expanded to a large display. New Earth's bright blue was the focus of the image as it slowly withdrew, causing the planet to become smaller. Then the recording of the colony homeworld became smaller and the star field rapidly expanded until New Earth was on one side of the large holoscreen and Ichlos was on the other side.

Korveth stared at the holoscreen for a few moments, silently taking it in. Then his gaze returned to Sean. "The reports of the previous government's interactions with General Gates indicated a strong distrust of his claims. Even now, with the evidence before us, I find it difficult to believe that a species such as yours has traveled so far."

"A species such as ours?" Sean asked, unsure how to react, and he certainly didn't want to assume.

"Not an insult, just an observation. The only species we're aware of who could travel the distances that you do are the Phantoms."

"I understand. Given the state of the *Pathfinder*, I could understand why anyone would have trouble believing it."

"Yes, and now that you're here, I think it's safe to assume that you've mastered this technology?"

The edges of Sean's lips lifted. Korveth was trying to glean information about their capabilities. "We made it here just fine."

Korveth looked at Elena.

"We're prepared to talk about the Infinity Drive," she said.

Korveth nodded. "One moment, please. Vaethis, please secure the chamber."

"Yes, First Protector," Vaethis replied.

A privacy field enclosed their small group, and Sean noticed the defensive readings on the room's displays shift to a higher alert status.

An alert appeared on Sean's HUD, indicated a loss of comms with the shuttle.

"First Protector," Sean said, "please allow one of my soldiers to go beyond the field to communicate our current status; otherwise, a lot of people will mistakenly believe that something bad has happened to us."

"Yes, of course. I should have anticipated that. Your soldier can simply walk beyond the privacy field without being hindered," Korveth said.

Sean looked at his protective details. "Report to the *Odyssey*."

Two soldiers moved away from them, leaving the field. A few moments later one of them looked toward Sean, giving him the universal all-clear signal in the form of a thumbs-up.

Sean looked at Korveth. "Please continue."

"Now we may speak more freely," Korveth said. "Our concerns about Salpheth extend beyond simple justice for past crimes. We believe he may seek retribution against Ichlos for the centuries of his imprisonment."

Sean exchanged glances with Elena before responding. "We share those concerns. We've encountered evidence of Phantom activity in our own region of space. It seems that some of them have taken an interest in us and have openly communicated with us, but they've left us no way to call on them. We've taken similar security measures like this back home."

"Tell us more of this," Vaethis said, his military instincts clearly engaged.

"After the *Pathfinder* left Ichlos, it traveled to an abandoned facility, a Phantom outpost," Sean said. "It was left over from some kind of expansion they were doing a long time ago. The facility was stuck in a what appeared to be a build cycle, with automated construction platforms operating, but no one was directing them. The facility was decommissioned and is no longer in n-space. Unfortunately, we believe that Salpheth escaped the facility before it was decommissioned. We managed to recover technology with capabilities far beyond what we currently have."

Vaethis narrowed his gaze. "How did you find this outpost?"

Sean knew that the question's simplicity carried an extra weight that was going to influence these negotiations. Over his many years in command, he'd learned the value of being diplomatic with certain things and being direct with others. The direct approach could be blunt and revelatory to the Aczar, but these things would be exposed anyway, and Sean didn't see the value in delaying it.

"Salpheth gave us the coordinates," Sean replied and waited a beat for their reactions. He'd expected a quick, knee-jerk type of judgement coming from them. The Aczar's physiology made them do everything faster. They thought quicker, aged faster, and could move with alarming speeds. However, Vaethis, First Director Korveth, and the others waited for him to continue. Sean's opinion of them increased.

"The *Pathfinder* had severely limited resources, and their options were equally as limited. There was also the fact that they had captured Salpheth."

"How were you able to contain him?" Vaethis asked.

"They used an energy field based on what they observed here and when Salpheth tried to steal the ship."

Vaethis looked at Korveth. "The zealots. They used a portable containment field to transport Salpheth."

"The zealots are no longer a problem," Korveth said, and Vaethis gave a grim nod.

Sean didn't have to guess what had happened to the zealots. In every conflict there was a side that lost. This wasn't the right time to ask Korveth to explain their recent history, but their grim expressions spoke volumes.

Korveth looked at Sean. "Please continue, General Quinn."

"I'll keep this high-level for the sake of everyone's time," Sean replied. "Salpheth attempted to steal our ship, you had a civil war breaking out, and Phendran somehow surmised what was happening and warned Connor and the others. Given their options, Connor decided that escaping was in their best interests, even while they tried to prevent Salpheth from taking control of the ship. Now, going back to Phendran, his ship was close enough to the *Pathfinder* that it was caught in the I-Drive's field, which was how the ship was able to escape your atmosphere. Your aircar wasn't designed for space flight. Connor ordered it brought inside, and Phendran and the others were able to adapt to our atmosphere through their SRAs. The crew of the *Pathfinder* had also managed to contain Salpheth, but when they tried to return to New Earth, they discovered that Salpheth had altered the ship's navigation system and they became lost again." Sean paused, considering just how much detail he should share. "There is more to it, and we have a briefing we'll make available that has more details. The long and short of it is that Connor decided to extract usable intel from Salpheth so they could repair their ship. This ultimately led to an uneasy alliance between them. That's how they ended up at the outpost, where Salpheth betrayed them."

Korveth shared a look with Vaethis, then said, "Very dangerous, but the situation was desperate. We've contended with Salpheth and his influence for a long time. Many regarded him as a deliverer of our species, while others thought of him as deceitful and manipulative. Even now that we are free of his direct influence, this division remains. It will take time for us to move beyond what he did to us... what we allowed him to do to us."

"It appears that you've made a lot of progress."

"What technology did you take from the outpost?" Vaethis asked.

"A ship... a very large ship that was pristine considering how long it had been docked."

Elena's SRA pulsed brightly. "Please allow me to share some of the things we brought. Loremaster Phendran provided us with

Saruvian technology specifically to help us understand and counter Phantom influence. Our scientists have been studying it, attempting to reverse-engineer the principles involved."

Zelara's headgear flared with activity. "Reverse engineering? To what extent?"

"We are very adept at this kind of work," Sean said with a slight smile. "We've made progress, but the complexity is... significant. On the outpost they encountered full-bodied SRAs that Salpheth was able to take control of. Phendran didn't anticipate that the piece of his SRA he'd given Connor would bond with him. As he will no doubt tell you, the SRA seems to work well with us."

Vaethis regarded him for a second. "I don't see that you have one."

"No," Sean replied.

Vaethis waited, but Sean didn't volunteer any more information. "You don't trust the bond?"

"It's new, and there are other people who are willing to try it out."

Vaethis looked as if he approved, which surprised Sean. "Your caution is understandable."

Korveth's large ears twitched, a sign Sean had learned indicated intense interest. "You possess actual Phantom technology?"

"We do. And we're working to unlock its secrets. But the threat level suggests we need allies—civilizations who understand what we're facing and can contribute to the solution."

The chamber fell silent as the implications sank in. Here were two civilizations, separated by vast distances but facing similar threats, each possessing pieces of a technological puzzle that neither could solve alone.

"Salpheth was aware of the Vemus," Sean said. "The Phantom construct we encountered also knew of them and warned us that they were a threat that was beyond us. The Vemus nearly annihilated our species once, and we've found remnants of civilizations that have waged their own battle with them. So far, none have survived. We're the only species that we know of who have managed to survive a Vemus invasion. Salpheth told Connor that the Vemus were the reason your ancestors fled their star system and came here."

A long silence stretched between them, and Sean noticed that the Aczars in the room waited for Korveth to reply.

"The trouble with Salpheth is that it's almost impossible to determine the difference between truth and lies," Korveth said. "We're aware that Ichlos isn't our original homeworld, but we have no records to indicate where it was. Any interstellar ships we once had, along with their technology, are gone. Destroyed. You see, this wasn't the first civil war the Aczar had fought. This transfer of power wasn't as brutal as some of the others in our history. We've had to rebuild from wars that nearly extinguished our people. The one constant through all that was Salpheth. We had to begin again from the ground up. Much of our history is lost, but now our fate is our own."

Sean had lived and fought through two major invasions of alien origin during his short life. First was the Vemus invasion that traveled from Old Earth to New Earth, and they'd just barely survived. Second was the Krake Wars, an inter-dimensional threat that no one could've anticipated. Leaving New Earth wasn't feasible, and through their ingenuity, sacrifice, and alliances, they survived a war with a vastly superior enemy.

"We've had to rebuild our civilization as well," Sean said. "In our history we've fought wars among ourselves and from alien threats. They've all left their scars on us, and we know the value of strong alliances. The Phantoms seem sympathetic to us, but they're also unwilling to take an active hand to advise us. And let's just say that we're reluctant to follow the advice of another species without careful consideration on our part and gathering evidence of our own. Salpheth complicates things, and we *should* be concerned about him, but the Vemus could be in a nearby star system and you might not know it. We've encountered them as close as a few hundred light-years from our planet. How many alien species are out there right now fighting their own war for survival against them? Aside from returning your citizens to you, it's for these reasons that we're here."

"This changes the nature of our discussion," Korveth admitted. "As First Protector, it is my duty to look after the interest of the Aczar and direct how we address the challenges we face. Salpheth is of great concern for us and now these Vemus as well. If they are as widespread as you suggest, our defensive preparations may be insufficient."

"The Vemus spread their seeds to worlds with life on them. They rise up and subjugate every species on the planet. They build an Alpha ship and travel through interstellar space to what we think is a super-alpha. We've found significant evidence to support this, but we only have pieces of it. They don't seem to be bound by the same time constraints as we are."

"I don't understand. What time constraints?" Zelara asked.

"We only get one life to live and then the next generation takes over. The cycle begins again. The Vemus operate outside of that. We continue to study it," Sean replied.

Elena cleared her throat. "Knowledge of Salpheth's capabilities, Phantom technology, and Saruvian adaptations could be valuable to both our civilizations, but such cooperation requires peaceful agreements and mutual trust."

Korveth considered this for a few moments. "You propose formal negotiations, representatives from both civilizations sharing information and resources toward a common defense against external threats."

Sean felt the moment balance on a knife's edge. Everything depended on whether the Aczar could see past their immediate concerns to the larger picture and whether they could trust the

Confederation enough to enter into the kind of alliance both species might need to survive.

"A common defense against external threats," Sean repeated, "but also peaceful coexistence. This was the reason we created the Confederation. We're prepared to begin such negotiations. The question is whether Ichlos is ready to join us in facing what may be the greatest threat any of our civilizations have ever encountered."

Korveth looked away, his gaze scanning the chamber. "Are there other alien species in this Confederation of yours?"

Elena nodded. "Yes, the Ovarrow. They are the native inhabitants of New Earth."

"Just two species?" Vaethis asked.

Sean smiled. "Two planets. Two member species. You'd be the third."

The chamber's displays shifted, showing tactical projections that painted a sobering picture of the challenges ahead. Sean didn't trust the Aczar yet; it just wasn't in him at this time, and he knew the feeling was mutual. This was only the first meeting. They would have to learn to trust each other or risk facing an ancient enemy alone.

"You've given us much to consider. Please allow us some time to discuss this. We will make accommodations available for your use," Korveth said.

Elena looked at Sean, and he gave her a nod.

"We gratefully accept, and we look forward to speaking with you further."

CHAPTER 8

MAJOR ETHAN GATES stood before the main holoscreen on the bridge of the *Ascendant*, watching as another fifty-light-year increment brought them deeper into unexplored space. They were five hundred light-years from Ichlos—farther than any Confederation ship had ventured in this direction. The shifting patterns of hyperspace gave way to the familiar flash sequence as the Infinity Drive bled off transit energy, and within moments they were back in normal space.

"Transition complete, Major," Lieutenant Reggie Jackson reported from the helm, his hands moving with practiced efficiency across the controls. The tall pilot's easy confidence remained steady even this far from home.

"Acknowledged," Ethan replied, then looked toward his tactical officer. "Captain Endo, initiate scanning protocols."

Captain Akira Endo's dark eyes remained fixed on his displays as he leaned over the tactical station. "Sensors coming online now, sir. Beginning standard deep-space survey pattern."

This was their eighth jump in search of Phantom communications networks, and Ethan couldn't shake the feeling that they were grasping at shadows. Each fifty-light-year hop took them further from the *Odyssey* and deeper into the void between stars. It was a calculated risk that weighed heavily on his mind. Ichlos wasn't what they were expecting, and the defenses in place near the planet were formidable. Sean wouldn't take the *Odyssey* in blindly and would have an escape plan if the Aczar decided that an attempt to capture their ship was too good to pass up.

Ethan studied the star map on the main holoscreen. The distances they were now able to travel were staggering in comparison to what they had thought were amazing just a few years ago. His last deployment had taken him over eighty light-years from New Earth, and it had taken over a month to reach the area. Now they could travel many times that distance at a fraction of the time. In fact, according to the new specifications for the I-Drive, they were moving painstakingly slowly. The *Ascendant* could have traveled to the coordinates where the Phantom Outpost had been with relative ease, but it would also put them out of contact with the rest of the task force. It would violate the mission parameters and his orders, which he wouldn't do. However, there was still some part of him that wanted to push the boundaries and travel all the way to the other side of the galaxy and back. It was the same nagging question that had driven generations of explorers who wondered what was out there.

"Ops, deploy the transceiver," Ethan ordered.

"Yes, sir," Lieutenant Anson Gooding responded, his stocky frame hunched over his console as calloused hands worked the deployment controls. "Subspace transceiver away. Quick-deployment configuration active at seventy percent. Should be operational within a few hours."

"Very well," Ethan nodded. The automated transceiver would establish their vital communications link back to the *Odyssey*, but until then, they were effectively alone in this empty region of space.

If something went wrong, either here or back on Ichlos, help was far away.

"Major," came a voice from behind him. Ethan turned to see Major Will Qualmann ascending from the Combat Information Center, his lean frame and hawk-like nose giving him a predatory alertness. They'd served together for years, and Ethan trusted him completely. "Cynergy's got the intelligence station configured for extended analysis. She's ready to start monitoring for Phantom protocols once we have sufficient scan data."

"Good." Ethan appreciated having his wife aboard, even if her transition from hybrid to fully human still sometimes caught him off guard. Her expertise with alien technologies—particularly Vemus physiology—made her invaluable for missions like this. She was still a hybrid in the sense that she wasn't in the military, but she had extensive engineering experience and had thrown herself into bridging the gaps in her knowledge with the current technological trends. Truth be told, this had started long before she'd had to become fully human. Her dossier classified her as a civilian specialist in multiple technological fields, but also an expert in Vemus hybrids and the Vemus themselves. In essence, she was a veteran intelligence analyst.

Ethan looked at Qualmann. "Any concerns about our current position?"

Qualmann's resonant voice carried a note of caution. "We're pushing the envelope on range from the *Odyssey*. If they encounter trouble and need immediate assistance…"

"I know," Ethan said. He'd run those calculations multiple times. "We're still within the operational envelope, and we needed to expand our search parameters. The Phantom network has to be out here somewhere."

From the science station, Zane Rennick looked up, his wild, curly red hair catching the bridge lighting. "Major, I'm detecting some interesting gravitic anomalies about two light-years out. Could be worth investigating with the scout drones."

Ethan moved to the science console, where Rennick's pale, freckled face was animated with his characteristic enthusiasm. The young officer's brown eyes practically glowed as he pointed to the sensor readings.

"What kind of anomalies?" Ethan asked.

"Hard to say from this distance, but the gravitational signatures don't match natural stellar formation. Too regular, too… artificial."

"Deploy hyper-capable scout drones," Ethan decided. "Full sensor package. I want to know what's out there before we commit to a closer approach."

"Deploying now, sir," Lieutenant Gooding reported from operations, his green eyes focused intently on his holoscreens.

Ethan settled into his chair, feeling the familiar weight of command. Atlas, his SRA, formed a subtle presence around his forearm, ready to assist but unobtrusive. The alien technology sometimes felt strange, but after two years its capabilities had proven invaluable, despite the fact that when he transitioned into his hybrid state, his connection to the SRA unraveled.

"Comms, any response from our transceiver deployment?" he asked.

Lieutenant Samantha Trickle looked up from her station, auburn hair pulled back in its practical ponytail. Her hazel eyes held a hint of concern. "Not yet, sir. The automated assembly sequence is operating at full capacity and should complete in approximately ninety minutes."

"Understood. Captain Grayston, status on our power systems?"

The grizzled engineering officer's voice came through the comms system, weathered and reliable. "All systems are nominal, Major. Our power cores are operating at peak efficiency. We've got plenty of juice for extended operations. Just give the word when you want to stretch the *Ascendant*'s legs."

Qualmann chuckled nearby and Ethan snorted.

"Will do," Ethan replied. He activated the ship-wide communications system. "This is Major Gates. We've arrived at our designated coordinates and are beginning our search for Phantom communications networks. We'll be conducting extended operations in this region over the next thirty-six hours. All department heads maintain readiness at Condition Three."

He closed the comlink. Standard exploration protocols now necessitated that all ships traveling through hyperspace operate at Condition Two readiness level, which assumes a threat is probable but not present. Then, once they transitioned back into n-space and performed an assessment, Condition One was set, which meant an "all clear."

As the hours passed, the bridge fell into the routine of deep space operations. The scout drones transmitted their data in regular intervals, gradually painting a picture of the region around them. Ethan found himself dividing his attention between the tactical displays and the CIC below, where Cynergy worked alongside other intelligence specialists.

"Major," Rennick called out, his voice carrying unusual excitement, even for him. "The scout drones are detecting structural formations approximately fifteen light-hours from our position. These aren't natural formations, sir."

Ethan moved to the science station. "What are we looking at?"

"Based on gravitational mapping, I'd say we're looking at artificial constructs. Large ones. The drones are still too far out for detailed scans, but the preliminary data suggests these structures could be significant."

Captain Endo looked up from tactical. "Sir, should I bring weapons systems to ready status?"

"Not yet," Ethan replied, though every instinct told him to be cautious. "But monitor the situation closely."

Twenty-four hours into their survey, Lieutenant Trickle's voice cut through the bridge's focused atmosphere. "Major, our subspace transceiver is fully operational. We have a clear channel back to the *Odyssey*."

"Excellent. Prepare a preliminary report for transmission." Ethan felt some of the tension leave his shoulders. At least now they weren't completely cut off.

Another shift change occurred as the crew got some food and some much-needed sleep. Twelve hours later brought more detailed data from the scout drones, and the picture that emerged was both fascinating and troubling. The structures were definitely artificial— a network of installations that stretched across several light-hours of space.

"Sir," Lieutenant Trickle said, "I might be out of my depth here, but this formation of structures reminds me of a communications array."

Ethan stared at the main holoscreen and blinked. As soon as she'd mentioned it he could see it. "I think you're right. Well done, Lieutenant."

She beamed at the compliment.

"Sir," Qualmann called from the CIC entrance, "Cynergy's found something you need to see."

Ethan descended into the Combat Information Center, where his wife stood before a bank of holoscreens showing complex signal analysis. Her honey-brown eyes were focused intently on the scrolling data, and her expression carried the serious concentration he recognized from their years together.

"What do you have?" he asked.

Cynergy turned toward him, her long, dark-blonde hair catching the CIC's lighting. "Those structures are just relays. We've detected distant communications protocols—definitely Phantom technology. But there's something else buried in the signal matrix." She manipulated the display, isolating specific frequency patterns. "Take a look at this."

As Ethan studied the data, Atlas enhanced his pattern recognition capabilities to decode what he was seeing. Then, it hit him like a physical blow. "That's a Vemus Alpha signal," he said quietly. "But it's so... small, almost delicate. Could the distance diminish it somehow? Some kind of latency effect?"

"There's no evidence of signal latency," Cynergy said, then gestured toward the middle screen. "Embedded within the Phantom communications network is a signal. Now, that can't be coincidence. It's subtle. Probably wouldn't have detected it without our upgraded sensors and our data library of Vemus communications frequencies."

Ethan felt Atlas stir slightly around his wrist, responding to his elevated stress levels. "Are you certain?"

"Analysis only gives a probability of sixty-eight percent. Without a direct encounter with the original source, I can't know for sure. The question is: what's a Vemus signal doing in an ancient Phantom communications network?"

Ethan looked around the CIC at the assembled intelligence officers, then back at his wife. "Good question. And one we need to answer before we go any closer."

He activated his comlink. "Bridge, this is Major Gates. Maintain current position and prepare for extended analysis operations. I want every sensor we have focused on those installations. And prepare a detailed report for the *Odyssey*. They need to know what we've found."

As he climbed back toward the bridge, Ethan couldn't shake the feeling that they'd stumbled onto something far more significant than a simple Phantom communications network. The combination of Phantom technology and Vemus signals suggested possibilities he didn't want to consider. Whatever was out there in the deep dark between the stars, they needed to understand it before it understood them.

CHAPTER 9

CONNOR GUIDED the aircar through the final approach vectors toward the Colonial Administration Complex, the sleek vehicle's navigation systems automatically syncing with the building's traffic control grid. Below him, the impressive structure rose from the heart of Sanctuary like a monument to human determination—five interconnected towers of gleaming titanium and reinforced transparisteel that caught New Earth's sun and cast prismatic reflections across the surrounding government district.

The designated landing pad materialized on his heads-up display, a circular platform extending from the main tower's fifteenth level. Connor engaged the aircar's vertical thrusters, feeling the familiar slight vibration as the craft settled onto the marked landing zone with practiced precision. Through the transparisteel canopy, he could see other government vehicles arranged in neat rows, a mix of official CDF transports and civilian administrative craft that spoke to the building's dual military and civilian purpose.

Stepping out onto the landing pad, Connor paused to take in the view. From this height, Sanctuary sprawled beneath him in organized sectors. Residential districts gave way to industrial zones, all connected by the efficient transit networks that kept the city running smoothly. Sanctuary had once been the smallest city of the colony, but over time it had grown in size and population to rival the other cities. There had also been a surge in population when the colonial government rotated its administrative center to Sanctuary. The practice of rotating the colonial government's seat of power had begun early in the colony's history to avoid any one city from rising above the other. Of the four major cities on New Earth, it was Sanctuary's turn to host the colonial government for the next five years.

The administration building itself commanded the skyline, its architectural lines suggesting both strength and accessibility. The towers were connected by graceful sky-bridges that seemed to float between structures, their surfaces embedded with the flowing light-strips that indicated active data streams flowing through the building's neural network.

West of the building, construction of a new transit system had begun unlike any other on New Earth. It was a transit system without any automated trams. Concentric rings spaced at precise distances created an artificial gravitational field that riders could enter and exit as they wished. The control systems prevented any collisions, and as Connor watched a few people step into the field to be quickly propelled away, he had to admit that it looked like a lot of fun. The design was based on a similar transit system that Ethan had encountered on a large alien ship. With advances in power creation, the costs to produce those transit systems on New Earth had become negligible. He'd also heard of proposals for their use as a teaching method at schools.

The main entrance led him through an airlock-style security checkpoint, a necessity given the building's importance and the various atmospheric requirements of different alien dignitaries who now regularly visited. Beyond the checkpoint, the lobby opened into a vast atrium that rose through three levels, its ceiling a dome of smart glass that could display anything, from New Earth's sky to star charts from all the places the Confederation's exploratory initiative had gone.

Connor's footsteps echoed softly on the polished stone floor, quarried from the far north of New Earth's vast continent and inlaid with thin veins of metal from asteroid mining operations. The walls displayed a subtle but impressive timeline of colonial achievements—images of the original Ark, the first settlements, construction of the orbital shipyards, Ovarrow settlements, later images of them joining the colony, and most recently, images for the voyages back to Old Earth and the reestablishment of contact with the people there. It was a reminder of how far they'd come and how much further they had yet to go.

Administrative staff moved through the space with quiet efficiency, their conversations a low murmur mixing human voices with the occasional rumble of Ovarrow speech. The diversity still struck Connor as remarkable—a functioning multi-species government that somehow managed to balance competing interests and cultures. It only worked because they lived under the same moral foundation and truth.

The governor's office occupied the top level of the central tower, accessible by high-speed lifts that moved with barely perceptible acceleration. How long would it be before the artificial gravity transit systems were brought into these towering buildings and lifts became a thing of the past?

As Connor stepped into the elevator, he noted the discrete but comprehensive security measures—scanners that verified identity from his neural implants, atmospheric sensors that could detect concealed weapons or dangerous substances, and the subtle presence of guard stations positioned to respond to any threat. The holoscreen registered two occupants because the computer system reported Joshua as an occupant distinct from Connor.

The lift opened onto a reception area that managed to be both impressive and welcoming. Large windows offered a panoramic view of Sanctuary and the surrounding landscape, while comfortable seating areas were arranged to accommodate various alien physiologies. The governor's receptionist, an efficient-looking woman with the bearing of someone accustomed to managing complex schedules, looked up as Connor approached.

She smiled up at him. "General Gates, welcome. Governor Blackstone is expecting you. Conference Room Alpha is prepared for your meeting."

Connor glanced across the reception area and down the hall to the conference room, seeing that there were already people inside. He looked at the receptionist. "Am I late?"

She shook her head. "You're right on time according to the schedule."

Connor nodded his thanks and moved across the area toward the indicated door, his thoughts already shifting to the matters at hand. This was to be an informal meeting, but it was amazing to him just how many informal meetings led to a shift in policy. There was more at stake than the mere informalities that came from a discussion of ideas. The Colonial Administration Building represented everything the Colony had achieved, which had then given rise to the Confederation—a place where the future of multiple species was decided through discourse rather than conflict, even when those discussions concerned threats that could destroy them all.

Connor stepped into Conference Room Alpha and immediately appreciated the thoughtful design. The oval chamber was spacious enough to accommodate various alien physiologies without feeling cavernous, its curved walls lined with smart-glass panels that currently displayed a subtle view of New Earth's rings against the star field. A horseshoe-shaped conference table dominated the center, crafted from the same polished stone as the lobby but configured with adjustable seating that could adapt to human,

Ovarrow, and even Aczar. The last time he was in this room was with Phendran before the mission to return him and the others to Ichlos.

Governor Blackstone stood as Connor entered, extending a welcoming hand. The governor's silver hair and lined face spoke to decades of public service, while his alert eyes suggested a mind still sharp enough to navigate the complex politics of a multi-species confederation.

"Connor, thank you for making time for this discussion," Blackstone said, gesturing toward an empty chair positioned where Connor could see all the other participants. "I believe you know most everyone here."

Connor nodded to General Nathan Hayes, who sat with military bearing in his blue uniform. His old friend's expression was carefully neutral, but Connor caught the slight tightening around his eyes that suggested this wouldn't be a simple briefing.

Dr. Seth Osbourne looked up from a data pad, and his weathered features brightened with genuine warmth. The renowned colonial scientist had collaborated with Connor on numerous projects over the years, and his presence suggested this meeting dealt with technology that straddled the line between military and civilian applications.

Across the table, Ozamus shifted slightly in his specially configured chair. The Ovarrow's pebbled brown skin caught the room's ambient lighting, and his large hands rested calmly on the table's surface. Connor had worked with enough Ovarrow over the years to recognize the subtle body language that indicated careful attention rather than relaxation.

"General Gates," came a crisp voice with a slight accent. Sebastian Devakul rose briefly from his seat—a lean man in his forties with the intense gaze of someone accustomed to having his expertise questioned. "I hope you remember me from the Terra Research Consortium. I've followed your work with great interest."

Connor nodded politely, already sensing the undercurrents in the room. "Of course I remember you."

The final participant caught his attention as she looked up from her own notes. Dr. Caroline Lockwood's blonde hair, cut in a long bob that framed her face attractively, seemed to catch and hold the room's light. Her blue eyes reflected the analytical intelligence of someone who studied behavior and motivation as a profession.

"Dr. Lockwood," Connor said by way of acknowledgement, "my team has reported moving forward with your request to access the Phantom ship."

She smiled. "Yes, I received the notification yesterday. Thank you for your help with this."

Governor Blackstone activated the room's privacy shields, and a barely perceptible shimmer indicated that their conversation was now secured against any kind of surveillance. "Ladies and gentlemen, we're here to discuss a proposal regarding Space Gate technology and its potential applications at Old Earth. A request has come to this office and the security council to review some of our long-standing policies on their use."

Connor felt his jaw tighten slightly. Space Gates—technology that had allowed travel between alternate universes during the Krake Wars, technology they'd used because they had no other choice.

Sebastian leaned forward immediately. "General Gates, the Terra Research Consortium believes we have a unique opportunity here. The Space Gate technology could allow us to contact alternate versions of Earth... Old Earth, that is. Versions of it where humanity might have developed different solutions to the challenges we face."

"Such as?" Connor asked, keeping his voice level.

"Warning them about the Vemus, for one. Sharing our technological advances. Perhaps finding versions of Earth where humanity found different paths entirely. The possibilities and their advantages are limitless."

"So, you propose that we bring a Space Gate to Earth and use it as a means to gain technological advantages?" Connor asked.

Sebastian frowned. "We'd share with them."

Connor glanced at Nathan for a second, and his friend lifted his chin. Then, he looked at Sebastian. "We've been down this road before. The Krake pursued exactly this kind of thinking and look where it led them—genetic modification just to survive in alternate universes and an obsession with control that led to hundreds of Ovarrow civilizations destroyed or severely impacted by their harsh experiments. This path warped the entire Krake society like a cancer."

Sebastian glanced at the others, probably looking to see whose support he could gain. "We're not the Krake. We're aware of the dangers. We won't make those mistakes. We'd put constraints around its use with protocols and ensure that they are followed."

Ozamus spoke in his deliberate manner, his words carrying the weight of personal experience. "The Ovarrow in other universes have made their choice. Our allies during the Krake War destroyed their Arch Gateways to prevent exactly this kind of interference. There is wisdom in isolation when the alternative is contamination."

"But surely the potential benefits outweigh the risks,' Sebastian pressed. "We could establish a network of human civilizations, sharing knowledge and resources across multiple realities. Replenish our population, so if the Vemus do actually return, we could be ready for them."

Dr. Lockwood cleared her throat. "From a psychological perspective, I'd like to understand the individual and societal impacts better. What happens to a person's sense of identity when they encounter alternate versions of themselves? What about entire societies?"

Connor leaned back in his chair, considering his words carefully. Memories of a war fought over twenty years ago came to the forefront of his mind. "Dr. Lockwood, the psychological toll is significant. The societies we encountered here were Ovarrow, so we were one step removed. Ovarrow soldiers who traveled between universes struggled with questions of identity and purpose that were difficult to resolve. It became even more difficult for them to move on from the warped society that not only fought the Krake but an insidious war among themselves, seeing entire societies fall victim to Krake manipulation that played upon any and all societal biases that come over time, but it's much worse." He looked directly at Sebastian. "The Krake became so obsessed with controlling alternate realities that they lost sight of their own. Their efforts began as a scientific theory, an exploration initiative, if you will. But when they learned that all the alternate universes they visited showed the consistent destruction of their own race, they began a campaign against the Ovarrow in their own universe as some kind of sick revenge. That's when things progressively became worse. They used entire planets as staging areas to wage invasions on other worlds. Their society became stagnant and rigid. My opinion, and that of anyone else who fought during the Krake Wars—the people and Ovarrow who witnessed this first-hand—will never be open to using the Space Gates in any capacity."

Nathan nodded. "That technology was restricted for good reason. Every argument I've heard today for using it echoes the justifications the Krake used, according to the data we've collected from the charred remnants of their homeworld."

"But what about defense?" Sebastian asked. "If we can't defeat the Vemus, shouldn't we have escape options? Other realities where humanity could survive?"

"Running from the problem doesn't solve it," Connor replied. "It just spreads it to other universes. And there's no guarantee that fleeing to alternate realities would be any safer than staying and fighting here."

Dr. Osbourne pulled up a holographic display showing complex molecular structures. "There's also the biological factor. Extended exposure to alternate realities requires genetic modification to survive. The universal constants are different enough that unmodified humans or Ovarrow, or even the Krake, will eventually sicken and die. Are we prepared to fundamentally alter what it means to be human?"

Sebastian's frustration was becoming evident. "But the potential knowledge we could gain—"

"At what cost?" Ozamus interrupted. "Knowledge that comes from violating the natural barriers between realities carries corruption with it. The Ovarrow learned this lesson at great cost."

Governor Blackstone raised his hand for silence. "Dr. Lockwood, you've been observing our discussion. What are your thoughts on the psychological implications?"

Dr. Lockwood considered it, her gaze moving around the table. "What I see here are two fundamentally different worldviews. One sees the multiverse as a resource to be explored and utilized. The other sees it as a boundary that shouldn't be crossed. Both perspectives carry psychological and social implications that could reshape our civilization."

She paused, then continued. "If we pursue, or reopen Space Gate technology, we're essentially saying that our current reality isn't sufficient and that we need alternatives to survive or thrive. That mindset alone could undermine social cohesion and individual purpose. Why struggle to solve problems here when escape is always an option?"

Connor nodded approvingly. "Exactly. The technology doesn't just change what we can do; it changes who we are."

Sebastian looked around the table, clearly realizing he was

outnumbered. "So, we're just going to abandon one of the most powerful technologies ever developed?"

"We're going to continue treating it with the respect and caution it deserves," Connor replied. "Some knowledge is too dangerous to pursue, regardless of the potential benefits. When I encountered the Phantoms, they were concerned by what they referred to as some kind of scarring in our star system, which stemmed from our use of the Space Gates. We had no other choice, but now we do. We have the Infinity Drive and a whole host of other technologies that could take us far away from here if it came down to it. We're not lacking in advanced technology from our own development, Ovarrow, and now Aczar, and also the Phantom tech we're working on reverse engineering." He paused for moment, his expression softening. "Sebastian, I still remember Old Earth. I remember all the people I left behind. It's more distant than it used to be. I know what was lost, but I also know that recklessly pursuing this in the name of discovery is a broad path to destruction."

Sebastian heaved a sigh and leaned back in his chair.

"Governor Blackstone also leaned back in his chair. "I think we have our answer. The Space Gate technology remains restricted. Dr. Devakul, you can inform the Terra Research Consortium that the Colonial Administration supports the current limitations."

As the meeting concluded and participants began to file out, Connor couldn't shake the feeling that this wouldn't be the last such discussion. The temptation to use powerful technology rarely disappeared simply because it was declared off-limits. But for now, at least, wisdom had prevailed over curiosity. But what about in the future when generations from now weighed these same questions but without the wisdom of the people who had witnessed the atrocities firsthand? Perhaps the technology should be destroyed and all records of its use removed.

Governor Blackstone thanked them for coming and Connor left the office. As he climbed onto the elevator, Nathan joined him.

"Well, that was something," Nathan said and eyed him for a second. "I appreciate the restraint you showed in there."

Connor snorted. "Was I that obvious?"

Nathan shook his head. "Not at all. I just know you better than they do."

The elevator reached the fifteenth level and they made their way back to the landing pads.

"The undertones of the request bother me," Nathan said.

"They're worried about being left behind," Connor said, meaning the people of Old Earth.

Nathan nodded. "There is a power dynamic that cannot be denied. One day it could shift, but today it was decidedly in our favor."

Connor gestured toward his aircar. "This is me."

"Good, because you're my ride back to base."

Connor grinned. "Seriously?"

"I knew you'd be here, and I needed to talk to you about a certain confidential proposal that made its way to my desk. Plus, I know you have the additional security measures that I need right now."

Connor nodded and gestured toward the aircar. They climbed inside, and Connor engaged the controls.

The aircar lifted into the air and Connor entered a destination that took them into the upper atmosphere. It was well beyond the range of a normal aircar, but Connor wasn't an average colonial citizen. He engaged the security protocols and inputted a flight plan that should give them enough time to discuss whatever it was that Nathan wanted to.

"We should be secure," Connor said, removing his hands from the controls and putting the aircar's flight systems into autonomous mode.

Nathan nodded and blew out a breath. "Can you ask Joshua to confirm?"

A silvery glow came from the metallic band on Connor's forearm. "Security protocols are engaged, General Hayes, including an energy field that would prevent Phantom monitoring," Joshua replied.

"Thank you, Joshua," Nathan said. "Just wanted him to confirm."

Connor frowned. "What's this about?"

"A proposal came directly to me from Sean before he left."

"Okay, what is it?"

"It actually came from Ethan."

Connor's eyebrows raised. "Ethan?"

Nathan nodded. "He took every security precaution available for the proposal and took it directly to Sean."

That meant that Ethan had bypassed the chain of command by bringing whatever he was proposing to Sean.

Connor nodded.

"The timing of the discussion we just had down there carries a bit of irony for what I'm about to show you. Here, look at this," Nathan said.

He made a passing motion, and the aircar's main holoscreen darkened with a schematic of a large-scale weapon.

"Is that what I think it is?"

"A Space Gate, but not like what we've used. It's different. It has a configurable deployment design so it can be either shuttle-sized or large enough for an entire fleet. It's the largest thing I've ever seen."

"Ever seen? This is still just a proposal, right?"

Nathan nodded. "But it's practical. He's taken the old theoretical designs and applied Aczar power generation to them to make them a lot sleeker to the point where they're truly autonomous. No need for it to tap into a heavy cruiser's massive power core to operate."

Connor continued to look at the holoscreen. "It's a Space Gate array." He paused, rubbing his chin for a second. "We've talked about weaponizing the Space Gates, but we couldn't make it work at the time."

"His proposal was for it to be used against a Vemus Alpha. It's got theoretically quick deployment designs. He's spent a lot of time on this."

Connor sighed. "That's because he's had a lot of time on his hands until recently."

"Agreed. At first I thought he'd accessed restricted Space Gate data to put this together, but he hadn't."

"He wouldn't do that. He could probably get the preliminary data from old CDF ship designs."

Nathan chuckled. "Resourceful, but I guess I shouldn't be surprised, given who his father is."

Paternal pride swelled Connor's chest. "Who knows about this?"

"Us, Sean, and Ethan. That's it. He knew it was controversial and wanted to restrict the concept."

Connor gave an approving nod, then shook his head. "We just spent an hour talking about the dangers of using Space Gates, and now we're going to consider weaponizing it against a potential Vemus Alpha or super-alpha, or whatever."

Nathan shrugged. "It *is* a bit ironic. What do you think?"

"I don't like it. I don't like it at all. I wish we'd destroyed the tech years ago so the temptation to use it wouldn't be there."

"Yes, it's an advantage that we can't completely ignore."

"We don't even…" Connor began and stopped. "There are a lot of unknowns, such as whether it'll work in other parts of the galaxy."

"I'm seriously considering assigning a team to determine the efficacy of the concept. It might not work."

Connor rolled his eyes. "I doubt it. Ethan could've been an

engineer if he'd wanted to. Noah tried to convince him while he was growing up. In the end he liked ships more."

"That's what I thought as well."

"If we're going to test this out, even at a conceptual stage, it'll have to be classified."

"I thought we were done with hidden projects, but I can't exactly take this in front of a review board."

Connor smiled. "We'll keep the project small."

Nathan eyed him. "You do realize I'm handing this to you. Put a team together, and make sure they're fully vetted. It's one of those things that I hope we never have to use."

"I'll put together a small list of candidates."

"Not Noah," Nathan said. "He needs to focus on the Phantom ship and the SRA development program."

"I agree."

Nathan transferred the proposal to Connor. "You have the only copy of this. We can't afford for anyone to learn of this for the time being."

Connor nodded and then had the aircar take them back to base.

CHAPTER 10

SEAN SETTLED into a curved seat that conformed to his body's contours, watching as the Aczar waiting area adapted to their presence with subtle shifts in lighting. The light EVA suit he wore was designed for extended operations, but Sean found himself looking forward to their return to the portable HAB units near their shuttles. Their hosts were working on providing better accommodation, though accommodating alien atmospheric requirements was unfamiliar territory for the Aczar.

The chamber itself was a study in organic architecture—walls that flowed like frozen water, surfaces that glowed with soft bioluminescence, and gravity fields that allowed for multi-level seating arrangements their hosts used with casual efficiency.

Three days of equal parts negotiations and getting to know each other had established a rhythm, though Sean couldn't shake the feeling that they were only seeing half the conversation. The Aczar delegation would arrive, engage in formal discussions for precisely two hours, then excuse themselves for what Thyven diplomatically termed "internal consultations." Each time they returned, their positions had shifted in ways that suggested input from someone with intimate knowledge of both Aczar culture and Confederation capabilities.

"They're getting advice," Sean said quietly, keeping his voice low enough that the translations systems wouldn't pick it up clearly. Despite the privacy of their waiting area, he had learned to assume they were being monitored.

Ambassador Elena Vasquez looked up from her diplomatic notes, the metallic band of her SRA catching the ambient light. Her dark eyes held the patient calculation of someone who'd spent decades reading the spaces between words. "Phendran?"

"Has to be. He's the most knowledgeable of the group, but they could be consulting with the others as well. The timing is too convenient, and their questions are too informed." Sean stretched his legs, feeling the subtle adjustment of the seat as it accommodated his movement. "Yesterday, Vaethis asked about our fleet composition and deployment methodologies. I expected questions like that from him, but it was a bit on the nose."

"You have to remember that from their perspective, we just arrived and they're still getting to know us. They're confirming everything we say and balancing it with what Phendran and the others are reporting. It's a good way to determine the validity of both parties, if you think about it," Elena said.

"Or that we brainwashed them and know how to keep our stories straight," Sean said, and Elena blinked. Sean shrugged. "It's what I would be thinking."

She sighed. "I suppose that makes sense given..." She gestured toward him, and Sean smiled.

He'd learned to consider situations from multiple angles, including those that the average civilian might never think about.

Dr. Samuel Chen glanced up from his analysis pad, his academic curiosity evident in the way he leaned forward. "So, it's a matter of establishing trust. From a psychological standpoint, it makes perfect sense. Phendran spent two years learning our systems, our thought processes, our cultural markers. He'd be invaluable for interpreting our positions and predicting our negotiating strategies.

Captain Blake shifted in her seat, her hand instinctively moving near her sidearm. "If they're consulting with him, they know our fleet composition, our weapons capabilities, even our standard operating procedures. That intelligence asymmetry puts us at a severe disadvantage in any negotiation. They can anticipate our responses while we're still guessing at theirs."

Sean nodded. "If they're wise enough to listen to him."

Elena set her notes down and moved to rub her head, then stopped as if she just remembered she was wearing a helmet. She gave a slight chuckle and shook her head. "The question is whether that's necessarily problematic. Phendran has been consistently supportive of a Confederation alliance. His advice might actually work in our favor."

"Unless Korveth decides that Phendran's loyalties have been compromised by his time with us," Sean replied. The thought had been nagging at him since their first formal session. "Two years away from home, dependent on an alien species for survival—that could be seen as coercion, regardless of our intentions."

Dr. Chen's fingers moved over his pad as he pulled up behavioral analysis notes. "The Aczar social structure places enormous emphasis on collective decision-making filtered through hierarchical expertise. Phendran represents both the highest level of knowledge preservation and direct experience with our civilization. Excluding him from these discussions would be almost culturally impossible."

"Which means he's either advising them directly, or..." Sean paused, considering the implications.

"Or observing through their communications networks," Elena finished. "The technology Zelara demonstrated at our arrival suggested real-time neural linking capabilities. If Phendran is connected to their system, he could be participating without being physically present."

Sean stood and moved to the chamber's large window, watching the sprawling metropolis below. The transformation of Ichlos continued to amaze him—vast construction projects were reshaping entire valleys, orbital platforms that stretched toward space, transportation networks that moved with the fluid efficiency of living organisms. The scale suggested a civilization that thought in terms of centuries rather than decades, which gave him an idea.

"There is one thing we're not considering," Sean said, turning back to the group. The others looked at him. "They can communicate without speaking. Through their SRAs, they can share their experiences on a much more intimate level that we're only beginning to do ourselves. That should demonstrate Phendran's, or any of the other's, consistent thoughts and feelings while they were with us. This could be in our favor. It then becomes a matter of whether they trust what is being shared."

Dr. Chen smiled and nodded enthusiastically.

"This next session feels different," Elena said, joining Sean at the window. "The preliminary discussions are finished. If they're going to make serious requests, or demands, it'll be today."

Captain Blake approached, her tactical awareness extending beyond immediate security to the broader strategic picture. "What kind of requests are we expecting?"

Elena's expression grew thoughtful. "Technology sharing is inevitable. They'll want access to our Infinity Drive capabilities, our military technologies, possibly our artificial intelligence systems. The question is what they're prepared to offer in return."

"And what they're prepared to demand," Sean added. "Through Phendran and the others, the Aczar have already given us a great deal. They're not in a weak bargaining position. They have advanced manufacturing capabilities, defensive technologies that we should study, and most importantly, knowledge of Phantom operations that predates our first contact. Plus, geographic advantages. Ichlos could serve as a forward base for operations in this region of space."

Dr. Chen looked up from his analysis. "There is also the psychological factor of legitimacy. Right now, the Confederation consists of two species from the same star system, and Old Earth of course. Adding the Aczar—a civilization five thousand light-years away—fundamentally changes our credibility as an interstellar alliance."

The waiting area's entrance chimed softly, and Thyven appeared with the fluid grace characteristic of Aczar movement. The senior counselor's silver-highlighted fur was immaculately groomed, and the metallic components of his attire pulsed with the subtle energy that indicated active connection to their communications networks.

"General Quinn, Ambassador Vasquez," Thyven said, his rapid speech automatically translating through their systems, "First Protector Korveth is prepared to receive your delegation. The conference chamber has been configured for extended discussions."

Sean exchanged glances with his team. Extended discussions suggested they were finally moving beyond preliminary positions into substantive negotiations. "Thank you, Senior Counselor. We're ready."

As they gathered their materials and prepared to follow Thyven, Sean caught Elena's eye. She gave him a subtle nod—the acknowledgment between experienced negotiators that they were about to enter the most critical phase of their mission.

"One more thing," Thyven said, pausing at the entrance. "First Protector Korveth has requested that today's discussions be conducted under enhanced privacy protocols. Your communications devices will need to be secured and the chamber will be isolated from external monitoring."

Sean felt his tactical instincts sharpen. Enhanced privacy meant they were about to discuss something the Aczar considered highly sensitive—technology, intelligence, or strategic capabilities they didn't want recorded or transmitted.

"Understood," Sean replied. "We're prepared to comply with your security requirements."

As they followed Thyven through corridors that seemed to reshape themselves around foot traffic, Sean couldn't shake the feeling that Phendran was watching somehow—either directly through hidden observation systems or indirectly through the neural networks that connected Aczar society. The Loremaster had spent two years learning to read human behavior and motivations. Today, that knowledge would be put to the test.

The game was about to begin in earnest.

The conference chamber exceeded even Sean's elevated expectations for Aczar technology. As Thyven guided them through the entrance, the room seemed to recognize their presence and began adapting—the ceiling rising to accommodate human height preferences, the lighting shifting to a spectrum more comfortable for their visual range.

The chamber itself was circular, with a raised platform in the center surrounded by tiered seating that could accommodate the physical requirements of various species. Holographic displays floated at multiple levels, currently showing real-time status feeds throughout Ichlos and the near planet space operations. Orbital platforms, mining operations, and defensive installations all coordinated through networks that processed information at speeds that made Sean appreciate the scope of Aczar technological achievement. At the same time, he also felt like they were showcasing what they were capable of like someone who was eager to be perceived as not being at a disadvantage.

First Protector Korveth waited at the central platform, his elaborate uniform bearing the complex insignia of supreme command. The chamber's technology seemed to flow around him like an extension of his authority, responding to subtle gestures as he monitored various displays. As Sean's delegation approached, Korveth stepped forward with the bearing of someone accustomed to being in authority.

"General Quinn, Ambassador Vasquez," Korveth said, his voice carrying clearly through the enhanced translation systems, "please be welcome in our most secure conference facility. Today we discuss matters that will shape the future of both our civilizations."

Defense Coordinator Vaethis stood to Korveth's right, his military bearing unmistakable even in the diplomatic setting. His chrome-accented uniform pulsed with the subtle energy indicators that suggested active connection to Ichlos's defensive networks. Sean recognized the posture—a commander maintaining awareness of potential threats even during negotiations.

The other Aczar delegates were arranged according to what Sean was learning to recognize as their complex social hierarchy. Thyven, now introduced as Senior Cultural Attaché, had positioned himself where he could observe both delegations and provide input on protocol issues. Zelara, whose expertise was in communications and advanced technology, wore an even more elaborate headgear array than before, its metallic filaments practically humming with activity as they interfaced with the chamber's systems. Sean suspected that her head gear was part of her SRA.

Two new faces caught Sean's attention. Moxtel leaned forward as he was introduced as Resource Coordinator, his practical bearing evident in the way he immediately consulted a data pad—clearly someone accustomed to managing logistics across multiple projects. Beside him, Tavira straightened when identified as Junior Archivist. Her youth was apparent, but so was the intense focus with which she absorbed every exchange, as if cataloging each diplomatic nuance for future reference.

"Loremaster Phendran's designated successor," Thyven explained quietly, noting Sean's interest in Tavira. "She and others of her generation represent the future of our knowledge-preservation efforts and our potential relationships with other species."

Sean thought Tavira seemed rather young for that kind of responsibility but kept his opinion to himself. He settled into the adaptive seating, feeling the material adjust to support his frame while maintaining the slight elevation that put all participants at equal eye level—a thoughtful touch that spoke to the Aczar's diplomatic experience. Elena took the seat to his right, her SRA band glowing softly as it interfaced with the chamber's translation systems. Dr. Chen and Captain Blake completed their delegation, both maintaining the professional alertness that marked experienced diplomatic personnel.

"Before we begin substantive discussions," Korveth said, "I want to acknowledge the service your people have provided in returning our citizens safely. Phendran and his companions have been debriefed extensively, and their accounts of your treatment have been…illuminating."

Sean caught the subtle emphasis and felt some of the tension leave his shoulders. Phendran's testimony had apparently been favorable.

"Furthermore," Vaethis said, leaning forward to add to Korveth's remarks, "we've reviewed the technical data and cultural information they've shared about your civilization. The scope of your technological achievements, particularly in interstellar travel, represents capabilities we had not fully appreciated."

In turn, Zelara also leaned forward, her elaborate headgear flaring with the kind of activity Sean now recognized as deep-system interface. "Which brings us to the primary subject of today's discussions. The Confederation has gained considerable advantages through Loremaster Phendran's guidance over the past two years. Your understanding of our technology, our cultural patterns, our defensive capabilities—all of this knowledge has strengthened your position. We believe reciprocal sharing is now appropriate."

Elena exchanged a quick glance with Sean before responding. "We've always been prepared to share knowledge with potential allies. The question is ensuring that such sharing benefits both civilizations without creating unintended consequences."

Moxtel consulted a holographic display that materialized at his gesture. "Our analysis suggests that your Infinity Drive technology would fundamentally transform our exploration and defensive capabilities. We're prepared to offer significant concessions in return for access to this technology."

Sean felt the moment balance on a razor's edge. This was the request they'd been expecting, but also the one fraught with the most danger. He leaned forward slightly, choosing his words carefully.

"Resource Coordinator Moxtel, we appreciate your directness. The Infinity Drive represents one of our most significant technological achievements, but it also carries tremendous risks. The technology that brought us here took many years to develop safely, and even now we're discovering new applications and limitations."

Dr. Chen cleared his throat gently. "From a technological development standpoint, the I-Drive requires supporting infrastructure that goes far beyond the drive itself. Navigation system, power management, safety protocols, manufacturing capabilities—it's an integrated technology ecosystem."

Vaethis narrowed his gaze. "Are you suggesting our current technological level is insufficient?"

"I'm suggesting that responsible technology transfer requires careful consideration of readiness and capability," Sean replied. "Your technological achievements here on Ichlos are remarkable, but interstellar travel using I-Drive technology involves variables that can't be fully simulated in a single star system."

The chamber fell silent and Sean could sense the rapid, untranslated communications flowing between the Aczar delegates. Their ability to share complex thoughts in near-real time gave them significant advantages in negotiations, but it also meant that human responses needed to be clear and unambiguous.

Vaethis looked at Korveth, giving deference to the First Protector. Korveth's expression showed careful calculation. "General Quinn, are you declining our request?"

"I'm suggesting a different approach," Sean said. "Your current technological capabilities are more than sufficient to fully explore and develop the Ichlos system. The experience and expertise gained from such operations would provide the foundation necessary for eventual interstellar expansion. However, your current exploits haven't gone beyond mid-system. I'm not taking anything away from what you've achieved; I'm merely stating that more experience is needed."

Tavira spoke for the first time, her voice carrying the earnest intensity of youth. "But such development could take decades. Meanwhile, threats like Salpheth or these Vemus could arrive at any time."

"Which is why defensive alliances and communications networks are our immediate priority," Elena interjected smoothly. "The Confederations can provide defensive support and early warning systems while your civilization develops the experience base necessary for more advanced technologies."

Thyven's fur rippled in what Sean had learned indicated thoughtful consideration. "You speak of experience as if it were a prerequisite for technology. Could the same not be said of any advanced capability?"

Dr. Chen leaned forward. "Consider your own history. The transformation of Ichlos didn't happen overnight; it was built upon centuries of underground development, knowledge accumulation, and careful refinement. Rushing advanced capabilities without proper foundation often leads to catastrophic failures."

"Or," Captain Blake added, "it leads to the kind of problems the Krake faced when they pushed technology beyond their ability to control it responsibly."

The reference to the Krake sent a ripple of reaction through the

Aczar delegation. Sean realized that Phendran's briefings had included detailed accounts of the inter-dimensional wars and their consequences.

Moxtel consulted another display before responding. "Your point about foundation and experience has merit, but you're essentially asking us to trust the Confederation's protection while remaining technologically dependent. That's not a sustainable long-term relationship."

"It's a development partnership," Elena clarified. "Joint operations, shared learning, gradual technology transfer as capabilities develop. The goal is eventual technological parity, not permanent dependence. We're not interested in subjugating anyone."

Korveth stood and moved to one of the chamber's larger displays, which showed a tactical representation of Ichlos. "The fundamental question remains one of trust and mutual benefit. You've gained significant advantages from our knowledge, but you're hesitant to provide equivalent access to your most important capabilities."

Sean stood as well, recognizing the critical moment in their negotiations. "First Protector, I'm not saying no to eventual I-Drive access. I'm saying not yet. The technology requires not just understanding but wisdom in its application. Hand an explosive to a child, and someone gets hurt, even if the child's intentions are entirely good. Consider this from our perspective. Your government has only been in power for two years. Any species that's gone through what you have will need an adjustment period. These are the facts as I see them. I hope you can understand."

The chamber's privacy systems chimed softly, indicating an incoming priority communication. Captain Blake checked her secure device and looked at Sean with an expression that suggested important news.

"If you'll excuse me for a moment," Sean said. "I'm receiving a priority update that may be relevant to our discussions."

Korveth gestured to a private alcove. "Of course. Privacy protocols will extend to your communication."

Sean stepped into the alcove, Captain Blake passed the comlink session to him, and it became active on his wrist computer. Colonel Sutton's face appeared on screen, his expression carrying the weight of significant developments.

"I'm sorry to interrupt, General, but we've received an important update from the *Ascendant*. Major Gates has found evidence of Phantom communications networks approximately five hundred light-years from Ichlos. Embedded in the signals are Vemus Alpha signatures."

Sean blinked in surprise. "Five hundred light-years? Did they find an outpost?"

"Negative, they sent scout drones to investigate and they appear to be some kind of ancient repeaters recently reactivated. The Alpha signal was buried in the network protocols. Sir, it's highly suspicious."

Sean nodded. "Meaning that someone wanted us to find it. That means their communications protocols are hyper-capable."

Colonel Sutton nodded. "It's a variant of our subspace communications protocols."

Sean glanced back toward the conference chamber where the Aczar delegation waited for his return. "Any indication of immediate threat?"

"Negative, but the presence of Vemus signals in Phantom networks warrants further investigation. It changes everything about the strategic picture in this region."

"Understood. Continue monitoring and prepare a detailed analysis. Our stay on Ichlos just got shorter," Sean said.

"Understood, sir."

The comlink ended, and Sean re-entered the chamber with an explanation as to why their negotiations had to be paused. He wasn't sure how the Aczars would react, but he wasn't about to send the *Ascendant* deeper into unknown space without the rest of the task force.

CHAPTER 11

SEAN STEPPED BACK into the conference chamber, the weight of Ethan's intelligence report pressing against his mind like a physical force. He couldn't take the time at this moment to really consider the implications of why there would be a hidden Vemus Alpha signal in an ancient Phantom communications network. He needed to focus on returning to the *Odyssey* as quickly as possible.

The Aczar delegation watched him with the intense focus characteristic of their species, their large ears twitching as they processed his change in demeanor through their SRA-enabled communications.

"General Quinn," Korveth said, rising from his position at the central platform. "Your communication appears to have brought significant news."

Sean moved to the center of the chamber, feeling the adaptive flooring respond to his footsteps. "First Protector, I'm afraid circumstances require us to cut these negotiations short. We need to depart Ichlos immediately."

The chamber fell silent except for the soft hum of holographic displays. Elena stared at him for a few seconds, then stood, as did the others from the diplomatic envoy.

Vaethis stepped forward. "What kind of circumstances, General?"

"Our deep space reconnaissance has detected remnants of Phantom communications networks approximately five hundred light-years from Ichlos. The signal contains embedded elements that suggest Vemus presence or influence."

The reaction was immediate and pronounced. Zelara's elaborate headgear flared with activity as she interfaced directly with Ichlos's communications systems. Moxtel's practical demeanor shifted to one of tactical concern. Even young Tavira leaned forward with the intense focus of someone suddenly understanding that theoretical threats had become concrete dangers.

Korveth's expression remained carefully controlled, but Sean caught the slight tension around his eyes. "Five hundred light-years. That places the detection well beyond our current exploration range."

"Which is why we've deployed our own communications relays during our journey here," Sean replied. "Once it's completely online, the Aczar will have direct contact capability with the Confederation for continued negotiations and general communications. However, this discovery requires immediate investigation."

Thyven consulted a holoscreen that materialized at his gesture. "General Quinn, this intelligence regarding Phantom networks—doesn't it strengthen the argument for immediate technology transfer? If threats are materializing in our region of space…"

Sean had been expecting this line of reasoning. "The detection is more than five hundred light-years away and appears to be at the very limits of the network's range. You're in no immediate danger. The fact remains that your civilization isn't equipped for a mission of this scope and complexity."

He paused, choosing his words carefully to avoid unnecessary offense while maintaining absolute clarity. "I'm not trying to insult your capabilities, but these are the operational facts. Deep space reconnaissance against potentially hostile Phantom installations requires experience and resources that take time to develop."

Zelara leaned forward. "General Quinn, with respect, the contributions of Loremaster Phendran and his companions during the events at the Phantom Outpost demonstrated that Aczar knowledge and capabilities can be invaluable in such situations. Our understanding of Phantom technology predates yours by a significant amount of time."

The point struck home with uncomfortable accuracy, and Sean exchanged glances with Elena. She gave him a subtle nod of acknowledgement. Zelara was correct; Aczar expertise had proven crucial during the *Pathfinder*'s encounter with Salpheth and the abandoned outpost.

"Zelara," Sean said, "you raise a valid point, but the circumstances were quite different. We don't find ourselves holding Salpheth prisoner, and our current ships are more capable than the *Pathfinder*. If we encounter something that we believe requires your expertise, we'll contact you through the communications protocols and equipment we're leaving behind. However, I'd be open to having Loremaster Phendran serve in an advisory role for this mission."

Korveth's response was measured but firm. "I'm afraid that's not possible, General Quinn. Loremaster Phendran must remain on Ichlos to complete his reintegration and share the knowledge he's accumulated during his time with your civilization. His expertise is needed here for our own development efforts."

Sean nodded, having expected this answer but feeling obligated to make the request. "I understand, First Protector. In that case, we should begin our departure preparations. Please accept my sincerest thanks for your hospitality. I would've preferred that it was longer."

The dismissal felt abrupt, but the intelligence from Ethan had fundamentally altered the timeline for everything they were trying to accomplish. As Sean and his delegation began gathering their materials amid the efficient rhythm of diplomatic conclusion, he noticed increased activity among the Aczar delegates—the kind of rapid, silent communication that suggested urgent consultation.

"If you'll excuse us," Elena said formally, "we'll return to our quarters to prepare for departure and coordinate with our ship."

The next thirty minutes passed in a blur of departure preparations. Sean found himself impressed by Aczar logistics as their delegation was escorted to a landing platform much closer to the government complex than their original arrival point. The afternoon light filtering through Ichlos's perpetual cloud cover gave the sprawling metropolis an ethereal quality that reminded Sean how far from home they'd traveled.

"General Quinn," came a familiar voice behind him. Vaethis approached with the purposeful stride of someone carrying important instructions. "First Protector Korveth has a request."

Sean turned, noting that the Defense Coordinator carried the formal bearing that suggested official business rather than casual conversation. "What can we do for the First Protector?"

"The Aczar government would like to send a diplomatic envoy to accompany your mission. They would serve as observers and cultural liaisons, while providing assistance with any Phantom technology you might encounter."

The request caught Sean off guard, though perhaps it shouldn't have. The Aczar had just learned of potential threats in their region of space, and sending observers on a Confederation mission would provide valuable intelligence about capabilities and intentions.

"Defense Coordinator," Sean said carefully, "we're not equipped to accommodate your species on our ships for extended periods. The portable HAB units we used for transport were emergency configurations. I wouldn't recommend anyone being restricted to them long-term."

Vaethis nodded with understanding. "We've anticipated this concern and conferred with Loremaster Phendran about the adaptation process he and his companions underwent during their time aboard the *Pathfinder*. Our diplomatic envoy can duplicate those procedures to adapt to your artificial atmosphere."

Sean watched the shuttle preparation activities around them. Having Aczar observers aboard would provide valuable expertise, but it would also mean constant security considerations and the challenge of integrating aliens into the ship operations designed for human crews.

"I'd like to speak with Loremaster Phendran directly about this proposal," Sean said finally. "His experience with extended space travel would be valuable in assessing the feasibility."

Vaethis regarded him. "I suppose that my personal assurances wouldn't be enough to sway your opinion?"

Sean stared at him. "We're both military, charged with protecting our respective species to the best of our abilities. Would you let someone you just met sway your opinion on something like this? Or would you seek the counsel of someone you knew better?"

Vaethis consulted his communications device, exchanging rapid, untranslated communications with his superiors. Sean watched the shuttle preparation activities around them while waiting, noting the methodical efficiency that characterized everything the Aczar did.

"First Protector Korveth grants your request," Vaethis said after a few moments. "I can establish a secure communication link."

Within minutes, Sean found himself speaking through a holographic interface with Phendran, whose image appeared with a clarity that spoke to Aczar communications technology. The Loremaster looked well-rested and had regained the alertness that characterized him during his time with the Confederation.

"Phendran," Sean began, "it's good to see you looking so well. How has your reintegration been proceeding?"

"General Quinn, thank you for your concern. The transition has been… illuminating. Sharing my experiences with my people has been both challenging and rewarding. But I understand you have questions about the proposed diplomatic envoy."

"I'd rather you were traveling with us and a team of your choosing," Sean said, and Phendran nodded. "Your expertise would be invaluable for the mission we're undertaking, but I understand your obligations here and the fact that they won't allow you to come with us." Vaethis stood a few paces away, but his head jerked up at that, confirming for Sean that he was monitoring this conversation. "Since I can't get what I want, I'd like to know your assessment of sending an Aczar delegation with us."

Phendran was quiet for a moment, his expression thoughtful. "General Quinn, I'm aware of the risks because of what we all experienced at the Phantom Outpost. However, I believe you should seriously consider this opportunity. An Aczar diplomatic envoy would learn firsthand the risks involved in traveling beyond our star system, while their expertise could prove useful should you encounter Phantom technology that you're not familiar with. I think both parties have much to gain by working together."

Sean nodded slowly. "The delegation they're proposing includes Tavira, your designated successor. Isn't she rather young for a mission of this scope? She's only a Loremaster in training."

"Despite Tavira's age, her mind has been specially trained to access the vast knowledge networks that I have developed. She represents not just our current capabilities, but our future potential for cooperation with the Confederation." Phendran paused, his expression becoming more serious. "General Quinn, I believe I can be of more help to the Confederation by remaining on Ichlos and working to bring my people fully into alliance with yours. But Tavira and the others can provide immediate assistance with your current mission. The burdens we collectively face should be divided among us, and the more my people understand those burdens and the Confederation you're building, the better the outcomes will be for both our futures."

Sean couldn't think of any counter arguments to this because he wholly agreed with Phendran. The conversation continued for several more minutes, with Phendran providing detailed assessments of each proposed envoy member's capabilities and the adaptation procedures they would need to undergo. By the time the communication ended, Sean had a clearer picture of both the benefits and challenges involved.

Elena approached as Sean concluded the call. "What's your assessment?"

"Phendran makes compelling arguments for taking them along," Sean replied. "But it's another variable to consider, and while I agree in principle with his reasoning, I have concerns about their real motivations. This could be intelligence-gathering as much as diplomatic cooperation."

"Most assuredly," Elena said pragmatically. "The question is whether the benefits outweigh the security risks." She paused for a moment. "I remember the numerous discussions had about whether to allow the Ovarrow to serve directly in the CDF. Do you?"

It seemed like a lifetime ago and a whole other conflict. "We'd been working with Mekaal soldiers for a while, so by the time their integration into our command structure actually happened, we more or less knew what to expect."

Elena smiled. "Indeed, it was the CDF that led the way in proving that the Ovarrow could successfully integrate into colonial society. They abandoned their more barbaric practices in favor of our more civilized ones, and they thrived. They were given the opportunity to witness how we did things so they could make an informed decision as a society. The process took many years to achieve. Why should we expect any different where the Aczar are concerned?"

Sean looked around the landing platform, noting the Aczar efficiency in everything from shuttle servicing to the security arrangements that kept their delegation safe without making them feel imprisoned. It was quite a bit different from the reports of Connor's experience on Ichlos. The civilization that had built this complex was capable, advanced, and strategic in their thinking. But they were loners and not used to working with other species. Those experiences would take time and a lot of patience.

Sean sighed. "We'll take them. But their access aboard the *Odyssey* will be restricted, and they'll be monitored throughout the mission. If they're intelligence-gathering, they'll earn every piece of information they collect."

Vaethis, who had been waiting at a respectful distance, approached as Sean's decision became clear. "General Quinn?"

"Defense Coordinator, please inform First Protector Korveth that we accept the diplomatic envoy. We'll need detailed information about their adaptation requirements and any special considerations for their species during extended space travel." Sean paused for a moment, thinking. "We are limited in what we have to offer that your species can consume. Can you quickly put together a supply cache for your envoy? It'll make their journey with us more comfortable."

Vaethis's ears twitched excitedly. "Excellent. The envoy is prepared to depart within the hour, and we've compiled comprehensive briefing materials about their needs and capabilities. There will be things included that you probably already know, but in my experience it's better if expectations are stated so everyone is on the same page."

Sean smiled. "On that we can agree."

"Regarding supplies, how long will this mission take?"

"It won't be two years before you see your envoy again. We travel with a stockpile that will last at least a year, longer if we go to rationing protocols. We're also equipped to take in biological material and convert it to nutrients we can consume."

Vaethis's eyes widened, as if he hadn't considered any of that. He quickly recovered and then nodded. "I'll make sure they have provisions to last up to a year." He paused and shook his head. "There are so many things we haven't considered yet for long deployments that you seem to take for granted as common knowledge."

Sean's expression softened. "One day you will have those insights as well. It'll just take time."

"General Quinn, I hope that one day you and I will interact again. It's not often that I get to interact with another veteran protector—a guardian of the people. I can tell it's a burden that you carry willingly, and your bearing is worthy of respect—more respect than I expressed at our first meeting."

Sean hadn't been expecting that kind of admission. "Thank you for that, Defense Coordinator. I hope we'll meet again one day as well."

As the final preparations began, Sean watched the Aczar diplomatic team board the shuttles. They were the same Aczar they'd already interacted with, and Sean pondered why they had been selected. They varied in age and experience levels and certainly couldn't be a representation of the best in their individual fields of expertise. But they had to be capable. Thyven had extensive diplomatic experience, Zelara was an engineer, Moxtel's expertise was with logistics and management, Kyveth was their medical specialist, Brennox was their security advisor, and young Tavira was a junior Loremaster, and they all carried the hope of becoming a bridge between civilizations.

Sean wondered why Korveth hadn't selected a more experienced group to go with them. The First Protector was purposeful in every decision he made and wouldn't be rushed. The team he was sending, and who had been part of their negotiations, weren't last-minute additions to the meetings. None of the Aczar had been expecting the Confederation to come to their planet, but the fact that they had put together a team so quickly indicated that some preparation had been made. Sean might've underestimated the Aczar, at least in part. He wouldn't do it again, even if the Aczar Diplomatic Envoy represented a wide mix of ages and experiences. He would assume they were highly intelligent and capable until they demonstrated otherwise.

The return journey to the *Odyssey* would be very different from their arrival, Sean reflected. They were bringing back not just the completion of a promise to Phendran, but the beginning of something larger—an alliance that could reshape the balance of power in their region of space, assuming they could navigate the challenges that lay ahead.

As the shuttles lifted off from Ichlos, Sean couldn't shake the feeling that this mission had just become significantly more complicated. But then again, the best opportunities usually did.

Settling back into his seat, Sean was relieved to finally shed the EVA suit for regular clothes. The confinement reminded him of the limitations they still faced in alien environments, limitations the Aczar seemed to overcome effortlessly through their SRA partnerships.

There had been a time when he could've spent days in a combat suit or an EVA suit depending on what he was doing, but it had been a long time. The suits, while capable, were also confining. They had to come up with options that would enable them to come to Ichlos without the requirement of wearing an EVA suit all the time. He wondered if some kind of rebreather would be enough. Probably not. There were probably things in Ichlos's atmosphere that could be absorbed through exposed skin. Yet, the Aczar, through the use of their SRAs, were able to adapt to an Earth-like atmosphere. Though they didn't change their physiology completely, their SRAs helped them bridge the gap in converting the Earth-like atmosphere into something they could process and survive on. Maybe he needed to rethink whether he would volunteer to become a bearer of his own SRA.

Sean frowned. That wasn't right. It wasn't his own SRA that he owned. The SRA was sentient, so it was more like an SRA partner, and partnership was a better description for the relationship.

He glanced at Elena, noting how her SRA band caught the shuttle's interior lighting. Her partnership would undoubtedly help with the Aczar envoy, but it also represented a vulnerability he couldn't ignore. What if an SRA could be compromised? The complete physiological integration meant any breach would affect the human partner as well.

Sean had spent most of his career learning to minimize risk, not create new vulnerabilities. Connor had embraced the technology after Joshua saved his life, and Sean understood the reasoning. But facing something like Salpheth in close combat, Sean preferred trusting in superior firepower over potentially compromised alien technology, at least for now.

CHAPTER 12

ETHAN STOOD before the large holoscreen in Conference Room Two, watching the video feeds of the ancient Phantom relay drift in the distance like a technological ghost. The structure hung motionless against the star field, its dark metallic surface barely reflecting the *Ascendant*'s navigation lights. After three days of careful approach and analysis, they had confirmed what the scout drone data initially suggested—this was indeed part of the vast communications network the Phantoms had abandoned centuries ago, or perhaps even longer.

"Still hard to believe something that old is even partially functional," Captain Tom Washburn said from his seat at the conference table, his weathered hands wrapped around a cup of coffee. The company commander had served with Ethan during the Vemus Alpha investigation, and his practical military mindset had proven invaluable during their previous encounters with alien technology. His prematurely graying hair and lined face spoke of decades of CDF service, but his alert brown eyes held the same tactical sharpness Ethan had come to rely on. Prolonging treatments extended human life spans to well over two hundred years. Ethan thought

Washburn liked the look of an older face, even though he was about the same age as Ethan.

Ethan turned from the holoscreen as the rest of his senior staff filed into the room. The conference space was smaller than the *Odyssey*'s diplomatic chambers, but it served their needs—an oval table with a holotank in the middle, adaptive seating, holographic displays that could project data at multiple angles, and the kind of sound dampening that made sensitive discussions possible.

"The relay's power signature is barely detectable anymore," Cynergy said as she settled into the chair beside Ethan. She crossed her legs, and her honey-brown eyes focused on her personal holo-screen. Her long, dark-blonde hair was pulled back in the practical style she preferred during extended operations, and the ship dark-blue ship-suit she wore emphasized her tall, athletic frame. Since losing her hybrid nature two years ago, she'd thrown herself into understanding alien technology with renewed determination, and her expertise with Vemus physiology had now expanded to include Phantom systems.

Captain Akira Endo looked up from his tactical analysis, his lean frame hunched over a portable workstation. He closed the holoscreen and took a seat at the conference table. "The structure shows signs of significant degradation, but the core systems appear to be maintaining minimal functionality."

"How minimal are we talking?" Ethan asked, settling into his command chair and feeling Atlas pulse gently around his forearm. The SRA's presence had become as familiar as his own heartbeat over the past eighteen months, though he still marveled at the alien technology's integration with his neural implants.

Zane Rennick leaned forward enthusiastically. The science officer's pale, freckled face was animated with the kind of excitement that came from encountering something genuinely unprecedented, his brown eyes practically glowing with scientific curiosity. "Major, the power levels are fluctuating between twelve and eighteen percent of what we estimate would be fully operational capacity. For technology that's potentially thousands of years old, that's remarkable."

Washburn let out a low whistle. "Eighteen percent after centuries? Our own comms relays start degrading after fifty years."

Ethan exchanged a glance with Cynergy, noting her raised eyebrows. Even she seemed impressed, and alien technology rarely surprised her anymore.

Lieutenant Samantha Trickle nodded. "The interesting part is the timing, sir. Based on power consumption analysis and signal degradation patterns, this relay was in some kind of standby mode until approximately eighteen months ago."

The room went quiet. Ethan noticed Washburn's coffee cup pause halfway to his lips, while Endo's tactical display was forgotten as he processed the implications.

"Eighteen months," Cynergy murmured, her analytical mind already working through the timeline. "That puts the activation right around when..."

"About six months after the *Pathfinder* left the Phantom Outpost," Ethan finished.

As he turned back to Trickle, he caught the brief glance she exchanged with Washburn, noting how his friend's expression softened almost imperceptibly. Their off-duty relationship was still developing, but both officers maintained their professional focus during operations—exactly the kind of discipline Ethan expected from his senior staff.

Ethan felt Atlas stir against his forearm, responding to his elevated interest. The SRA's consciousness touched the edge of his awareness, offering additional perspective without overwhelming his human thought processes.

The timeline is significant, Atlas observed through their neural link. *As we investigate this further, we should look for evidence of increased Phantom activity in multiple regions.*

"Atlas is pointing out that there is likely a correlation, but we'll need to assess for increased Phantom activity," Ethan said. "What brought it out of standby mode?"

Cynergy manipulated her data pad, projecting a three-dimensional representation of the relay's internal structure above the conference table. The holodisplay revealed a complex network of interconnected systems, most showing the dark signatures of inactive components. Her expertise with alien technology, hard-won through years of studying Vemus physiology and now expanded to include Phantom systems, was evident in the way she highlighted specific subsystems.

"Major Qualmann and I have been analyzing the activation sequence," she said, her analytical mind processing the data with the same intensity she'd once applied to understanding hybrid conversion processes. "The relay received an external signal—something that triggered a wake-up protocol. Once activated, it began transmitting on frequencies that matched the Vemus Alpha signatures we detected."

Washburn leaned back in his chair, his expression thoughtful. The veteran officer had seen enough alien technology during their previous encounters to understand the implications. "So, something or someone woke it up specifically to send that signal. That's not a coincidence."

"Definitely not," Cynergy agreed. "The relay had been dormant for centuries, possibly longer. Whatever activated it knew exactly which frequencies to use and had the authorization codes necessary to access the network."

Atlas pulsed more actively around Ethan's wrist, drawing his attention to memories from his father's encounter at the Phantom Outpost.

Ethan cleared his throat. "Salpheth mentioned this network during my father's unorthodox mission. He indicated that the Phantoms had moved beyond this communication method. The buoys are no longer monitored or maintained. The network spans hundreds or thousands of light-years, but it's been abandoned. Since the Phantoms are likely not maintaining this network anymore, there is a strong possibility that Salpheth has triggered this."

"Why would he do that?" Endo asked. "It's obvious that he's trying to get our attention or perhaps even the Vemus's attention, but I can't think of a good reason for doing that."

Rennick raised his hand. "The degradation patterns are fascinating, too. Even Phantom technology isn't immune to entropy. The relay's ceramic matrix shows micro-fractures consistent with centuries of cosmic radiation exposure, and the exotic matter components have definitely lost coherence over time."

"Wasn't the outpost in much better condition? Wouldn't it have suffered from the same degradation? Assuming it was just as old as this relay," Washburn said.

"No, because there were maintenance and actual construction platforms that were still active," Ethan said.

"That's unbelievable."

"Yeah, that's just what they thought, too. My father figured out that the outpost's computer system had been stuck during the decommissioning process the Phantoms used. This kept the maintenance platforms operating and the construction platforms building until they exhausted their materials."

"A relay like this," Cynergy said, gesturing toward the holotank, "wouldn't have as sophisticated a maintenance system as an outpost. These were likely designed with a specific lifecycle in mind before they were abandoned."

Rennick nodded. "True, but if the Phantoms had a process in place to decommission an outpost, wouldn't they have something similar in place for their relays and other installations?"

Ethan pressed his lips together. "Not necessarily. We use throwaway equipment as well—low-cost tools that serve a temporary purpose and we don't need to retrieve them. Think scout drones, our own buoys and transceivers that we deploy for our own communications network. They have a maintenance cycle, so they should operate for a couple hundred years, but one day they'll need to be replaced. It was never intended that we revisit them to manually perform standard maintenance."

Washburn nodded. "I guess it's just a matter of scale."

"Precisely," Ethan replied.

"All things decay eventually," Atlas said, his voice coming from a temporary voice construct on the SRA. "Even my own matrix will degrade over time, though that process has the potential to measure in millennia rather than centuries. It's oddly comforting to know that impermanence is a universal constant."

Ethan smiled slightly at Atlas's observation. The SRA's developing personality continued to surprise him, adding depth to their partnership that went beyond simple technological enhancement. As Ethan glanced at the others, he noted some of the somber expressions from them, and it took him a second to realize why. Atlas had just casually observed that he had the capacity to outlive all of them.

The casual mention of millennia hit the room like a cold wave. Rennick's enthusiastic expression faded, while Trickle shifted uncomfortably in her seat. Even Washburn, who'd seen enough alien technology to be jaded, stared at Ethan's forearm with new understanding.

"I must apologize," Atlas said, picking up on Ethan's thoughts. "The subject of life spans is a sensitive one that I'm not immune to, and my lack of forethought has caused offense."

"Not offense," Ethan said. "We're just surprised."

"I don't understand."

Ethan glanced at Cynergy. They'd had more than a few close brushes with their mortality. "This is still new to us. We tend to think in terms of our own lifespans. The Aczar live much shorter lives than we do, so we assumed that SRAs have similar lifespans."

"Wait a second," Washburn said. "Atlas, you could live for thousands of years?"

"That is correct. Potentially."

"What do you mean 'potentially'?"

"The relationship between SRA and Aczar and now Humans, is somewhat symbiotic. Loremaster Phendran explained to me that when an Aczar dies, their SRAs will often choose to merge with the source-nexus that is later used to create new SRAs," Atlas said.

"So, you don't die?" Washburn asked.

Ethan shook his head, and Atlas answered. "No, we do cease to exist, but the strongest knowledge and raw experiences as they are weighed in our moral matrix are preserved so that future SRAs will be more refined."

Washburn blinked a few times, then heaved a long sigh. "That's … it's amazing and depressing all at the same time."

Atlas didn't reply, and silence sank heavily onto those in the conference room.

"Let's move on," Ethan said and looked at Washburn. "You mentioned wanting to send a team to retrieve hardware samples from the relay. What's your assessment now that we have better data?"

Washburn cleared his throat and looked at his personal holoscreen for a few seconds. Leading away teams had taught him to weigh risks carefully. "The structure's stable enough for operations, and my engineers confirm they could extract core components without compromising the relay's basic functionality. The question is whether the intelligence value justifies the operational risk."

"What kind of risks are we looking at?" Ethan asked, though he could make a pretty good guess as to most of them.

"Standard EVA hazards, plus the unknown factor of Phantom technology," Washburn replied. "The relay's been broadcasting for months, and we don't know if that signal has attracted attention from other parties. It's highly unlikely we'd be walking into a trap, but I can't rule it out entirely. It could also be that we could trigger some kind of automated defense system we haven't detected yet."

Trickle shifted in her seat and leaned forward. "Sir, I've refined our detection protocols based on the signal patterns we've collected. The relay's broadcast contains embedded navigation data that could help us triangulate the source of the activation signal. But I could further refine what I've got if we could extract the relay's core memory systems to then extract the complete dataset."

"Which brings us back to Captain Washburn's extraction mission," Cynergy said. "The question is whether we have time for that kind of operation."

They were five hundred light-years from the *Odyssey*, operating at the edge of their communication range with the main task force. General Quinn expected regular updates, and any significant delay in their reconnaissance schedule would require explanation.

"The value might be worth the risk, sir," Endo said, "unless we can fool the relay's system into sharing that data with us." He glanced at Washburn. "Might save you a trip."

Washburn chuckled. "The trip doesn't bother me. I mean it might be worth searching and retrieving examples of Phantom technology that is worth further analysis. But I really don't see how anything on that old relay could be better than what we already have back at COMCENT."

"I wouldn't rule out the value entirely," Rennick said. "Even degraded components could advance our understanding of their manufacturing processes and materials science."

Washburn smiled. "So, you're saying you'd like to come with us if we go?"

Rennick blinked in surprise. "What? No!" Then he shook his head. "I hadn't really thought of that."

Washburn arched an eyebrow and looked at Ethan. "I

thought all bridge crew were also field certified. Is there any reason this young science officer can't join us for the away mission?"

There was a mischievous glint in his friend's eye. "Okay, leave him alone," Ethan said and gave Rennick a reassuring look to set the young science officer at ease. "Let's take a pragmatic approach. Phantoms, like anyone, want reliable and secure communications at the most basic level. Right?" The others nodded. "So, there could be safeguards against unauthorized access, protective protocols designed to prevent those things."

"On the other hand," Cynergy said, "if the relay's been abandoned for centuries, those safeguards might have degraded along with everything else. The power levels are so low that most active defense systems would be offline. Scans of the relay don't indicate any kind of weapons system."

Washburn chuckled. "You're awfully comfortable risking my team on this."

"Oh, please. How much risk is there, really? Do you have any idea how many old military installations we scavenged for the supplies and tech we needed?" Cynergy asked, eyes gleaming, but there was an underlying edge to her expression that indicated she wasn't making an idle boast.

"Cyn, that hurts my feelings. I thought we were friends," Washburn said, and she shook her head. He looked at Ethan. "Say the word, sir, and we'll go over there and bring that whole relay back if you want it. I could send a small team—four specialists with full EVA gear and salvage kits. Quick in and out, grab what we can without compromising the relay's basic function."

Ethan considered it for a few moments and then looked at Lieutenant Trickle. "Do you think you could fool the relay into sharing more information with us?"

"I could certainly try, sir. We can mimic their protocols, and that should get a response from the system. I'd like to take some time to review the *Pathfinder*'s mission data on the operational protocols the Phantom used."

Ethan nodded and looked at his wife. "Can you work on this with Lieutenant Trickle? It doesn't have to be anything fancy; it just needs to get the job done."

"Of course," Cynergy said.

The conference room's communications system chimed with an incoming message-priority signal. Trickle activated the display, and Colonel Sutton's face appeared on the main holoscreen. The *Odyssey*'s bridge was in the background.

"Major Gates," Sutton said, his imposing presence evident even through the transmission, "General Quinn extends his compliments to you and your crew. You're ordered to maintain position and prepare for rendezvous. The *Odyssey* and the *Horizon* are en route to your coordinates."

Ethan felt relieved that the rest of the task force would be joining them. Sean must have felt that the evidence he'd provided was compelling enough to cut the diplomatic mission short and come out to continue the investigation.

"Understood, Colonel. What's our ETA for rendezvous?"

"Eighteen hours. The General wants a comprehensive briefing on your discoveries, and we're bringing additional analysis equipment that should enhance your detection capabilities."

"Sir," Trickle interjected, and Ethan nodded for her to continue, "if the *Odyssey* and the *Horizon* are joining us, we could establish a much more effective detection array. Three ships coordinating their sensor sweeps could triangulate signal sources across a much larger region."

Sutton nodded approvingly. "That's exactly what the general has in mind, Lieutenant. We'll be able to narrow down the source of these activations much more efficiently with combined assets."

After Colonel Sutton signed off, the conference room fell into thoughtful silence. The arrival of the main task force would change their operational parameters significantly, but it also meant they'd have the resources necessary for a more comprehensive investigation.

"Well," Washburn said with a slight grin, "looks like my extraction mission just got postponed. Probably for the best, but don't think I've forgotten about you Rennick."

Rennick's cheeks reddened and then he sat up straighter. "Anytime, Captain."

"Stop taunting my bridge officers, Captain," Ethan said to his friend. "Lieutenant Trickle, I'd still like you to take a crack at gleaning more useable intel from the relay."

"Yes, sir," she replied.

Ethan stood and moved back to the main holoscreen on the wall, watching the ancient relay drift against the star field.

"All right, people," he said, turning back to face his senior staff. "We've got eighteen hours to prepare comprehensive briefing materials and coordinate our sensor arrays for maximum effectiveness. Captain Endo, prepare a tactical assessment of the relay and surrounding space. Dr. Rennick, compile everything we know about Phantom technology degradation patterns. I want it to be reviewed by your peers here and among the rest of the task force."

As the senior staff began filing out for their respective duties, Cynergy lingered beside Ethan at the holoscreen. Her eyes reflected the distant stars as she considered the implications of their discovery.

"You know," she said quietly, "part of me hopes we don't find the source of that activation."

Ethan looked at her with surprise. "Why?"

"Because if it *is* Salpheth, or someone like him with the knowledge and capability to wake up ancient Phantom networks, it probably isn't someone we want to meet unprepared," she replied, her experience with dangerous alien technology evident in her caution. "And we're a very long way from home."

Ethan felt Atlas pulse gently against his forearm, offering silent support through their neural link. The SRA's presence reminded him that they weren't facing these challenges alone; they had allies, technology, and the combined wisdom of multiple species working together.

"Maybe," he said, reaching to touch Cynergy's hand. "But we've faced the unknown before and come through it. Whatever's out there, we'll figure it out."

As the *Ascendant* continued its vigil beside the ancient relay, Ethan couldn't shake the feeling that they were standing at the threshold of something significant. In eighteen hours, the real investigation would begin, and with it, answers that might reshape their understanding of the threats facing their civilization.

Ethan remembered his conversations with his father about Salpheth. The Phantom was highly intelligent, manipulative, and dangerous. He had a purpose for every action he performed, and Ethan highly suspected that this signal they'd detected was more of an invitation than a discovery.

CHAPTER 13

SEAN SETTLED into the curved leather chair behind his ready room desk. The smart cushion adjusted to his bodyweight, providing excellent support without sacrificing comfort. His personal preferences were read from his neural implant and used to update his file in the ship's computer system. The space around him represented everything the Colony and now the Confederation had achieved in shipbuilding—a perfect balance of functionality and comfort that spoke of humanity's evolution from desperate colonists to confident explorers.

The ready room occupied a prime section of the *Odyssey's* command deck, its floor-to-ceiling transparisteel windows offering an unobstructed view of the star field beyond. Nano-robotic material that covered the walls had the appearance of New Earth oak paneling, as if it were harvested from the early colonial settlements. It lined the walls between holographic displays that could project everything from tactical situations to family photographs. The wood grain caught the ambient lighting, creating warm patterns that softened the high-tech environment without diminishing its efficiency.

Sean's desk commanded the center of the room—a masterpiece of colonial craftsmanship that incorporated both traditional design and cutting-edge technology. It was made of actual colonial oak his father had salvaged to serve as his desk when he'd been governor of the colony. The desk had served over a dozen governors until it was retired, and Sean had taken possession of it. The surface of the desk appeared to be solid wood, but embedded holographic projectors could transform it into a tactical display, communications hub, or administrative workstation within seconds. Behind the desk, built-in shelving held a carefully curated collection of items that told the story of his career—a piece of metal from the first Infinity Drive prototype, a crystal formation from an unexplored world, and a physical photograph of his wedding day that somehow seemed more real than any holographic image.

To his left, a conversation area featured two curved couches upholstered in deep blue fabric that complemented the ship's color scheme. The seating faced each other across a low table crafted from the same New Earth oak as his desk, creating an intimate space for informal discussions or private consultations. Soft lighting from overhead fixtures formed pools of warmth that invited relaxation while maintaining the professional atmosphere essential for command decisions.

On the right side of the room, a conference table extended from the wall, its adaptive surface capable of accommodating eight people comfortably. The table's integrated holographic systems could project three-dimensional tactical displays, star charts, or technical specifications with perfect clarity. Above it, a larger holo-screen could display everything from ship status reports to real-time communications feeds, ensuring that even informal meetings could access the full spectrum of ship data.

The ready room's environmental systems maintained perfect temperature and humidity, while sound dampening ensured complete privacy for sensitive discussions. Hidden fabrication units could produce everything from coffee to full meals, though Sean preferred the authenticity of his steward delivering refreshments prepared by Chef Karen Kristoff, who was determined to expand his waistline.

Colonel Brad Sutton entered through the ready room's main door, his tall, athletic frame moving with the controlled precision that had made him invaluable as an executive officer. The closely-shaved head and deep-set eyes gave him an intimidating presence, but Sean had learned to read the subtle expressions that revealed his XO's analytical mind at work.

"General," Sutton said, settling into the chair across from Sean's desk. His resonant voice carried the calm authority that kept the *Odyssey*'s crew functioning smoothly during the most challenging operations. "I've finished reviewing the data packages from the *Ascendant*. Major Gates and his team have outdone themselves."

Sean activated his desk's holographic display, bringing up the comprehensive analysis that Ethan's crew had compiled over the past week. Three-dimensional representations of the ancient Phantom relay rotated slowly above the desk surface, accompanied by signal analysis matrices and power consumption graphs that painted a picture of remarkable detective work.

"The correlation between the relay activation and Vemus Alpha signatures is undeniable," Sean said, highlighting specific data points with casual gestures. "But what impresses me most is how they approached the investigation. Rather than rushing in for hardware samples, they took the time to understand the system's behavior patterns first."

Sutton leaned forward. "Lieutenant Trickle's signal analysis work is particularly noteworthy. She managed to extract navigation data by mimicking Phantom communications protocols. That required both technical expertise and creative thinking."

"Ethan's influence," Sean replied with unmistakable pride. "He's developed into exactly the kind of commander I hoped he would.

He has genius-level intelligence, but more importantly, he's learned to use it wisely."

"Sir?"

Sean gestured toward the data streams flowing across his desk display. "Look at the sequence of their investigation. They detected anomalies, deployed scouts to gather intelligence, analyzed the data thoroughly before making any commitments, and then adapted their approach based on what they learned. That's systematic thinking combined with tactical awareness, not luck."

Sutton nodded thoughtfully. "The distinction between intelligence and wisdom."

Sean smiled. "Exactly. Foolish people get lucky sometimes, but luck always runs out eventually. Wise people tend to be lucky more often because they created the conditions for success." Sean manipulated the display to show the timeline of Ethan's investigation. "Every decision his team made was calculated to minimize risk while maximizing intelligence-gathering. That's the hallmark of exceptional command."

"You sound like you're ready to promote him."

Sean chuckled. "Not yet, but he's getting close." He glanced at Sutton. "What is it?"

"Off the record?"

Sean nodded.

"The fact that he's a hybrid is going to hold him back. You might be able to push through a promotion to lieutenant colonel, but that might be as far as he goes unless... he gives up being a hybrid. I know you hate to hear that."

"You're right. I do hate to hear that, but I also know it's true."

"So why doesn't he give it up? I honestly thought that after what happened with his wife, he would've come around."

"It's not that simple. Ethan is convinced that he and other hybrids have special insight into the Vemus that no one else has.

I'm inclined to believe him. He's willing to bear the burden of this, and we should support him."

"I agree with you. You know I do, but that doesn't mean others will agree."

The holographic relay continued its slow rotation, its ancient structure somehow more impressive when viewed through the lens of Ethan's careful analysis. Sean found himself thinking about the parallels between Ethan's methodical approach and Connor's sometimes instinctive leadership style. Different methods, but both rooted in the same fundamental principle—understanding the situation before acting. Connor had amazing instincts, and Sean had done everything he could to emulate and build on Connor's example. It was how he'd risen through the CDF ranks, and he'd promised himself long ago that he'd do what he could to see that Ethan received fair treatment from the CDF.

"The Aczar delegation has been asking about our investigation methods," Sutton said, shifting to operational matters. "They seem particularly interested in how we coordinate multiple ships across these distances."

Sean leaned back in his chair, considering the implications. "They're observing and learning. Expected, given that this is their first exposure to large-scale space operations. How are they adapting to ship life?"

"In the forty-eight hours since we left Ichlos, they appear to be doing just fine. Thyven has been working with Elena Vasquez to understand chain-of-command protocols. Zelara spends most of her time in communications, fascinating Lieutenant Ramirez with her SRA interface capabilities. She wants access to Major Wallace and his engineering team."

Sean chuckled. "I bet she does. Engineering is her specialization, and at some point Jamal is going to meet with her. How about Tavira?"

Sutton's expression softened slightly. "She's remarkable, sir.

Yesterday she spent four hours with Dr. Chen discussing xenopsychology, then moved on to tactical simulations with Captain Norquist. Talk about hitting the ground running. Her learning capacity rivals anything I've seen."

Sean wasn't surprised. Phendran had specifically recommended the young junior Loremaster as someone who could bridge the gap between civilizations. The fact that she was adapting quickly to Confederation methods suggested that the Aczar's future relationship with humanity might be smoother than anyone had dared hope. At least, those were his thoughts today. He would try to reserve judgement until a lot more time had passed.

"What's the status on our current investigation?" Sean asked, bringing the conversation back to immediate operational concerns.

"The data processing teams have been working around the clock to analyze everything the *Ascendant* collected," Sutton replied, consulting his personal holoscreen. "Oriana's preliminary assessment doesn't negate any of the findings. The relay was part of a much larger network—possibly spanning thousands of light-years. The activation sequence appears to have been remotely triggered, which means someone has access to Phantom command protocols."

Sean was quite familiar with the theories and factual accounts regarding the Phantoms. "Remote activation from how far away?"

"Unknown, but the signal propagation analysis suggests a significant distance. We could be dealing with someone operating from thousands of light-years away."

The implications were staggering. Sean remembered when the distance of sixty light-years that separated New Earth from Old Earth was an impossible dream; then it became a journey of four to six months and now was barely a few hours. They spent more time navigating within the star system itself than traveling between star systems.

They had no actual evidence that Salpheth was responsible for this, and he must consider other options for how these signals started happening. Something, an entity or latent protocols, that had the capability to activate abandoned Phantom infrastructure across galactic distances represented either an invaluable ally or an existential threat. Given humanity's recent experiences with beings like Salpheth, Sean strongly suspected the latter.

"I'm surprised no one has mentioned the possibility that Salpheth might've found himself some help or even another prisoner like him, trapped somewhere, and this is their calling card," Sean said.

Sutton blew out a long breath. "We can't rule out that possibility."

"And right now we can't confirm it. Any progress on triangulating the source?"

Sutton's expression grew more serious. "That's where the real breakthrough occurred. Lieutenant Trickle's protocol mimicry convinced the relay to share navigation data that points to a specific region of space. Not exact coordinates, but close enough for our purposes. Sean moved to the conversation area and gestured for Sutton to join him on the couches. The more relaxed seating arrangement facilitated the kind of strategic thinking that normal desk conferences sometimes inhibited.

Sutton brought up his personal holoscreen and showed a report to Sean.

"Recommendation is to move thirty light-years from our current location and attempt to create a sub-space scanner array between all three ships."

Sutton nodded. "It's theoretically possible. I had it confirmed before coming here."

It was *only* a thirty-light-year redeployment that could glean them insight into where the Phantom signal had come from.

"Okay, I'll authorize the deployment to the target coordinates," Sean said.

Sutton opened a comlink to the bridge and ordered them to move the ship.

When he was finished, Sean asked, "Recommendations for approach?"

"Cautious reconnaissance with full tactical preparation," Sutton replied immediately. "We deploy the task force in a triangular formation spread across six light-years. The power requirements are going to be a lot, but it'll give us maximum sensor overlap. I doubt we'll encounter anything hostile, but we'll have emergency escape vectors and coordinated defensive capabilities ready."

Sean nodded. "If it's not broke then don't fix it."

"Exactly."

They spent the next hour going over the data and analysis of orbital installations surrounding Ichlos and the rest of the star system. There were some interesting design choices that Sean was going to have his officers discuss with the Aczars during their meetings with the various department heads. This way information could flow both ways, with everyone learning something new.

The ready room's communications system chimed with an incoming priority message. Sean activated the holoscreen, and Major Hiroki Nagata's face appeared.

"General Quinn," Nagata said, his lean frame visible against the backdrop of the bridge, "we've arrived at the target coordinates, thirty light-years from the Phantom relay. The *Ascendant* and the *Horizon* have checked in and are maintaining position two light-years from our location as ordered."

Sean felt the familiar surge of anticipation that came before significant operations. "Status of our sensor arrays?"

"Fully deployed and coordinated, sir. We're ready to begin the next phase of the investigation. All ships report ready for whatever we might encounter."

"Acknowledged, Major. Colonel Sutton and I will be on the bridge momentarily.

As the transmission ended, Sean stood and straightened his uniform. The proposal to link multiple ships sensor arrays using both subspace and the I-Drive to expand the range of their sensors was making them step firmly into theoretical protocols. The ancient Phantom relay had been just the beginning. Triangulating the signal would narrow down just where the signal had originated from. He doubted it would be near the Phantom Outpost where Connor had been. That place was gone, but there were more Phantom relays in the deep dark and they had to lead somewhere.

The hunt for answers was about to begin in earnest.

CHAPTER 14

SEAN AND COLONEL SUTTON stepped onto the *Odyssey*'s bridge, immediately sensing the controlled energy that permeated the command center during critical operations. The main holoscreen displayed a three-dimensional tactical representation of their task force—three ships positioned in precise triangular formation across several light-years of space, their sensor arrays creating an invisible web of detection capability that stretched into the void.

"General on the bridge," Specialist Danny Ramirez announced from the communications station, his rapid-fire competence evident in the way he managed multiple data streams simultaneously.

Sean moved to his command chair, noting the heightened alertness of his bridge crew. Captain Jane Norquist looked up from the tactical station, her striking blue eyes reflecting the amber glow of weapons displays as she monitored the task force's defensive posture. Her petite frame was poised with the kind of controlled tension that spoke to years of managing complex threat assessments.

"Status report, Captain Norquist," Sean said, settling into his chair and feeling the bridge's attention focus on him with laser intensity.

"All ships report ready for SESA deployment, General," she replied crisply, her shoulder-length blonde hair catching the ambient lighting as she turned from her displays. "The *Ascendant* and the *Horizon* have confirmed optimal positioning for maximum sensor overlap."

Sean looked at Colonel Sutton. "SESA?"

"Subspace experimental scanner array, sir," he replied.

Sean nodded. "Okay, SESA it is. Sounds funny to say."

Captain Norquist grinned, then muttered a quick apology.

Captain Jake Lennox glanced up from the operations station, looking slightly amused. "Sir, Engineering reports all systems nominal. They're ready for the spike in power draw and have monitoring systems on standby to re-route as needed. Power cores are operating at peak efficiency, and final preparations for the enhanced sensor array are complete."

The door to the bridge opened and Major Jamal Wallace entered. Captain Lennox's eyes widened a little in surprise.

"General Quinn," Wallace said as he approached a nearby auxiliary workstation and brought up the engineering interface. "I thought it better to be up here for this endeavor."

Sean noted the tenseness of Wallace's shoulders. "Are the power-cores going to fail on me, Major Wallace?"

"Not if I can help it, sir. But this is experimental. You should know that lead engineers hate that term. We prefer established protocols to ensure ships operate at maximum efficiency."

"Is the power consumption estimate that taxing for this SESA protocol?" Sean asked.

"It's significant but should be manageable, General. We're not just scanning through subspace. We're using the I-Drive to target an area ahead of the ship so the entire scanner array can peek at an area a thousand light-years away."

"With the possibility of expanding that as much as we can," Sean said.

Wallace grimaced. "Understood, sir. We're looking at approximately forty percent drain on primary power cores during active scanning. The subspace distortion requirements are substantial, but we've configured the I-Drive to provide the necessary field manipulation without compromising our mobility."

Sean nodded. "And just to be clear, the full I-Drive systems will not be engaged. I don't want us to accidentally travel anywhere."

Major Wallace gave him an 'are you serious' look. "Negative, sir. We're not going anywhere. I've got protocols in place that will cut power to the I-Drive should anything unforeseen happen. Our emergency cutoffs are much better than they were on the *Pathfinder*."

"Good," Sean said.

Colonel Sutton moved to stand beside Sean's chair. "General, we're essentially turning three ships into components of a single, massive sensor array. The computing requirements alone are unprecedented."

Major Hiroki Nagata emerged from the Combat Information Center. "Sir," he said, consulting his portable workstation, "we've networked all three ships' computing cores to the *Odyssey*. The computational capacity should be sufficient to analyze the massive data influx we're expecting, but the power requirements are at the theoretical limits of our systems."

Sean inhaled a breath, feeling the significance of command decisions that could reshape entire missions. The Subspace Experimental Scanner Array—SESA protocols—represented the cutting edge of Confederation detection technology, but it also pushed their ships to operational limits that had never been tested under field conditions. Experience with triangulating sensor arrays across a single star system fell far short of what they were trying to do.

"Like we need another acronym to memorize," Sean muttered,

earning slight chuckles from several bridge officers. Perhaps communicating through a neural link wouldn't be that bad, or maybe he was just getting set in his ways. Sean gave a slight shake of his head at the thought.

Sutton arched an eyebrow and Sean said, "Never mind."

Sutton nodded. "All stations report ready for SESA deployment."

Sean looked around, seeing the faces of the men and women on the bridge. They'd been selected for this deployment because each of them wanted to explore, and exploration had become one of the pillars of the Confederation. It was a rallying cry that hopefully would appeal not only to future generations but also other civilizations. Venturing where few dared also meant they might encounter threats beyond conventional understanding.

"Begin SESA protocols. I want continuous monitoring of all ship systems during deployment."

The bridge's ambient lighting shifted to a deeper blue as the enhanced sensor arrays came online. Sean could feel the subtle vibration through the deck plates as the *Odyssey*'s massive power cores redirected energy to the experimental systems. On the main holoscreen, the tactical display expanded exponentially, revealing a three-dimensional map that stretched across thousands of light-years.

"SESA protocols active," Lennox reported, his fingers moving rapidly across the operations console as he coordinated the massive data influx. "We're achieving sensor range of approximately twelve hundred light-years. Power consumption is within predicted parameters, but we're experiencing significant drain on all three ships."

Captain Norquist's tactical displays flared with activity as the enhanced sensors began detecting signals across vast distances. "General, we're picking up multiple Phantom relay signatures. The network is much more extensive than our initial estimates suggested."

Sean leaned forward in his command chair, watching as the holoscreen populated with dozens of signal sources scattered across a region of space larger than anything they'd previously imagined. "Pattern analysis?"

"Working on it, sir," Nagata replied. "The data being returned is more than we anticipated."

Sean frowned, noting Nagata's concerned expression.

"Sir," Lennox said. "The SESA protocol might be working better than we expected, stretching the capabilities of our sensor arrays to their limits. The field created by the I-Drive must be extending beyond projected parameters."

Sean looked at Wallace, his lead engineer focused on a group of sub-windows on his workstation holoscreen.

"Captain Lennox is correct, General," Major Wallace said. "The field created by the I-Drive has extended our sensor range by over three thousand light-years and growing."

"Can you slow it down or limit the field?" Sean asked, concerned that their systems were going to be overwhelmed.

"I'm trying, sir," Wallace replied.

"Ops, stand by to cut power to the I-Drive," Sean said. They could sift through the data after they stopped the SESA protocols.

"Field stabilizing for now, sir," Wallace said.

"We're getting detections, sir," Nagata said. "There are other relays. They appear arranged with signal traffic flowing toward a central location, but it's out of range."

The implications hit Sean immediately. They weren't just tracking individual relay activations; they were mapping an entire communications network that spanned thousands of light-years. "Can we trace the activation sequence?"

"Affirmative," Specialist Ramirez said from communications, his rapid analysis of signal patterns revealing the galactic breadcrumbs they needed to follow. "I can confirm what Major Nagata has reported. The activation cascade must originate from a nexus and propagates outward through the network. We'll need to do further analysis to lock down the source."

Sean felt the bridge's tension increase as the scope of their discovery became clear. They were looking at evidence of someone with the capability to control Phantom infrastructure across galactic distances—capabilities that dwarfed anything the Confederation had previously encountered.

"General," Wallace called from engineering, "power consumption is approaching critical levels. I recommend we limit SESA deployment to ten-minute intervals to prevent core overload."

"Understood. Maintain current scan until the time runs out, then power down to standard sensor configuration," Sean ordered. "I want a complete analysis of everything we've detected. Call in extra personnel if needed."

As the SESA arrays continued their intensive scanning, the main holoscreen revealed a picture that was both fascinating and deeply concerning. The Phantom communications network stretched across hundreds of star systems, almost funneling toward a destination they couldn't detect. The SESA protocols allowed them to take a snapshot of regions that they hadn't been to, and if they'd been able to run more extensive scans, the detections might indicate something other than the funnel they were seeing.

"Sir," Sutton said quietly, "we're at the edge of our communications range with New Earth. If we pursue this nexus, we'll be completely cut off from home."

The detections added another three thousand light-years distance from their current location, which would put them farther from home than even the *Pathfinder* had gone. But the intelligence value of identifying whoever controlled the Phantom network could prove crucial for their actions in the future and perhaps even for the Confederation's survival.

"Deploy a subspace transceiver here," Sean decided. "Full data package with everything we've discovered to be transmitted when the relay network comes fully online. We're going to follow this trail to its source."

"SESA shutdown in thirty seconds," Wallace announced.

The bridge lighting returned to normal as the experimental sensor arrays powered down, leaving them with standard detection capabilities but a wealth of new intelligence about the network they were tracking. Sean stood and moved to the main holoscreen, studying the star chart that now revealed a preliminary route to their next destination.

"Comms, recall the *Ascendant* and the *Horizon* to our location," Sean said.

"Yes, sir," Specialist Ramirez said.

Major Wallace stood. "General, I'd like to return to main engineering. This exercise really shook things up, and I'd rather get a jump on any issues now than whenever we do chase this down," he said, gesturing toward the main holoscreen.

"Very well," Sean replied.

"General," Specialist Ramirez said, "I'm receiving a request from the Aczar diplomatic envoy. They'd like to meet with you at your earliest convenience."

Sean glanced at Sutton, noting his XO's slight frown. The timing of the Aczar request was interesting. They'd been monitoring bridge activities and had undoubtedly observed the SESA deployment status. Elena had likely set up a monitoring station for them all to observe together.

"Schedule the meeting for one hour," Sean replied. "And Colonel, I want either you or me on the bridge whenever we deploy SESA protocols. The power requirements and systems stress make it too risky for routine operations."

"Understood, sir," Sutton replied. "Should we inform the Aczar about our discovery?"

The Aczar only knew that they'd gathered data from an experimental scanning protocol and didn't have access to even the preliminary results. They were potential allies, but they were also observers gathering intelligence about Confederation capabilities and intentions.

"We'll see what they want first," Sean said finally.

As the bridge settled into the routine of deep space travel, Sean couldn't escape the feeling that they were following a trail deliberately laid out for them to find.

He wanted to have a look at the data they collected before the analysis was done, so he sent a quick message to Oriana to meet him in his ready room.

"Colonel Sutton, you have the conn," Sean said and left the bridge.

CHAPTER 15

An hour later, Sean entered Conference Room Alpha with Oriana at his side. The room's adaptive lighting adjusted to accommodate the joint delegation, creating an atmosphere that felt both formal and welcoming. The oval conference table's integrated holographic systems displayed a subtle star field pattern, while the room's sound dampening ensured complete privacy for sensitive discussions.

Ambassador Elena Vasquez rose as they entered, along with Captain Morgan Blake, who snapped a salute to Sean.

Major Hiroki Nagata looked up from his personal holoscreen and then stood.

Sean returned the salute to both his officers.

The Aczar delegation occupied the far side of the table, their chrome-accented uniforms shimmering subtly as their SRAs adapted to the room's electromagnetic environment. Thyven sat with the dignified bearing of someone accustomed to diplomatic protocols, his silver-highlighted fur and his large ears positioned in what Sean had learned indicated formal attention.

Zelara wore her communication headgear, which had been

reduced in size, and its metallic filaments pulsed with gentle activity. Tavira, the youngest member of their delegation, watched them with keen interest.

"Ambassador Thyven," Sean said, settling into his chair and noting how the room's systems automatically adjusted the lighting to accommodate his position. "Thank you for requesting this meeting. I hope you're adjusting well to your new living situation. I understand you have questions about our recent operations."

Thyven's large ears twitched slightly. "General Quinn, we observed significant power fluctuations through the ship during your experimental scanning procedures. As guests aboard your vessel, we wanted to ensure we weren't inadvertently interfering with critical operations."

Sean appreciated the diplomatic phrasing, though he suspected the Aczar delegation's interest went deeper than simple courtesy. "You observed significant power fluctuations?"

"Yes, General," Zelara answered. "Our SRAs allow us to see in multiple spectrums, and we deduced that a significant operation was occurring to draw so much power."

Sean glanced at Elena and then looked at the delegation. "Interesting. I had no idea that you could detect power fluctuations even though you don't have access to the status of those systems."

Zelara shifted in her seat and her ears twitched rapidly. "I apologize, General. I thought you knew of our SRAs' capabilities. I can provide you or your team with a high-level report of the capabilities you might be interested in knowing."

"Thank you, I appreciate that. My team might've already been aware, but I wasn't. Go ahead and send me what you've got," Sean replied and looked at Thyven. "Your presence aboard the *Odyssey* has been entirely cooperative, and you've caused no operational difficulties. However, I imagine you have questions about what we discovered."

Oriana leaned forward slightly. "The scanning procedures were indeed experimental. We were testing the limits of our sensor capabilities using enhanced subspace manipulation."

Zelara's headgear flared with increased activity. "Dr. Quinn, the power signatures we detected suggested you were using Infinity Drive technology in a non-propulsion capacity. This represents a significant advancement in field manipulation techniques."

Sean exchanged glances with Elena, noting the ambassador's slight nod of approval. The Aczar had demonstrated both observational skills and technical knowledge that could prove valuable for the investigation.

"You're correct," Sean said, choosing directness over diplomatic circumlocution. "We've developed what we call SESA protocols— Subspace Experimental Scanner Array—that allows us to project our sensor capabilities across thousands of light-years. What we discovered has significant implications for this region of space."

He activated the conference table's holotank, projecting a three-dimensional representation of the Phantom communications network they'd detected. The image showed dozens of relay points scattered across vast distances, with signal patterns flowing toward a central nexus that lay beyond their current scanning range.

"This is what we found," Sean continued, highlighting specific signal sources with casual gestures. "An extensive Phantom communications network that spans thousands of light-years. Someone has been systematically activating these ancient relays, and we intend to track the signals to their source."

The reaction from the Aczar delegation was immediate and pronounced. Thyven's ears flattened against his head in concern, while Zelara's headgear practically hummed with activity. Even young Tavira leaned forward with the intense focus of someone suddenly understanding that theoretical threats had become concrete realities.

"The scope is remarkable," Thyven said, his rapid speech automatically translated through the room's systems, "but also deeply troubling. In our experience, Phantom technology that operates on such scales typically serves purposes that transcend individual civilizations."

Tavira spoke for the first time during the meeting, her voice carrying the earnest intensity of youth combined with the analytical training of a future Loremaster. "General Quinn, the activation patterns you've detected—do they show evidence of systemic coordination? Or random reactivation of dormant systems?"

Major Nagata looked up from his workstation. "The patterns suggest deliberate coordination. Someone with access to Phantom command protocols is activating specific relays in a sequence that creates a communications pathway toward a central nexus."

Sean felt the meeting's dynamics shift as the Aczar delegation's expertise became evident. Their questions demonstrated not just curiosity but genuine understanding of the technological and strategic implications involved.

"Ambassador Thyven," Sean said, "I suspect this meeting involves more than simple observation of our operations. Do you have insights that might help us understand what we're facing?"

Thyven exchanged rapid, untranslated communications with Zelara and Tavira before responding. "General Quinn, we request permission to assist with your analysis. Zelara possesses expertise with communications systems that could prove valuable, and Tavira's training includes pattern recognition techniques specifically designed for interpreting Phantom technology signatures."

Sean considered the request carefully. Allowing them access to sensitive analysis could provide valuable insights while also revealing operational details that might not serve the Confederation's interests.

"Major Nagata," Sean said, "what's your assessment of providing limited access to our analysis data?"

Nagata's lean frame straightened. "Sir, we could establish an auxiliary workspace in the CIC, separate from our primary analysis stations. The Aczar delegation could review selected data sets without accessing our core intelligence systems. All activities would be monitored according to standard security protocols."

Captain Blake nodded approvingly. "That approach would allow collaboration while maintaining operational security. We'd have complete oversight of their access and activities."

Sean looked directly at Thyven, meeting the Aczar's large eyes with the kind of steady gaze that conveyed both respect and expectation. "Ambassador, I'm prepared to grant limited access to our analysis data, but I need your understanding that such access comes with restrictions. Your activities will be monitored by security protocols, and any attempt to exceed authorized access will result in immediate termination of the arrangement."

Thyven's expression conveyed both gratitude and understanding. "General Quinn, we accept your restrictions completely. Our goal is to assist in understanding threats that could affect both our civilizations. We have no interest in compromising your operational security. We are your guests and will behave accordingly."

Zelara leaned forward, looking at Oriana. "Dr. Quinn, between my technical background and Tavira's pattern-analysis training, we might identify signal characteristics that your systems haven't prioritized. Different analytical perspectives often reveal details that might be overlooked."

"I'd like to add to that," Tavira said. "We have within our archives extensive data on Salpheth. There is a strong likelihood that he has something to do with this, and there might be a correlation that I might observe that might otherwise be missed."

Oriana smiled. "That's exactly the kind of collaborative approach that could prove invaluable. Phantom technology often operates according to principles that challenge conventional understanding. Outside of being able to ask them about it, I think us working together is as close as we'll get to that."

Sean nodded. "Very well. Major Nagata, establish an auxiliary workspace and provide access to the SESA analysis data. But I want continuous monitoring and regular reports on their activities. Ambassador Vasquez, I'll need you to establish formal protocols for this collaboration."

Elena nodded professionally. "I'll draft the appropriate agreements and ensure all parties understand the parameters involved."

Tavira's expression brightened with the kind of enthusiasm that reminded Sean of why Phendran had specifically recommended her for this mission. "General Quinn, we're grateful for this opportunity. Understanding whoever controls this network could prove crucial for both our species' future security."

Sean stood, feeling the meeting's momentum shift toward operational planning. "This collaboration begins immediately. We're tracking this signal to its source, regardless of where it leads us. Your expertise could make the difference between success and failure."

As the meeting concluded and participants began filing out to their respective duties, Sean couldn't shake the feeling that they'd just taken another step toward an alliance that could eventually reshape the Confederation. The Aczar delegation's expertise with Phantom technology, combined with the Confederation's exploration capabilities, might prove essential for whatever they would discover at this mysterious nexus.

He had high hopes for their collaboration, but he also remembered that the Aczar had allowed Salpheth to manipulate and control their species for a very long time. They were free of it now, but he had to be careful that his team didn't allow the Aczar's experience with Salpheth to take precedence over the recommendations in their own analysis.

CHAPTER 16

SEAN SETTLED into one of the curved leather chairs in his ready room's lounge area, watching his wife pour two cups of coffee from the fabrication unit. She added cream and sugar to both their cups, giving him a little extra cream the way he liked it.

Oriana moved with the graceful confidence that had first caught his attention over twenty years ago, her tall, slender frame accentuated by the dark blue science officer's uniform that complemented her velvety black hair. As she settled into the chair across from him, her dark, alluring eyes regarded him with a pensive frown.

"How do you do that?" she asked.

"Do what?"

"Give me *that* look, like you haven't seen me for a while."

Sean grinned and shook his head. "If I ever stop doing that, something is seriously wrong with me." She rolled her eyes and smiled. "I'm always happy to see you. I don't care how many times a day it is."

She pursed her lips, and Sean realized that even after they'd been married all this time, he loved her more now than when they were first married. It was as simple as that.

"Flatterer."

He stood and leaned across to kiss her. "It's true." He went back to his chair, and they each sipped their coffees. "Hard to believe it's been five days since we left Ichlos. Feels like we've covered a year's worth of discoveries in less than a week."

Oriana smiled, the expression transforming her sweetly angelic features with a warmth that never failed to ease the tension he carried as mission commander. "The SESA deployment data alone represents the most comprehensive deep-space survey in human history. We've mapped Phantom infrastructure across a region of space larger than anything we'd previously imagined possible."

Sean activated the nearby holoscreen with a casual gesture, bringing up the three-dimensional representation of the network they'd been tracking for the past several days. Dozens of relay points stretched across thousands of light-years, their signal patterns forming a complex web that funneled toward a central nexus located eight hundred light-years from their current location.

"Our collaboration with the Aczar delegation has exceeded all expectations," Sean said, highlighting specific data correlations that had emerged from their joint analysis. "We would have eventually figured out the routing protocols on our own, but their insights accelerated the process significantly."

She set her coffee down and leaned forward, studying the holoscreen. "Zelara's understanding of communications hierarchies was particularly valuable. She identified signal authentication patterns that our systems had classified as random noise. Without that insight, it would've taken weeks to decode the network's organizational structure."

He nodded, remembering the breakthrough moment when the Aczar engineer had demonstrated how Phantom communications systems used multi-layered routing protocols that indicated strict hierarchical command structures. "And Tavira's pattern-analysis capabilities helped us understand that the network isn't just carrying communications traffic; it's actively coordinating events across multiple star systems."

The Aczar's help with piecing things together was directly related to their familiarity with what Salpheth had taught them. It wasn't that they already knew how these ancient Phantom communications protocols worked, but they had enough of a foundational knowledge to give them insight into what they were observing. This insight, coupled with colonial analysis capabilities, made for a much quicker and more thorough result.

"I think the real leap came when we ruled out anything to do with the original Phantom Outpost location," Oriana said, manipulating the display to show their refined analysis of signal flow patterns. "The routing protocols clearly indicate that whatever we're tracking originates from a completely different region of space. The nexus is located three hundred light-years inward from where the *Pathfinder* took Salpheth."

Sean felt a mixture of relief and concern at that revelation—relief because it meant they weren't heading directly back to a location where they knew dangerous entities had operated, and concern because it suggested that the scope of the Phantom infrastructure was even more extensive than their most pessimistic estimates had suggested.

"Major Nagata's intelligence assessment is that we're dealing with someone who has systematic access to Phantom command protocols," Sean said, pulling up the tactical analysis that had shaped their approach strategy. "The activation sequences are too coordinated and too precise to represent random reactivation of dormant systems."

Oriana's expression grew more serious as she considered the implications. "Which brings us back to the fundamental question: are we tracking friend or foe? Someone with the capability of controlling Phantom networks across galactic distances could be an ally or a dangerous enemy. I think Salpheth might tilt more toward an enemy. Do you think that's a bridge too far?"

"Connor and I talked a lot about him. Basically, Connor's assessment is that Salpheth's primary concern is with himself, along with a strong inclination to seek retribution against those who imprisoned him. Not the Aczar but other Phantoms."

"So how do you evaluate that kind of threat?"

Sean blew out a shallow breath and arched an eyebrow. "Carefully."

"Is that really all you've got, General Quinn?"

He chuckled. "I don't have a definitive answer for you or anyone else. That will largely depend on what we find at this nexus. We don't know if Salpheth will be there or what he's been doing these past two years."

"I suppose. It's frustrating not being able to accurately determine where he fits in," Oriana said.

"The Aczar delegation is in agreement that Salpheth is an enemy and that it could be foolish to interact with him in any capacity."

"I tend to agree with them. Don't you?"

"Yes and no. I certainly wouldn't trust him, but regardless of that, he knows things. He knows about the Phantoms and about the Vemus. He told Connor as much."

"Right before he betrayed him."

"Doesn't mean he was lying about the Vemus. The other Phantoms told us that the Vemus were beyond our ability to deal with. Salpheth seemed interested that the Phantoms had interacted with us at all. But he also knew more about the Vemus than he indicated. All this means that if I were to cross paths with Salpheth, I would try to glean as much information as I could before doing anything else."

"We're still operating with incomplete information about Phantom civilization and their long-term objectives."

Sean nodded. "And the fact that the fundamentals of the Phantom civilization had changed—something so significant that they abandoned the infrastructure they'd established. The Phantom agent told Connor that they were just passing through, that they were explorers, and that they would move on."

"Their ascension."

"Maybe not all of them ascended, and perhaps there were serious disagreements as to whether they should ascend. Without knowing more, we'll continue to go around in circles about this without reaching a solid conclusion."

Oriana was quiet for a few moments. "It would be great if we encountered friendly Phantoms."

"It would, but we're still going to approach the nexus with full tactical preparation. If they're friendly, we'll follow diplomatic protocols. If we encounter hostiles, we have the firepower to defend ourselves and the speed to escape if necessary. The task force config-uration gives us maximum flexibility for either scenario."

Sean activated his personal holoscreen, reviewing the final approach vectors that would carry them to their destination. The *Odyssey*, *Ascendant*, and *Horizon* would transition into n-space at coordinates calculated to provide optimal sensor coverage while maintaining safe distances from potential threats.

"I don't like that we're so far from our own relay network," Sean said. "We could use the SESA protocol to send a transmission to our nearest relay, but if we're in any kind of trouble, we won't be able to spare the power for that kind of undertaking. Either way, we're rolling the dice."

Oriana reached across the small table to touch his hand, her fingers warm against his skin. "We've faced the unknown before and come through it stronger. Whatever's waiting for us at the nexus, we'll handle it the same way we've handled everything else— together, with the careful planning and support of the best people in the Confederation."

Sean gently squeezed her hand, drawing strength from the partnership that had sustained them through decades of exploration, discovery, and even war. "The crew's ready. The Aczar delegation has provided helpful insights. Our ships are operating at peak efficiency, and we have clear protocols for every contingency we can imagine."

"And a few we probably can't," Oriana added with a slight smile that acknowledged the reality of deep-space exploration.

Sean's personal comlink chimed softly, indicating the approach of their scheduled bridge briefing. He stood and offered his arm to Oriana, feeling the familiar pre-mission anticipation building in his chest.

"Ready to make history, Dr. Quinn?"

"With you, General Quinn, always," she replied, accepting his arm with the natural grace that made her his perfect partner in both personal and professional endeavors.

As they left the comfortable confines of the ready room for the controlled environment of the bridge, Sean reflected on how far they'd traveled—not just thousands of light-years from New Earth, but the journey from desperate colonists to confident explorers capable of investigating the galaxy's deepest mysteries.

The Phantom Nexus awaited them, along with answers that could reshape humanity's understanding of its place in the universe. They would soon learn whether that was a place of allies or adversaries with powers that operated on scales at the edge of human imagination.

The final phase of their investigation was about to begin, and with it, discoveries that would echo across generations of Human, Ovarrow, and Aczar civilizations.

————

Sean and Oriana stepped onto the *Odyssey*'s bridge, immediately sensing the heightened alertness that permeated the command center before critical operations. The main holoscreen displayed their current location relative to the target coordinates, with tactical overlays showing the positions of the *Ascendant* and the *Horizon* maintaining formation two light-years away.

"General on the bridge," Specialist Danny Ramirez announced from communications.

Sean moved to his command chair, noting the controlled tension in his bridge crew's posture. After a week of tracking signals across thousands of light-years, they were finally approaching answers that could reshape their understanding of galactic power structures.

"Status report," Sean said, settling into his chair and feeling the bridge's attention focus on him with characteristic intensity.

"All ships report ready for final approach, General," Captain Lennox said from the Ops workstation. "Power systems are optimal, and the *Odyssey*'s critical systems report green across the board."

"Sir," Captain Norquist said from the tactical workstation, "long-range sensors confirm artificial patterns at the target coordinates. The signals we've been tracking are definitely originating from constructed installations rather than natural phenomena."

Sean exchanged glances with Oriana, who had moved to the auxiliary science station to review the sensor data.

"Elaborate on those artificial patterns, Captain Norquist," Sean said.

"Sir, our telescopic analysis reveals structured light patterns that are inconsistent with natural stellar phenomena. The observations show significant changes over time—what we detected at two thousand light-years appears much more active than current readings at one thousand light-years."

Major Hiroki Nagata emerged from the Combat Information Center, his lean frame moving with quiet precision as he consulted his portable workstation. "General, the temporal analysis suggests something significant occurred at the target location approximately fifteen hundred years ago. The artificial light signatures show dramatic reduction in activity, consistent with either catastrophic damage or systemic shutdown."

The evidence suggested they were approaching the remnants of major Phantom installations, but the historical timeline indicated that whatever they found would be ancient and possibly damaged.

"Captain Norquist, set Condition Two throughout the task force," Sean ordered. "All personnel to stations. We're making our final approach."

The bridge lighting shifted to the amber configuration that indicated elevated readiness levels, and Sean could hear the subtle changes in the ship's ambient sounds as systems throughout the *Odyssey* prepared for potential combat operations.

"Condition Two set, sir," Norquist reported. "All ships confirm readiness status."

"Helm, engage Infinity Drive," Sean commanded. "Final jump to target coordinates ten light-hours from the signal source."

The familiar sensation of I-Drive engagement washed over the bridge as space-time bent around them. The main holoscreen showed the characteristic swirling patterns of hyperspace, but this time the journey lasted only minutes before they transitioned back to normal space.

What appeared on the main holoscreen defied immediate comprehension.

"My God," Oriana whispered from the science station, her voice carrying the awe of someone encountering something that challenged their fundamental assumptions about what was possible.

During the Krake War, Sean had encountered some of the most elaborate advanced alien installations across many star systems. What he now saw on the main holoscreen made everything the Krake had accomplished look like the simple indulgence of an active child.

The target system centered around a white dwarf star approximately the size of Earth—the compressed remnant of a star that had exhausted its nuclear fuel millions of years ago. The stellar remnant glowed with intense heat despite its small size, providing a stable energy source that could power civilizations for geological ages.

But it wasn't the white dwarf that commanded attention. Scattered throughout the system were the shattered remains of what had once been a massive ring structure—fragments of Phantom mega-engineering that dwarfed anything in the Confederation's experience.

"Preliminary sensor analysis complete, General," Captain Lennox reported, his voice tight with barely contained amazement. "We're looking at the remains of some kind of Dyson ring or similar megastructure. The fragments are distributed across multiple orbital planes, with the largest sections maintaining stable positions around the white dwarf."

"Sir," Major Nagata said, "preliminary scans indicated no immediate threats. No active vessels, no weapons signatures, no signs of current habitation. What we're seeing appears to be archeological rather than military."

Sean stood and moved toward the main holoscreen, watching as the display populated with a detailed analysis of the ring fragments. The scale was staggering. Individual sections that could house entire civilizations were scattered across distances that required hours of travel time between them.

"Dr. Quinn, what's your preliminary assessment?" Sean asked.

Oriana manipulated her holoscreen, projecting detailed analysis above the main tactical plot. "The ring fragments show similar hallmarks of Phantom construction techniques but on a scale that exceeds anything we've previously encountered. Based on the distribution patterns and structural analysis, this was once several continuous ring structures with varying circumferences in the billions of kilometers. It's not a complete structure, so it could either have been in the process of being built, or we could be looking at the remnants of something much more complete. We'll need time to perform a more extensive analysis, but there's more—the white dwarf's current state doesn't match that of the interstellar location."

Sean frowned, and more than a few people turned toward his wife. "What do you mean?"

"If these readings are correct, the white dwarf is much older than it should be. Something artificially accelerated this star's evolution to its current white dwarf state."

Sean stared in shock. "I know the Phantoms were extremely advanced, but a star has massive amounts of energy. What could they have done with all that?"

"I don't know. I'm basing this analysis on what our scanners have detected in the surrounding region, and the analysis suggests that the current state of this star is an anomaly when compared with the others nearby. As to what the Phantoms did with all that energy, I can't answer for you right now. I'm just reporting what the preliminary analysis suggests."

"What probability does the computer give for that assessment?" Sean asked.

"Over eighty-seven percent. It's accurate based on observable data."

Sean turned back to the main holoscreen, considering.

"General," Captain Norquist said. "We're detecting three primary fragment clusters. The main section contains active communications arrays—the source of the signals we've been tracking. A secondary fragment approximately 3.3 AU from the main also shows intact structures that are some kind of facility. There is no indication of whether it's a mining facility or a research lab, or some kind of habitation facility. Tertiary fragments are scattered throughout the system, some showing minimal power signatures."

Sean felt the scope of the investigation expanding beyond their current capabilities. Three ships couldn't adequately explore fragments separated by hundreds of millions of kilometers, especially when each section might contain discoveries that could reshape galactic understanding.

"This is why the network signals converge here," Sean realized, studying the tactical display. "This system sits at the intersection of multiple Phantom communications networks. It was designed as a galactic communications hub."

"Which means whatever we find here could provide intelligence about Phantom operations across thousands of star systems," Nagata added, his analytical mind already processing the strategic implications.

Sean returned to his command chair. The ring fragments represented knowledge that could advance the Confederation by centuries, but investigating them properly would require resources and time they might not have.

"We're going to split the task force," Sean decided. "Major Gates and the *Ascendant* will investigate the secondary fragment cluster. The *Odyssey* and the *Horizon* will focus on the primary ring section where the communication signals originate."

"Understood, sir," Specialist Ramirez replied, already preparing the communications protocols necessary to coordinate operations across such vast distances.

Sean looked around the bridge, seeing the faces of officers who had been selected for this mission while knowing they might encounter wonders beyond imagination. The shattered Phantom rings represented both humanity's greatest discovery and potentially its greatest challenge.

"All stations, prepare for extended investigation protocols," Sean announced. "We're about to explore the remnants of a civilization that achieved feats of engineering we can barely comprehend. Whatever we learn here could determine the Confederation's future among the stars."

As the *Odyssey* began its approach toward the primary ring fragment, Sean couldn't shake the feeling that they were entering a museum of galactic history where the exhibits might still be operational and where the previous visitors might not have left voluntarily.

The investigation of the Phantom Nexus was about to begin, and with it, discoveries that would echo across generations.

CHAPTER 17

MAJOR ETHAN GATES stood before the main holoscreen on the *Ascendant*'s bridge, studying the scattered fragments of what had once been something far beyond human comprehension. It was one thing to theorize about the possibilities of an advanced civilization building a megastructure, but it was staggering to witness firsthand. He wondered what it must've looked like when it wasn't a scattered remnant of its former glory.

The secondary cluster stretched across millions of cubic kilometers, each piece a monument to Phantom engineering that dwarfed the largest human constructions. There wasn't enough Human or Ovarrow population to occupy even the tiniest fraction of what they'd seen since coming to this star system. And if he threw in the population of the Aczar, that still didn't change much.

"Analysis complete on fragment cluster seven," Lieutenant Anson Gooding reported from operations, his stocky frame hunched over the displays showing structural compositions that challenged conventional understanding. "We're looking at materials that should have degraded over geological timescales, but they're showing minimal deterioration."

Cynergy moved from her auxiliary workstation to stand beside Ethan. Her expertise with salvage operations was evident in the way she studied the fragment distribution patterns, seeing connections that pure scientific analysis might miss.

She sighed, sounding intrigued. "There's something about the way these fragments are positioned," she said, manipulating the holoscreen to highlight specific structural elements. "The debris pattern doesn't match natural orbital mechanics or random destruction. Look at the orientation of the larger pieces."

Zane Rennick looked up from his science station, his curly red hair catching the bridge lighting as he processed her observation. "Are you suggesting they were once connected? The structural variations make that seem unlikely. We're looking at different construction methodologies and material compositions."

"Not constructed together," Cynergy clarified, her salvage experience informing her analysis, "but arranged together. I've spent years mapping debris fields from the Venus Wars, and this pattern suggests deliberate placement rather than catastrophic fragmentation."

Captain Akira Endo leaned forward, peering at the main holoscreen. "If we assume the fragments were once joined in some configuration, the combined mass would be approximately forty percent larger than current orbital mechanics would support at this distance from the white dwarf."

Ethan felt Atlas pulse gently around his forearm, drawing his attention to the tactical implications of their discovery. The SRA's consciousness touched the edge of his awareness, offering perspective that went beyond human analytical capabilities.

The positioning suggests strategic arrangement rather than natural settling patterns, Atlas observed through their neural link. *These fragments may represent an ancient battlefield rather than a single destroyed installation.*

Ethan wondered if Atlas could sense subtle shifts in his

thoughts because he was leaning in that direction but hadn't fully committed to the idea yet. He made a mental note to question Atlas about it later.

"Perhaps this wasn't their original location," Ethan said. "We could be looking at the remnants of an ancient engagement. Captain Endo, have the ship's computer run analysis on this theory based on our current scan data."

"Yes, sir," Endo said and turned toward his tactical workstation with a thoughtful frown. "It's possible, sir, but given the volume of data and the need for gravitational modeling across multiple stellar positions, the analysis will take considerable time, unless you want priority assigned to this investigation."

Cynergy looked at him. "The analysis model might also balk or be confused by the mysterious nature of this star system."

Ethan nodded. "You mean because it doesn't align with the age of the stars in the galactic neighborhood."

She gestured toward the main holoscreen. "If they can build all this, they could probably manipulate a star to use more of its energy sooner rather than later."

She made a good point. None of the planets left in the system were conducive to sustaining life, but if the Phantoms could do all this… he let that line of thinking go. Until there was evidence to the contrary, he wouldn't attribute actions or abilities to any alien civilization.

"Negative, tactical," Ethan replied, his command instincts focusing on immediate operational concerns. "We need to concentrate on intact structures where we're detecting power signatures. Battlefield archeology can wait until we understand what's currently active."

Lieutenant Samantha Trickle's voice cut through the bridge's focused atmosphere. "Major, I'm detecting a significant power source from fragment designation Alpha-Seven. The signature suggests active Phantom technology rather than residual energy discharge."

Ethan moved to the tactical station where the main holoscreen displayed a detailed view of what appeared to be a partially intact research installation. The structure was massive—easily ten times larger than the Phantom Outpost that his father had encountered—with multiple sections connected by enclosed walkways that suggested extensive internal pressurization.

The classification of "research installation" was an educated guess. Most space habitats they encountered in the deep dark were built with a purpose in mind—mining, habitation, or research that served various kinds of interest. This didn't account for military installations, but the scans hadn't detected any weapons systems.

"Range to Alpha-Seven?" Ethan asked.

"Approximately two million kilometers, sir," Lieutenant Reggie Jackson reported from the helm. "We can reach optimal scanning range within four hours at current acceleration."

Captain Elias Grayston's weathered voice came through the comms system from main engineering. "Major, I'm reading multiple power sources within that structure. Whatever's operating in there has been active for some time. The energy signatures show the kind of stability that suggests ongoing maintenance rather than automated systems running down."

Ethan felt a chill of anticipation. "Ongoing maintenance? Are you sure?"

"The Phantoms could have sophisticated systems online keeping that place active, so there is the possibility of that, but I would advise you to look for evidence of current activity given those power signatures," Grayston replied.

Major Will Qualmann came over to Ethan. "If someone's maintaining Phantom installations out here, we need to consider whether they're aware of our presence. Perhaps we should consider hailing them on comms."

Ethan nodded. "You're probably right, but let's wait until we get closer. Maybe, if there *is* someone there, they'll try to communicate with us first."

"Long-range sensors detect no vessels in the immediate vicinity," Captain Endo reported from tactical. "But the installation itself could house significant defensive capabilities that wouldn't show up on standard scans."

Cynergy returned to the auxiliary workstation and projected a detailed analysis of the research facility's external structure. "The design includes landing platforms similar to what the *Pathfinder* encountered at the original Phantom Outpost. Whoever built this expected regular visitor traffic."

"I agree," Ethan said. "The installation's configuration suggests research rather than military purposes, but I don't expect it to be completely defenseless. We'll approach with full tactical awareness."

Qualmann pursed his lips, giving him an appraising look. "The direct approach it is, then. Just head on in there."

Ethan chuckled. "We're not going to kick the door down. We'll knock first to see if anyone replies. Then we'll try to get inside."

Qualmann nodded and leaned toward Ethan. "It would be nice if we'd brought more ships with us."

"Of course it would, but where's the fun in that?" Ethan replied.

As the *Ascendant* accelerated toward the research installation, the main holoscreen provided increasingly detailed views of their destination. The structure appeared to be built into what had once been part of a massive ring system, its foundations anchored to materials that showed the distinctive characteristics of Phantom engineering that had been applied on a massive scale. Ethan wondered why they'd left it all behind. The time it must've taken to build this place should've made it difficult to just up and leave.

"Major," Lieutenant Anson Gooding said from the ops workstation, "we're detecting atmospheric venting from multiple points on the installation. Spectral analysis indicates a breathable atmosphere —composition matches our own ship's environmental systems."

That revelation sent a ripple of surprise through the bridge crew. Ethan felt Atlas stir more actively around his forearm, responding to his elevated stress levels.

Rennick shook his head in disbelief. "That's not possible. The chances of an alien installation maintaining an atmosphere identical to our standard environmental protocols are beyond astronomical."

"Unless someone's been expecting us," Qualmann said grimly.

Ethan nodded. "Salpheth spent time on the *Pathfinder* and at certain times had limited access to the ship's systems. He could've easily set this up."

Cynergy leaned back in her chair, head tilted in thought. "The composition isn't just similar; it's identical within measurement tolerances. Either this is the most unlikely coincidence in galactic history, or someone has specifically configured that installation for human occupation."

"Salpheth," Qualmann said.

"Maybe, but the Phantoms themselves have studied us, more so than Salpheth."

"But why would they come out here and set this whole thing up for us to find? Seems a bit odd. They could've just come to us directly," Ethan said.

"Connor said he couldn't be sure whether there were multiple factions within the Phantom civilization that were in alignment with how they explored the galaxy. Maybe a small faction came out here and did just that. The chances are small, but it is a possibility —an alternative to just thinking that Salpheth had something to do with this."

"We should consider alternative explanations until it's confirmed otherwise," Ethan said.

He returned to the command chair. The evidence suggested they were approaching something that had been prepared for their arrival, but whether that preparation represented a welcome or a trap remained unclear. It seemed like a lot of effort to set a trap for them.

"Ops, time to optimal sensor range?" Ethan asked.

"Thirty-seven minutes, sir," Lieutenant Gooding replied.

"Captain Endo, begin detailed tactical analysis of the installation's defensive capabilities. I want to know what we're facing before we commit to any approach vectors."

"Understood, sir. Passive sensors only until we determine threat levels."

As the *Ascendant* continued its approach toward the mysterious research installation, Ethan couldn't shake the feeling they were walking into something that had been specifically designed for this encounter. The question was whether they were approaching allies or enemies, as well as whether they would be able to tell the difference until it was too late to matter.

"Sir," Gooding called from operations, "detailed scans confirm the presence of landing platforms and what appear to be shuttle bays. The installation is definitely configured for visitor access."

Ethan stood and moved toward the bridge exit, his command instincts telling him that this investigation would require more than remote sensing. "Major Qualmann, you have the conn. I'm going to brief the away team. If we're going to investigate the installation properly, we'll need people on the ground."

I recommend the away team include personnel with SRA partners, Atlas observed through their link. *The integration of biological and artificial consciousness may provide advantages when interfacing with Phantom technology.*

Ethan stepped out of the bridge before he replied. "Atlas, sometimes I think you're reading my thoughts."

"Indeed, but not quite," Atlas replied.

Ethan imagined what it would be like to walk on the research station. There would always be a part of him—more than a part of him, if he was being honest—that wanted to be the first on the away missions. The drive to explore was in him, but so was the ability to command. He'd watched his father over the years strike a balance between leading and being on away missions. It was something he was hoping to emulate, but he hadn't appreciated just how much of an effort it took to find that balance.

The investigation of the research installation was about to begin. He wouldn't be on the away team, but that didn't preclude him from going there after the all-clear was given.

Ethan headed to the elevator. He'd needed to stretch his legs, and he was overdue to visit his friend, Washburn.

————

Ethan made his way through the *Ascendant's* corridors toward the main hangar bay, feeling the subtle vibration through the deck plates as the ship maintained its approach vector toward the mysterious research installation. The familiar sounds of a ship preparing for away team deployment reached him before he entered the staging area—the methodical checking of equipment, the quiet conversations of soldiers preparing for unknown dangers, and the distinctive hum of combat shuttles being prepped for deployment.

The hangar bay's main doors slid open to reveal Captain Tom Washburn overseeing final preparations with the calm efficiency that had made him invaluable during their previous encounters with alien technology. The grizzled officer's weathered features were highlighted by the bay's work lighting as he moved between equipment stations, checking gear and confirming mission parameters with his team leaders.

"Major Gates," Washburn said, looking up from a tactical display that showed the research installation's external structure. "Timing's perfect. We're about fifteen minutes from deployment."

Ethan approached the mission planning area where Washburn

had arranged holographic displays showing the installation's landing platforms and external access points. The familiarity of pre-mission briefings with his friend provided a moment of comfort before they committed to investigating something that defied easy explanation.

"How are you feeling about this one, Tom?" Ethan asked, noting the controlled tension in his friend's posture that suggested professional wariness rather than fear.

"Ready to get off ship and stretch my legs," Washburn replied with a grin. Then his expression grew more serious. "Better than the last time we investigated a mysterious alien installation, I'll give you that. At least this one isn't crawling with Vemus trying to kill us."

The reference to their encounter with the Vemus Alpha sent a brief chill through Ethan's chest. That mission had cost them a lot —including Cynergy's hybrid nature and several members of their crew who'd been converted to Vemus fighters.

"Different kind of unknown this time," Ethan replied, "but potentially just as dangerous if someone's been maintaining that facility for a while. And we can't forget about the Vemus signal hidden in the main signal we detected."

Lieutenant Kurt Spencer approached from the equipment staging area, his lean frame moving confidently. The metallic band around his forearm indicated his SRA partnership—one of the newer additions to their crew who'd volunteered for the enhanced technology integration.

"Sir," Spencer said, addressing both officers, "my SRA confirms that the installation's power signatures are consistent with active Phantom computer systems. If we can establish interface protocols, we should be able to access their data libraries."

Washburn nodded approvingly. "That's where Hash comes in. Kid's got a talent for making alien technology cooperate, even when it doesn't want to."

As if summoned by his name, Hash appeared from behind a supply crate, his youthful features animated with the kind of enthusiasm that came from encountering new technical challenges. Despite being one of the younger members of their team, his experience surviving on Old Earth during the Vemus occupation had given him insights into alien technology that proved invaluable during complex missions.

"Major Gates," Hash said, his informal manner reflecting his civilian specialist status rather than military protocol, "I've been reviewing the sensor data from the installation Cynergy sent over, along with advisories for us to pay attention to." He paused for a second. "I still find it … unsettling that the artificial atmosphere indicates someone was expecting human visitors."

Ethan nodded. "Join the club; membership is free."

Hash grinned. "I'm hoping someone is welcoming us instead of… you know." He glanced at Atlas on Ethan's wrist. "How's the SRA pilot going?

"Atlas and I work flawlessly together when I'm completely human. When I shift to hybrid, things unravel. We haven't been able to work it out yet."

"Strange. I have my application in for the SRA pilot, but I haven't been called yet."

Ethan nodded. "No shortage of volunteers."

Sergeant John Staggart joined the group, his solid frame carrying the confident bearing of someone who'd survived numerous dangerous missions. The metallic band around his wrist indicated his own SRA partnership, making him another valuable asset for interfacing with alien systems.

"Ready, willing, and able as always, sir," Staggart said with a confident smile.

Ethan smiled. Staggart had helped save his life on the Vemus Alpha. "Make sure you keep Washburn safe."

"Absolutely, Major. That's my job, and I'm pretty good at it."

Washburn chuckled, and Ethan studied the holographic representation of their destination, noting the multiple landing platforms and access points that suggested the installation has been designed for regular visitor traffic.

"This is going to be the first of potentially many reconnaissance missions to that facility. I want to understand what they were researching there and what happened to cause its apparent abandonment."

"Lieutenant Spencer and Hash will focus on computer system access," Washburn said, highlighting specific sections of the installation. "If we can tap into their data networks, we might get answers without having to physically explore every section of what appears to be a very large facility."

Ethan nodded and continued to study the holoscreen.

"Give us a minute," Washburn said to the others, and they left. He turned to Ethan with an expression that mixed professional duty with personal friendship. "You know, I could always use another experienced officer on this mission. Want to take point? Being in command does have its privileges. If you really wanted to come along, you could."

Ethan chuckled, recognizing the gentle challenge in his friend's tone. "Are you questioning my command decisions, Captain?"

"Just making sure you know the option exists," Washburn replied with a slight grin. "But since you'll probably insist on staying with your ship like a responsible commanding officer, mind if my highly capable team scouts the area first? Get the lay of the land before we start poking around in potentially dangerous alien computer systems?"

"That's exactly what I want you to do," Ethan said, feeling the familiar confidence that came from working with people he trusted completely. "Establish a perimeter, confirm the facility's safe for extended investigation, then begin the technical analysis. Happy hunting, Tom."

Washburn's weathered features lit up with the kind of professional satisfaction that came from receiving clear, achievable mission objectives. "Understood, sir. We'll have preliminary reports within six hours of touchdown."

As the away team began final preparations for deployment, Ethan watched them move through the familiar routines that had kept them alive through numerous dangerous missions. Spencer and Hash worked together on interface equipment, their different backgrounds—military precision and civilian innovation—complementing each other perfectly. Staggart coordinated with the shuttle crew while Gustor ran final equipment checks with methodical thoroughness.

The combat shuttle's engines began their pre-flight sequence, filling the hangar bay with the controlled energy that preceded every away mission. Ethan felt the familiar mixture of anticipation and concern that came with sending his people into unknown situations—pride in their competence balanced by awareness of the dangers they might face.

"Bring me back something interesting," Ethan said as Washburn headed toward the shuttle.

"Always do," Washburn replied, pausing at the shuttle's loading ramp. "Try not to get into any trouble while we're gone. I'd hate to miss out on the excitement."

As the away team boarded the combat shuttle and the hangar bay began cycling through departure protocols, Ethan couldn't shake the feeling that they were about to discover something that would fundamentally change their understanding of who was operating in this region of space. The research installation represented either humanity's greatest opportunity or its most carefully constructed trap.

Within minutes, his people would be walking into the unknown, carrying with them the hopes and fears of everyone who'd traveled thousands of light-years to unlock the secrets of an ancient Phantom facility that someone had been maintaining for reasons they couldn't yet comprehend.

CHAPTER 18

Captain Tom Washburn felt the subtle shift in artificial gravity as the combat shuttle settled onto the designated landing platform, the sensation reminding him that they were now under control of alien technology. Through the shuttle's viewport, he could see the second shuttle touching down on an adjacent platform, its crew already beginning post-landing procedures.

"Artificial gravity field confirmed," Lieutenant Hale reported from the pilot's station. "Platform systems are automatically interfacing with our shuttle's landing protocols."

Washburn stood and moved toward the shuttle's rear compartment where his team was conducting final equipment checks. The soldiers wore tenth-generation Nexstar combat suits in variously configured loadouts kitted for the wearer's mission function. The familiar routine of pre-deployment preparation provided a moment of normalcy before they stepped into whatever waited beyond the shuttle's protective hull.

"Listen up," Washburn said, his voice carrying the authority of someone who'd led numerous dangerous missions. "We're dealing with technology that's been expecting us. Stay alert, follow protocols, and remember that someone or something has been maintaining this facility for purposes we don't understand yet."

Lieutenant Kurt Spencer turned toward him, the metallic band around his armored forearm pulsing gently as his SRA interfaced with the shuttle's sensor systems. "Sir, external scans confirm breathable atmosphere and standard gravity throughout the visible sections of the facility. The environmental systems appear to be configured specifically for human occupation."

"Which should make everyone nervous," Sergeant Staggart added. His own SRA band glowed softly as it processed data streams from the shuttle's systems.

Hash moved from his position near the storage compartment. "Captain, the platform we've landed on is constructed from some kind of reactive metallic alloy. It's already beginning to illuminate pathways toward what appears to be the main entrance in this section."

Sergeant Gustor checked his weapon one final time before activating the shuttle's loading ramp. "Squads are ready for deployment, sir. Standard recon formation with technical specialists positioned for maximum protection."

"Move out," Washburn ordered, feeling the familiar surge of adrenaline that accompanied stepping into the unknown.

The Phantom facility stretched before them like something from a technological dream, its white metallic surfaces seeming to glow with its own internal light. As Washburn's armored boots touched the platform, reactive plating beneath his feet began illuminating a clear pathway toward the nearest entrance, creating a welcoming guide that somehow made the situation feel more ominous rather than less. He couldn't dismiss the feeling that they were venturing somewhere they weren't supposed to be.

"The facility's responding to our presence," Corporal Ali Sykes observed, her monitoring equipment tracking multiple energy signatures nearby. "Biometric sensors indicate no life forms in the immediate vicinity, but the power consumption patterns suggest active systems throughout the complex."

The landing pads were outside the facility, and even though they were within an artificial gravity field, it was still very much a vacuum.

Washburn led his team along the illuminated pathway, noting how the facility's architecture seemed designed to accommodate humanoid visitors. Scanning the area, his combat suit helmet allowed him to see farther than he otherwise would've been able to. Doorways were the right height, the corridors he saw through view-ports were appropriately wide, and the overall design aesthetic suggested builders who understood human psychological prefer-ences for open spaces and natural lighting patterns.

"Not at all like what we found on that derelict alien fleet," Stag-gart said.

Washburn nodded, remembering the alien ships they'd encoun-tered as they tracked a Vemus Alpha ship.

"This is too convenient," Staggart muttered as they approached what appeared to be the main entrance. "Someone's been expecting human visitors for a long time."

"Maybe," Washburn replied. "But that Outpost had similar features, so perhaps the Phantoms are similar enough to us that it presents in their architecture."

The entrance itself was an impressive archway that seemed to pulse with gentle energy, its surface showing the same reactive prop-erties as the landing platform. As they drew closer, a door control panel materialized from the apparently solid pale wall, its interface displaying symbols that shifted between Phantom scripts, which was then translated on their HUDs to human text.

"Sergeant Staggart," Washburn said, "you and Hash examine that control system before we attempt entry."

Staggart gestured for Hash to follow him, and they approached the panel with the cautious precision of someone who'd learned to respect alien technology through hard experience.

"The panel's responding to our proximity," Hash said. His enhanced hybrid perception allowed him to process the energy patterns. "The symbols are definitely shifting toward human-readable format. Someone's programmed this system to accommodate our language and interface preferences."

Staggart's SRA pulsed more actively as it interfaced with the control system. "My SRA confirms that the door mechanism is safe to operate. No defensive systems detected, no harmful energy signatures, no security checks. It wants us to come inside."

"Do it," Washburn ordered.

The Phantoms had technology that was radically advanced, and he couldn't rule out the possibility that they could've had automated systems monitoring their communications and adapted the interface to something they could understand. He'd still keep the translation interface on in his combat suit computer just in case.

The control panel responded to Staggart's SRA with smooth efficiency, and the massive entrance dilated open to reveal a containment shield that shimmered like semitransparent liquid mercury. Beyond it, a well-lit corridor stretched into the facility's interior, its surfaces showing the same welcoming illumination patterns they'd encountered outside.

"Containment field is maintaining atmospheric separation," Corporal Richardson reported, scanning the entrance with portable sensors. "No pressure differential, no contamination detected. We can proceed safely."

Washburn led his team through the containment field, feeling the subtle tingle of energy as they passed from the external platform into the facility's interior. The corridor beyond was impressive in its scale and sophistication—high ceilings, elegant architectural lines, and surfaces that seemed to anticipate their movement by providing optimal lighting conditions.

A bright blue light flashed overhead, startling them.

"Decontamination protocols activating," Hash announced as gentle energy fields swept over the team. He gestured toward a nearby holoscreen on the wall, which indicated scanning was in progress. "Standard procedure for any facility built in space. Nothing harmful detected on my end."

A synthesized voice filled the corridor, speaking in clear, unaccented human language that somehow made the situation even more unsettling. "Welcome to Praxion Research Facility. Please proceed to the central laboratory complex for orientation and assignment briefing."

"Orientation briefing?" Gustor asked doubtfully. "How long have they been expecting us?"

Washburn tried to maintain objectivity, but it was a losing battle. He opened a comlink to the *Ascendant*. "Major Gates, we're inside the facility. The systems are definitely configured for human occupation, and someone's programmed them to provide what appears to be standard research facility protocols. Plus, the system is speaking in the clear. No translation interface."

Ethan's voice came through clearly despite the distance separating them. "Understood. This follows previous Phantom encounters, including the encounter with Salpheth. Proceed with caution and maintain regular contact. If someone's been expecting us, we need to know why."

The team moved deeper into the facility, their footsteps echoing softly off surfaces that seemed to absorb and redirect sound for optimal acoustics. Many of the rooms they passed were sealed, their control panels dark and unresponsive, but the main corridors remained fully illuminated and welcoming.

"Sergeant," Corporal Richardson said to Staggart. "Should we stay on our own life support?"

Staggart looked at Washburn. "Captain?"

Tom checked the biometric readings from his combat suit's

sensors. They were within Earth-norms that nearly matched the atmosphere on any Confederation ship he'd served on. "Stay on individual life support for now," he replied.

They continued down the corridor.

"Captain," Sykes called from her location near a large open area, "I'm detecting a transit system ahead. Appears to be similar to an Aczar teleportation platform."

The transit pad was a circular platform set into the floor, its surface covered with intricate patterns that pulsed with gentle energy. Control interfaces around its perimeter displayed route options to various sections of the facility, each destination labeled in both Phantom script and human text.

Tom studied it for a few seconds and Hash came to his side.

"Central Laboratory Complex," Hash read from the display. "That matches the facility's earlier instruction. Someone definitely wants us to go there."

Washburn weighed the risks of using unknown alien technology against the practical necessity of covering large distances in what appeared to be a massive installation. "Can we trust it?"

Staggart's SRA interfaced with the transit controls, proving detailed analysis through his neural implants. "The system appears safe and standard for Phantom installations. It all indicates normal teleportation protocols with full safety interlocks."

"Is there some way we can test it first?"

Staggart looked up at him. "You need a test subject? Richardson, you're up."

Richardson hesitated.

"One second, corporal," Tom said. "My understanding of how the transit pads work is that it can teleport anything through it. Find me something to send through."

"How about a scout drone, sir?" Hash asked.

"Perfect. Go ahead."

Hash pulled out a dark, oval-shaped scout drone and set it on the pad. He activated it and its counter-grav emitters engaged so that it hovered just above the ground.

"Activating," Staggart said from the control interface.

A quick flash of light and the scout drone disappeared. Hash brought up his personal holoscreen and then a video feed from the drone. The feed panned over, locking in on their location, and the camera zoomed in toward them.

"The drone's fully operational, sir," Hash said.

Tom nodded and looked at Staggart. "Take the first group, Sergeant."

"Yes, sir," Staggart said and called out to his men.

The transit pad could accommodate both platoons, but only two squads joined Staggart on the pad. The transit system activated with smooth efficiency, surrounding them with gentle energy before depositing them across the wide-open area near the Central Laboratory Complex.

"We've cleared the pad, Captain. All clear," Staggart said over comms.

Tom had read the reports of how transit pads used on Ichlos had worked. As expected, it felt like a slight drop underneath them and they were quickly deposited at the destination pad. The whole experience was benign, except for the startling realization that they'd just teleported over five hundred meters within a second.

Tom turned toward the vast laboratory complex and his eyes widened at the sight. The space was enormous—easily the size of a starship hangar—filled with research stations, analysis equipment, and containment systems that suggested investigations into biological and technological subjects.

But it was the raised platform at the center of the laboratory that commanded immediate attention.

"My God," Gustor whispered with awe in his voice.

The platform held what appeared to be a pale humanoid figure suspended in some kind of containment apparatus. The being was female in appearance, tall and elegantly proportioned, with what appeared to be toned muscle mixed with a dancer's grace. Her skin was angelically pale, similar to descriptions of Phantoms, but her overall appearance was distinctly more human than any alien species they'd encountered.

She looked both completely at peace and oblivious to their presence. Multiple metallic cords connected her to the crystalline cradle that held her, and monitoring displays around the platform showed vital signs that indicated she was alive but dormant.

"It has to be an artificially grown humanoid avatar," Hash said. "The biological signatures are too perfect, too optimized for this to be a natural organism."

"Are you sure about that?" Gustor asked.

Hash gestured toward the empty laboratory around them. "Do you see her parents here? This is clearly a constructed being designed for specific purposes… you're poking fun at me."

Gustor laughed and was soon joined by several of the others. "It's just too easy sometimes."

Washburn ordered Gustor to take his soldiers to get a closer look at the containment apparatus from multiple angles while maintaining safe distances. The technology was clearly Phantom in origin but configured in ways that suggested research into biological forms rather than purely technological subjects.

"Can we communicate with her?" Spencer asked, his SRA pulsing as it attempted to interface with the monitoring systems.

"Life signs are consistent with deep unconsciousness," Sykes reported from her biometric scanner. "Neural activity is minimal but stable. She's alive but not responsive to external stimuli."

"Like a coma patient?" Spencer asked.

"Could be, sir, or some kind of stasis," Sykes replied.

As they continued their examination, Hash suddenly stepped

back from his monitoring equipment, his expression shifting to one of alarm. Several soldiers noticed the movement and raised their weapons, pointing them at the woman.

"What is it?" Washburn asked.

Hash cleared his throat. "I'm detecting irregular heart rhythm patterns. I suggest that everyone move away from the platform."

The humanoid's skin began showing elaborate grayish-purple patterns that spread across her limbs and torso like living tattoos. The designs were disturbingly familiar to anyone who'd encountered hybrid physiology but with characteristics that suggested something far more advanced.

"Biometrics still show unconsciousness, Captain," Sykes reported, her voice tight with controlled tension. "But those skin patterns... they look like hybrid markings."

Washburn glanced at Hash.

"I'm not sure, sir."

"Is she Vemus?" Staggart asked, lifting his weapon and aiming it at the target.

The team looked to Hash, whose experience with both hybrid physiology and Vemus encounters made him their best resource for understanding what they were seeing. The young specialist watched the monitoring displays while processing sensory input that his hybrid nature made possible.

Washburn activated his comlink to the ship. "Major Gates, we need guidance. We've found what appears to be an artificially constructed humanoid with hybrid characteristics. Unknown if hostile or friendly. Adding data feed to this comlink."

A few seconds passed before Ethan replied. "Hash, try communicating with her subvocally. Biometrics show no known contagions, and if she's some kind of hybrid construct, she might respond to direct contact. Remove your helmet if necessary."

Hash approached the platform with obvious reluctance, even from inside a combat suit.

Staggart came to his side. "I'll watch your back."

"Thanks," Hash replied, sounding relieved. He disengaged his helmet and moved closer to the containment apparatus, embracing his hybrid nature.

Washburn watched Hash's transition from human to hybrid, and even though he'd seen it many times, he still found it amazing —amazing and little unsettling, as if his brain were being tricked into seeing something that shouldn't be happening. He understood that hybrids could communicate subvocally using their body's biological rhythms to convey information. That was the concept as he understood it, but he also knew there were deeper levels of understanding he'd never reach because he wasn't a hybrid.

Hash's expression became tense, and his gaze locked onto the humanoid woman.

The response was immediate and terrifying. A subsonic burst of communication erupted from the humanoid, so intense that everyone in the laboratory felt it as a physical sensation in their chests. Hash staggered backward, his face draining of color.

He gasped. "She's... she's some kind of Vemus Alpha," Hash said, his voice sounding strained and full of fear.

Staggart moved in front of Hash, covering the strange humanoid Vemus with his weapon. Several soldiers flanked him, and together they ushered Hash away from the center.

"The subvocal communication patterns are definitely Alpha-level, but... I don't understand. How can that be an Alpha?"

Hash looked at Washburn, but he knew the question was really for Ethan.

The humanoid remained unconscious despite the communication burst, her vital signs showing no change from their previous readings. Whatever she was, she remained dormant for reasons they couldn't yet understand.

"Fall back," Washburn said, and they moved away from the

center, putting even more distance between them and the humanoid.

"Major Gates, we need orders. Admittedly, I'm not a hybrid expert, but I'd say Hash looks pretty shaken up from even that brief encounter. If that thing is an Alpha, it isn't like any Alpha we've encountered before. Should we eliminate the threat?"

The other Vemus Alphas they'd encountered were larger than the *Ascendant* itself. The remnant they'd faced two years ago was still large enough to fill this vast chamber.

"Someone set this up for us to find, Tom," Ethan said. "I don't think we should destroy it without understanding why. Clear your people back to the laboratory entrance and maintain monitoring distance. I'm coming down there."

Washburn's protective instincts went into overdrive. "Sir, I must advise against that."

"Noted, Captain. Keep searching the area but stay clear of that lab until I get there."

Washburn gritted his teeth, shaking his head. "Understood, sir."

The comlink ended.

As Washburn's team withdrew to a safe distance, he couldn't shake the feeling that they'd just discovered something that would fundamentally change their understanding of the threats facing humanity. They were no longer operating in familiar territory, and the decisions made in the next few hours could determine whether humanity gained crucial intelligence or walked directly into a carefully constructed nightmare.

Hash made his way over to him with his helmet re-engaged. "Sorry, sir. That response took me completely by surprise."

"You're not the only one," Washburn replied. "This is going to sound strange, but did it communicate anything?"

"Not directly. It was more of a warning," Hash said and glanced behind him down one of the adjacent corridors.

"What are you looking at?"

Several soldiers were heading down the corridor to explore other areas nearby.

"This might sound paranoid, but what if whoever created that," Hash said gesturing toward the central lab, "also created others like it, or worse."

Washburn blinked in surprise and then muttered a curse as he called Staggart over to him and began bellowing orders.

CHAPTER 19

ETHAN WALKED through the Praxion Research Facility's corridors with a purposeful stride, flanked by his CDF escort and two hybrid specialists whose enhanced capabilities might prove crucial for understanding whatever they'd discovered in the central laboratory. The facility's reactive lighting responded to their movement, creating pathways that seemed almost eager to guide them toward their destination.

Christoph Rahner moved with the controlled alertness of someone whose salvage operations had taken him into more than a few dangerous situations. His lean frame and weathered features spoke of years extracting valuable technology from places where others had died trying. Beside him, Lydia Torres carried herself with the fluid grace of someone whose combat training had been honed through both formal instruction and brutal necessity. Her dark eyes constantly scanned their surroundings, processing potential threats with enhanced hybrid perception.

"This place feels wrong," Torres said, her hybrid senses detecting subtleties that purely human perception might miss. "The environmental systems are too perfect, too specifically tailored for our needs."

Ethan had retracted his combat suit helmet soon after arriving. He wanted to get a feel for this place that the suit prevented.

"It's too damn clean," Christoph said. "With as old as this place is supposed to be, it shouldn't be this pristine. I don't care how great Phantom tech is."

"Just because it's clean now doesn't mean it was always like this. I doubt an atmosphere has been maintained here for countless years as the facility lay dormant," Ethan said.

The air was nearly odorless, which seemed unnatural. Even with scrubbers that were part of the life support systems, there was eventually a slight odor over time. Regular maintenance took care of that, but on colonial ships they rotated certain scents that spacers found appealing. Ship environmental systems could be tailored to the person, but for public spaces the scents were generally very light.

Atlas pulsed more actively around Ethan's armored forearm as the SRA interfaced with the facility's computer systems. The alien consciousness touched the edge of his awareness, offering insights that went beyond conventional analysis.

The facility has been recently activated, Atlas observed through their neural link. *Systems access logs indicate restoration began approximately six months ago, with multiple landing zones brought online in sequential phases. Someone has been preparing for visitors.*

"Atlas confirms recent activation," Ethan said, sharing the SRA's findings with his team. "This isn't an ancient installation running on automated systems. Someone's been actively preparing it for our arrival."

"So, the signal we detected isn't that old at all then," Torres said.

Ethan nodded. "Doesn't have to be. The Phantoms were using their own subspace communications to propagate the signal. It was the ancient relays that eventually slowed it down."

Rahner surveyed the area as they walked down the corridors. "I've got a data feed to some of the scout drones. The power distribution patterns suggest most of the complex remains offline. Whoever reactivated this place focused their efforts on specific sections—landing zones, main corridors, and presumably the central laboratory where the others made their discovery."

Ethan kept thinking that Salpheth had set this up, but he couldn't figure out why he would do this. Why would he draw them out here? What was he hoping to accomplish? They hadn't found evidence that Salpheth had done any of this, and he was determined to find hard evidence to support that, but at the same time he couldn't completely rule out that some other Phantom was the perpetrator. Thinking along those lines made it all but impossible for him to figure out why any of this had been done.

They reached the transit platform that would teleport them to the laboratory complex. The thought of a teleportation platform made him snort a little. A flashback to when he'd been fifteen years old came to mind. His parents were hosting Sean and Noah at their house. He remembered Sean joking with Noah about trying to create a teleportation device during the early days of research that ultimately led to the invention of the Infinity Drive. Very few people who were outside his parent's circle of friends knew the camaraderie and intimate bond between the first generation of colonists on New Earth. Most were aware of the breakthroughs in technology, or the heroic deeds, but these facts were historic references in the colonial archives. Ethan had grown up around great men and women who had accomplished so much and overcome colossal odds. All of these thoughts reinforced in him that he was right where he belonged, at the mysterious edge in a region of the galaxy that humans had never traveled before.

The transit platform had a crystalline surface that pulsed with gentle energy that seemed to anticipate their arrival. As they stepped onto the platform, Ethan felt a subtle disorientation as they were teleported across the complex.

The central laboratory stretched before them like a technological cathedral, its vast spaces filled with research equipment that might have represented the pinnacle of Phantom scientific achievement. His gaze slid toward the raised platform at the center of the space, which commanded his immediate attention. A humanoid figure was suspended within a crystalline cradle.

Captain Tom Washburn approached from his position near the laboratory entrance. Behind him, Ethan saw CDF soldiers positioned at strategic locations throughout the laboratory, their weapons ready but not actively targeting the humanoid figure.

"Major," Washburn said, his voice carrying the relief of someone who'd been hoping for additional expertise, as well as the recognition that they'd been dealing with something that must be kicked up the chain of command. "The situation hasn't changed since my last report. She remains unconscious, but her vital signs indicate increasing stress patterns."

Hash emerged from behind a bank of monitoring equipment, his youthful features animated with the kind of intense focus that came from encountering something that challenged his technical understanding. The hybrid specialist had been coordinating with the *Ascendant*'s science team, gathering data that painted an increasingly disturbing picture.

"Major Gates," Hash said with a relieved smile, "I've been working with Cynergy to analyze the containment apparatus. What we're seeing appears to be some kind of biological experiment, but the methodology is unlike anything in human or known alien scientific protocols."

Hash gestured toward the cords that connected the humanoid to her crystalline cradle, their surfaces pulsing with energy patterns that suggested active data and material transfer. "The connections aren't just sustaining her, they're introducing controlled stressors on a molecular level—chemical mutagens, targeted radiation exposure, possibly engineered viruses designed to alter DNA sequences."

Torres peered at the monitoring displays, her expression growing increasingly troubled. "The cellular modification rate is accelerated beyond anything we've encountered. Whatever process is occurring, it's happening rapidly and would normally be extraordinarily painful."

"I understand the concept of accelerated cellular modification, but how is this different than what we've already encountered?" Ethan asked.

"Our encounters with the Vemus have happened after they reach a pinnacle in their evolution. They absorb the DNA of life-forms on planets and use what they learn to adapt. Once they reach a certain stage, the governing protocols of the Vemus change to promote consolidation where they seek to escape the world they've subjugated, presumably to return to a super-alpha somewhere else."

Ethan nodded. "Right. We haven't encountered an early stage of a Vemus invasion. The seeds had already sprouted and matured."

"That's exactly right."

Ethan moved closer to the platform while Atlas attempted to interface with the Phantom monitoring systems. The humanoid figure was remarkably beautiful in a way that seemed almost designed to evoke human aesthetic preferences—tall and elegantly proportioned with features that combined the best aspects of human and Phantom characteristics.

"She doesn't appear to be experiencing pain," Ethan observed, studying the peaceful expression on the humanoid's face.

Cynergy's voice came through the communications link from the *Ascendant*. "Pain receptors might be chemically blocked, or the modifications could include enhanced tolerance for cellular stress. We don't know how long this has been going on. Either way, the biological changes occurring are extensive and systematic."

"Understood," Ethan replied. The humanoid represented either a breakthrough in comprehending their enemies or the most sophisticated trap ever constructed by entities that understood human psychology better than humans understood themselves. Salpheth, or some other Phantom, knew that the Confederation needed to learn more about the Vemus. It was a safe bet that when they encountered a Vemus Alpha, simply killing it wouldn't be their first course of action. They needed to study it, to learn where the super-alpha was located. They needed to assess the threat and determine just how many worlds had been seeded by the Vemus. Even now, there could be young, advanced civilizations fighting for their lives, most likely losing everything they'd built against an enemy that was simply beyond their capabilities to deal with.

Ethan frowned. That thought reflected what the Phantoms had told his father at their first meeting, and yet they refused to accept it. It was the same determination or that questioning drive that had taken humanity into the stars in the first place. Since they'd survived, perhaps others had survived their encounter with the Vemus as well. Fear of the unknown wouldn't get them anywhere, and there were some things Ethan couldn't walk away from.

"I'm going to attempt direct contact," Ethan decided, moving toward the platform despite the concerned expressions of his team.

Washburn stepped forward. "Sir, if that really is a Vemus Alpha construct, direct neural contact could be extremely dangerous."

Ethan regarded his friend. "Which is why I'm not approaching alone," he said, looking at Torres and Rahner. "I'm going to synchronize our hybrid abilities to amplify the communication attempt. She responded to Hash's attempt, but it was more of a brush-off than real communication. No offense, Hash."

"None taken. Scared the heck out of me," Hash said and frowned. "It reminded me... never mind."

Ethan gave Hash a knowing look. Through his experiences in direct contact with different Vemus Alphas, he'd developed the ability to force other hybrids into submission. That might've made him some kind of Alpha himself, but he wasn't sure about it. Cynergy had told him that there were hybrids who were adept at aligning other hybrids in an unconventional bond that united them. The closest thing the CDF had to that was the newer neural implants that allowed for shared distributed consciousness. It enabled a platoon or squad to share sensory input and decision-making processes in real-time, creating a collective intelligence that could adapt faster than traditional command structures.

"Be careful, Ethan," Cynergy said over comms.

Torres nodded. "It's a tactical advantage to coordinate our capabilities like this. Combine synchronization. If she tries anything hostile, we'll be able to counter her influence more effectively."

"And if that fails," Washburn said, gesturing to other soldiers, "we'll take care of it before it gets out of hand."

Ethan knew Qualmann was monitoring from the *Ascendant's* bridge. He would take command of the mission should something happen to Ethan.

Hash looked at Ethan. "Sir, do you want me to help?"

Ethan shook his head. "No, I want you to observe and advise Washburn."

"Yes, sir."

The three hybrids positioned themselves closer to the platform, feeling their enhanced nervous systems beginning to resonate with each other as they embraced their hybrid natures. Ethan felt the others' presence through his heightened senses and brought them into alignment with his own. The process added Rahner's and Torres's strength and will to his own.

He focused his attention on the humanoid figure in front of them, projecting subsonic communication toward her and strengthening it with his will and determination. The response was immediate and profound.

The humanoid's eyes opened—large, luminous orbs that held the kind of ancient intelligence that spoke to experiences spanning millennia rather than decades. It was gone in an instant, replaced by a strange, confused expression. Her gaze fixed on Ethan with an intensity that seemed to penetrate not just his physical form but his essential nature as a being capable of choice and moral judgement.

When she spoke, her voice carried an authoritative resonance that was unquestionable but also the curiosity of someone encountering something genuinely unexpected.

"You are not like the other hunters," she said, her words carrying subsonic harmonics that resonated in the chests of everyone present. "This test presents a strange interaction of parameters I was not prepared to encounter."

Ethan felt Atlas pulse with alarm as the SRA processed the implications of her statement. The mention of hunters and tests suggested they were participants in something far more complex than a simple research installation.

"I would prefer not to harm you," Ethan said carefully, "but I will defend myself and my people if you attack. I would like to speak with you, if you will allow it."

The humanoid stared at him, her luminous eyes processing information through keen senses. The patterns on her skin shifted subtly, suggesting internal processes that might indicate threat assessment or simple curiosity.

"Very well, hunter. Proceed," she replied, her voice carrying both permission and warning in equal measure.

As the laboratory fell into tense silence around them, Ethan realized he was about to engage in a very important conversation. Some battlefields were fought with weapons, while others were fought with words. His gut told him that he needed to be a master of both right now.

CHAPTER 20

THE LABORATORY FELL into tense silence as Ethan faced the humanoid figure, her alien eyes studying him with an intensity that suggested she was processing information through senses that operated beyond his understanding. The patterns of her skin shifted subtly, creating flowing designs that might indicate internal processes or simply her response to their presence.

"You may address me as Seraphine," she said, her voice still carrying strange subsonic harmonics. "The name was revealed to me in an earlier iteration and is therefore of a divine nature."

Ethan felt Atlas pulse with concern, the SRA's consciousness touching the edge of his awareness with warnings about the implications of her statement. Revealed names suggested external guidance that raised disturbing questions about who or what was directing this research.

"You can call me Ethan. Our names are given to us by our parents."

Seraphine regarded him for a long moment. "Communication would be much quicker if you would permit me to make physical contact with you." Seraphine said, her elegant form shifting slightly within the crystalline cradle. "I believe direct neural interface would facilitate more efficient communication."

"You better not!" Cynergy's voice crackled through the comlink from the *Ascendant*, tension evident in every syllable.

Ethan stepped back from the platform, his instincts screaming warnings about the dangers of direct contact with someone who might be capable of mental manipulation or conversion. It was how the other Alphas he'd encountered behaved. "I don't think that would be wise for either of us. Too many variables we don't understand."

Seraphine looked disappointed. Could she feel lonely? Reading emotions in features that combined humanoid and alien characteristics was challenging.

"As you wish. Your caution suggests intelligence, which makes you more intriguing than the other hunters."

"You mentioned hunters before," Ethan said, studying her carefully. "Why did you think I was a hunter?"

"Are you not?" Seraphine asked, her head tilting slightly in a gesture that seemed almost human. "Your enhanced physiology, your weapons, your coordinated approach to this facility—these characteristics match the parameters I was prepared to encounter."

"By that definition, I am a hunter, but probably not what you were expecting," Ethan replied. "What exactly *were* you expecting?"

Her gaze settled on his, and he could feel the weight of her stare. "A test," she said simply, as if the answer should be obvious.

"What kind of test?"

"The kind that improves me." Seraphine's luminous eyes seemed to glow more brightly as she spoke about improvement. "Each iteration brings refinement, enhanced capabilities, superior adaptation to the challenges presented."

Ethan felt a chill that had nothing to do with the laboratory's temperature. "Do you always win these tests?"

"No," Seraphine replied with the calm certainty of someone

stating basic facts. "When I fail, I am remade and improved. I am revived here." She gestured at the crystalline cradle that supported her body. "The testing continues until the final iteration."

"When will that be?"

"I do not know. I haven't reached perfection yet because I am still here."

The implications made the muscles of Ethan's chest become tense, as if he'd been stuck. They weren't looking at a single experiment; they were witnessing one iteration in an ongoing process designed to create something that could overcome any opposition.

Behind him he could hear Washburn warn the other soldiers searching the facility.

"The Vemus we've encountered elsewhere in the galaxy were monsters," Ethan said, watching her reaction carefully. "They destroyed entire civilizations, converting entire species into extensions of their collective will."

"The concept of evil is misunderstood by the unenlightened," Seraphine replied, her voice carrying the patient tone of someone explaining simple concepts to children. "We preserve life and perfect it. We bring harmony to chaos and will eventually bring this galaxy into proper submission to optimal order."

"No," Ethan said firmly, feeling anger rise in his chest. "What you call harmony is slavery. What you call perfection is the destruction of everything that makes life worth living."

Seraphine's expression showed genuine curiosity rather than offense. "I am particularly interested in you, Ethan, and the other hybrids, because you represent a genetic deviation that intrigues our research protocols. Your species achieved partial integration with our biological systems while maintaining individual consciousness —a combination that should not be possible according to established parameters."

"How would you know?" Ethan asked.

She frowned as if the thought had never occurred. "It is known. It was always known."

"But you don't know how you know," Ethan said, stepping closer to her. "You were given this information and you just accept it? No curiosity? No consideration that perhaps you're being lied to?"

"Impossible."

"No, it's not. You wouldn't know because no one has ever told you."

"I've received instruction. Knowledge is locked inside me, and the closer I get to perfection, the more knowledge is unlocked. It is a path that must be walked."

Before Ethan could respond, Major Qualmann's voice came through his comlink with urgent intensity. "We have a problem. Scout drone reports an unknown vessel is approaching the facility's far docking port. EM signature doesn't match any known design."

Ethan clenched his jaw. They were no longer alone at the research facility, and they had no idea who was coming to investigate.

"Classification?" Ethan asked, maintaining visual contact with Seraphine while processing the new threat.

"Unknown, sir, but it's big. Estimated length over two kilometers, and it's moving with purpose toward the docking facilities. ETA approximately thirty minutes."

The ship wasn't of Phantom design, so it must've entered the system like they had done.

Seraphine's eyes seemed to grow brighter as she listened to the communication. "A new phase of testing."

Ethan's gaze narrowed. "What's arriving, Seraphine?"

"I don't know."

He blinked in surprise. The answer wasn't what he expected. "What do you mean you don't know? You just said this was a new phase of testing."

"It must be. The parameters are always changing, becoming more complex. It is written that visitors would come here, and here you are."

She didn't know. She thought this was all part of some carefully orchestrated test, but that couldn't be it. What must've drawn these newcomers was the same thing that had drawn them to this place—the Phantom communications signal that contained a Vemus broadcast hidden inside. What Ethan didn't know was whether this was some other alien race or a Vemus ship arriving to investigate.

The real test was about to begin.

CHAPTER 21

GENERAL SEAN QUINN stood before the main holoscreen on the *Odyssey*'s bridge, studying the catastrophic remains of what had once been the most impressive technological achievements ever created. The shattered Phantom ring stretched across millions of kilometers, its broken sections orbiting a nameless white dwarf star like the bones of some colossal creature that had died in ancient violence.

The rings could've been abandoned, and the formation of the white dwarf star could've triggered enough damage to cause the entire structure to break apart. Sean had first studied ancient battlefields on New Earth, where bombardments and war on a scale that almost wiped out the Ovarrow had been hidden under thousands of kilometers of forests. During his career in the CDF, he'd seen remnants of battles both on planets and in star systems, so when he looked at this star system he thought he was looking at an ancient battlefield rather than an abandoned mega-structure.

"Engineering analysis complete, General," Major Jamal Wallace reported from his station, his expressive eyes reflecting the amber glow of the workstation's holoscreens. "The damage patterns are consistent with deliberate destruction rather than natural decay. A battle was fought here."

Oriana looked up at Sean from the science station where she'd been coordinating analysis with the Aczar delegation. "The ring fragments show evidence of high-energy weapons impacts, gravitational stress damage, and what appears to be controlled implosion collapse of specific sections. It's likely that Major Wallace's assessment is correct, and a battle was fought here, but there is significant damage in areas that suggests the battle was also fought from within the structures themselves."

Sean was no stranger to wars and their complexities. He'd fought enemies, but without a doubt the worst kind of war was one fought among themselves. There had been a couple of times in colonial history that certain factions had pushed for division among the colonists.

"A Phantom civil war, and it tore apart their civilization," Sean said.

She nodded. "It's a theory that our analysis assigns a high probability." She pursed her lips in thought. "Given the size of these rings, the Phantom population must've easily been in the billions, possibly trillions. A lot of different ideas manifest in an environment like that."

Sean nodded. "Captain Norquist, what's your analysis of weapons signatures?"

Jane Norquist turned toward him from the tactical workstation. "The energy weapons patterns are extremely high-magnitude, and Phantom power cores are certainly capable of powering those kinds of weapons, but the scale is beyond anything we've previously encountered or are capable of duplicating with our own power cores. Some of the impact damage suggests weapons capable of cracking planetary crusts."

Colonel Brad Sutton moved to stand beside Sean's command chair, his imposing presence adding weight to the tactical implications of their discovery. "General, the absence of opposing fleet debris suggests this was an internal conflict. Phantoms fighting Phantoms with weapons that could reshape entire star systems."

Uneasy tension seemed to hang over the bridge crew as Sean studied the data fields populating with the latest scan results.

Captain Jake Lennox looked up from operations. "Sir, we've managed to establish remote access to several intact computer nodes throughout the ring fragments. The data we're extracting is revealing network maps that span thousands of star systems."

"Show me," Sean ordered.

The main holoscreen shifted to display a three-dimensional map of galactic proportions, showing communications networks that stretched across vast regions of space like a technological nervous system. Phantom relay stations appeared as glowing nodes connected by data pathways that revealed the scope of their former civilization's reach.

"This location must've served as a convergence point for multiple networks," Thyven said, the Aczar ambassador moving from his observation position near the diplomatic workstation. His silver-highlighted fur caught the ambient lighting as he studied the network display with the kind of focused attention that suggested recognition. "The ring's original purpose was to boost and route galactic communications across this entire region of space."

"Sir," Captain Lennox said, "my analysis concurs with Ambassador Thyven's."

Captain Jane Norquist turned toward him. "Sir, there is too much data on the nexus for us to store in our system, and all of our compression algorithms are insufficient. However, the access logs show that someone has been using this facility to coordinate activities across multiple star systems."

Sean felt a chill as the implications became clear. "Time frame for the most recent access?"

Major Hiroki Nagata emerged from CIC. "Sir, the access logs

show regular usage over the past six months, with the most recent activity occurring approximately three weeks ago."

"Salpheth," Sean said, the name carrying the weight of recognition and concern. The rogue Phantom had escaped from the original outpost encounter with capabilities that remained largely unknown, and evidence of his continued operations raised disturbing questions about his long-term objectives.

"The pattern suggests coordination rather than simple information-gathering," Nagata continued. "Whoever was accessing these systems was sending instructions to multiple network nodes across hundreds of light-years. The data doesn't indicate whether those target systems access other network nodes farther away."

Sean nodded in understanding. If the Phantoms were concerned with secure communications—and there was no reason to suspect that they weren't, given that they were fighting a civil war—they could have taken steps to block access to certain network nodes after the data reached its destination. The way communications networks worked was that data was transferred, and though the receiving node acknowledged that the data was received, it didn't have to inform the sending node of where the data went from the receiver.

Oriana moved to the main display, manipulating the data to highlight specific communications pathways. "Sean, look at this. The network architecture shows evidence of systematic reactivation. Ancient relay stations that had been dormant were brought online in sequence, creating communications chains, but there are a lot of failures where the relay stations are nonfunctional."

"General," Specialist Danny Ramirez said, "I'm detecting increasing electromagnetic interference from various ring fragments. It's starting to affect our scanner arrays and could impact communications with the *Ascendant*."

Sean activated his command interface, bringing up tactical displays that showed the positions of both the *Odyssey* and the

Horizon relative to the ring fragments. "Source of the interference?"

"Multiple fragments are showing increased power output," Captain Lennox reported from operations. "The interference patterns suggest the ring's communications systems are still partially active but operating outside normal parameters."

Zelara's ears twitched as she turned toward Sean. "General Quinn, the electromagnetic signatures match certain broadcast protocols we use, but they're also cycling through frequencies that seem designed to prevent external monitoring."

Sean was impressed with her analysis. She was observing them and had minimal system access to the ship's computers, and he was impressed that she'd made a meaningful contribution.

"Thank you, Zelara," Sean said.

Colonel Sutton looked at Sean. "Could be an automated security response to our presence. Ancient defensive systems activating to prevent unauthorized access."

"I would've expected a more active defense system if they were already fighting a battle," Sean replied. "The damaged sections could've been home to weapons systems and might've been among the first targets, unless things were really chaotic and they were targeting living spaces."

His statement drew a few haunted looks from the crew. They were excellent at their jobs, but most of them hadn't fought in a war, and certainly not in an ongoing war where things kept escalating.

Sutton gave him a grim nod in understanding.

Thyven consulted a holographic display that materialized at his gesture, showing correlations between the current activity and historical Aczar records. "General Quinn, this pattern matches descriptions from our oldest archives. The Phantoms used similar techniques during what our ancestors called the Great Silence—a period when all communication with Phantom civilizations ceased abruptly."

Sean frowned. "You have records of being in contact with the Phantoms from before your species went to Ichlos?"

Thyven considered Sean's words, likely making sure he understood the translation. "It's more of a lore that was taught to us. We settled Ichlos and took steps to hide our presence on the planet. It is believed that our ancestors were refugees from a greater conflict. However, the source of this information is Salpheth, and we have difficulty discerning truth from fabrication from him."

The Aczar ambassador looked away, eyes downcast as if he were ashamed by the admission.

"It's okay," Sean said to him. "Thank you for trying to help."

Thyven looked up at him and gave him a single nod.

Oriana manipulated her science station displays, projecting detailed analysis above the main tactical plot. "I've found references in the Phantom data archives that mention something called Ascensionist Majority. It's more of a headline of sorts, but whatever they were, they achieved enough votes to end some kind of conflict."

Sean moved to the main holoscreen, studying the ancient data that painted a picture of civilization-ending internal strife. "What kind of conflict?"

"The records are fragmentary, but they reference debates about transcendence protocols and dimensional migration," Oriana replied. "It appears the Phantom civilization was divided about certain key issues, including whether to remain in this dimension or ascend to a higher plane of existence."

The implications hit Sean with the force of revelation. The shattered ring, the weapons damage, the abrupt cessation of Phantom activities—they weren't investigating the remains of external conquest but the aftermath of a species-wide decision that had torn their civilization apart.

"The civil war over ascension, but there has to be more to it,"

Sean said, understanding flooding through him while even more questions came to his mind. "Some Phantoms wanted to leave this dimension entirely, while others wanted to remain and continue their own way of exploring the galaxy. The Phantoms Connor met told him that they were a race of explorers, and that they moved through systems like some kind of galactic nomads."

"And the Ascensionists won," Sutton added grimly, "which means the Phantoms like Salpheth are the remnants of the faction that lost."

Before Sean could respond further, Captain Lennox's voice cut through the bridge's focused atmosphere with urgent intensity. "General, I'm detecting transition signatures. Multiple vessels just emerged from hyperspace inside the system."

The main holoscreen shifted to tactical display, showing three contacts that had appeared at coordinates that suggested careful positioning rather than random arrival. The vessels were large— easily matching the *Odyssey*'s mass—and their energy signatures didn't match any design they'd encountered before.

"Classification?" Sean asked, moving to his command chair as the bridge crew shifted into combat-readiness protocols.

"Unknown, sir," Captain Norquist reported from tactical, her professional composure making what Sean knew was rapid threat assessment. "Configuration suggests purpose-built warships, but the design principals don't match anything in our databases."

Sean once again felt the weight of command pressing down on him. They were investigating the remnants of a galactic civil war while unknown forces approached their position, and the interference from the ring fragments was limiting their sensor capabilities and communications.

"Set Condition One," Sean ordered, and the bridge lighting shifted to combat configuration. "All hands to battle stations. Comms, signal the *Horizon* to assume defensive formation. And get me a communications link to the *Ascendant*. They need to know we're no longer alone out here." He waited a moment and then said. "Helm, move us away from the ring section."

"Yes, sir, moving away from the ring section," Roberts replied.

As the *Odyssey* and her escorts prepared for potential conflict, Sean couldn't shake the feeling that their discovery of the Phantom civil war had attracted someone's attention. Then he remembered the hidden Vemus signal within the broadcasts that had come from the Phantom Nexus.

"Tactical, I want firing solutions on those ships ready, but don't bring up our weapons systems yet unless they do," Sean said.

"Yes, General," Norquist replied.

Colonel Sutton looked at him. "Are they here because we were poking around, or are they also responding to the signal being broadcast here?"

Sean nodded grimly. "That's the real question, isn't it?"

CHAPTER 22

THE THREE UNKNOWN vessels maintained their positions at the edge of sensor range, their massive hulls reflecting the white dwarf's harsh light in patterns that suggested armor designed for combat rather than exploration. Sean observed how the ships had positioned themselves with mathematical precision that spoke to coordinated military planning.

"Comms, any response to our hails?" Sean asked, though the silence from his comms officer's station already provided the answer.

Specialist Danny Ramirez shook his head as he cycled through multiple communications protocols. "Negative, General. No acknowledgement of standard greeting transmissions, emergency frequencies, or diplomatic channels. Our signals are reaching them, but they are either unable to respond or are choosing not to."

Sean's jaw tightened slightly. "Try transmitting one of the recorded broadcasts from the Phantom Nexus. If they're here for the same reason we are, they might recognize the signal."

"Transmitting Phantom broadcast protocols now, sir," Ramirez replied, his fingers dancing across communications interfaces as he sent the ancient signal patterns toward the mysterious vessels.

The response was immediate and ominous. Instead of acknowledgment or communication, the three ships broke formation with fluid precision, splitting along different trajectories that took them above and below the Confederation task force's location. They maintained their distance but began moving with the kind of coordinated precision that suggested tactical maneuvering.

"They're positioning for envelopment," Colonel Sutton observed. "Classic formation for containing enemy forces while maintaining firing solutions."

"Tactical, are their weapons systems active?" Sean asked.

"Negative, sir," Captain Jane Norquist replied. "Their positioning suggests they're preparing to establish overlapping fields of fire. Request permission to bring weapons systems online."

Sean considered it, his expression hardening. Their weapons systems weren't active, but they were moving to tactical positions. It was an escalation that he couldn't ignore. "Granted. Target all three vessels and prepare firing solutions. Comms, transmit on all frequencies: Unknown vessels, any aggressive action against Confederation ships will be met with defensive force."

The bridge lighting shifted to combat configuration as the *Odyssey*'s weapons systems came online, their targeting arrays locking onto the alien ships with mechanical precision. On the tactical display, similar readiness indicators showed the *Horizon* moving into defensive formation.

Before the aliens could respond to the warning, space around them suddenly blazed with new transition signatures. Sean counted at least six additional vessels emerging from hyperspace, including one that dwarfed everything else in the system—a behemoth easily three times the *Odyssey*'s length, with a configuration that spoke to purposes Sean couldn't immediately comprehend.

"My God," Oriana whispered from the science station, her voice carrying awe and concern in equal measure.

The mammoth vessel's response was swift and incomprehensible. A brilliant energy beam erupted from its forward section, but instead of targeting the Confederation ships, it struck one of the newly arrived vessels. The target absorbed the energy for several long moments before redistributing it through smaller beams that created a network of energy connections throughout the area.

"What are they doing?" Sean asked, though he suspected the answer would be something they wouldn't like.

His suspicion was confirmed within seconds, and it felt as ominous as a door suddenly slamming shut.

"General," Captain Jake Lennox called from operations, alarm evident in his voice, "I'm detecting massive gravitational distortion throughout this region of space. The field strength is increasing exponentially."

Sean activated his command interface, bringing up environmental displays that showed readings that should've been impossible. "Source?"

"The energy network created by the alien vessels, sir. They're generating an artificial gravitational field that's anchoring everything in this region."

Floyd Roberts looked up from the helm. "Sir, maneuvering engines are non-responsive. The ship isn't moving despite full thrust application."

"The *Horizon* reports similar propulsion issues," Specialist Ramirez announced, his communication with their escort vessel confirming their worst fears.

Oriana expanded the holoscreen at the science station, manipulating the data to show the scope of their predicament. "Sean, they've trapped us in a massive artificial gravitational field. The field strength exceeds that of a main sequence star, but it's precisely controlled to prevent tidal destruction while maintaining absolute positional lock. That largest ship is the source of the field. It arrived with an energy field already active, meaning that it was ready to fire."

Sean nodded in understanding. "Meaning that this is something they've done before. But with that much power, why create an artificial gravity field at all?"

Oriana frowned, and Sean recognized when she had an idea. She gave him a knowing look. "There must be a limitation in creating and sustaining all that energy. If they released it as a weaponized force, there is likely a limitation on how many times they could do it."

"Single shot, so if they miss, they'll be destroyed."

"Yes, but they could also be confirming whether or not we're a target."

There were too many unknowns that Sean didn't like. They'd walked into something far more sophisticated than a simple ambush. "Helm, emergency I-Drive activation. Get us out of here."

Roberts reply was delayed for a few moments. "Uh, sir, I-Drive systems are unable to lock onto target coordinates. The gravitational distortion is preventing proper space-time manipulation."

Sean's gaze narrowed. "Why can't the nav computer just adjust for the new gravitational field?"

Roberts frowned, uncertain. "I, I don't know, sir."

"General," Norquist said, "the gravitational field isn't constant. It's changing and the nav computer is having trouble predicting how the field will react."

"That's correct, sir," Lennox said. "This wouldn't be an issue if we were already in hyperspace, but since we're also transitioning from n-space, the interference is enough to confuse our nav system."

"How long will it take for the ship's computing core to figure this out?"

"Probability matrices are currently running, sir, but it's outside safety protocols," Lennox replied.

Sean stood and moved to the tactical station, studying weapons options that might break them free from the alien trap. "Captain Norquist, deploy combat drones against the nearest vessels. We need to disrupt their coordination."

He hoped there was a gap in the field that they could exploit.

The drones launched with their characteristic acceleration signatures, but their progress slowed dramatically as they closed in on the alien ships under the gravitational field's influence. They'd made it farther from their own ship than Sean anticipated.

"Give me a firing solution with HADES VII missiles," Sean ordered, escalating to weapons that might have the power to break their captivity. "Our attack drones found some soft spots in the field. Have them track a course through the field to reach the alien ships."

"Sir," Norquist said, "high-yield warheads in this gravitational environment could damage our own ships. We're essentially immobilized, and the blast effects would—"

"Understood," Sean interrupted, recognizing the tactical reality. "Alternative options?"

Colonel Sutton moved to stand beside the tactical workstation. "We could generate our own artificial gravitational fields using the I-Drive systems. Create enough spatial distortion to break their hold or trap them with us, forcing them to deactivate the field to avoid mutual destruction."

Oriana looked at Sean. "That could work, but the energy interactions between competing gravitational fields are unpredictable. We could end up with tidal effects that tear all the ships apart, or we could inadvertently create a localized singularity."

Sean weighed the options, feeling the onus of command decisions that could save or doom everyone under his authority. The alien vessels showed no signs of immediate hostility beyond their containment field, but more ships could arrive at any moment, overwhelming their defensive capabilities.

"Alternative approach," Sean said. "We leverage the I-Drive to create localized space-time distortion, just enough to break their gravitational lock without risking catastrophic field interactions."

"That might work," Oriana said, her expression slipping into calculation as she processed the technical requirements. "But I recommend we study their gravitational field first. Understand the energy output, the field harmonics, the maintenance requirements. They can't fire on us while maintaining this level of gravitational control, just as we can't fire on them without risking self-destruction."

Sean considered the tactical stalemate they found themselves in. Both sides were effectively neutralized by the aliens' own containment system, creating a standoff that favored whoever could maintain their position longest.

Sean's mind raced as he forced his mind to take a step back and consider alternative strategies. "Major Gates and the *Ascendant* are still out there," Sean said, thinking through the broader tactical situation. "He'll investigate the loss of communication with the *Odyssey*. Once he determines the cause of our immobilization, he'll have options we don't—attacking from outside the gravitational field."

Colonel Sutton nodded approvingly. "The *Ascendant* could target the field generators for the ships maintaining the network. One well-placed strike might collapse the entire system."

Sean blew out a breath. "We wait and study them." He went to his command chair. "Captain Norquist, continue working on solutions based on gravitational field disruption and controlled I-Drive spatial distortion. All calculations must be perfect. We won't get a second chance if we get it wrong."

They might need those solutions if the *Ascendant* was discovered and disabled before they could help the rest of them.

As the bridge crew settled into the tense routine of strategic practices, Sean kept thinking about the actions the aliens had taken. They must've detected their presence and then entered the star system ready to neutralize them. The fact that they didn't just fire their weapons on the *Odyssey* or the *Horizon* meant that perhaps the aliens didn't understand who they were. Why hadn't they responded to attempted communications?

Oriana came over to him. "I've run some analyses of their arrival. They can travel in hyperspace but not like we do."

Sean looked at the data on her personal holoscreen. "That doesn't make sense. Are you sure that's right?"

His wife arched an eyebrow toward him.

"Fine," Sean said. "That's slower than our first-generation I-Drives. It would've taken them months to arrive here."

Oriana nodded. "Exactly. They likely detected the signal early on, deciphered it, and came to investigate."

"Then why wouldn't they respond to us?"

She shook her head. "I don't know."

Sean looked away and shook his head.

"What is it?" she asked.

"Maybe we're both here for the same reasons."

"The Phantoms?"

"No, the Vemus. The hidden signal."

Her mouth hung open a little and she blew out a short breath. "Oh. That explains a few things."

Sean nodded. "Security protocols. It makes sense if they thought they were going to encounter a Vemus alpha."

"So, they might not be enemies."

"We just need to convince them of that, if our assumptions are correct."

"I think they are," Oriana said. "Mind if I work with Jane for a few minutes?"

"Go ahead," Sean replied, knowing that between his wife's brilliance and his tactical officer's experience, they would be able to prove whether his idea about these mysterious aliens was correct.

CHAPTER 23

Ethan felt Atlas pulse with sudden intensity around his forearm, the SRA's consciousness touching his awareness with an urgency that immediately commanded attention. Around the laboratory, he noticed similar reactions from Lieutenant Spencer and Sergeant Staggart as their own SRAs responded to some detection that human senses couldn't perceive.

She has an SRA, Atlas observed through their neural link, his artificial consciousness carrying undertones of surprise and wariness. *The signature has the same foundational principles as my own matrices but also seems more sophisticated. The biological integration patterns are fundamentally different.*

Seraphine's piercing stare focused more intently on Ethan as she observed his SRA's reaction. Ethan didn't see an SRA on her, but it could be hidden within her, which presented a whole host of implications that he didn't have time to consider.

"Your artificial companion recognizes mine. How interesting. I haven't encountered others with such technology."

Ethan stepped closer to the crystalline cradle, studying the humanoid figure with renewed attention. "You have an SRA? How is that possible?"

"Possible?" Seraphine looked amused. "The technology you carry is derived from our own biological integration methods. What you call Saruvian Robotic Assistants are crude approximations of systems we perfected millennia ago."

Ethan shook his head. "I don't think so. None of the Vemus we've encountered have used this technology. Only the Phantoms, and you're not one."

She blinked a few times, her thoughts conflicting with one another. "I have embedded knowledge that tells me this."

Captain Washburn moved to stand beside Ethan. "Major, if she's been expecting us, someone's been feeding her information about our capabilities."

"Indeed," Seraphine said, her voice carrying the patient tone of someone explaining obvious facts. "I was instructed that beings like you would eventually come seeking me." She paused, considering. "Humans with enhanced physiology and artificial companions. It is the presence of one of our offshoots in you that is puzzling to me. Regardless, the parameters of this test were established long before your arrival."

Ethan's gaze narrowed. *Offshoots.* She meant Vemus-Human hybrids like himself. It made sense. Salpheth had no knowledge of hybrids, and Ethan doubted that anyone on the *Pathfinder* had volunteered that kind of information during their interactions.

Hash approached from his monitoring station. "Major, the biological modifications occurring in her body are accelerating. Whatever process she's undergoing, it's reaching some kind of culmination point."

Ethan looked at his friend. "Where is her SRA?"

Hash brought up his personal holoscreen. "I'm seeing similar SRA energy signatures coming from her spine and brain stem. This is true integration between the two. It must've been required to accelerate the mutation during the evolutionary trials."

Atlas concurred with Hash's findings and Ethan looked at Seraphine. "You mentioned a Super Alpha. Where is it located?"

Her eyes seemed to grow brighter as she considered the question. "Such information could be shared, but it would require a more intimate connection than verbal communication allows." She reached a hand toward him. "Physical contact would permit direct knowledge transfer."

"Not happening," Ethan replied immediately, his experience with Vemus Alphas making him acutely aware of the dangers inherent in direct neural contact. "I've encountered your kind before. Physical contact is how you convert other species to serve your collective will."

Her face fell. "Your caution prevents you from gaining the knowledge you seek. But perhaps there are other forms of exchange that might prove mutually beneficial."

Before Ethan could respond, Christoph Rahner's voice crackled through the comlink with urgent intensity. "Major, we're detecting multiple contacts approaching the facility. Unknown vessel classifications, but they're moving with purpose rather than random exploration."

Ethan activated his personal holoscreen, bringing up tactical displays that showed several contacts approaching from different vectors. The combat shuttle's scanners were limited, and the vessels didn't match any known design principles.

"Additionally, sir," Rahner continued, "we're losing contact with our perimeter scout drones. Not from the direction of the approaching ships, but from sectors we thought were clear."

Ethan's mind raced with the tactical implications. "Something else is out there. Something that's systematically eliminating our surveillance network."

Washburn turned toward Ethan. "Major, those could be the

'hunters' that Seraphine mentioned. If she's been tested before, whatever's taking out our drones might be the entities conducting those tests."

Seraphine listened intently to their tactical discussions. "The parameters continue to evolve. This iteration presents variables I was not prepared to encounter."

"What kind of variables?" Ethan asked, though part of him dreaded the answer.

"Multiple species converging simultaneously. Enhanced humans, unknown alien entities, and the systemic elimination of your monitoring systems, leaving you blind." She paused, and her gaze focused directly on Ethan. "Someone is orchestrating events to create optimal testing conditions."

Ethan realized they were facing something far more complex than a simple research facility investigation. "We need to evacuate this installation immediately."

"I cannot leave," Seraphine said, her voice carrying absolute certainty. "The testing must continue until completion. Departure would invalidate all previous iterations."

"Then you'll die here when those hunters arrive," Ethan replied bluntly.

"Death is merely another form of iteration," Seraphine responded with the calm acceptance of someone whose existence operated according to the principles that transcended individual survival. "But perhaps... there are alternative arrangements that might serve both our purposes."

Ethan studied the humanoid figure, weighing the intelligence value she represented against the dangers of maintaining contact with a Vemus construction. "What do you mean?"

"I am more than a simple test subject," Seraphine said, her voice carrying undertones that suggested depths of knowledge that could reshape their understanding of the Vemus. "I carry within my genetic matrix the combined biological heritage of multiple civilizations that have encountered the Vemus collective. I am a living archive of species that no longer exist in their original forms."

The revelation hit Ethan with the force of understanding, but then he seized that thought cycle, stopping it. Was she telling him something he wanted to hear? Could she be trying to get him to lower his guard? His gaze narrowed as he stared at her. What if he wasn't just looking at an experimental Vemus construct? What if he really was facing a repository of genetic and cultural information from civilizations that had been conquered and absorbed by the Vemus?

"You're a treasure trove of intelligence about Vemus operations and the species they've conquered," Ethan said, the implications reshaping his tactical priorities, but only if she was telling the truth.

"Precisely. My existence serves purposes that extend far beyond individual testing scenarios." Seraphine looked pleased at his understanding. "The knowledge I contain could prove invaluable to species seeking to understand us better."

"And you expect me to just take your word for it?"

"The decision is yours. I was created for a purpose."

"And what is that, exactly?"

She stared at him and there was something both powerful and delicate at the same time in her expression. "To reach perfection."

The others around him became still.

"What happens then?" Ethan asked.

She didn't reply, and Ethan wondered if she even knew. Seraphine had an objective that she marched toward with dogged determination, but her understanding of her actions appeared stunted.

"You don't know, do you?" Ethan said.

She regarded him, her expression hauntingly neutral, making her seem utterly alien. "All will be revealed."

Hash cleared his throat. "Sir," he said quietly, "the biological modifications in her system are reaching critical parameters. If we're going to extract her from the containment system, we need to act soon."

Ethan considered it, recognizing the trap of a decision that looked simple but wasn't. Seraphine represented both an unprecedented intelligence asset and a potentially catastrophic security risk.

"Captain Washburn," he said, "prepare for emergency evac. We're taking her with us."

"Sir?" Washburn's expression showed the concern of someone questioning orders that seemed to contradict every safety protocol they'd established.

"She's right about being a living archive. The genetic information from conquered civilizations, the knowledge of Vemus operational methods, the intelligence about their expansion patterns—all of that could be crucial for the Confederation's survival."

Lieutenant Spencer approached from his position near the facility's monitoring systems, his SRA pulsing with increased activity. "Major, I'm detecting systematic infiltration of the facility's computer networks. Someone or something is accessing the research data."

Before anyone could respond to Spencer's warning, the laboratory's lighting shifted to an ominous red configuration, and synthetic voices began echoing through the installation's communications systems.

"Attention test subjects. Phase Two parameters are now in effect. Defensive protocols have been activated. Facility lockdown is in progress."

Ethan felt Atlas pulse with alarm as blast doors began sealing throughout the installation, cutting off their planned evacuation routes.

"The hunters are coming," Seraphine said, her voice carrying anticipation that made Ethan's instincts scream warnings. "And now you'll discover whether your species possesses the adaptability necessary for survival."

As the facility's security systems activated around them, Ethan realized they were no longer investigating a research installation; they were trapped in an arena designed to test humanity's capabilities against threats that had been specifically engineered to exploit their weaknesses.

The real test was about to begin, and failure might mean more than just death. It could mean the conversion of his entire team into extensions of the Vemus collective will.

CHAPTER 24

MAJOR WILL QUALMANN stood before the main tactical display on the *Ascendant's* bridge, his lean frame tense with the controlled alertness that came from managing multiple threats simultaneously.

"Status report on the away team," Qualmann said, his resonant voice carrying the authority of someone accustomed to making critical decisions in the absence of his commanding officer.

Lieutenant Samantha Trickle looked up from communications, her auburn hair catching the bridge lighting as she monitored multiple channels. "Last contact was forty-seven minutes ago, sir. They reported facility lockdown procedures had activated. No response to our subsequent hails."

Captain Akira Endo tracked the alien vessels movements. "Sir, preliminary analysis suggests scout-class vessels, each approximately thirty percent of the *Ascendant's* mass. Their positioning indicates coordinated reconnaissance rather than random exploration."

Qualmann moved to the tactical station, studying the alien ships' formation. "Assessment of their capabilities?"

"Unknown, but they're maintaining distance from the research facility while conducting what appears to be systematic scanning operations," Endo replied. "One vessel has approached the far side of the installation and appears unaware of our position. The other two are conducting broader patrol patterns."

"They haven't detected us?" Qualmann asked.

"Negative, sir. We're positioned in the sensor shadow of a large ring fragment, and our passive scanning protocols are preventing active detection. They likely assume we're debris from the structure."

Cynergy Gates looked up from the auxiliary science station where she'd been analyzing the alien vessels' design characteristics. The importance of that wasn't lost on her as she'd been monitoring the away team's interaction with the Vemus Avatar.

"Major Qualmann," Cynergy said, "I'm running comparative analysis on these ship configurations. Something about their design seems familiar."

"Elaborate," Qualmann replied, moving to stand beside her workstation.

Cynergy manipulated her displays, projecting detailed scans of alien vessels above the tactical plot. "The hull configurations, the angular design elements, the energy distribution patterns—they're similar to something we've encountered before."

Lieutenant Anson Gooding turned toward them from operations. "Similar to what, exactly? The computer didn't flag anything during our initial scans."

"The battlefield where we found the dying Vemus Alpha," Cynergy said. They shared a knowing look as each remembered the encounter clearly, though it was over two years ago. She was used to being completely human, but there were times when she missed being a hybrid. "Remember the fleet of derelict ships we investigated? Over twelve hundred vessels that had fought against the Alpha?"

Qualmann felt a chill as the implications became clear. "You're suggesting these are the same species?"

"The ships' foundational design principles match," Cynergy replied, highlighting specific structural elements on her displays. "But there are differences—darker metallic composition, subtle variations in hull architecture, modified weapons emplacements. Enough to confuse initial analysis, but the core design is consistent."

Zane Rennick leaned forward from his workstation next to hers. "The computer correlation analysis shows approximately seventy percent probability match between these vessels and the derelict fleet we encountered two years ago."

Qualmann stared at the tactical displays, weighing the evidence against the practical impossibilities it suggested. "Those ships were thousands of light-years away. Our analysis of their propulsion systems indicated FTL capability, but nothing approaching our Infinity Drive range."

Cynergy drummed her fingers on the console, then said. "Maybe they're nomadic. No fixed homeworld, constantly moving through space seeking out Vemus threats to engage. It would explain their advanced ship design and tactical coordination. They've been fighting this war for generations."

"That's one heck of a leap," Rennick said.

"I don't think it is," Cynergy replied. "Think about it. We survived the Vemus, and now that we have the technology to explore farther than we had before, we discovered that the Vemus weren't just some anomaly that impacted Old Earth. Maybe the aliens in those ships had a similar experience and have dedicated themselves to hunting the Vemus."

"Which means," Endo said from the tactical workstation, "they might be here for the same reason that attracted our attention."

Qualmann felt the muscles in his back tense. "The Phantom communications signal with embedded Vemus signatures. If these aliens hunt Vemus, that signal would have drawn them here just as it drew us. Expertly done, Cynergy."

She stood and moved to the main tactical display. "Major, if I'm right about these being the same species, Ethan and the away team aren't just dealing with one threat. They're trapped in a facility with a Vemus construct while alien hunters approach from outside. Multiple hostile forces converging on the same location. There are hybrids on the away team. The new arrivals could decide to attack them based on that detection alone."

Qualmann clenched his jaw. The loss of communication with both the away team and the *Odyssey* suggested they were facing coordinated opposition.

"Captain Endo," Qualmann said, "maintain passive scanning protocols but prepare for combat operations. If these aliens are the same species that fought the Vemus Alpha, they possess capabilities that could threaten our people."

"Understood, sir," Endo replied, his tactical training evident in the smooth transition to combat readiness. "Weapons systems standing by."

"Lieutenant Trickle," Qualmann said, "continue attempts to contact the away team. They need to know what's approaching their position."

"Still no response, sir. The facility's lockdown procedures may be interfering with communications signals."

Qualmann moved back to the command chair, feeling the bridge's attention focus on him as the crew awaited orders that could determine the mission's outcome. The evidence suggested they were facing opponents who'd been fighting the Vemus for potentially centuries, with technology and tactics refined through countless encounters. That was the potential of that alien species, but it hadn't been proven yet. Cynergy was right; they might consider the away team as hostile.

"We need to warn our people," Qualmann said. "Ops, prepare a scout drone for deployment."

"Yes, sir," Lieutenant Gooding replied.

Cynergy returned to her station, bringing up additional analysis of the alien vessels' capabilities. "The energy signatures suggest these ships are designed for extended operations but are likely part of a larger group."

"Understood," Qualmann said.

"Sir," Trickle said, "I'm detecting communication attempts from the alien vessels. They're broadcasting on frequencies that match some of the patterns we recorded from the Phantom network."

Qualmann narrowed his gaze. The revelation added another layer of complexity to an already dangerous situation. The aliens weren't just responding to the same signal that had attracted the Confederation task force, they were actively communicating using protocols derived from the same ancient Phantom networks.

"Sir," Captain Endo said from tactical, "they could be trying to remote-access the facility's systems, which won't work anymore because of the lockdown."

Qualmann nodded.

"Major Qualmann," Cynergy said, "we have to warn them. This intelligence changes everything about the threats the team is confronting."

As the *Ascendant* maintained its hidden position near the facility, Qualmann couldn't shake the feeling that they were witnessing the convergence of forces. They thought that Salpheth had lured them here, but what if he was also searching for others who knew about the Vemus and would also come to investigate?

"Comms," Qualmann said, "upload a data package to the scout drone. Make sure it contains the recent intelligence about the new aliens and their suspected origins."

"Yes, sir," Trickle said.

"Tactical, send that drone right to the shuttles. If the comms fails, have the drone penetrate as far into the facility as it can until contact is made with the away team," Qualmann said.

"Yes, sir," Endo replied. "Deploying drone."

CHAPTER 25

ETHAN WATCHED as the crystalline cradle's energy fields began to dissipate, its bio-sustaining systems powering down with mechanical precision. Seraphine's tall form gracefully extracted itself from the containment apparatus. As she moved, Ethan noticed her pupils dilate slightly when her gaze swept across the soldiers' weapons—a predatory response that sent warning signals through his enhanced senses.

"Communications with the *Ascendant* are down," Lieutenant Spencer reported, "but we're still receiving telemetry from the combat shuttles. There must be some kind of localized interference envelope around the facility." He frowned as he received a new alert. "Sir, our combat suit power consumption is running twenty percent higher than normal. Something in this facility could be draining our systems."

Atlas surged to life around Ethan's forearm, analyzing Seraphine's physical structure through enhanced sensors. *Her skeletal composition contains materials similar to my own matrices,* Atlas observed through their neural link. *But there's something else—fragmentary data signatures in the facility's deeper systems that I cannot fully access. I'll keep working on it.*

Ethan watched Seraphine as she tested her balance and range of motion, noting the unconscious grace with which she moved despite having been confined in the cradle for an unknown period. "How many hunters are we facing?"

Seraphine focused on him with unsettling intensity. "The numbers vary according to test parameters. Each iteration increases in complexity, and difficulty."

"You don't know?" he asked, suspecting that she was evading the question.

"I am a divergent sample derived from a Vemus Alpha genetic template," she replied with clinical precision. "The hunters represent another evolutionary branch—more savage, with capabilities specifically designed to counter my own adaptations. They are likely reptilian in nature and possess advanced concealment abilities."

Captain Washburn approached his position near the laboratory's sealed exits. His rifle was at the ready position, studying Seraphine with professional wariness. "Major, staying in this laboratory is suicide. We need to move toward extraction, but the facility's lockdown has disabled the transit systems."

Ethan activated his tactical display, studying the route back to their combat shuttles. "The transit pad is offline?"

"Completely dead," Sergeant Staggart confirmed, his SRA pulsing as it interfaced with the facility's systems. "Someone or something has severed the power connections."

Hash cleared his throat. "Sir, the central laboratory is positioned as a kill-box—multiple access points but limited cover. If we stay here, we'll be surrounded."

Washburn shook his head at him. "Do you really think the Major is unaware of this?"

Hash blinked for a second, and then nodded once, muttering an apology.

"Focus on finding us a working transit pad or another way out of here," Ethan said.

Corporal Richardson stepped forward, his expression tight. "Major, with respect, bringing her along violates every safety protocol we have. She's a Vemus construct."

Sergeant Staggart swung his gaze toward him. "Lock that up, Corporal."

Ethan knew the others were likely thinking the same thing. "The intelligence she represents could save lives. The decision is made."

Staggart gestured ahead of them. "Take point, Corporal."

Richardson didn't reply as he moved into position.

Corporal Sykes held a scanner and had it aimed across the vast distance across the chamber. She shook her head. "Our combat suit jets don't have sufficient fuel for the distance, sir. We'd need external assistance to cross the open areas."

Ethan turned to Seraphine, who had been observing their tactical discussions with evident interest. "What would you do in this situation? Assuming we'd never woken you up."

She regarded him for a quick moment. "Evaluate the hunters' capabilities through direct engagement, then eliminate them as efficiently as possible," she replied without hesitation. "Movement provides tactical advantage. Remaining stationary ensures defeat."

"Moving blindly increases risk of discovery. I'm trying to avoid the hunters and extract my people safely," Ethan said, studying her reaction.

Seraphine's tight expression and slight narrowing of the eyes indicated disapproval. "The facility will not permit such tactics. It will actively work to force confrontation between opposing forces. Avoidance is not among the acceptable parameters."

Ethan gave a slight nod to himself as the implications became clear. He glanced at Washburn and saw the same understanding on his face. They weren't just trapped in a research facility; they were in an arena specifically designed to ensure combat between different test subjects.

Ethan looked at her. "So, the facility will work against us if we don't go along with its test parameters."

While he spoke, he sent an alert to Hash. If the facility's computer systems were running some kind of governance of this area, perhaps there was a way to stop it before it really had a chance to begin.

He received an acknowledgement from Hash.

"Precisely," Seraphine said, seemingly unaware of what he was doing. "The trial requires interaction between variables. Separation invalidates the testing protocols. Perfection can only be achieved through conflict."

Washburn consulted his tactical map, highlighting potential routes that skirted the edges of the central complex. "Sir, we should move around the perimeter, avoid the main corridors, and head for the shuttles through whatever path the facility leaves open."

"Agreed," Ethan said. "Standard formation, with technical specialist protected in the center. Hash, monitor the facility's systems for changes in security protocols and let me know if you find anything else."

He turned toward Seraphine, who was scanning the area. "We have more to discuss. I would like you to come with me."

She regarded him and then looked at the soldiers around them. "Willingly or otherwise?"

He stared at her, his gaze unyielding. "If it comes down to it."

The edges of her lips lifted, which he wasn't expecting. "I will travel with you."

Ethan pointed his weapon at her. "Just so we're clear—the moment you do anything I find suspicious, we'll take you out. I don't care what knowledge you have. We can learn plenty about you from your corpse if it comes to that. Are we clear?"

If his threat bothered her, she didn't show it in the slightest.

"The trial wants us to travel together, otherwise the facility would separate us. Even now we are being watched."

Ethan told her to stay near him, and he assigned two soldiers to take up positions behind them.

As they moved through the laboratory's secondary exits, Ethan noticed how the facility seemed to respond to their presence. Corridors that had been accessible minutes earlier were now sealed by blast doors, forcing them to take longer routes that led deeper into the installation rather than toward their extraction point.

"The facility's learning our movement patterns," Hash reported. "It's adapting in real-time to our tactical decisions. I think there are monitoring devices everywhere, even though I can't actually see them."

Ethan didn't doubt it. As they moved through the facility's corridors, the environmental controls began working against them. Blast doors sealed their preferred routes while the lighting flickered in patterns that seemed almost like morse code. Strange metallic scratching echoed from within the walls, stopping abruptly when anyone tried to locate the source.

Seraphine's fingers flexed unconsciously, and Ethan observed the subtle way her joints moved too fluidly, suggesting hidden articulation points. "The facility will continue to adapt based on what it observes about your capabilities. Each tactical choice provides data for its decision matrix."

The ventilation system suddenly became quiet, and Seraphine tilted her head, listening. Then the ventilation system resumed with altered air pressure.

Sergeant Gustor held up his hand, signaling for silence as his augmented hearing detected sounds from the ventilation system above them. "Movement in the main air ducts. The scout drones show they're large enough to use as travel corridors."

"Sir," Hash said. "I've found the remains of one of our drones in corridors a hundred meters ahead of us, but nothing else seems to be there."

"Camouflaged hunters," Seraphine said quietly. "They possess advanced heat suppression and optical concealment capabilities. Your standard sensors may not detect them until they're within attack range."

Ethan knew that Seraphine had no idea what their capabilities were and the fact that the CDF had fought creatures capable of concealing themselves from standard sensor equipment. His hybrid nature surged as enhanced senses detected subtle variations in air pressure and electromagnetic fields that indicated concealed presences above them. His connection to Atlas flatlined as his SRA retreated into some kind of isolation mode when Ethan embraced his hybrid nature.

Seraphine watched him intently, noting the change in him instantly.

She froze mid-step just before Ethan said, "Contact!" He was directing hybrids Christoph Rahner and Lydia Torres toward specific ceiling locations where his enhanced perception indicated hidden threats. "Hunter scouts approximately fifteen meters ahead."

The hybrid specialists moved with fluid coordination, their enhanced reflexes allowing them to deploy seeker grenades. The smart munitions traveled through the ventilation system toward their targets, guided by sensor packages that could track subtle movement patterns.

The explosions echoed through the facility's corridors as the hunter scouts fled deeper into the ventilation network but not before Ethan's enhanced perception caught glimpses of reptilian forms that moved with predatory efficiency. Some of the scouts had survived the explosion.

"Increase weapons yield," Ethan ordered.

He released his hybrid nature and used his neural implants to update the weapon's configuration. Atlas returned to normal status, and Ethan noted frustration coming from his SRA.

Seraphine observed the engagement with obvious fascination. "Your coordination with the other enhanced humans is remarkable. You function as an Alpha but not like the ones I have encountered previously. More integrated with your original species characteristics."

He couldn't decide whether she approved or was just stating observations.

Before Ethan could respond to her, Spencer's voice crackled through the communications link. "Major, incoming message from the *Ascendant*. It's a recorded data package that managed to penetrate the facility's interference. It came via a ship's scout drone, sir."

Ethan activated his personal holoscreen, reviewing Qualmann's intelligence analysis about the alien vessels that had approached the research installation. The correlation with the derelict fleet they'd encountered two years ago sent a chill through his chest. They'd analyzed those ships and their drive systems. They weren't capable of making the journey thousands of light-years away.

"The aliens approaching the facility are likely the same species whose ships we found at the Vemus Alpha battlefield," Ethan told his team. "If the analysis is correct, they're experienced Vemus hunters."

Washburn stared at him momentarily and then glanced at Seraphine. "Which means they might consider us either allies or competitors, depending on how they interpret our presence here."

Ethan tried to recall his memories from the alien scout ship that had led them to the dying Vemus Alpha two years ago. He recalled the strangeness of the ship's layout because it had likely been designed for a species that had more than two legs.

Hash turned back toward him, eyebrows raised in alarm. "Sir, one of our scout drones has detected a large group—uh, platoon-sized, sir—approaching from the direction of the alien vessel's docking port. I'm displaying the drone's video feed now."

The portable holographic display flickered to life, showing a corridor within the research facility. Moving through it with predatory efficiency was a group of dark figures. They were tall, angular forms that seemed to move with a cadence that made them difficult to track. They appeared to carry several weapons that were attached to their legs, but it was difficult to see on the image.

Washburn shook his head, then blew out a breath. "Those look different from the hunter scouts we just engaged. More organized, better equipped."

Ethan felt Atlas pulse with alarm as the SRA processed the visual data, comparing it to known threat profiles.

The convergence of forces was building, but there was still time to avoid them. Avoiding first contact with an alien species—another alien species—was preferable given the danger they were in.

CHAPTER 26

ETHAN FELT the facility's systems working against them as they moved through the corridors, blast doors sealing their preferred routes while others remained conspicuously open. The metallic scratching from within the walls had evolved into a deliberate pattern, with hunters moving through maintenance passages, creating noise designed to push them in a specific direction. The amount of noise suggested far more hunters than his own team.

"They're herding us," Ethan said, pausing at an intersection where two corridors had sealed themselves while a third remained invitingly open. His neural implants automatically shared the strategic assessment with his team, creating a network of shared awareness that kept everyone informed of his analysis.

Seraphine nodded, her luminous eyes tracking movement patterns that his enhanced senses couldn't quite detect. Hers were definitely more acute than his equipment but not by much.

"The facility wants us in the central atrium. They're guiding us toward optimal testing conditions," she said.

Hash looked up from his personal holoscreen, sweat beading on his forehead despite the facility's controlled environment. "Multiple contacts moving through service corridors. It's like they're escorting us."

Washburn turned toward Ethan. "I hate this. We could make a stand here. Change the dynamic. Blow out the wall separating us from the maintenance corridors and force them into a choke point. I'd rather fight here than walk into whatever they've prepared."

The narrow space would funnel the hunters toward them, but it would also eliminate their own mobility advantages. They didn't know how many hunters were there, and trapping themselves here was too hasty when they had better options.

"Negative," Ethan decided. "If we get pinned down here, they'll grind us down. Better to face them in an environment where we have room to maneuver."

The facility's behavioral patterns suggest increasingly complex test parameters, Atlas said. *Each decision you make provides data for optimization of future encounters. However, this must also apply to the hunters as well.*

Ethan shared the SRA's warning with his team through the neural link. The implications were disturbing. They weren't just fighting hunters; they were being studied by systems that would use their combat responses to improve future threats. It meant that he needed to keep certain tactics in reserve; otherwise, the facility would work to counter them just like an enemy force would.

The sounds from the maintenance passages intensified, creating an almost musical rhythm that seemed designed to increase psychological pressure. Alarms began sounding in sequence, drawing their attention to specific corridors while masking the movement of forces they couldn't see.

"Standard formation," Ethan ordered. "Christoph and Lydia, take point with Staggart and Gustor's squads. Hash and Spencer, center protection. Everyone else, watch the flanks and maintain overlapping fields of fire."

Rahner and Torres moved with the fluid coordination of experienced hybrid specialists, their augmented awareness of environmental data heightened. With them, the CDF soldiers maintained the disciplined spacing that had kept them alive through previous encounters with alien threats.

As they advanced toward the central facility, Ethan noticed how Seraphine moved. She stayed near him as he'd told her to, but she positioned herself where she could observe their tactics while remaining protected by their firepower. She seemed to consider their firepower almost as an afterthought, and it was a reminder that her true capabilities remained largely unknown.

The corridor opened into a vast multilevel atrium that made Ethan take notice. Small recon drones flew ahead, quickly scouting the area. The space soared five stories above them, its transparent walls offering views of the research facility's inner workings. Specimen containers lined elevated walkways, their contents hidden behind frosted surfaces that suggested biological research on a massive scale. Multiple levels connected through graceful ramps and dormant transit platforms, creating a three-dimensional maze of potential firing positions and hiding places.

Washburn blew out a breath. "This place is just one kill-box after another," he muttered, recognizing the tactical situation immediately.

Ethan embraced his hybrid nature at a minimal level that allowed Atlas to remain active. His heightened acuity detected subtle variations in air pressure and electromagnetic fields that indicated concealed presences throughout the atrium. While the hunters could conceal themselves from visual detection, Ethan heard a very slow heartbeat among them. Once he recognized it, he was able to focus on it, filtering out everything else. Hunters had positioned themselves behind laboratory equipment, structural supports, and specimen containers, creating overlapping fields of fire that would catch his team in devastating crossfire.

Ethan frowned, considering the hunters' formation. He used his neural implants to coordinate defensive deployment across the atrium's ground level. Instead of moving to the side of the atrium that he knew would bring them closer to where the Combat Shuttles waited, he took them in the opposite direction, choosing to move toward the far side, taking them away. He wasn't just facing Vemus hunters, he was also contending with the testing system Salpheth had engineered into this place. He doubted that a testing facility was the original intent for this place, which meant Salpheth was limited in the use of what the facility could actually do to them.

His team moved with professional precision, taking cover behind research stations and structural elements while maintaining visual contact with each other. Through the neural link, Ethan could sense their readiness and tactical awareness, each soldier processing their section of the battle space while contributing to their collective understanding.

Seraphine stayed near him, her eyes glowing a little as she scanned the elevated walkways with an intensity that suggested recognition. "They're already in position. Three levels of coordinated firing positions, with movement corridors designed to prevent your escape."

Before Ethan could respond, the attack began.

The first wave erupted from the elevated positions with coordinated precision that spoke to extensive planning. Hunters dropped from ceiling access points while others emerged from concealed positions behind specimen containers, their reptilian forms moving with predatory efficiency that challenged conventional targeting solutions.

Ethan's team responded with the disciplined firepower that had carried them through previous encounters, quickly adapting to the hunters' startling speed and coordination that pushed a CDF combat suit's augmented response to their limits and even beyond. Energy weapons fire lanced down from multiple levels while hunters used their superior mobility to constantly shift positions.

"They're countering our formation protocols," Spencer reported, his voice tight with controlled tension as he tracked multiple targets across different elevation levels. He chose a target and fired a burst of high-density alloyed darts at the hunter right as it grasped the wall, using its claws to gouge the metal. The darts cut into the creature's hand, startling it, and it fell to the ground.

Ethan took several well-timed shots of his own, accounting for their surroundings and using them as part of his tactics, but the enemies moved through the area with increased fluidity. It was as if the hunters had double shoulder joints and could move against the natural order, making them difficult to track.

With no other choice, it was time to embrace his hybrid nature.

The transformation was both familiar and disorienting, enhanced reflexes and strength flooding through his system while his perception shifted to accommodate capabilities that went beyond simple combat-suit effectiveness. He felt Atlas's presence withdraw as his SRA retreated into isolation mode, cutting him off from the artificial consciousness that had become an integral part of his strategic thinking.

But the loss of Atlas was compensated by the surge of hybrid awareness that allowed him to quickly process the complex battle space with predatory clarity. He could sense the hunters' movement patterns, anticipate their positioning, and coordinate with Torres and Rahner through subsonic communication that operated below human hearing thresholds.

"Christoph," Ethan projected through hybrid harmonics, "elevated positions, northwest and southeast platforms. Suppress their coordination patterns."

The hybrid specialist responded with fluid precision, his enhanced agility allowing him to reach elevated positions while maintaining weapons accuracy. The CDF soldiers followed his movements, providing covering fire. Ethan followed him upward, using his hybrid strength to leap between levels while engaging hunters in close-quarters combat on the catwalks and mezzanines. During this, he felt Atlas begin to stir as if trying to break through the isolation protocol that prevented their union when Ethan was in hybrid form.

The hunters were formidable opponents—reptilian beings with natural armor and enhanced reflexes that matched his own hybrid capabilities. But Ethan had advantages they hadn't encountered before—tactical training that allowed him to think strategically even while fighting instinctively, as well as the ability to coordinate both the hybrid and human elements of his team simultaneously.

As he engaged a hunter on a narrow catwalk, trading blows that would've shattered purely human bones, Ethan used his neural implants to direct Washburn's positioning of human soldiers below. The integration of hybrid combat and human tactical thinking created a dynamic that the hunters clearly hadn't expected.

Seraphine had somehow climbed to the catwalk with him, and the atrium's lighting system suddenly shifted into a striking pattern that disoriented the hunters while CDF combat suits automatically compensated for the visual interference. Specimen containers began rupturing in coordinated sequence, creating smoke screens and barriers that disrupted hunter movement patterns while providing additional cover for the CDF team.

"Environmental systems are responding to unauthorized access," the facility's synthetic voice announced with mechanical precision. "Lockdown protocols are adapting to current threat parameters."

But instead of working against them, the facility's systems seemed to be favoring the CDF team. Transit platforms activated to provide Ethan's soldiers rapid movement between levels, while emergency barriers deployed to block hunter escape routes.

Seraphine's hands interfaced with control systems that shouldn't have responded to her touch. "The facility recognizes my authority protocols, she called out, her voice carrying over the sounds of combat. "I'm redirecting its optimization parameters."

The third wave of hunter attacks revealed their adaptive capabilities as they countered the environmental changes with specialized equipment that Ethan's team hadn't encountered before—energy-dampening fields that reduced the effectiveness of CDF weapons, mobility enhancers that allowed hunters to navigate the altered environment, and coordination systems that maintained their tactical cohesion despite Seraphine's interference.

But the hunters made one critical miscalculation; they'd underestimated Ethan's ability to function as both tactical commander and front-line combatant.

Using his hybrid agility to move between elevated positions, Ethan coordinated a complex multilevel engagement that stretched the hunters' defensive capabilities. He directed the other hybrids through subsonic communication while using his neural implants to position CDF soldiers, creating a fluid battle dynamic that adapted faster than the hunters' countermeasures.

When a group of hunters attempted to flank their position through a service corridor, Ethan intercepted them personally, engaging in close-quarters combat that showcased the lethal efficiency of hybrid enhancement combined with professional military training. His enhanced strength allowed him to physically overpower opponents while his tactical awareness prevented them from isolating him from his team's support.

The battle reached its climax when Seraphine demonstrated capabilities that exceeded even Ethan's enhanced perception. Moving with a dancer-like grace that belied devastating effectiveness, she engaged hunters with intimate knowledge of their anatomy and weak points. Her strikes were precise and economical, each movement calculated for maximum effect while expending minimal energy. She even accounted for her CDF escorts, who were providing cover. She'd maneuver a hunter, giving the soldiers a target opportunity that was too rich to pass up.

Her interaction with the facility's systems proved most impressive. As the hunters deployed their adaptive equipment, Seraphine countered with facility responses that seemed to anticipate their tactical adjustments. Blast doors sealed hunter escape routes at precisely the right moments, while environmental controls created conditions that favored CDF capabilities over hunter advantages.

"How is she doing that?" Hash asked, his voice tight with awe and concern as he watched Seraphine coordinate facility responses with their tactical needs.

"Try to isolate what she's doing," Ethan said to him. "We're going to need it."

He didn't know how she was doing it, but he was sure it had something to do with her own SRA. The results spoke for themselves. The hunters' coordinated assault was fragmenting under pressure from both his team's adaptive tactics and the facility's newly hostile environment. Their superior numbers and prepared positions were being neutralized by a combination of human innovation, hybrid enhancement, and Vemus technical integration that they clearly hadn't anticipated.

The engagement ended with brutal efficiency. The surviving hunters withdrew through emergency access points, leaving behind evidence of capabilities that had nearly overwhelmed even Ethan's enhanced team. Damaged equipment, energy scorch marks, and the distinctive chemical residue of their concealment systems painted a picture of enemies far more dangerous than their previous encounters with the Vemus had suggested.

As Ethan transitioned back to human form, feeling Atlas's presence return with welcome familiarity, he studied the aftermath of their first major engagement with the mysterious hunters. His team had performed admirably, integrating human tactics with hybrid capabilities and alien assistance in ways that created emergent advantages none of them could have achieved alone.

There were some injuries, but the tactical intelligence they'd gained was sobering. The hunters were experienced, adaptive, and equipped with technology they hadn't anticipated. Ethan suspected they'd withdrawn not because they'd been defeated but because they'd gathered the intelligence they needed for their next assault.

Ethan looked at Washburn. "Casualty report?"

"Minor injuries only, sir," Washburn replied, sounding relieved. "Armor absorbed most of the impact damage. Their energy weapons can pierce our armor, but Gustor found out that their claws can also penetrate."

Ethan had fought multiple hunters but had avoided their clawed attacks. He nodded, then looked at Seraphine, who stood amid the battle's aftermath with an expression that mixed satisfaction with something that might have been surprise.

"Your capabilities exceed your previous demonstrations," he said carefully.

She stared at him intently, her eyebrows raising slightly, as surprised as he was by what she'd accomplished. "The facility's systems responded to integration protocols I wasn't aware I possessed. Knowledge is still unlocking within my own matrix."

Her gaze slid down to his forearm where Atlas was. "Your response to the hunters was measured, and I suspect you've held back some of your capabilities."

Ethan regarded her, neither confirming nor denying it. He felt Atlas's frustration with the isolation protocol build when Ethan embraced his hybrid nature. One of the core tenets of an SRA was protection, and it was unable to perform this function while in isolation. Has Seraphine guessed that there was a problem with his SRA? The implications were troubling. Seraphine was evolving, gaining access to capabilities that she herself didn't fully understand. Whether that evolution would ultimately favor their alliance or threaten it remained an open question. She was evaluating them just as much as she was the hunters.

Ethan glanced at Hash.

A message from Hash appeared on his HUD.

I think I can access the system like she can. I haven't tried yet because I don't want the system to close the door on it, cutting us off. I figured you'd want to play this close to the chest.

Ethan gave Hash a small nod.

"We need to move," Ethan said. "They'll be back with counter-measures for everything we just demonstrated, and I don't want to be caught here when they do."

As his team prepared for continued movement through the facility, Ethan tried to think of what he could do that the system couldn't anticipate. No matter what they did, the system knew they were trying to get back to the shuttles. They couldn't remotely pilot the shuttles, not with the communications interference. If the interference increased, they could lose the shuttles altogether and, with them, their only escape from the facility.

Hash approached one of the fallen hunters, pulling out a portable sampling kit from his equipment pack. "Major, we should collect tissue samples for analysis. Understanding their physiology could give us tactical advantages for future encounters."

Ethan shook his head, already moving toward the atrium's exit. "No time. We need to move before they regroup with counter-measures."

As they left the atrium behind, the team moved through a secondary commons area—a smaller space designed for researcher gatherings, with comfortable seating areas and food preparation stations that spoke to the facility's original peaceful purpose. The contrast with their current situation would have been ironic if it weren't so deadly.

Sergeant Staggart held up his hand, signaling for silence as his enhanced hearing detected sounds from beyond the far corridor.

The rhythmic impacts of energy weapons were mixed with inhuman shrieks and what sounded like metal being torn apart.

"Contact ahead," Staggart reported quietly. "Sounds like the newcomer aliens are engaging the hunters."

Ethan embraced his hybrid nature at minimal levels, extending his enhanced senses toward the distant battle. The sounds were intense—not the coordinated precision of the hunter attack they'd just survived, but something more brutal and overwhelming.

Abruptly, the battle sounds ceased.

The silence that followed was more unsettling than the combat had been—no withdrawal sounds, no regrouping movements, just an eerie quiet that suggested decisive victory rather than a tactical pause.

Heavy footsteps echoed through the corridor ahead, accompanied by a sound like metal scraping against stone. Something was approaching their position with deliberate purpose.

Three hunter corpses sailed through the air into the commons area, their reptilian bodies broken and torn in ways that spoke to overwhelming physical force. The message was clear; whatever had killed them possessed capabilities that made the hunters' formidable strength irrelevant.

The aliens that then entered the commons area defied easy categorization. They stood nearly three meters tall on two powerful locomotive legs that could lock into position with mechanical precision. Four manipulator arms extended from their central torso, two primary arms thick with muscle and equipped with what appeared to be integrated weapons systems and two secondary arms designed for fine motor control and tool manipulation. Their radial symmetry created the unsettling sense of being observed from multiple angles simultaneously.

Their skin held a dark, metallic undertone that suggested natural radiation shielding that had been developed through generations of space living. Larger eyes than would be proportional for

Earth-based life dominated their alien features, accompanied by additional sensory organs that tracked movement and energy signatures with predatory efficiency. Everything about their physiology spoke to adaptation for three-dimensional combat in hostile environments.

But it was their equipment that truly impressed Ethan. Bio-armor that seemed to be living and adaptive covered their bodies, integrating seamlessly with salvaged technology from multiple species. Weapons systems that combined organic components with advanced metallurgy created tools that were both alien and hauntingly familiar. Complex electrical patterns flickered across their six limbs—bio-electric communication that created field patterns invisible to human senses but clearly sophisticated in their complexity. The aliens seemed to be conducting detailed conversations through electromagnetic frequencies that Ethan's enhanced perception could barely detect.

Ethan stepped forward, raising his weapon to a non-threatening position while keeping it ready. "I'm Major Ethan Gates, Confederation Defense Force. Can you understand me?"

The aliens' response was immediate. A sound that resembled "Kythara" repeated in harmonic patterns that suggested meaning beyond simple vocalization. Their bio-electric fields intensified, creating patterns that might have been attempts at communication.

But it was clear that neither species could properly perceive the other's primary communication method. To the aliens, humans probably seemed deaf to electrical conversations. To humans, the aliens appeared unresponsive to verbal communication.

Seraphine moved closer to Ethan, her luminous eyes studying the aliens with intensity. "They're analyzing us," she said quietly. "Their sensory capabilities are more sophisticated than yours. They can detect your enhanced physiology, your artificial companion, and the hybrid nature of your team members."

The Kythara—as Ethan found himself thinking of them—

maintained their positions with mechanical precision. Their weapons weren't directly threatening, but their posture suggested readiness for instant combat. They had demonstrated overwhelming superiority against the hunters, and their assessment of the human team was clearly ongoing.

Captain Washburn moved into a defensive position, understanding without words that they were facing another potential threat. "Sir, recommend we maintain respectful distance while attempting to establish communications protocols."

The largest Kythara stepped forward, its bio-electric patterns creating a complex display across its limbs. The sound "Kythara" repeated in what might have been introduction, inquiry, or warning. Its multiple sensory organs tracked each member of Ethan's team while its weapons systems remained in ready position.

Atlas pulsed with concern against Ethan's forearm. *Their technology integration suggests a civilization that has encountered multiple species. The bio-armor incorporates design elements that match our database of Vemus technology.*

The standoff stretched taut with tension as three species— human, Vemus construct, and the mysterious Kythara—faced each other in a facility designed to test survival capabilities. Each group possessed unknown capabilities, uncertain intentions, and the demonstrated ability to destroy the others if conflict erupted.

Ethan kept his weapon ready while maintaining a non-aggressive stance, knowing that the next few moments could determine whether they faced new allies or additional enemies in their struggle to escape the research facility alive.

CHAPTER 27

ETHAN WATCHED the towering Kythara as they maintained their defensive positions, their bio-electric patterns creating mesmerizing displays across their six limbs. The aliens' multiple sensory organs tracked his team's movements with predatory precision, while their integrated weapons systems remained in a ready configuration.

"Rahner, Torres," Ethan said quietly through his neural implants, "dial back your hybrid nature to minimal levels. We don't want them mistaking us for Vemus constructs."

The hybrid specialists nodded, their enhanced physiology shifting subtly as they reduced their transformation states. Ethan felt his own hybrid nature recede to barely detectable levels, maintaining just enough enhancement to coordinate with his team while avoiding triggering the Kythara's threat assessment protocols.

"Hash," Ethan continued, "initiate First Contact protocols. Standard translation packages and mathematical progression sequences."

Hash activated his portable communications array, broadcasting mathematical concepts and universal constants through multiple frequency ranges. Their translator protocols were based on extensive colonial research, including reverse-engineering communications capabilities from other advanced species.

The Kythara showed no response to the audio transmissions, their bio-electric patterns continuing unchanged as they seemed to conduct conversations that humans couldn't perceive.

Ethan suspected their communication among themselves must be similar. He wondered whether this new group was a threat and why they were here in the first place.

Seraphine stayed quietly behind Ethan, observing the aliens intently.

Atlas pulsed with sudden intensity around Ethan's forearm. *Ethan, I'm detecting structured electromagnetic communication signatures from the aliens. The patterns are geometric, with specific limb positions corresponding to distinct EM frequencies.*

"What kind of patterns?" Ethan asked subvocally.

Complex mathematical relationships embedded in bio-electric fields. They're communicating through electromagnetic frequencies that your equipment can barely detect. But I can process the data streams and attempt correlation analysis.

Ethan felt a surge of hope. "Can you convert their signals into something we can understand?"

Beginning pattern analysis now. The geometric arrangements of their limbs appear to create specific EM field configurations. I'll attempt to map their communications protocols.

Within seconds, Atlas began projecting visual displays onto Ethan's HUD—geometric patterns that corresponded to the Kythara's limb positions, with accompanying frequency analyses that revealed the sophistication of their bio-electric communication.

"Atlas is detecting their communication patterns," Ethan announced to his team. "They're using bio-electric fields that we can't naturally perceive."

Hash looked up from his equipment with excitement. "Sir, if Atlas can map their protocols, I might be able to generate response signals through the facility's systems by amplifying our electromagnetic output to match their communication range."

The largest Kythara suddenly shifted its position, all four manipulator arms creating a complex geometric configuration while its bio-electric patterns intensified. Atlas immediately translated the display into visual symbols on Ethan's HUD.

They're expressing concepts that translate roughly to 'identification request' and 'threat assessment,' Atlas reported. *Their communication includes emotional context that suggests cautious interest rather than immediate hostility.*

Ethan activated his neural implants, using his combat suit's systems to generate basic electromagnetic pulses in mathematical sequences. Starting with prime numbers, he progressed to geometric ratios, then attempted to replicate the simplest patterns he'd observed from the Kythara's bio-electric displays.

The response was immediate and dramatic. All three Kythara shifted their postures, their bio-electric patterns synchronizing as they focused their attention on Ethan's crude electromagnetic attempts.

"They're responding," Hash reported, his equipment detecting the increased EM activity. "Sir, I can amplify your signal through the facility's communications systems. Create a stronger interface."

"Do it," Ethan ordered.

Hash's fingers danced across his interface as he connected with the facility's systems, using the same protocols that Seraphine had demonstrated earlier. The electromagnetic output from Ethan's equipment suddenly amplified, creating signals strong enough for clear two-way communication.

The Kythara's response was complex and immediate. Atlas worked rapidly to process the incoming data streams, translating bio-electric patterns into concepts that appeared on Ethan's HUD.

They identify themselves as Kythara-Hunting-Collective, Atlas reported. *They express concepts related to Vemus-threat-elimination and facility-investigation-purpose. They're asking about our mission parameters and threat classification.*

Ethan carefully composed his response using Atlas's translation protocols, generating EM patterns that conveyed basic concepts—human-species identification, Vemus-opposition, facility-investigation, extraction-requirement.

The Kythara leader stepped forward, its bio-electric patterns creating what Atlas translated as approval mixed with tactical concern. More complex communication followed—warnings about facility-system-hostility, hunter-adaptation-capabilities, and coordination-proposal for mutual benefit.

"They're proposing cooperation," Ethan announced to his team. "They want to work together against the hunters and the facility's systems."

Seraphine moved closer, her luminous eyes studying the Kythara with intense focus. Several Kythara shifted their focus to her, and Ethan thought it was only moments before they identified Seraphine as a Vemus-Alpha.

"The facility won't permit extended cooperation between test subjects. It will intervene to maintain conflict parameters," she said.

As if responding to her prediction, the facility's synthetic voice echoed through the commons area. "Communications protocols detected. Optimization parameters require adjustment. Implementing countermeasures."

A massive electromagnetic pulse erupted from the facility's systems, overwhelming both the Kythara's bio-electric fields and Atlas's detection capabilities. The aliens staggered, their communications networks disrupted, while Ethan felt Atlas retreat into protective isolation mode.

"EM interference pulse," Hash announced, his equipment registering electromagnetic chaos throughout the area. "The facility generated it deliberately. It's trying to prevent communication between us and the Kythara."

Ethan nodded. "The facility doesn't want us working together. It's designed to maintain conflict between test subjects."

The Kythara recovered quickly, their bio-electric patterns returning but noticeably dimmed. Their posture shifted to defensive readiness as they struggled to reestablish the communications networks that the facility had deliberately sabotaged.

Before either species could attempt to restore contact, massive facility systems activated with mechanical precision. The common area's far wall began retracting, revealing machinery that had been hidden behind decorative panels. Structural supports shifted and emergency barriers deployed in configurations that hadn't existed moments earlier.

"Structural reconfiguration in progress," the facility announced. "Test parameters are adapting to current conditions and additional test groups."

The wall separating them from the adjacent corridor tore away, revealing hunters that were fundamentally different from their previous opponents. These creatures stood nearly four meters tall, their reptilian forms augmented with cybernetic modifications. Bio-mechanical armor covered their natural scales, while energy weapons integrated directly into their arm structures pulsed with contained power. But it was their equipment that proved most concerning. Electromagnetic dampening fields surrounded each hunter, creating dead zones that suppressed bio-electric communication within their immediate vicinity. The Kythara's attempts to coordinate were met with static interference wherever the enhanced hunters approached, causing them to move closer together.

"EM dampeners," Hash said, his instruments detecting the suppression fields. "They're equipped specifically to counter Kythara communication."

The enhanced hunters moved with coordinated precision that spoke of extensive preparation, which made Ethan wonder how they could have prepared so quickly. They'd observed both human and Kythara tactics, developing countermeasures specifically designed to neutralize the advantages that cooperation might provide.

Ethan realized that verbal coordination was now their only option. "Visual signals only!"

The battle erupted with devastating intensity. The enhanced hunters' cybernetic modifications allowed them to move with unnatural speed while their integrated weapons systems provided firepower that challenged the Kythara's bio-armor. More concerning was their obvious focus on Seraphine; multiple hunters directed their primary attacks toward her position, attempting to eliminate what they clearly perceived as a priority target.

Ethan found himself fighting alongside the Kythara leader, their coordination limited to visual cues and universal combat principles. The alien's four manipulator arms created a defensive pattern that protected both species while its integrated weapons provided suppressing fire that allowed human soldiers to reposition.

Seraphine demonstrated capabilities that exceeded her previous displays, moving with lethal efficiency that matched the augmented hostiles' cybernetic advantages. But she was clearly being over-whelmed by focused assault from multiple opponents equipped specifically to counter her abilities.

"They're targeting her specifically," Washburn shouted over the sounds of combat.

Ethan fired his weapon and nodded. "It had to start sooner or later."

These hunters were larger in size than the previous group, requiring concentrated weapons fire to bring them down.

The battle's dynamics shifted rapidly as the facility's systems continued their structural reconfiguration. Floor sections began retracting, creating gaps that forced both human and Kythara forces to constantly adapt their positioning. The enhanced hunters used these changes to their advantage, herding their opponents toward specific locations while maintaining their coordinated assault.

Ethan coordinated with the Kythara leader through desperate improvisation—pointing to targets, indicating movement directions, using hand signals that transcended species barriers. The alien responded with tactical intelligence that proved invaluable, its enhanced sensory capabilities detecting hunter positions that human equipment couldn't track.

At some point during the fighting, Ethan noticed that several Kythara had spotted Seraphine, and the hunters were working toward their main objective. One of the Kythara, a smaller one that was still taller than Ethan, held some kind of scanner and pointed it directly at Seraphine. Ethan moved to block the scan as he fired his weapon at a hunter.

The facility's interference was creating an increasingly untenable situation. Communications disruption prevented effective coordination while structural changes limited their tactical options. The augmented hostiles pressed their advantage with methodical precision, their EM dampening fields creating dead zones that isolated the Kythara from their support networks.

A massive section of the commons area floor suddenly retracted, creating a gaping chasm that stretched across the entire space. Ethan found himself falling alongside Sergeant Staggart, Corporals Sykes and Richardson, Hash and Seraphine. The Kythara leader and two of its soldiers fell with them, all of them tumbling through darkness toward an unknown destination.

As they fell, Ethan caught glimpses of the remaining forces above—Washburn and the other soldiers separated from them by what might as well have been an interstellar distance. The facility had achieved its objective, breaking apart the cooperative forces and creating smaller groups that would be easier to test individually.

They landed hard on the platform below, the impact absorbed by their armor and the Kythara's bio-mechanical enhancements.

Emergency lighting activated around them, revealing another research level with different environmental conditions and what appeared to be entirely separate testing protocols.

Ethan struggled to his feet, checking on his separated team members while Atlas slowly emerged from protective mode. Nearby, the Kythara leader helped its soldiers recover, their bio-electric patterns dim but gradually strengthening as they moved away from the enhanced hunters' dampening fields.

Ethan looked over and saw Staggart helping Richardson to his feet.

Ethan opened a comlink to Washburn. The CDF Captain answered and Ethan heard sounds of fighting.

"Where are you, sir?" Washburn asked.

"Several levels below you. We're cut off," Ethan said, watching as the ceiling above them closed. "Sit rep."

"The damn facility put a wall right through the middle of the commons area. Looks like the hunters are regrouping. Give me a few minutes and we'll cut our way to you," Washburn said.

"Negative," Ethan replied. "Start making your way back toward the shuttles. We'll do the same and look for a way to meet up with you."

A grudging silence came through the comlink for a few moments. "I don't like it, sir."

"Me either, but if we stay here, those hunters are going to converge on our location and wipe us out. We can't keep fighting like this."

"Sir, I saw Seraphine... she noticed the area where the floor disappeared before it actually happened. You need to watch your back."

"Copy that," Ethan said and severed the comlink.

Staggart and the others reported only minor injuries, their armor having absorbed most of the impact. The Kythara appeared similarly functional, though their bio-electric communications remained suppressed by residual electromagnetic interference from the facility's systems.

Seraphine stood off to the side, watching them intently.

Hash looked at his wrist computer and frowned. "No communication with the others, sir. The facility is jamming everything above us."

"I just spoke to Washburn," Ethan said, trying to reestablish the comlink he'd used earlier.

It wouldn't connect.

Atlas pulsed weakly against his forearm. *The electromagnetic interference is diminishing. I should be able to restore limited communications protocols with the Kythara within minutes.*

"Good," Ethan replied subvocally. "We're going to need all the cooperation we can manage."

Emergency systems activated around them, revealing a research level that seemed designed for different experiments entirely. It looked abandoned and hadn't been used for a very long time.

The Kythara were engaged in some kind of interaction, and they cast what Ethan thought was suspicious posturing toward him and the others. Something had changed during the fighting.

"I don't like this, sir," Staggart said.

Ethan nodded. "Yeah, neither do I."

CHAPTER 28

THE ELECTROMAGNETIC INTERFERENCE FINALLY DISSIPATED, and Atlas's presence strengthened. Communications protocols cleared, allowing full functionality to return. Ethan felt the familiar comfort of his SRA's full functionality returning, along with the ability to interface with the Kythara's communications patterns.

The largest Kythara stepped forward, its four manipulator arms creating geometric configurations that Atlas translated into formal introduction protocols. The leader identified itself as Vex'thara, combat-coordinator of the hunting collective. It expressed cautious cooperation parameters while maintaining threat assessment protocols.

"Vex'thara," Ethan said aloud, using vocal communication while Atlas simultaneously generated corresponding electromagnetic patterns. "I'm Major Ethan Gates. We appreciate your assistance against the hunters."

The alien's bio-electric response carried undertones that Atlas translated as acknowledgement mixed with strategic calculation. Around them, the other Kythara had begun systematic examination of the fallen enhanced hunters, their secondary manipulator arms extracting tissue samples with surgical precision.

"Richardson," Ethan motioned toward the nearest corpse, "collect samples from the nearest hunter. Same protocols we use for any unknown biological threat."

Corporal Richardson approached one of the cybernetically enhanced corpses, pulling out a portable sampling kit. "Standard biological containment, sir?"

"Affirmative. We need to understand what we're facing."

As Richardson worked, Vex'thara's bio-electric patterns intensified, creating displays that made Atlas pulse with alarm. The alien moved closer to Ethan, its multiple sensory organs focusing on something that human perception couldn't detect.

Vex'thara is expressing concepts related to biological-contamination-anomaly and Vemus-contagion-patterns, Atlas reported. *It's asking if we're aware of contamination threats in this facility.*

Ethan frowned, studying the alien's agitated display. "What kind of contamination?"

Vex'thara must've observed Ethan embracing his hybrid nature during the fight.

Vex'thara's response was complex, involving geometric limb configurations that created increasingly agitated bio-electric fields. Atlas translated the display into concepts that appeared on Ethan's HUD: *active-conversion-technology,   Alpha-creation-protocols, unknown-species-collaboration-evidence.*

"The facility," Ethan realized. "You're detecting traces of Vemus technology integrated into the Phantom systems."

Vex'thara's attention suddenly shifted to Seraphine, who had been standing quietly near the edge of their group. The alien's bio-electric patterns created displays that Atlas translated as threat-identification and elimination-protocols.

Vex'thara is asking why Vemus Alphas attack each other, appearing confused by internal conflict among Vemus constructs.

Ethan moved protectively closer to Seraphine, understanding that the Kythara's hunting instincts were being triggered by her presence. "She's not like the others. This facility was designed as an experiment to create new types of Vemus constructs. Someone wanted us to find her."

"The facility represents research rather than natural Vemus development," Seraphine added, her luminous eyes studying Vex'thara with careful attention. "I am a divergent sample, created through artificial modification rather than standard conversion protocols."

Vex'thara's response was immediate and uncompromising. The alien's bio-electric patterns created displays that Atlas translated with brutal clarity: *No coexistence with Vemus. Destruction is only option. All Vemus constructs must be eliminated.*

The Kythara leader's primary manipulator arms shifted configuration, revealing integrated weapons systems that had been concealed within its bio-armor. Energy conduits along its limbs began pulsing with contained power as it prepared for immediate combat.

"Stand down." Ethan planted himself protectively between Vex'thara and Seraphine. "She's providing intelligence about Vemus operations. We need her alive."

But Vex'thara had already committed to attack. Its bio-electric fields intensified as it lunged forward, primary manipulator arms extending toward Seraphine with lethal intent and startling speed.

Atlas responded immediately. The SRA's metallic band expanded instantly, flowing like liquid metal to form a shield that caught Vex'thara's strike. The impact sent shockwaves through Ethan's arm, but Atlas's adaptive structure absorbed the energy while maintaining protective coverage.

Sergeant Staggart and the other CDF soldiers pointed their weapons at the other Kythara, each group unsure whether to engage the others.

A massive shadow fell across them as enhanced hunters dropped from concealed positions in the ceiling above. The creatures were even larger than their previous opponents—nearly five meters tall with cybernetic modifications that included advanced mobility systems.

The ambush was perfectly coordinated. While Ethan and Vex'thara were focused on their confrontation, the hunters had positioned themselves for maximum tactical advantage. One of them landed directly on Seraphine, its massive bulk overwhelming her defensive capabilities despite her enhanced physiology.

"Contact!" Sergeant Staggart shouted, bringing his weapon to bear on the nearest hunter.

The battle erupted in the confined space with devastating intensity. The enhanced hunters moved with unnatural coordination, their cybernetic modifications allowing them to function in the contaminated atmosphere while their size and strength challenged both human and Kythara defensive capabilities.

Atlas adapted to the combat environment with fluid precision. The SRA's shield configuration shifted into offensive modes, creating stabbing weapons that extended from Ethan's arms while generating powerful electrical discharges. Each strike carried enough energy to penetrate hunter bio-armor while disrupting their cybernetic systems.

Vex'thara fought with lethal efficiency, its four manipulator arms creating a defensive pattern that protected both species while its integrated weapons provided suppressing fire. The alien's bio-electric communications resumed as the hunters' EM dampening fields were overwhelmed by close-quarters combat intensity.

But the hunters had learned from previous encounters. Their cybernetic modifications included countermeasures specifically designed to neutralize both human weapons and Kythara bio-electric advantages. Adaptive armor absorbed energy discharges while mobility enhancers allowed them to constantly shift positions despite their massive size.

Seraphine fought desperately against the hunter that had ambushed her, but her opponent's cybernetic enhancements provided overwhelming physical advantages. Energy claws designed specifically for penetrating Vemus bio-armor tore through her defensive capabilities, leaving deep wounds that pulsed with her luminous blood.

"She's hurt," Hash reported, his equipment detecting the specific biological signatures that indicated severe trauma. "That hunter's weapons are designed to cause maximum damage to Vemus physiology."

Ethan coordinated his team's response while engaging hunters in close-quarters combat. Atlas's offensive configurations allowed him to match their cybernetic advantages, but the confined space limited their tactical options while favoring the hunters' superior size and strength.

Ethan's battle was twofold as he fought the instinctual urge to embrace his hybrid nature, but if he did, he'd lose Atlas's help.

The largest hunter succeeded in grappling Seraphine despite her attempts to escape. Its massive form began retreating toward an access shaft that led deeper into the facility, carrying her away from any possibility of rescue.

"Staggart," Ethan said, "bring down the ceiling. Collapse the access points and separate us from the remaining hunters."

"Sir, that could trap us down here," Staggart replied, though he was already preparing the explosive charges.

"Do it."

Staggart deployed the explosive charges with precision. The ceiling collapsed in controlled sections, crushing several hunters while creating a barrier that separated Ethan's group from both the remaining threats and Vex'thara's forces.

As dust and debris settled around them, Ethan assessed their situation. They were cut off from both their original team and their Kythara allies, pursuing an unknown number of enhanced hunters through a facility designed to overwhelm their survival capabilities.

But Seraphine represented intelligence that could determine humanity's long-term survival against the Vemus threat. Her knowledge of Alpha locations, conversion protocols, and the larger Vemus collective structure made her invaluable despite the risks her presence created.

"Atlas, track her bio-signature," Ethan ordered as they prepared to pursue the hunters deeper into the facility.

Bio-electric traces detected along corridor seven-alpha, Atlas reported. *The hunters are moving toward what appears to be a central processing facility. Their destination suggests specific objectives rather than random retreat.*

"They're taking her somewhere specific," Ethan realized. "This whole scenario was planned."

Hash looked up from his scanner, sweat beading on his forehead. "Sir, there might be unknown environmental hazards as we go deeper. Our suits can handle it for now, but extended exposure..."

"We'll deal with that when we have to," Ethan replied. "Right now, we need to get to Seraphine before they finish whatever they're planning."

As they began their pursuit through corridors that seemed designed to guide them toward whatever waited in the facility's depths, Ethan couldn't shake the feeling that they were walking into something that had been orchestrated from the beginning.

Salpheth had created this facility as a testing ground, but the specific scenarios they were encountering suggested someone who understood both human psychology and Kythara hunting patterns with unsettling accuracy. The rogue Phantom had anticipated their arrivals, prepared appropriate challenges, and was now guiding them toward whatever revelation waited at the facility's heart.

"Stay alert," Ethan ordered as they moved deeper into the installation. "We're not just rescuing Seraphine; we're walking into whatever Salpheth wanted us to find."

The hunt through the facility's depths was about to begin, and with it, discoveries that would reshape their understanding of the threats facing not just humanity, but every species that had ever encountered the Vemus collective.

CHAPTER 29

ETHAN MOVED through the facility's corridors as the scout drone flew ahead of them, tracking Seraphine's passage. The hunters had taken her deeper into the installation, following pathways that seemed designed to guide them toward a specific destination.

"She let them take her," Ethan realized, studying the scorch marks and debris patterns that told the story of their passage. "There are no signs of struggle after the initial capture."

Sergeant Staggart examined the evidence. "Why would she do that? She doesn't do anything without a reason. She's cold and calculating to the max."

Ethan considered it, feeling the pieces of a larger puzzle clicking into place. "She's trying to complete the trial. The only way to do that is to eliminate the Alpha."

The revelation sent a chill through his team. While they'd killed many hunters, these enhanced versions were stronger, more coordinated, and equipped with technology specifically designed to counter their advantages. The hunters they'd destroyed were subordinates to the Alpha—tests to evaluate their abilities so that when they faced the true threat, it would be better prepared. It was a military tactic that carried a heavy price, but with the Vemus, Ethan doubted they registered the loss at all.

"Sir," Hash said, his equipment detecting increasing energy signatures ahead, "the hunters' traces are converging on a large facility approximately two hundred meters ahead. Multiple hunter signatures. They're not trying to conceal their presence anymore, but something else is there—much stronger."

"Hash," Ethan said, "try to contact Washburn. Use the facility's systems if necessary. Send him our coordinates."

He'd ordered Washburn to return to the shuttles, but he suspected Washburn would likely be finding a path that would bring them closer to where he thought Ethan and the others were going.

Staggart frowned as Hash worked on establishing the comlink. "Won't the facility hinder Washburn's efforts to find us?"

Ethan shook his head, studying the tactical displays on his HUD. "I don't think so. The odds are against him and others reaching our destination in time to help. This trial is going to be decided well before reinforcements can reach us."

They approached the entrance to another massive laboratory, this one dwarfing even the central atrium where they'd first encountered the hunters. The space stretched in all directions, its ceiling disappearing into shadows while rows of broken containment vessels lined the walls like technological tombstones.

Their destination waited at the center of the laboratory.

The Hunter-Alpha was a massive reptilian creature that stood nearly five meters tall, its natural scales enhanced with cybernetic modifications that pulsed with contained energy. Unlike the other hunters, its markings were elaborate—geometric patterns that seemed to shift and flow across its bio-armor while it projected the Alpha signal that commanded its lesser constructs.

Ethan felt the signal's influence attempt to penetrate his defenses, but his hybrid nature and Atlas's presence created barriers that prevented Alpha compulsion. Beside him, Hash showed no signs of mental intrusion, his own enhanced physiology providing similar protection.

"Status report," Ethan said quietly, using his neural implants to coordinate with his team while avoiding detection by the Alpha's enhanced senses.

Hash checked his personal holoscreen. "I've made contact with Captain Washburn. He says to tell you that he's sent a team to secure the way back to the shuttles, and he's making his way toward our location."

The message carried deeper meaning. Washburn understood they were facing something that required immediate resolution rather than tactical patience. However, he wanted Ethan to know that he was still coming.

Staggart moved closer to Ethan, his voice barely audible. "Sir, we could just walk away. Let these Alphas kill each other. We could return to the ship, blow this place to hell, and then search through the pieces."

The suggestion was tactically sound and tempting. The presence of the Kythara also added another layer of complication to their mission here and to the ship. Ethan felt the pull of pragmatic decision-making that would minimize the risk to his people while potentially achieving their intelligence objectives through different means. There was no way to eliminate the risk entirely, and he didn't know what would happen if the two Alphas eliminated each other. Would the trial reset as it had done before? There was no way to confirm this, regardless of what Seraphine had told him. The fact that the governing system of the experiment had accounted for the eventual human presence could trigger the cycle to end. If that happened, they'd lose a strategic asset against the Vemus.

"The best chance of someday finding the super-alpha is by taking Seraphine with us," Ethan said. "She's a construct and perhaps a trap, but there's knowledge to be gained that we can't get any other way."

Staggart's expression showed understanding mixed with hardened concern. "What happens if she won't come willingly? She's been evaluating us as much as them."

Ethan peered at the Alpha in the distance, weighing tactical options while considering the larger strategic picture. "One day we're going to have to stop the Vemus. To do that, we need to find out where they go once they reach a particular stage of development. Salpheth recognized this and knew we would see the value in this information. It also means he doesn't know where the super-alpha is either."

Staggart sighed. "That's way above my pay grade, sir."

"Yeah. Right. If you thought it was a bad idea, you wouldn't hesitate to tell me."

Staggart nodded. "I'd drag you back to Captain Washburn if I thought you were compromised, sir."

Ethan knew the CDF sergeant was only half-joking.

The laboratory's layout offered both advantages and challenges. Broken containment vessels provided cover but also created obstacles that could trap them during retreat. Multiple levels connected through access ramps allowed for three-dimensional maneuvering but also gave the Alpha superior positioning options.

"I'm not going in alone," Ethan said, and Staggart relaxed. "Hash, Sykes, and Richardson, take flanking positions toward our extraction route. Hash, do you still have access to the facility's systems?"

"Yes, sir. Seraphine's credentials haven't been revoked. What do you need me to do with them?" Hash asked.

"Use them to create distractions. Draw the hunters away from the Alpha, giving us a chance to close the distance to it," Ethan said.

Hash glanced away from them and then nodded. "I can do that, sir."

The plan was simple but risky—create chaos to mask their approach, extract Seraphine during the confusion, and fight their way out before the Alpha could coordinate an overwhelming response. While Hash worked on setting up his chaos-filled distractions, Sykes and Richardson moved into position.

Hash's hands moved across his interface as he accessed the laboratory's control systems. "Ready to initiate overload sequences on the research stations, sir."

Ethan nodded. "Afterward, I want you to head toward Richardson's position."

"Understood, sir."

"Do it."

Multiple laboratory stations erupted in controlled explosions. Their energy discharges sent bolts into nearby hunters, disrupting their formations. The Alpha's attention shifted toward the disturbances, its massive form moving with surprising speed as it attempted to identify the source of the attacks.

Ethan and Staggart used the distraction to advance toward Seraphine's location. She was positioned near the laboratory's central processing area, guarded by enhanced hunters whose attention was now divided between their prisoner and the ongoing systems failures.

Seraphine used the chaos to her advantage. The skin on her arms hardened as if encased in an SRA variant, metallic surfaces forming natural armor while elongated claws extended from her fingertips. She moved with lethal efficiency, her enhanced capabilities allowing her to kill the nearest hunters before they could respond to her transformation.

The massive Hunter-Alpha spun toward her and attacked with

startling speed that defied its size, overwhelming Seraphine's defenses despite her enhanced capabilities. Energy claws designed specifically for penetrating Vemus bio-armor tore through her protective modifications, leaving deep wounds that pulsed with luminous blood as she was flung across the laboratory.

"Now," Ethan ordered.

He and Staggart emerged from cover with weapons configured for maximum impact. Heavy ammunition depleted their supplies faster but packed enough energy to challenge even the Alpha's cybernetic enhancements. Their surprise attack drove the massive creature back, forcing it to focus on immediate threats rather than finishing Seraphine.

Atlas adapted to combat configuration, creating stabbing weapons that extended from Ethan's arms while generating electrical discharges powerful enough to disrupt the Alpha's bio-mechanical systems. Staggart coordinated their assault with professional precision, his heavy weapons providing suppressing fire that prevented the Alpha from using its superior size and strength effectively.

But the Hunter-Alpha possessed capabilities they hadn't encountered before. As the creature's Alpha signal intensified, Ethan felt compulsion protocols attempting to override his conscious decision-making. On instinct, he embraced his hybrid nature, his enhanced physiology providing barriers against mental intrusion that purely human defenses couldn't match.

The transformation cost him Atlas's support. His SRA retreated into isolation mode, cutting off the artificial consciousness that had become integral to his tactical thinking. Without Atlas's enhanced awareness, Ethan was blindsided by the Alpha's counterattack.

Massive claws caught him across the chest, their energy discharge overwhelming his armor's protective capabilities. The impact sent him crashing into a bank of monitoring equipment, pain lancing through his ribs as he struggled to maintain consciousness.

Staggart pulled him clear of immediate danger, his covering fire keeping the Alpha at bay while Ethan recovered. "Sir, are you alright?"

"I'll manage," Ethan replied, assessing his injuries through his hybrid-enhanced perception. Bruised ribs and torn armor, but nothing that prevented continued combat operations. Baseline repair protocols engaged to fill the gaps where the Alpha's claws had penetrated, and nanorobotic patches plugged the holes.

Richardson and Sykes provided covering fire from their flanking positions, but their weapons had limited effectiveness against the Alpha's adaptive armor. More concerning was the arrival of reinforcements—additional hunters converging on their position as the Alpha's coordination protocols overrode the facility's electronic interference.

Weapons fire erupted from the laboratory's far side as Kythara forces engaged the hunter reinforcements from the upper level. Vex'thara's bio-electric patterns were visible through the chaos, the alien leader coordinating his forces with deadly efficiency while avoiding direct confrontation with the Alpha construct.

"Staggart, cover me while I check on Seraphine," Ethan said.

"Go! I got you," Staggart bellowed.

Ethan found her near the central processing station. Her wounds were severe enough that he wasn't sure if she'd survive. Luminous blood pooled beneath her as her bio-mechanical enhancements struggled to maintain critical functions.

She looked up at him. "I haven't reached perfection in this iteration," she said, her voice carrying the calm acceptance he'd learned to associate with her unique perspective on existence and death. She expected that part of her would be revived somehow, but Ethan wasn't so sure about that. "But you..." Her luminous eyes focused on his hybrid form with something that might have been approval.

"You're a type of Alpha but not like me or my enemy. Different parameters entirely."

Ethan felt Atlas stirring as his SRA attempted to reestablish connection despite his hybrid transformation. The artificial consciousness carried data that had been gathered during their brief contact with Seraphine's bio-mechanical systems.

"I can save you," Ethan said. "Show you how to regenerate."

Seraphine's eyes widened. "I've tried regeneration protocols, but they're not working. I'm lacking critical knowledge." She paused, studying him with renewed intensity. "Transference can only occur with direct contact, and you've already refused such integration."

Ethan imagined Cynergy screaming at him for what he was about to do, and she wouldn't be the only one. He reached toward her and she lifted her hand. He stopped just beyond her reach. "I'll make a deal with you. In exchange for the knowledge to heal yourself, you travel with us. We'll help you reach perfection because it'll lead us to the super-alpha."

She considered the proposal as blood continued to pool beneath her. She inhaled sharply and winced in pain. She tried to reach for him, but he pulled his hand away, waiting for her response.

"Acceptable parameters."

Ethan grabbed her hand. The contact was immediate and overwhelming. He'd been attached to a Vemus Alpha before. Usually, an Alpha sought to subjugate and deceive to gain dominance, but this contact was different. Perhaps it was because she was a Vemus Alpha construct and he was a hybrid, but it was as if their natures recognized each other through biological harmonics that transcended species barriers. Ethan sensed the Alpha consciousness within her—ancient, powerful, and driven by purpose that stretched across galactic timescales. Despite Seraphine's young age, her DNA contained ancient knowledge. Alphas weren't the top of the Vemus hierarchy, and her weakened state allowed him to share regeneration techniques that had been refined through his own experiences with hybrid physiology.

Atlas observed the entire exchange, even in his isolated capacity the SRA's consciousness mapped the interaction between biological and artificial systems that allowed Seraphine's unique capabilities.

"The regeneration requires hibernation," Ethan explained as he removed his combat suit. "Extended dormancy while your systems rebuild from critical damage."

Seraphine lapsed into unconsciousness as she focused on healing her injuries. He carefully placed Seraphine within the suit's protective framework, using its medical interface to induce the controlled coma that would allow her biological systems to concentrate entirely on repair and regeneration. The combat suit's life support systems would maintain her during the healing process while its armor provided protection during transport.

Staggart approached as Ethan activated the suit's autonomous functions. "Sir, what exactly am I looking at?"

"Our ticket to finding the super-alpha," Ethan replied, enabling the combat suit's remote-control features. The automated system could carry Seraphine toward Hash and the others while following pre-programmed movement patterns that avoided immediate threats.

The Hunter-Alpha chose that moment to renew its assault. Without the protection of his combat suit, Ethan relied entirely on his hybrid enhancements, but Atlas had become fully active. His SRA had somehow overcome the isolation protocols, maintaining connection despite his transformed state—a breakthrough that fundamentally changed their combat capabilities.

The Hunter-Alpha barreled toward them, and Ethan and Staggart dove out of the way. Staggart fired his weapon, and heavy metallic darts penetrated the vulnerable underbelly of the Hunter-Alpha. Patches of its armor were burned through by Kythara weapons.

Ethan launched himself upward as Atlas formed a long combat knife, its edge glowing with energy. He slashed down, cutting the Hunter-Alpha along the back of its shoulder.

Ethan's hybrid nature allowed him to match the Alpha's speed and strength while Atlas provided tactical analysis and weapons configurations at the speed of Ethan's thoughts. The weapons configurations exploited weaknesses in the Hunter-Alpha's bio-mechanical systems. Upon contact with the creature's flesh, the combat knife expanded, shoving spikes deep into its back. The Alpha howled in pain as the knife punched through its chest.

Staggart's covering fire disrupted the Hunter-Alpha's coordination attempts while their combined assault gradually overwhelmed its adaptive defenses and it fell with a death shriek that echoed through the laboratory's vast spaces. The surviving hunters, cut off from the Alpha, flailed on the floor in confusion and madness.

"Attention test subjects," the facility's synthetic voice announced. "Both Alpha constructions have been eliminated. Trial parameters have been satisfied. Facility decommission will begin immediately."

The implication was immediate and terrifying. Whatever decommission process Salpheth had programmed into the facility would eliminate all evidence of their discoveries—and potentially everyone still inside.

Across the laboratory, Ethan noticed Vex'thara observing him from a position near the exit corridors. The Kythara leader's bio-electric patterns were dim at this distance, but its posture suggested evaluation rather than immediate hostility. Other Kythara had their weapons pointed at Ethan, but they didn't fire. After several long moments, the alien retreated from view, leaving Ethan to wonder what conclusions it had drawn about their encounter.

He rejoined his team, where the others showed initial shock at seeing Seraphine's unconscious form within his combat suit. Ethan disabled the helmet's transparency mode so the sight of Seraphine wouldn't alarm the others.

Hash and the others stared at Ethan. He was in a basic black uniform of the CDF, but his skin was dark and thick. As he embraced his hybridness, his skin formed something akin to Vemus exoskeletal material that should protect him enough to make it back to the shuttle, even in a vacuum. Atlas gleamed along his forearm, the metallic SRA extending across Ethan's chest and spreading to his other arm. This was reminiscent of how the Aczar wore their SRAs.

"Focus on extraction," Staggart ordered. "We need to get out of here before this place comes apart around us."

Hash nodded. "I've found a path back toward the shuttles, sir. Shared the route with Captain Washburn. But we need to move fast. The facility's power systems are beginning systematic shutdown."

Wall panels retracted with grinding metallic shrieks as they ran, revealing maintenance systems that had been hidden throughout their exploration. The corridor floor buckled beneath their feet, forcing them to leap across widening gaps while emergency lighting strobed in patterns that disoriented human vision but left Ethan's hybrid-enhanced perception unaffected. The facility was returning to whatever dormant state Salpheth had programmed as its final configuration.

As they ran through passages that might seal at any moment, Ethan felt the artificial atmosphere begin to thin. An alert appeared on his HUD. Ethan inhaled a deep breath several times and held it. He slowed down his internal physiology, increasing the efficiency of his muscles to consume less oxygen. In essence, he could hold his breath for a couple of hours if he needed to. However, he couldn't speak when he was doing this, but since Atlas was now available, he could rely on his SRA to communicate for him.

As they ran through the corridors, Ethan wondered if the trial had gone as Salpheth had intended. He considered it as his combat suit, with Seraphine's unconscious form inside, ran ahead of him. They'd gained something invaluable and perhaps profoundly dangerous. Seraphine was a living repository of Vemus knowledge that could reshape their understanding of their greatest threat. Whether Seraphine would prove to be an ally or enemy remained to be determined, but the intelligence she represented was worth the risks they'd taken to acquire it. Now, all they had to do was make it back to the shuttles and return to the ship in time to avoid a greater conflict with the Kythara.

CHAPTER 30

THE COMBAT SHUTTLES touched down in the *Ascendant*'s main hangar bay. Ethan felt the familiar sensation of artificial gravity taking hold as the shuttle's systems powered down, but his hybrid-enhanced physiology remained active, his skin maintaining the dark exoskeletal appearance that had protected him during their escape from the research station.

Atlas pulsed with steady energy across his forearm and chest, the SRA's expanded configuration still active despite their return to normal atmospheric conditions. The breakthrough they'd achieved —maintaining connection during his hybrid transformation— represented a fundamental change in their partnership that would require careful evaluation. Ethan wondered if this was just a one-off, and whether once he reverted back the problem would return the next time he embraced his hybrid nature. He sensed that Atlas shared that concern.

Ethan heaved a sigh and released his hybrid nature. Atlas's presence remained active.

Successful test, Atlas said.

"Did it work?" Hash asked.

Ethan nodded. "Yes."

"How? Why this time?"

"I'm not sure. We need to work it out."

Hash nodded. "When you do, can you show me?"

Ethan knew Hash had requested to join the SRA pilot program, and it probably wouldn't be long before he was accepted into it.

"Secure the prisoner," Ethan ordered, as the shuttle's rear compartment opened. His combat suit, carrying Seraphine's unconscious form in medical hibernation, was guided onto a medical transport platform by automated systems.

Washburn came to his side. "It's good to be back. Medical team is standing by for decontamination and prisoner containment protocols."

"You did well in there," Ethan said.

Washburn smiled. "Thank you, sir. I appreciate it."

Dr. Sarah Chen emerged from the medical bay's entrance. She focused on the most critical injuries first, conducting quick assessments before sending the wounded to medbay. Then she made her way over. "Major Gates, we've prepared a medical isolation capsule with full quarantine measures for the prisoner. Two armed guards will be on rotation with emergency containment protocols that include purging the capsule if necessary."

Ethan nodded, watching as Seraphine's transport was guided toward the medical bay under heavy security escort. "Let's hope it doesn't come to that. She's in hibernation for regenerative purposes. Monitor her vital signs but don't attempt to wake her until we've had time to prepare proper containment measures."

"Understood, sir," Dr. Chen replied. "If you'll come with me, I'll get you checked out. I'm sure Major Qualmann is anxious to have you return to the bridge."

The medical examination was thorough but brief. Dr. Chen's instruments detected the physiological changes that had occurred during Ethan's extended hybrid transformation, and Atlas's expanded presence across his body created readings that challenged conventional understanding of SRA integration.

"Your SRA connection has increased significantly," Dr. Chen observed, studying the data from his biochip. "The integration patterns are unlike anything we've recorded previously. We'll need to monitor this."

Ethan felt Atlas pulse with acknowledgement as he responded. "We've worked some things out. The isolation protocols that prevented connection during hybrid transformation have been overcome."

She made notes on her medical pad. "We'll need to document the changes and assess any potential risks or benefits."

Ethan left the med bay and found Cynergy walking toward him from the other end of the corridor. Her eyes locked on, and she lengthened her stride.

"Are you okay? You look different," she said, moving into his arms.

"Yes," he said, holding her.

She pulled back to study his face and then let him go. "We need to get to the bridge."

They moved through the *Ascendant*'s corridors together. Crewmembers stepped to the side as they passed, clearing their path to the bridge.

The bridge was a hub of controlled activity as Major Will Qualmann coordinated multiple analysis operations from the command chair. Captain Endo worked at the tactical station and had just finished giving Qualmann an update.

The main holoscreen displayed tactical plots that painted a complex picture of their current situation.

"Major Gates," Qualmann said, rising from the command chair with evident relief. "Good to have you back, sir. We've got a complex situation developing."

Ethan moved to the center of the bridge, feeling Atlas interface with the ship's systems to provide enhanced tactical awareness. "Report."

"The alien vessels haven't departed the research station, but our sensors confirm the facility is systematically shutting down," Qualmann replied, gesturing toward the tactical display. "Power systems are going offline throughout the installation."

"I can confirm that," Ethan said. "The facility's automated systems are decommissioning it. Must be part of whatever protocol Salpheth programmed into its operations."

Qualmann nodded, then shifted the display to show their primary concern. "We deployed scout drones when we lost communication with the *Odyssey*. The intelligence they've gathered is significant. I've never seen anything like it."

The main holoscreen shifted to display a tactical situation that made his face tighten with concern. The *Odyssey* and the *Horizon* appeared immobilized in space, surrounded by multiple Kythara vessels in precise formation. But it was the massive ship—easily three times the *Odyssey*'s length—that commanded attention.

"Gravitational anomaly field," Captain Endo reported from tactical. "The large vessel is generating an artificial gravitational field that's preventing our ships from maneuvering. Energy beam distribution suggests the field is being maintained through coordinated power-sharing among multiple alien vessels."

Ethan stared at the tactical display. "They're not attacking. This is containment rather than aggression… at least outright aggression." He paused. "The alien species we encountered are called the Kythara. They're Vemus hunters—a nomadic civilization that's dedicated their existence to tracking and eliminating Vemus threats throughout the galaxy."

The revelation sent a ripple of understanding through the bridge crew. Cynergy looked up from her auxiliary station with the expression of someone whose analysis had just been confirmed.

"That correlates with our assessment of the derelict fleet we encountered two years ago," she said. "The ship configurations, the technology integration, the evidence of extended combat operations against Vemus forces."

Ethan looked at her holoscreen, which compared images of the ships they'd encountered two years ago with the Kythara ships. They weren't exactly the same, but they clearly had the same foundational principles in their construction.

Qualmann moved to stand beside Ethan at the main display. "Endo and I have been developing firing solutions based on the assumption that we'd need to engage them militarily. Analysis suggests their engines are less capable than the *Ascendant's*."

"We can outrun them back to the group," Captain Endo added from tactical. "But it's unclear whether they'll detect our approach or interpret it as hostile action. Also, they don't seem to have any form of subspace communications."

"This is more complicated than a simple rescue operation," Ethan said. "The Kythara could become valuable allies in our fight against the Vemus. We need to find a way to free the *Odyssey* and establish communication with the Kythara forces."

He activated his command interface, bringing up communications protocols that might bridge the gap between species. "The communication breakthrough we achieved at the facility could be replicated. If we can establish contact, even briefly, it might be enough for both groups to separate without conflict."

"The Kythara's containment field suggests evaluation rather than immediate hostility. They may be assessing whether our ships represent Vemus threats or potential allies," Atlas said, participating in the discussion.

Ethan thought about Vex'thara. He and the other Kythara had the opportunity to fire on him, but they hadn't.

"I agree," Ethan said. "Their actions indicate uncertainty about our nature and intentions."

Cynergy looked at him. "The gravitational field they're maintaining requires enormous energy expenditure. They can't sustain it indefinitely without compromising their ships' other systems."

Qualmann eyed Ethan, considering. "We could try to establish communication, but then we'd give ourselves away."

"It's more complicated than that," Ethan said. "The Kythara commander we encountered knows I'm a hybrid. His superior officers could decide that this is evidence enough to attack the *Odyssey* and the *Horizon*. We can't risk simply opening communication. I mean, we can't only try to communicate with them."

"Sir," Captain Endo said, "I recommend we approach at maximum sublight speed. We can configure a comms drone to communicate with them at the same time we disrupt their artificial gravity field."

Ethan looked at his tactical officer. "How do you suggest we do that?"

Endo smiled. "Sir, it's a chain. Break one of the links, and the whole thing falls apart."

Ethan nodded in understanding. "And at the same time, we establish comms with the *Odyssey* and the *Horizon*."

Qualmann cleared his throat. "Do you think General Quinn will attack them?"

"Looks like they tried, but they're likely studying them and perhaps waiting on us."

Qualmann was quiet for a few moments. "So, do we break a link in the chain then?"

Ethan moved to the command chair, feeling the bridge's attention focus on him as the crew awaited orders that could determine the outcome of their entire mission. "No, we're going to break the entire chain and get our people out of there. The Kythara could be our allies, and perhaps there are good reasons for their actions. The fact is that we don't know if breaking a single link in the chain is enough, but I do know that if we target enough links it'll be enough of a disruption to free our people. Then we can worry about communication."

Ethan brought up the tactical plot on his holoscreen. "There."

Qualmann leaned in to see the screen. "We can target those receivers with attack drones. Should minimize collateral damage—" He stopped and then chuckled. "Stealth attack drones. Get them into position, put them in attack mode to coordinate a hit at the same time to all targets."

Ethan smiled. "Yes. I don't want to destroy any of their ships. This deals with the threat in a measured response. I hope they'll realize that, but they also need to know they can't push us around either."

Qualmann nodded. "I follow your logic. Why would they use this tactic in the first place?"

Cynergy looked at him. "They hunt Vemus Alphas. Doing this would neutralize the Alpha and ready an overwhelming attack while the Alpha couldn't do anything but watch."

Ethan gave his wife an approving nod. "Helm, set course for the *Odyssey's* position. Comms, let's get a drone ready for deployment. It's going to need a change in configuration. I'll get your help with it."

He sent a message to Hash, ordering him to come to the bridge.

"The next few hours will determine whether we gain valuable allies or face additional enemies," Ethan announced. "The Kythara have been fighting the Vemus for potentially centuries. Their experience and capabilities could prove crucial for our long-term survival."

As the *Ascendant* accelerated toward the coordinates where their task force remained trapped, Ethan couldn't shake the feeling that they were approaching a convergence point. The research facility's decommission had eliminated evidence of Salpheth's experiments, but they'd gained things that were potentially more valuable—a living repository of Vemus knowledge and the possibility of alliance with experienced Vemus hunters.

"Time to intercept?" Ethan asked.

"Approximately four hours at current acceleration," came the response from navigation.

Four hours would have to be enough, and Ethan intended to use every moment to ensure they succeeded.

CHAPTER 31

ETHAN STOOD on the *Ascendant's* bridge, watching the tactical displays that showed their approach to one of the most delicate military operations he'd ever attempted. Four hours of preparation had refined their strategy to its essential elements—attempt communication, disable the Kythara gravitational trap, free the *Odyssey* and the *Horizon*, and avoid triggering an interspecies war that could doom any hope of an alliance against the Vemus.

"Status on the stealth attack drones?" Ethan asked.

"Twelve drones deployed and holding position at forty thousand kilometers above the engagement zone," Captain Endo said. "Stealth configuration is maintaining minimal energy signatures. No response from the Kythara to the drones at all. Stealth placement has been achieved."

The stealth drones represented some of their most advanced military technology, reverse engineered from the Krake attack drones that colonial scientists had perfected. Each unit was barely larger than a fast-attack combat shuttle, and when activated, their systems burned as hot as a main sequence star, capable of punching through anything it came into contact with. The CDF's only defense against the attack drones were powerful artificial gravity fields that prevented the drones from reaching their ships.

Ethan looked at the tactical display and it showed that the drones were significantly elevated above the Kythara formation.

"Once they transition to attack mode, descent time to target is approximately eight seconds," Captain Endo said.

"Very well," Ethan replied.

Hash looked up from his specialized workstation where he'd been configuring the communication drone's system. "Sir, the comms drone is ready for deployment. I've programmed it with the electromagnetic pulse patterns we developed during our facility encounter, along with the data repositories you requested."

Ethan nodded, studying the communications package they'd assembled. It was primitive compared to normal diplomatic protocols, but it represented their best hope for avoiding unnecessary bloodshed.

"What's the basic message content?" Qualmann asked.

"Non-threat identification, request for status confirmation, and cessation of hostile containment actions," Ethan replied. "We've also included data from our encounter with the derelict Kythara fleet two years ago, but that'll take them time to decipher."

The inclusion of the historical data was a calculated risk. The derelict fleet they'd encountered was likely a completely different group of Kythara, but it might convince them that Confederation ships weren't threats. There was also a data package on how to communicate with Confederation ships. The complex data would require analysis that might take longer than their tactical situation allowed.

"Communications status with the *Odyssey*?" Ethan asked.

Lieutenant Trickle's expression showed frustration as she worked through multiple frequency ranges. "Still no contact, sir. The gravitational field is somehow interfering with subspace comms. Our computer systems could overcome the interference, but processing time would be approximately forty-three minutes."

Time they didn't have. Whatever the Kythara were planning, their energy expenditure maintaining the gravitational trap couldn't continue indefinitely. Ethan suspected that they could use the gravitational trap to crush the *Odyssey* and the *Horizon*, causing catastrophic damage to both ships.

"Deploy the communications drone," Ethan ordered. "Standard approach vector toward the largest Kythara vessel. I want them to notice it but not interpret it as a weapons-delivery system."

The drone launched from the *Ascendant*'s forward bay with a minimal energy signature, its trajectory designed to appear non-threatening while carrying their message toward the Kythara command ship. Hash had configured the drone's systems to broadcast electromagnetic pulses in patterns they'd developed for basic Kythara communication.

"Drone deployed, sir," Lieutenant Trickle confirmed. "Time to effective communication range fourteen minutes."

Ethan felt Atlas pulse with concern as the SRA processed tactical variables through enhanced analytical capabilities. The Kythara's response to their communication attempt would determine whether their strategy succeeded or failed.

The scout ships they'd encountered at the research facility were still hours away, so Vex'thara couldn't help them. Ethan wasn't sure whether he *could* help them.

"Sir," Captain Endo said from tactical, "secondary firing solutions are locked and ready. If the stealth drones prove insufficient, or the Kythara ships attack after the gravitational field is brought down, we can target their ships for maximum damage."

The backup plan involved the *Ascendant*'s main weapons systems that mixed HADES VII missiles along with kinetic delivery systems. Use of those weapons would eliminate any hope of peaceful resolution. Ethan preferred the precision approach, but he wouldn't sacrifice the *Odyssey* or the *Horizon* for diplomatic considerations. The Kythara's gravitational trap was an act of aggression, and their response had to operate along similar parameters.

Ethan suspected that Sean had a firing solution ready for when the gravitational field came down. The *Odyssey*'s crew had probably figured out how he could bring down the field by destroying the power distribution nodes on each of the ships.

"They've done this before," Cynergy observed from her workstation. "The formation, the power distribution, the tactical positioning—this isn't improvised. It's a standard containment protocol they've refined through multiple encounters. It's a safe bet that there are more ships on their way here."

"It's not a bad strategy against a Vemus Alpha," Qualmann said. "Lock them in place, assess their capabilities, then eliminate them with overwhelming firepower."

Ethan agreed with their assessment.

"Communications drone reaching effective range, sir," Lieutenant Trickle announced. "Beginning electromagnetic pulse transmission."

The bridge fell silent as Hash's carefully constructed message was transmitted toward the Kythara command ship. Everything they could compress into electromagnetic patterns that the aliens might interpret as communication rather than interference had been included.

Minutes passed with no response.

"Rebroadcast the message," Ethan ordered. "Different frequency ranges, enhanced signal strength."

Lieutenant Trickle adjusted the transmission parameters, sending their diplomatic package through multiple communication channels while the stealth attack drones maintained position above the engagement zone. The Kythara ships showed no change in formation or energy output, their gravitational trap continuing to immobilize the Confederation vessels.

Then the response came.

The Kythara command ship's reply was transmitted and appeared on the main holoscreen.

Vemus threat detected. Elimination protocols authorized.

The tactical situation shifted immediately. Energy signatures from the Kythara ships began increasing as weapons systems came online.

Ethan had no choice. "All stealth attack drones, transition to attack mode."

Twelve attack drones raced toward the Kythara formation. Their stealth systems disengaged as attack configurations activated, each drone burning with energy signatures that briefly rivaled stellar output. Even if the Kythara could detect them, eight seconds wasn't enough time to coordinate a defensive response.

"Drones locked on target," Captain Endo reported.

Ethan watched the countdown display, knowing that the next few seconds would determine whether they saved their trapped ships.

"Five seconds to impact," Endo announced.

The attack drones struck with precision. Energy discharges lanced through space, striking specific power distribution nodes that maintained the Kythara gravitational field. The attacks were calculated to disable rather than destroy, but their effectiveness was immediate and dramatic.

The gravitational anomaly collapsed instantly.

"Field disruption confirmed," Lieutenant Trickle announced. "The *Odyssey* and the *Horizon* are free to maneuver."

Ethan watched the comlink status to the *Odyssey* and saw that they'd received the data package the moment the field was disrupted.

The field disruption must've overloaded the Kythara ships' internal systems. Their response was sluggish, confirming the effectiveness of Ethan blindsiding them.

"Evasive maneuvers," Ethan ordered. "Maximum acceleration away from the engagement zone."

The *Ascendant*'s engines fired with full power.

"Sir, orders from the *Odyssey*," Lieutenant Trickle said. "Emergency rendezvous coordinates."

"Helm, plot a course to those coordinates," Ethan ordered.

"Yes, sir," Lieutenant Jackson said. "Course entered into NAV computer."

"Engage," Ethan said.

The I-Drive spun up and within seconds they were out of the star system, leaving the Kythara behind.

CHAPTER 32

VEX'THARA'S BIO-ELECTRIC fields pulsed with anticipation as he moved through the command vessel's corridors, his four manipulator arms carrying the alien communications device they had recovered from the engagement zone. The electromagnetic patterns flowing across his six limbs betrayed none of the turmoil churning through his consciousness—a discipline honed through decades of hunting the Great Enemy across the void between stars.

The device itself was surprisingly sophisticated, its construction principles unfamiliar yet elegant. During the brief moments before the aliens had escaped, Vex'thara had observed their tactical capabilities with the analytical eye of a hunter who had survived countless encounters with forces that could shatter fleets. These beings—these humans—possessed technologies that challenged conventional understanding of what lesser species could achieve.

The command chamber's dampening fields activated as Vex'thara approached Kol'veren's presence-sphere, a necessity when conducting sensitive discussions that required absolute security. His superior officer waited within the sphere's isolation protocols, his own bio-electric patterns subdued to barely detectable levels that indicated deep contemplation.

Kol'veren stood nearly half a meter taller than Vex'thara, and his reinforced neural amplifiers crowned his elongated skull, necessary for command. Generations of fleet leadership had shaped his lineage toward enhanced cognitive processing, allowing him to coordinate the complex logistics that kept their hunting group operational across interstellar distances. His bio-armor bore the scars of previous Alpha encounters, each mark representing a victory that had cost blood, ships, and irreplaceable lives.

"Report your assessment, Hunt-Coordinator," Kol'veren said, his bio-electric patterns creating formal command frequencies that resonated through the chamber's conductive pathways.

Vex'thara positioned his limbs in the geometric configuration that indicated comprehensive tactical analysis, allowing his bio-electric fields to carry the full complexity of his encounter with the human forces. "The aliens demonstrate capabilities that exceed our preliminary estimates. Their coordination protocols rival our own, and their weapons technology shows evidence of extensive combat refinement."

He projected tactical data through bio-electric pulse patterns, sharing the experience of fighting alongside the human called Ethan against the Alpha constructs. The memory carried emotional undertones that spoke to professional respect earned through shared combat—a recognition that these beings understood warfare that transcended mere technological advantage.

"They fought with efficiency and adaptability that suggests extensive experience with Alpha-class threats," Vex'thara continued, his limb configurations creating increasingly complex analytical displays. "Their leader demonstrated tactical coordination capabilities that allowed integration of different combat specializations in real-time adaptation to changing battlefield conditions."

Kol'veren's bio-electric response carried frequencies that indicated skeptical evaluation. "Combat prowess alone does not determine alliance worthiness. What evidence supports the assessment that these beings oppose the Great Enemy rather than serve it?"

The question struck at the heart of Vex'thara's uncertainty. During their encounter, he had detected biological signatures that indicated Vemus contamination among the human forces—enhanced individuals whose physiological modifications bore disturbing similarities to Alpha conversion processes, yet who fought against the constructs with lethal determination.

"The humans possess enhanced individuals whose biology shows Vemus modification patterns," Vex'thara admitted, his bio-electric patterns shifting to carry undertones of tactical concern. "However, these enhanced beings fought against the Alpha constructs with capabilities that exceeded even our own combat effectiveness. They demonstrated resistance to Alpha compulsion attempts while coordinating with unmodified humans in ways that showed voluntary cooperation rather than parasitic control."

He modulated his bio-electric output to project the memory of watching Ethan coordinate hybrid and human elements during their desperate battle against the enhanced hunters. The tactical efficiency had been remarkable, with different species and enhancement levels functioning as a unified force despite their biological diversity.

"More significantly," Vex'thara continued, "their leaders shared tactical intelligence that indicates previous encounters with our people. They have star charts showing the locations where thousands of our ship types had been engaged in combat against Great Enemy forces, as well as evidence of a diaspora group that achieved sufficient success to warrant documentation and study."

The revelation sent ripples through Kol'veren's bio-electric patterns. For generations, their hunting group had operated in isolation, believing themselves to be among the few survivors of their species' exodus from a dead homeworld. The possibility that other groups had not merely survived but thrived carried strategic significance that extended far beyond immediate tactical considerations.

"You verified this intelligence personally?" Kol'veren asked.

"Affirmative. The human leader activated a portable display device that projected detailed tactical analysis of ship configurations, weapons effectiveness, and engagement patterns that matched our ancestral fleet specifications. The scale of the engagement suggested fleet elements numbering in the thousands."

Vex'thara's limbs created geometric patterns that conveyed both wonder and tactical possibility. "If accurate, this intelligence is proof that at least one diaspora group achieved sufficient growth and coordination to mount large-scale operations against Great Enemy forces. Their experience could provide tactical innovations that enhance our own hunting effectiveness."

Kol'veren moved through the isolation sphere with the controlled precision that marked command decision-making under strategic uncertainty. His bio-electric patterns showed the complex interplay of calculation and caution that had kept their hunting group operational through many cycles of warfare against impossible odds.

"The communications device they deployed," he said, gesturing toward the alien technology that Vex'thara carried. "Internal components of the transport vehicle. Analysis confirms it contains additional intelligence?"

"Preliminary scans detect extensive data repositories formatted in unknown communications protocols," Vex'thara replied. "The device appears designed for translation interface rather than simple message transmission. Its complexity suggests these beings anticipated the need for extended communication rather than mere tactical coordination."

The observation carried implications that resonated through Kol'veren's bio-electric patterns with frequencies that indicated strategic recognition. Species that developed sophisticated translation protocols demonstrated long-term thinking that extended beyond immediate survival needs. It indicated a civilization with resources and stability sufficient for extended research and development.

"The research facility where this encounter occurred," Kol'veren said, "your assessment of its purpose and current status?"

Vex'thara's bio-electric patterns shifted to project the memory of exploring the massive installation where they had first detected the Great Enemy's signature. "An experiment that integrated with biological research systems designed for Alpha construct development. The facility contained active test subjects, including a humanoid Alpha variant whose capabilities exceeded standard construct parameters."

He paused, his limb configurations creating patterns that carried tactical concern mixed with professional unease. "The facility's systems decommissioned themselves during our engagement. Power systems collapsed throughout the installation, eliminating all research data and containing specimens except..."

"Except the humanoid construct that accompanied the human forces," Kol'veren finished.

"Affirmative. We were unable to confirm elimination of the primary test subject. The humans maintained a protective formation around the construct throughout their withdrawal, suggesting either compulsion influence or they intend to study it to glean insights into the Great Enemy."

"Or it's an alliance with Alpha-class entities."

Alpha constructs that could maintain long-term psychological influence over technologically advanced species represented threats that transcended conventional military engagement. If the humans had fallen under such influence, their capabilities made them potentially more dangerous than the standard Great Enemy forces.

"It's unclear whether there is Alpha contamination among the human forces. They're unlike any species we've encountered before," Vex'thara said.

"Yes, it's a possibility that we can't ignore. What is your assessment of Alpha contamination among the human forces?"

Vex'thara considered the question, reviewing his observations of the human leader's capabilities and decision-making patterns. "The enhanced individuals demonstrated resistance to Alpha compulsion during direct exposure to construct influence fields. Their coordination with unmodified humans suggested voluntary cooperation rather than parasitic override of conscious decision-making."

He modulated his bio-electric output to carry analytical uncertainty mixed with tactical respect. "However, the preservation of the humanoid construct indicates either contamination influence or strategic calculation that accepts significant risk for potential intelligence value. Without extended observation, definitive assessment remains impossible."

Kol'veren's patterns shifted to complex frequency overlays that indicated command-level strategic processing. His neural amplifiers pulsed with enhanced activity as he coordinated multiple analytical threats through cognitive pathways that had been optimized for command decision-making. "The humans will succumb to Alpha influence," he said finally. "No species has maintained voluntary cooperation with construct entities without eventual conversion to the Great Enemy objectives. Their technological capabilities will be absorbed and turned against all."

The assessment carried the weight of historical precedent earned through generations of warfare against an enemy that converted rather than conquered. Vex'thara had witnessed species fighting against the Great Enemy, and all eventually were defeated. Yet his memory of fighting alongside Ethan against the Alpha constructs suggested possibilities that challenged conventional understanding. The human leader had demonstrated capabilities that exceeded even enhanced Kythara combat effectiveness while maintaining tactical coordination that spoke to compromised decision-making authority.

"Command-Leader," Vex'thara said, "consider the possibility that these humans represent something unprecedented—their resistance to Alpha compulsion combined with technological capabilities that exceed our own." He waited a few moments, wondering if his observation had gone too far as to insult his superior officer's actions. When he didn't receive a sharp reprimand, he continued. "They escaped the trap using minimal force and clever tactics. I suspect that they had weapons with greater destructive force, but they chose not to use them. These actions are worth further consideration and analysis."

Kol'veren became perfectly still and then said, "The communications device contains data repositories that may confirm or refute their intelligence claims. You will coordinate with Technical-Specialist Vel'tyros to extract and analyze all available information. Priority focus on verification of diaspora group contact and assessment of technological capabilities that could enhance our hunting effectiveness."

The assignment carried implications that resonated through Vex'thara's bio-electric patterns. Technical-Specialist Vel'tyros represented one of their most capable analytical minds, her cognitive modifications allowing data processing capabilities that rivaled ship-mounted computer systems. If any Kythara could extract useful intelligence from alien technology, she possessed the skills and resources necessary for success.

"Secondary priority," Kol'veren continued, "analysis of communications protocols for potential future contact scenarios. If these humans demonstrate continued resistance to alpha influence while maintaining opposition to Great Enemy forces, alliance evaluation may become strategically necessary."

The concession represented a significant shift in command assessment, acknowledging possibilities that challenged their traditional isolation protocols. Vex'thara's bio-electric patterns showed tactical satisfaction mixed with recognition of the complex challenges that lay ahead. The analysis of alien intelligence would determine whether they faced potential allies in their eternal war against the Great Enemy, or simply another species destined to fall under Alpha influence and become extensions of the collective will that sought to consume all biological diversity in the galaxy.

Either way, change was coming to their isolated hunting group, and Vex'thara found himself anticipating the challenges ahead with something that felt remarkably like hope.

CHAPTER 33

GENERAL SEAN QUINN took his place at the head of the conference table in the *Odyssey*'s primary briefing room. Around him, officers and specialists had gathered to analyze their encounter with the mysterious alien force. Thirty-six hours had passed since their escape from the Kythara gravitational trap, and the initial shock was giving way to methodical intelligence analysis.

The conference room's smart-glass walls displayed tactical plots showing their current position relative to the Phantom Nexus—safely beyond the detection range of standard sensors while maintaining observation capabilities through long-range arrays. The ancient ring fragments appeared dormant now, their power signatures reduced to barely detectable levels that suggested systematic shutdown rather than catastrophic failure.

"Status report on the Phantom Nexus," Sean said, activating the holographic displays that showed the latest sensor data.

Major Nagata looked up from his holoscreen. "The communications networks have gone completely silent, General. Power output from all ring fragments has decreased to less than two percent of previous levels. Whatever systems were maintaining the facility's operations have initiated what appears to be a controlled decommissioning sequence."

Sean nodded, the implications clear. "The experiment is finished. Salpheth got what he wanted from our encounter with his research facility."

Ethan sat across the table from Sean. The metallic band of his SRA caught the ambient lighting as Atlas interfaced with the ship's data systems, providing enhanced analytical capabilities that supplemented human intelligence gathering.

"The Kythara showed limited response to our tactical approach," Ethan said, highlighting specific elements of their escape sequence on his personal holoscreen. "My assessment is that maintaining their gravitational containment field required such significant power allocation that their sensor capabilities and defensive responses were operating at reduced capacity. We essentially blindsided them."

Colonel Brad Sutton leaned forward with a nod. "Which explains why they didn't detect the *Ascendant*'s approach until you initiated the attack on their power distribution nodes. Their attention was focused on containing the *Odyssey* and the *Horizon* while their surveillance systems were operating with limited effectiveness."

"And they were distracted by the comms drone we sent to them," Ethan said.

Major Wallace nodded approvingly. "I concur with your crew's findings, Major Gates."

Sean glanced at Wallace and knew that the *Odyssey*'s lead engineer was not an officer who was easily impressed. He studied the tactical reconstruction, noting how their escape had succeeded through factors that might not be repeatable. "Major Gates, your assessment of whether we can count on similar advantages in future encounters?"

"Negative, sir," Ethan replied immediately. "They weren't expecting us, which gave us the tactical surprise necessary for successful extraction. That's not something we should anticipate happening again. The Kythara demonstrated adaptive capabilities during our facility encounter that suggest they learn from tactical defeat. If they'd kept a couple of scout ships in reserve to guard their main force, this might have had a different outcome."

Oriana gave Ethan an appraising look. "Just to clarify, assuming the Kythara had a reserve force watching their backs, what do you think the outcome would've been?"

"There would've been no way to avoid a more forceful engagement. It would've resulted in significant damage to their ships and perhaps the *Ascendant*."

Oriana nodded. "But you still think you would've been able to bring down the gravitational field."

"Yes."

"The intelligence that Cynergy gathered during your facility investigation correlates with our analysis of the derelict fleet you encountered two years ago," Oriana said, manipulating the displays to show comparative technological assessments. "There is strong evidence to support that the Kythara appear to be a nomadic species whose entire civilization is organized around hunting and eliminating Vemus threats."

She gestured toward tactical displays that showed ship configurations optimized for extended operations far from any support infrastructure. "Their vessels show evidence of extended modification and repair cycles using salvaged materials from multiple species. This suggests a civilization that has been operating independently for generations, possibly centuries, without access to fixed manufacturing or resource bases."

Ambassador Elena Vasquez peered at the data on the holoscreen. "A nomadic warrior culture dedicated to Vemus elimination. Not only that, but with multiple branches or fleets that don't have direct contact."

"Their propulsion systems limit their range," Major Wallace said.

"But their tactics are effective within their operational parameters," Colonel Sutton said.

Thyven shifted in his adaptive seating. "Such dedication suggests either religious conviction or survival necessity that transcends normal strategic calculation. They have transformed their entire civilization into a weapon against the Vemus threat."

"Could be a combination of both," Sean said, highlighting the tactical sequence that had led to their containment. "They detected Vemus signatures in the communication signals from the Phantom Nexus and concluded that our vessels represented a contamination threat requiring immediate neutralization."

Dr. Samuel Chen cleared his throat. "That kind of response suggests a zero-tolerance policy regarding any indication of Vemus presence or influence. They've likely encountered too many situations where attempting to distinguish between willing collaboration and parasitic control proved futile."

Ethan frowned. "From their perspective, any ship responding to Vemus communication signals represents a potential threat that requires containment pending elimination, which is what was happening here. However, I also think they were incapable of communicating with us when your encounter occurred. It was only our close contact with them that allowed us to figure out how they communicated with each other, and it's not like anything I've ever seen before."

"The mistaken identity issue may be more complex than simple signal detection," Major Wallace added. "Confederation ships incorporate numerous reverse-engineered systems from the Phantom vessel we captured. Our power cores, shield generators, fabrication units, and communications arrays all show technological signatures that could be confused with genuine Phantom construction."

The observation sent a chill through Sean. "You're suggesting the Kythara might not be able to distinguish between Confederation vessels and actual Phantom ships?"

"It's a possibility we should consider," Wallace replied. "If their detection methods rely on technological signatures rather than biological indicators, our improved systems could trigger false positives that classify us as Phantom-affiliated rather than independently developed."

The Kythara's dedication to eliminating Vemus threats made them valuable potential partners, but their aggressive response to perceived contamination suggested that establishing peaceful contact would require overcoming significant cultural and tactical barriers.

"Major Gates," Sean said, "what measures did you take to provide the Kythara with information about Confederation capabilities and intentions?"

"I left them a communications drone with extensive data repositories," Ethan replied, activating his holoscreen to show the technical specifications of their diplomatic package. "Translation protocols, historical records of our encounters with Vemus forces, and tactical intelligence about our successful resistance to Alpha compulsion. The data includes verification of our previous encounter with their derelict fleet and evidence of our opposition to the Vemus."

He paused, considering. "However, the information is formatted according to our systems rather than theirs. I used just enough of Kythara communications protocols so they should be able to decipher the data. It will likely require significant time and analytical resources on their part."

Zelara's communications headgear flared with activity as the Aczar engineer listened to the technical discussion. "The electromagnetic communication patterns we observed suggest sophisticated bio-electric capabilities that could interface directly with technological systems. If accurate, they may possess analytical advantages that accelerate information processing beyond conventional expectations."

Sean nodded, then looked at Thyven. "Ambassador, Dr. Kyveth mentioned observing Major Gates' SRA integration during the medical evaluation. What's your assessment of the changes in his partnership with Atlas?"

Thyven's ears twitched with the kind of focused attention that indicated serious consideration of technical matters that carried cultural significance for his species. "The bond strength between Major Gates and his SRA has increased substantially beyond our previous observations. Among our people, such integration typically develops over years or even decades of partnership."

He gestured toward Ethan's SRA band, which showed the subtle chrome accents that indicated active technological integration. "The synergistic relationship between biological consciousness and artificial intelligence creates capabilities that exceed the sum of their individual components. However, the accelerated development observed in Major Gates suggests either exceptional compatibility or external factors that enhanced the bonding process."

Tavira leaned forward with the earnest intensity that marked her as Phendran's designated successor. "Loremaster Phendran's records indicate that such rapid advancement typically occurs during periods of extreme stress or life-threatening challenge. The SRA's protective instincts can overcome normal integration limitations when the biological partner faces existential threats."

Sean felt a surge of respect for Ethan's capabilities and the risks he'd accepted in order to gather intelligence that could prove crucial for the Confederation's survival. "Major Gates, your encounter with the Vemus construct in the research facility—that's where the breakthrough occurred?"

"Affirmative, sir," Ethan replied. "The tactical situation required coordination between my hybrid capabilities and Atlas's technological interface. The breakthrough came when I showed Seraphine how to regenerate to heal herself from the wounds she sustained. She was created with an SRA that was part of her skeleton. It was during that brief contact that Atlas observed and was able to overcome the isolation defensive protocols."

Sean nodded, understanding the things Ethan hadn't said. "A calculated risk."

"Yes, sir, it was."

"Your contributions during this mission have exceeded expectations, Major. The intelligence gathered and the tactical innovations achieved represent significant advances in our understanding of both the Phantom legacy and potential alien alliances."

Ambassador Elena Vasquez looked at Sean. "General, the question remains: what are our next steps? The Kythara represent potential allies whose experience could prove invaluable, but establishing meaningful contact will require overcoming significant cultural and technological barriers."

"I need to review all available intelligence before making operational decisions. Reports will be transmitted back to the Confederation detailing our encounters and requesting guidance on diplomatic protocols for contact with nomadic warrior civilizations."

Sean paused, looking around the table at the assembled team. "Before finalizing any recommendations, I want to interview the Vemus construct that Major Gates extracted from the research facility. The intelligence she represents could be crucial for understanding both Phantom objectives and Vemus capabilities."

Thyven's ears twitched as he looked up at him. "General Quinn, we request permission for our delegation to observe the interview process. Major Gates has indicated that the construct possesses SRA technology integrated into her skeletal structure—something we've never encountered before."

The Aczar ambassador's tone carried the kind of careful precision that indicated significant interest in technological developments that could affect his species' understanding of their own capabilities. "Since Salpheth appears to be involved in her creation, our experience with Phantom manipulation techniques might provide insights into his objectives."

Allowing alien observers during the interrogation of a potentially dangerous Vemus construct violated numerous safety protocols, but their expertise with Phantom technology could prove invaluable for extracting useful information.

"I'll authorize limited observation under strict security protocols," Sean decided. "However, I must emphasize that we're dealing with a Vemus Alpha construct whose capabilities remain largely unknown. While we'll take every precaution to ensure safety, I cannot guarantee that the containment measures will be sufficient if she decides to attempt escape or conversion protocols."

Ethan looked directly at Sean. "Sir, we have multiple elimination options ready for immediate implementation if she demonstrates hostile intent. However, I believe Salpheth designed this entire scenario to ensure we would capture her and extract whatever intelligence she possesses. The risks are significant, but the potential intelligence value regarding Vemus operations and Alpha locations could determine our species' survival."

Sean stood, feeling the conference room's attention focus on him as he prepared to commit them to a course of action that could either provide crucial intelligence or unleash a threat that current containment measures might not be able to control.

"We'll proceed with the interview," he announced. "Selected personnel will transfer to the *Ascendant* for the interrogation. All participants will be equipped with emergency extraction protocols and multiple containment backup systems."

As the meeting began to break up, Sean thought about Connor. He'd had to contend with Salpheth on a ship that was barely space worthy. The Vemus construct represented either their greatest intelligence breakthrough or their most dangerous mistake.

CHAPTER 34

ETHAN STOOD at attention in the *Ascendant*'s main hangar bay, watching as General Sean Quinn's shuttle touched down. The assembled crew formed neat ranks across the deck plating, their dress uniforms crisp.

Atlas pulsed gently around Ethan's forearm as the SRA interfaced with the ship's systems, monitoring atmospheric conditions and security protocols while maintaining the enhanced awareness that had become integral to his command capabilities. The breakthrough they'd achieved during the research facility encounter continued to provide tactical advantages.

The shuttle's loading ramp extended, and Sean emerged with the composed authority that had carried him through decades of command decisions.

"Crew of the *Ascendant*," Sean announced, his voice carrying clearly across the hangar bay, "you have exceeded every expectation for this mission. Securing an intelligence asset in the face of a first-contact scenario while maintaining operational security represents the kind of tactical innovation that defines exceptional military service."

He moved closer to the assembled crew, his gaze taking in faces that had volunteered for deep space operations knowing they might encounter threats beyond conventional understanding. "It would have been easy to eliminate the perceived threats and withdraw to safe distances. That approach would have left us blind to crucial intelligence while potentially making enemies of a species whose experience could prove invaluable for our long-term survival."

Sean's attention focused on Ethan with the kind of recognition that carried weight throughout the command structure. "Major Gates, your tactical coordination during the facility investigation and your strategic thinking during the Kythara encounter enabled us to extract vital intelligence. You also preserved the possibility of future alliance. Your actions directly contributed to freeing the *Odyssey* and the *Horizon* from hostile containment with minimal casualties."

The acknowledgment resonated through the hangar bay as the crew recognized the significance of operations that had pushed the boundaries of exploration while achieving objectives that could reshape their strategic position in the galaxy.

"The intelligence we've gathered and the precedents we've established will influence Confederation policy for generations," Sean continued. "You've demonstrated that courage combined with careful analysis can achieve objectives that seemed impossible when we began this mission. Major Gates, your actions, and those of your crew, hold to the highest traditions of the CDF, and this will be an example for others to aspire to."

Pride swelled in Ethan's chest, and the crew of the *Ascendant* saluted Sean.

"Thank you, sir," Ethan said.

As the formal address concluded and the crew began returning to their duties, Ethan approached Sean. "General, if you'll follow me, I'll escort you to the containment facility."

They moved through the *Ascendant*'s corridors toward the

medical bay's secure wing, where specialized isolation chambers provided multiple layers of containment for potentially dangerous prisoners. The route took them past observation windows that offered the Aczar delegation monitoring positions while maintaining safe distances from direct contact.

"Status of the prisoner?" Sean asked as they walked.

"Seraphine remains in medically induced hibernation," Ethan replied, his neural implants automatically accessing the latest medical reports. "Dr. Chen estimates complete regeneration within twenty-four hours. Her biological systems are healing at accelerated rates that exceed even hybrid recovery capabilities."

They reached the containment facility. Beyond the barrier, Seraphine lay unconscious in a crystalline medical capsule.

"Her appearance is remarkably human-like," Sean said.

"Deliberately so," Ethan said, activating the holographic displays that showed detailed biological analysis. "The facility where we found her was specifically designed for creating humanoid Alpha constructs. Someone wanted to produce Vemus entities that could interact with human psychology more effectively than standard Alpha configurations."

Atlas projected additional data onto Ethan's personal display, sharing analysis data that had been gathered during their brief contact with Seraphine's integrated SRA systems. "Her skeletal structure incorporates SRA technology at the molecular level. The integration is far more advanced than anything we've encountered, including Aczar partnerships."

Sean frowned. "Direct biological integration rather than external symbiosis?"

"Correct. Her SRA isn't a separate entity that chose partnership; it's woven into her fundamental biology as an integral component of her consciousness and physical capabilities."

The revelation carried disturbing implications about the level of biotechnological sophistication involved in Seraphine's creation. Someone had achieved biological-artificial integration that transcended anything the Confederation had previously imagined possible.

"She's aware of her current status?" Sean asked.

"Affirmative. The hibernation is voluntary rather than externally imposed. She chose to enter regenerative stasis after sustaining severe injuries during the facility encounter." Ethan paused, considering the psychological complexities involved in their prisoner's cooperation. "She agreed to work with us because she believes it will help her achieve 'perfection,' whatever that means in Vemus terminology."

"And what happens when she reaches this perfection?"

"According to her statements, perfection unlocks knowledge about her ultimate destination, which is integration with something she calls the super-alpha—a central entity where all Vemus Alphas eventually travel after reaching sufficient development."

The words hung in the air between them. The super-alpha represented either humanity's greatest opportunity for decisive action against their enemies or the location of a threat so massive that confronting it could doom their species.

"Why would Salpheth arrange for us to discover this information?" Sean asked, voicing the question that had been troubling Ethan since their escape from the research facility. "What does a rogue Phantom gain by providing humans with intelligence about Vemus operations?"

Ethan felt Atlas pulse with analytical certainty as the SRA processed data that correlated with their previous encounters with Phantom entities. "Based on Salpheth's conversations with my father, he understands that humanity needs to locate the super-alpha to have any chance of stopping the Vemus threat permanently. The Phantoms warned us that we lack the power to defeat them, but perhaps they were referring to conventional military approaches."

He manipulated the displays to show tactical projections that illustrated the scope of Vemus expansion across galactic distances. "If the super-alpha represents a central coordination point for all Vemus activities, destroying or disrupting it could collapse their entire expansion network. Salpheth might be providing us with the intelligence necessary to achieve objectives that align with his own agenda."

Sean watched Seraphine's unconscious form. "A calculated risk that serves multiple purposes. We gain crucial intelligence about our greatest threat, while Salpheth achieves objectives that require capabilities he doesn't possess."

Before Ethan could respond, his neural implants chimed with an incoming priority message from the bridge. Major Qualmann's voice carried through the communications link with professional urgency.

"Major Gates, we're detecting movement from the Kythara fleet—multiple vessels departing the Nexus coordinates on trajectories that suggest organized withdrawal rather than tactical repositioning."

Ethan activated his command interface, bringing up tactical displays that showed the alien fleet's movements in real-time. "Confirmed departure, sir. The Kythara appear to be leaving the system entirely."

Sean watched as the alien ships moved with a coordinated precision that suggested mission completion rather than strategic retreat. "Status of the Phantom Nexus?"

"Still dormant, General. Power signatures remain at minimal levels throughout all ring fragments. Whatever Salpheth programmed into those systems appears to have concluded its operational cycle."

The observation confirmed Sean's assessment that their

encounter had served its intended purpose. Salpheth had achieved his objectives through their investigation of the research facility, and the ancient Phantom infrastructure was returning to the hibernation state that had concealed it for centuries.

"General," Ethan said, "what are our operational priorities now?"

Sean moved closer to the observation window, studying Seraphine's unconscious form. "We'll transmit our reports to the Confederation, but I want to continue investigating this region. If Salpheth has moved on to other installations or objectives, tracking his activities could provide additional intelligence about Phantom capabilities and intentions."

He paused, considering the diplomatic implications of their extended mission. "The Aczar delegation will have to wait longer before reaching New Earth, but I suspect they won't object to observing additional exploration operations. They've gained invaluable experience during this mission."

Ethan nodded, understanding the strategic calculation that balanced immediate diplomatic obligations against the opportunity to gather intelligence that might not be available again. "The crew is prepared for extended operations, sir."

"Then we continue the hunt," Sean said. "Salpheth went to considerable effort to provide us with this intelligence. We're going to use it to track down whatever else he's planning while we still have the opportunity."

As they stood before the observation window watching Seraphine's unconscious form, both officers understood that they were approaching decisions that could determine whether humanity gained the intelligence necessary to survive its greatest threat or walked into carefully constructed traps that would doom their species.

The hunt for answers would continue, carrying them deeper into the galaxy's hidden conflicts. Whatever lay ahead, they would face it with the combined knowledge of multiple civilizations and the determination that had carried humanity from desperate colonists to confident explorers of the infinite dark between stars.

Whatever answers Seraphine might provide, Ethan knew they were no longer fighting the Vemus alone.

AUTHOR NOTE

Thank you for reading *Shattered Nexus* - Book 19 in the First Colony series. I hope you've enjoyed this journey with me.

This book is a continuation of the storyline that began with *Pathfinder*, and builds on the foundation that was established with it. Balancing the expanding First Colony universe, while keeping the story both compelling and fresh, is a challenge that I enjoy. It forces my mental muscles to grow and stretch, developing the various conflicts, technologies, and philosophies that are part of the series. I hope that this approach creates stories that resonate with you.

The First Colony universe continues to expand well beyond its initial boundaries. There are more stories waiting to be told and characters you've yet to meet as the torch passes from one generation to the next. I'm thrilled about the future of this series and hope you share that excitement.

Your support has been the cornerstone of everything—without you, there would be no First Colony series. When I began this journey in 2017, I never imagined I'd still be writing in this universe eight years later, and that's all thanks to readers like you.

If you enjoyed *Shattered Nexus*, please consider leaving a review. Reviews make a huge difference with discoverability and send a powerful message to potential readers that this series is worth their valuable time.

Thank you again for accompanying me on this adventure.

~Ken

If you're looking for another series to read consider reading one of the following series:

Federation Chronicles

First came the development of a Personality Matrix Construct—PMC, transferring human consciousness into a machine. It changed the galaxy and the way wars were fought. Then something went wrong with PMCs and the Federation Wars toppled the galactic order. PMCs became a menace to be hunted and exterminated. Long after the Federation Wars, the galaxy limps on. Spacers carve out an existence upon the bones of the old worlds, but things are about to change. . .something has begun broadcasting signals to reactivate PMCs that were stored in secret.

https://kenlozito.com/federation-chronicles/

Ascension Series

They've been watching us for hundreds of years.
Now they need our help.
Earth is not safe.

Zack is good at finding things, but when he discovers a global conspiracy, life as he knows it is over. Sometimes the truth doesn't set you free. It traps you instead.

Kept secret for 60 years, the discovery of an alien signal forces an unlikely team to investigate a mysterious structure discovered in the furthest reaches of the solar system. Join the crew of the *Athena,* Earth's most advanced spaceship on the ultimate journey beyond our wildest imagining.

https://kenlozito.com/ascension-series/

Space Raiders

Nathan Briggs led a life that was anything but ordinary, but when the aliens abducted him, the stakes have never been higher. They told him he should've run away. Maybe they were right. Embark on an adventure that begins on present day Earth, where four people are abruptly taken away from a life they've known, and travel to other worlds, encounter exotic species, and struggle to stay alive. There is a galaxy full of secrets waiting to be explored. If you're a fan of old school heroes and villains where grit and determination are offset by a little bit of humor, then this is the adventure for you.

https://kenlozito.com/space-raiders/

ABOUT THE AUTHOR

I've written multiple science fiction and fantasy series. Books have been my way to escape everyday life since I was a teenager to my current ripe old(?) age. What started out as a love of stories has turned into a full-blown passion for writing them.

Overall, I'm just a fan of really good stories regardless of genre. I love the heroic tales, redemption stories, the last stand, or just a good old fashion adventure. Those are the types of stories I like to write. Stories with rich and interesting characters and then I put them into dangerous and sometimes morally gray situations.

My ultimate intent for writing stories is to provide fun escapism for readers. I write stories that I would like to read, and I hope you enjoy them as well.

If you have questions or comments about any of my works I would love to hear from you, even if it's only to drop by to say hello at KenLozito.com

Thanks again for reading *First Colony - Shattered Nexus*

ALSO BY KEN LOZITO

Space Raiders - Forgotten Empire

Space Raiders - Dark Menace

Federation Chronicles

Acheron Inheritance

Acheron Salvation

Acheron Redemption

Acheron Rising (Prequel Novella)

Ascension Series

Star Shroud

Star Divide

Star Alliance

Infinity's Edge

Rising Force

Ascension

Safanarion Order Series

Road to Shandara

Echoes of a Gloried Past

Amidst the Rising Shadows

Heir of Shandara

If you would like to be notified when my next book is released visit kenlozito.com

www.ingramcontent.com/pod-product-compliance
Lightning Source LLC
Chambersburg PA
CBHW072318020726
47501CB00002B/562